James Fenimore Cooper The Pilot

The Pilot

James Fenimore Cooper

*Introduction by John T. Winterich
and illustrated with woodcuts by
Robert M. Quackenbush*

THE HERITAGE PRESS, NEW YORK

Introduction

IN Washington's Potomac Park stands the simulacrum of a uniformed figure which at first glance somewhat resembles a traffic officer. The conception is not so incongruous as might appear, for the figure stands at a three-road junction where it is itself something of a menace to navigation (the terrestrial variety, that is). Closer inspection will reveal the effigy as a representation of Admiral John Paul Jones, whose name wasn't Jones at all. He was born at Kirkbean, Kirkcudbrightshire, Scotland, the son of John Paul, gardener to a local worthy, on July 6, 1747. At the age of twelve he became an apprentice in the British merchant marine service and signed aboard a vessel engaged in the tobacco trade with the American colonies, and the die was cast. Nine years later he received his master's certificate. In the year of independence he went to Philadelphia and took his captain's commission in the fledgling United States Navy directly from the hand of the presiding officer of the Continental Congress, John Hancock. Thenceforward his career was that of a story-book hero. In the early 1770's John Paul had added Jones to his name, probably to establish a reasonably innocent alias, for his pugnacity had won him considerable notoriety, though he was only five foot six.

The sea fighting of the American Revolution was made to order for John Paul Jones. He reached the summit of his career on September 23, 1779. On that day, commanding the *Bonhomme Richard*, named for Benjamin Franklin as compiler of the Poor Richard Almanacs, Jones fought it out in the eastern Atlantic with the British frigate *Serapis*, named for an Egyptian deity. Finding himself outmanned and outgunned, Jones reacted on the principle of "if you can't lick 'em, join 'em." He grappled with the *Serapis* and boarded her. When the commander of the *Serapis* asked Jones if he was ready to quit, Jones gave voice to an utterance that has made all the quotation books: "I have not yet begun to fight."

Now there have been—and still are—novelists who transfer people, real people, into their books. There can be no doubt at all, for instance, that Charles Dickens' father, John Dickens, is embalmed forever in the pages of *David Copperfield* as Wilkins Micawber. Why do some authors adopt this stratagem? Sometimes, perhaps, by way of affection, or revenge, or convenience, or novelty, or total collapse of the creative function.

I mention this proclivity because it may be germane to the book you now hold in your hands. James Fenimore Cooper may have taken John Paul Jones as the prototype for his fictional pilot, or again he may not have. In his pocketable biography of Cooper, Robert E. Spiller quotes Cooper's denial of having "any original in mind" for one of his characters, and Cooper thereafter generalizes: "A leading character in a work of fiction has a fair right to the aid which can be obtained from a poetical point of view of the subject." On the other hand, James Grossman, whose study of Cooper launched the American Men of Letters series, described *The Pilot* as a story "about a fictitious raid by John Paul Jones on the English coast."

Whoever the Pilot may have been, *The Pilot* was Cooper's fourth novel. That figure would not be regarded as astronomical today, but in America in the first quarter of the nineteenth century it was prodigious. Only one native author had so far exceeded it. He was a Philadelphian named Charles Brockden Brown, who had died at the age of thirty-nine after producing six works which, for want of a more precise characterization, are usually catalogued as prose fiction.

Cooper's first novel, *Precaution*, published in 1820, was written on a sort of dare. Unlike a good many literary legends, this one may be accepted as authentic, for the chronicler of the incident was Cooper's daughter Susan Augusta Fenimore Cooper. Susan was only seven years old at the time, but that fact by no means invalidates her testimony, for Susan had the story later from her mother. Cooper, it appears, was reading aloud a new English novel;

and in the past century and a half, much scholarly detective work has been devoted to attempting to identify it. Finally Cooper tossed the book aside, remarking that he could do better than that, which naturally brought from his wife the retort, "Well, why don't you?" or words to that effect. It can well be doubted whether *Precaution* was any improvement over the English book, whatever that may have been. *Precaution* itself was an English book to all intents and purposes; the scene was English and the characters were English, and since it was issued anonymously, there was no telling the author's nationality or even sex. Few were *Precaution*'s readers on either side of the ocean. A ranking non-reader was William Cullen Bryant, who was the Pooh-Bah of American letters at the time of Cooper's death in 1851, and who presided at a memorial service in Cooper's honor in which Bryant confessed he was not acquainted with *Precaution* save for its name.

A brief further word on Susan Cooper. As was fit and proper and altogether filial, she was a devoted admirer of her father, and much of our knowledge of him is due to that devotion. They were even literary collaborators. In 1845 a London publisher brought out a work entitled *Elinor Wyllys, A Tale*, "Edited by J. Fenimore Cooper, Esq.," and a year later the book appeared in America with slight changes in the title and with the by-line of "Amabel Penfeather" (plus Cooper's name as editor). In 1850 Susan brought out *Rural Hours*, "by a Lady," the dedication of which read: "To the Author of *The Deerslayer*, These Notes Are Very Respectfully, Gratefully, and Most Affectionately Inscribed by the Writer." Susan was a good reporter; every writer should have at least one daughter like her.

Cooper's second novel, *The Spy*, appeared in 1821. It was subheaded "A Tale of the Neutral Ground," the name given during the American Revolution to the stretch of country along the Hudson River north and west of the Harlem River where both British and American bands and individuals foraged and plundered in a sort of guerilla warfare. Today we would call such a stretch of territory a Demilitarized Zone. Cooper had had the idea for *The Spy* handed to him on a platter by John Jay, first Chief Justice of the United States. In his pre-Chief Justice days, Jay had had the story from General George Washington (two good and reliable authorities, one would think). Cooper's third novel was *The Pioneers*, published in 1823, the first unit in the Leatherstocking Tales, which recited the adventures and exploits of Natty Bumppo.

He wrote thirty or so other novels, but only one of these need concern us here. Cooper must have approached the composition of *The Pilot* with high satisfaction. He would be operating in a field with which he was thoroughly conversant, a field in which he was by way of being an expert. Actually he was about to assemble the first American novel of the sea. Let us glance for a moment at his qualifications for the job.

The son of an upstate New York politico and landowner (at a time and place when real estate was computed not as acreage but as square-mileage), Cooper had attended Yale College briefly but was dropped for hell-raising. His father paid the bills which James had run up and then arranged for his joining as a foremast hand the crew of a merchantman about to sail for the Mediterranean. James did not regard this step as punishment at all. The voyage lasted just short of a year. Back home, James was ready and eager to take his warrant as a midshipman in the fledgling United States Navy. He served just over two years, including shore duty as a recruiting officer in New York City and port duty in Oswego, New York, at the eastern end of Lake Ontario, where several gunboats were under construction. Altogether it was not an exciting hitch, but it thrilled Cooper to the marrow. He never forgot a minute of it, and much of it he put into his novels. Most Americans regard Cooper primarily as the author of the five Leatherstocking Tales, but at least ten of his stories are largely blue-water yarns. And he capped his marine career by publishing in 1839 a two-volume *History of the Navy of the United States of America* which proved immensely popular.

In Cooper's day, and for a considerable time thereafter, copyright in America was effected by the simple deposit of the title-page (and that was as far as some books ever got). The title-page of Volume I of *The Pilot* was deposited August 1, 1823. Volume II followed on December 29th. (Within a matter of days, a dramatic version appeared at New York's Adelphi Theatre —whoever wrote it, Cooper did not.) The book's publisher was Charles Wiley, whose address was 3 Wall Street, today probably the most valuable fragment of real estate on earth. None of Cooper's books were things of beauty; almost without exception they were bound in paper over boards. The color of the paper that enclosed the sheets of *The Pilot* was blue, and the white paper shelfback supported a paper label.

A few days after *The Pilot*'s publication, Cooper addressed a long and newsy letter to his old messmate of Navy days, William Branford Shubrick, which included this paragraph: "Pilot comes on but slowly—I have not look'd at it in near two months—the first volume however is printed and the second in part. Among the rest the *dedication* is struck off and I send you a rough proof sheet that you may see yourself in print—I would keep it close until the book appears." (Cooper probably italicized *dedication* to be sure Shubrick would get the point.) Of all Cooper's correspondents, Shubrick received the longest and most entertaining letters. During the War of 1812 he had served with distinction on the *Hornet*, the *Constellation*, and the *Constitution;* and he saw active service in the Mexican War of the 1840's, which not many Americans think of as having had a naval phase. Cooper's affection for him is certified in a single glowing sentence, written when Cooper hoped to make a trip from New York to Boston, where Shubrick was stationed: "I should like to be there ten days and not see a soul beside yourself."

In a letter addressed to "My Dear Shu" in February, 1824, Cooper submitted a progress report on *The Pilot:* "Pilot is decidedly successful—the sale is the best criterion in such matters, and that is very great—it is very little if any short of Spy in popularity, though opinions are as various as men's minds —I found Wiley had the book in the hands of five printers on my return for a reprint—If it has not been as much commended it has certainly been less assailed than any book I have ever written—so much for our *joint* efforts." Shubrick, we may be sure, was delighted with the little joke inherent in that *joint.**

The reader of *The Pilot* is the recipient of an unannounced and unusual bonus. Not only is he introduced to the first novel of the sea written by an American author. He is also present at the first whale hunt in our native literature. A few years before Cooper began writing *The Pilot,* he had acquired a share in a Long Island whaler. From this experience he gained an expert's knowledge of the economics of whaling and certainly some familiarity with its technique. The whale hunt in *The Pilot*—you will find it in Chapter XVII —is brief, exciting, and thoroughly professional, and it has nothing at all to do with the main current of the story. Cooper simply wanted to demonstrate that he knew considerable about the art and practice of whaling, and it is good for a man to share his knowledge with his fellow men.

The pursuit of the whale occupies only a few pages of the novel, but they are lively and spirited pages. The hero of the episode, one might even say its instigator, is, of course, the coxwain, Long Tom Coffin, a Nantucketer by birth who absorbed his keenness for whaling with his mother's milk (incidentally, an adult female whale could provide enough milk to keep the human population of Nantucket in fresh milk for as long as she continued lactating).

Cooper's handling of the whale hunt exposes one of his weaknesses as a manager of English prose. He hated to repeat words. He therefore took refuge in an awkward device which, nearly a century later, was christened the Ele-

* The extracts from Cooper's letters are quoted from texts included in *The Letters and Journals of James Fenimore Cooper*, edited by James Franklin Beard, which reached its sixth and final volume in the spring of 1968.

gant Variant. (The man who invented the label was Sir Arthur Quiller-Couch, the first occupant of the King Edward VII chair of English literature at Cambridge University.) If you are writing an essay on Byron, for instance, you will have to include Byron's name from time to time. A writer caught in the toils of the Elegant Variant, however, will shy away from repeating *Byron, Byron, Byron* and will refer to his subject as the *lame poet, the author of Sardanapalus, the hero of Missolonghi,* or *the noble libertine.* Writing about a whale, Cooper had to use the word *whale* occasionally, but he could and did contrive awkward occasional switches to *the sluggish animal, the monster of the deep, their foe, their formidable antagonist, the alarmed animal, the terrified and wounded victim, the fish, the terrible monster, the enormous black mass, the fish, the fish,* and at this point the author of *The Pilot* runs out of variants, elegant or otherwise, and a whale isn't a fish anyway. So much for Cooper the non-stylist. But you will find other Elegant Variants, and they will amuse you or irritate you, or both.

JOHN T. WINTERICH

Springfield, Massachusetts

Color Illustrations

Author's Preface

IT is probable a true history of human events would show that a far larger proportion of our acts are the result of sudden impulses and accident, than of that reason of which we so much boast. However true, or false, this opinion may be in more important matters, it is certainly and strictly correct as relates to the conception and execution of this book.

The Pilot was published in 1823. This was not long after the appearance of *The Pirate*, a work which, it is hardly necessary to remind the reader, has a direct connection with the sea. In conversation with a friend, a man of polished taste and extensive reading, the authorship of the Scottish novels came under discussion. The claims of Sir Walter were a little distrusted on account of the peculiar and minute information that the romances were then very generally thought to display. *The Pirate* was cited as a very marked instance of this universal knowledge, and it was wondered where a man of Scott's habits and associations could have become so familiar with the sea. The writer has frequently observed that there was much looseness in this universal knowledge, and that the secret of its success was to be traced to the power of creating that *vraisemblance*, which is so remarkedly exhibited in these world-renowned fictions, rather to any very accurate information on the part of their author. It would have been hypercritical to object to *The Pirate*, that it was not strictly nautical, or true in its details; but, when the reverse was urged as a proof of what, considering the character of other portions of the work, would have been most extraordinary attainments, it was a sort of provocation to dispute the seamanship of *The Pirate*, a quality to which the book has certainly very little just pretension. The result of this conversation was a sudden determination to produce a work which, if it had no other merit, might present truer pictures of the ocean and ships than any that are to be found in *The Pirate*. To this unpremeditated decision, purely an impulse, is not only *The Pilot* due, but a tolerably numerous school of nautical romances that have succeeded it.

The author had many misgivings concerning the success of the undertaking, after he had made some progress in the work, the opinions of his different friends being anything but encouraging. One would declare that the sea could not be made interesting; that it was tame, monotonous, and without any other movement than unpleasant storms, and that, for his part, the less he got of it the better. The women very generally protested that such a book would have the odor of bilge-water, and that it would give them the *maladie de mer*. Not a single individual among all those who discussed the merits of the project, within the range of the author's knowledge, either spoke, or looked, encouragingly. It is probable that all these persons anticipated a signal failure.

So very discouraging did these ominous opinions get to be, that the writer was, once or twice, tempted to throw his manuscript aside and turn to something new. A favorable opinion, however, coming from a very unexpected quarter, put a new face on the matter, and raised new hopes. Among the intimate friends of the writer was an Englishman, who possessed most of the peculiar qualities of the educated of his country. He was learned even, had a taste that was so just as always to command respect, but was prejudiced, and particularly so in all that related to this country and its literature. He could never be persuaded to admire Bryant's "Water-Fowl," and this mainly because if it were accepted as good poetry, it must be placed at once among the finest fugitive pieces of the language. Of the "Thanatopsis" he thought better, though inclined to suspect it of plagiarism. To the tender mercies of this one-sided critic, who had never affected to compliment the previous works of the author, the sheets of a volume of *The Pilot* were committed, with scarce an expectation of his liking them. The reverse proved to be the case—he expressed himself highly gratified, and predicted a success for the book which it probably never attained.

Thus encouraged, one more experiment was made, a seaman being selected for the critic. A kinsman, a namesake, and an old messmate of the author, one now in command on a foreign station, was chosen, and a considerable portion of the first volume was read to him. There is no wish to conceal the satisfaction with which the effect on this listener was observed. He treated the whole matter as fact, and his criticisms were strictly professional and perfectly just. But the interest he betrayed could not be mistaken. It gave a perfect and most gratifying assurance that the work would be more likely to find favor with nautical men than with any other class of readers.

The Pilot could scarcely be a favorite with females. The story has little interest for them, nor was it much heeded by the author of the book in the progress of his labors. His aim was to illustrate vessels and the ocean, rather than to draw any pictures of sentiment and love. In this last respect the book has small claims on the reader's attention, though it is hoped that the story has sufficient interest to relieve the more strictly nautical features of the work.

It would be affectation to deny that *The Pilot* met with a most unlooked-for success. The novelty of the design probably contributed a large share of this result. Sea-tales came into vogue as a consequence; and, as every practical part of knowledge has its uses, something has been gained by letting the landsman into the secrets of the seaman's manner of life. Perhaps, in some small degree, an interest has been awakened in behalf of a very numerous, and what has hitherto been a sort of proscribed class of men, that may directly tend to a melioration of their condition.

It is not easy to make the public comprehend all the necessities of a service afloat. With several hundred rude beings confined within the narrow limits of a vessel, men of all nations and of the lowest habits, it would be to the last degree indiscreet to commence their reformation by relaxing the bonds of discipline, under the mistaken impulses of a false philanthropy. It has a lofty sound, to be sure, to talk about American citizens being too good to be brought under the lash upon the high seas; but he must have a very mistaken notion who does not see that tens of thousands of these pretending persons on shore, even, would be greatly benefited by a little judicious flogging. It is the judgment in administering, and not the mode of punishment, that requires to be looked into; and in this respect there has certainly been a great improvement of late years. It is seldom, indeed, that any institution, practice or system, is improved by the blind interference of those who know nothing about it. Better would it be to trust to the experience of those who have long governed turbulent men, than to the impulsive experiments of those who rarely regard more than one side of a question, and that the most showy and glittering, having, quite half of the time, some selfish personal end to answer.

There is an uneasy desire among a vast many well-disposed persons to get the fruits of the Christian Faith, without troubling themselves about the Faith itself. This is done under the sanction of Peace Societies, Temperance and Moral Reform Societies, in which the end is too often mistaken for the means. When the Almighty sent his Son on earth, it was to point out the way in which all this was to be brought about, by means of the Church; but men have so frittered away that body of divine organization, through their divisions and subdivisions, all arising from human conceit, that it is no longer regarded as the agency it was so obviously intended to be, and various contrivances are to be employed as substitutes for that which proceeded directly from the Son of God!

Among the efforts of the day, however, there is one connected with the moral improvement of the sailor that commands our profound respect. Cut off from the most of the charities of life, for so large a portion of his time, deprived altogether of association with the gentler and better portions of the other sex, and living a man in a degree proscribed, amid the many signs of advancement that distinguish the age, it was time that he should be remembered and singled out, and become the subject of combined and Christian philanthropy. There is much reason to believe that the effort, now making in the right direction and under proper auspices, will be successful; and that it will cause the lash to be laid aside in the best and most rational manner—by rendering its use unnecessary.

Cooperstown
August 10, 1849

The Pilot

Sullen waves, incessant rolling,
Rudely dashed against her sides.

Song

A SINGLE glance at the map will make the reader acquainted with the position of the eastern coast of the Island of Great Britain, as connected with the shores of the opposite continent. Together they form the boundaries of the small sea that has for ages been known to the world as the scene of maritime exploits, and as the great avenue through which commerce and war have conducted the fleets of the northern nations of Europe. Over this sea the islanders long asserted a jurisdiction, exceeding that which reason concedes to any power on the highway of nations, and which frequently led to conflicts that caused an expenditure of blood and treasure utterly disproportioned to the advantages that can ever arise from the maintenance of a useless and abstract right. It is across the waters of this disputed ocean that we shall attempt to conduct our readers, selecting a period for our incidents that has a peculiar interest for every American, not only because it was the birthday of his nation, but because it was also the era when reason and common-sense began to take the place of custom and feudal practices in the management of the affairs of nations.

Soon after the events of the Revolution had involved the kingdoms of France and Spain, and the republic of Holland, in our quarrel, a group of laborers was collected in a field that lay exposed to the winds of the ocean, on the northeastern coast of England. These men were lightening their toil, and cheering the gloom of a day in December, by uttering their crude opinions on the political aspects of the times. The fact that England was engaged in a war with some of her dependencies on the other side of the Atlantic, had long been known to them, after the manner that faint rumors of distant and uninteresting events gain on the ear; but now that nations, with whom she had been used to battle, were armed against her in the quarrel, the din of war had disturbed the quiet even of these secluded and illiterate rustics. The principal speakers on the occasion were a Scotch drover, who was waiting the leisure of the occupant of the fields, and an Irish laborer, who had found his way across the Channel, and thus far over the island, in quest of employment.

"The nagurs wouldn't have been a job at all for ould England, letting alone Ireland," said the latter, "if these French and Spanishers hadn't been troubling themselves in the matter. I'm sure it's but little reason I have for thanking them, if a man is to kape as sober as a praist at mass, for fear he should find himself a sholdier, and he knowing nothing about the same."

"Hoot! mon! ye ken but little of raising an airmy in Ireland, if ye mak' a drum o' a whiskey-keg," said the drover, winking to the listeners. "Noo, in the north, they ca' a gathering of the folk, and follow the pipes as graciously as ye wad journey kirkward o' a Sabbath morn. I've seen a' the names o' a Heeland raj'ment on a sma' bit paper, that ye might cover wi' a leddy's hand. They war' a' Camerons and McDonalds, though they paraded sax hundred men! But what ha' ye gotten here? That chield has an ow'r liking to the land for a seafaring body; an' if the bottom o' the sea be onything like the top o't, he's in gr'at danger o' a ship-wreck!"

This unexpected change in the discourse drew all eyes on the object toward which the staff of the observant drover was pointed. To the utter amazement of every individual present, a small vessel was seen moving slowly round a point of land that formed one of the sides of the little bay, to which the field the laborers were in composed the other. There was something very peculiar in the externals of this unusual visitor, which added in no small degree to the surprise created by her appearance in that retired place. None but the smallest vessels, and those rarely, or, at long intervals, a desperate smuggler, were ever known to venture so close to the land, amid the sandbars and sunken rocks with which that immediate coast abounded. The adventurous mariners who now attempted this dangerous navigation in so wanton, and apparently so heedless a manner, were in a low, black schooner, whose hull seemed utterly disproportioned to the raking masts it upheld, which, in their turn, supported a lighter set of spars, that tapered away until their upper extremities appeared no larger than the lazy pennant, that in vain endeavored to display its length in the light breeze.

The short day of that high northern latitude was already drawing to a close, and the sun was throwing his parting rays obliquely across the waters, touching the gloomy waves here and there with streaks of pale light. The stormy winds of the German Ocean were apparently lulled to rest: and, though the incessant rolling of the surge on the shore heightened the gloomy character of the hour and the view, the light ripple that ruffled the sleeping billows was produced by a gentle air, that blew directly from the land. Notwithstanding this favorable circumstance, there was something threatening in the aspect of the ocean, which was speaking in hollow but deep murmurs, like a volcano on the eve of an eruption, that greatly heightened the feelings of amazement and dread with which the peasants beheld this extraordinary interruption to the quiet of their little bay. With no other sails spread to the action of the air than her heavy mainsail, and one of those light jibs that projected far beyond her bows, the vessel glided over the water with a grace and facility that seemed magical to the beholders, who turned their wondering looks from the schooner to each other in silent amazement. At length the drover spoke in a low, solemn voice:

"He's a bold chield that steers her! and if that bit craft has wood in her bottom, like the brigantines that ply between Lon'on and the Frith at Leith, he's in mair danger than a prudent man could wish. Ay! he's by the big rock that shows his head when the tide runs low, but it's no mortal mon who can steer long in the road he's journeying and not speedily find land wi' water a top o't."

The little schooner, however, still held her way among the rocks and sand-pits, making such slight deviations in her course as proved her to be under the direction of one who knew his danger, until she had entered as far into the bay as prudence could at all justify, when her canvas was gathered into folds, seemingly without the agency of hands, and the vessel, after rolling for a few minutes on the long billows that hove in from the ocean, swung round in the currents of the tide, and was held by her anchor.

The peasants now began to make their conjectures more freely concerning the character and object of their visitor; some intimating that she was engaged in contraband trade, and others that her views were hostile, and her business war. A few dark hints were hazarded on the materiality of her construction, for nothing of artificial formation, it was urged, would be ventured by men in such a dangerous place, at a time when even the most inexperienced landsman was enabled to foretell the certain gale. The Scotchman, who, to all the sagacity of his countrymen, added no small proportion of their superstition, leaned greatly to the latter conclusion, and had begun to express this sentiment warily and with reverence, when the child of Erin, who appeared not to possess any very definite ideas on the subject, interrupted him, by exclaiming:

"Faith! there's two of them! a big and a little! sure the bogles of the saa likes good company the same as any other Christians!"

"Twa!" echoed the drover; "twa! ill luck bides o' some o' ye. Twa craft a sailing without hand to guide them, in sic a place as this, whar' eyesight is na guid enough to show the dangers, bodes evil to a' that luik thereon. Hoot! she's no yearling the tither! Luik, mon! luik! she's a gallant boat, and a gr'at"; he paused, raised his pack from the ground, and first giving one searching look at the objects of his suspicion, he nodded with great sagacity to the listeners, and continued, as he moved slowly toward the interior of the country, "I should na wonder if she carried King George's commission aboot her; weel, weel, I wull journey upward to the town, and ha' a crack wi' the good mon; for they craft have a suspeecious aspcct, and the sma' bit thing wu'ld nab a mon quite easy, and the big ane wu'ld hold us a' and no feel we war' in her."

This sagacious warning caused a general movement in the party, for the intelligence of a hot press was among the rumors of the times. The husbandmen collected their implements of labor, and retired homeward; and, though many a curious eye was bent on the movements of the vessels from the distant hills, but very few of those not immediately interested in the mysterious visitors ventured to approach the little rocky cliffs that lined the bay.

The vessel that occasioned these cautious movements was a gallant ship, whose huge hull, lofty masts, and square yards loomed in the evening's haze, above the sea, like a distant mountain rising from the deep. She carried but little sail, and though she warily avoided the near approach to the land that the schooner had attempted, the similarity of their movements was sufficiently apparent to warrant the conjecture that they were employed on the same duty. The frigate, for the ship belonged to this class of vessels, floated across the entrance of the little bay majestically in the tide, with barely enough motion through the water to govern her movements, until she had arrived opposite to the place where her consort lay, when she hove up heavily into the wind, squared the enormous yards on her mainmast, and attempted, in counteracting the power of her sails by each other, to remain stationary: but the light air that had at no time swelled her heavy canvas to the utmost began to fail, and the long waves that rolled in from the ocean ceased to be ruffled with the breeze from the land. The currents and the billows were fast sweeping the frigate toward one of the points of the estuary, where the black heads of the rocks could be seen running far into the sea, and, in their turn, the mariners of the ship dropped an anchor to the bottom, and drew her sail in festoons to the yards. As the vessel swung round to the tide, a heavy ensign was raised to her peak, and, a current of air opening for a moment its folds, the white fields and red cross, that distinguish the flag of England, were displayed to view. So much even the wary drover had loitered at a distance to behold; but when a boat was launched from either vessel, he quickened his steps, observing to his wondering and amused companions that "they craft were a'thegither mair bonny to luik on than to abide wi'."

A numerous crew manned the barge that was lowered from the frigate, which, after receiving an officer, with an attendant youth, left the ship, and moved with a measured stroke of its oars directly toward the head of the bay. As it passed at a short distance from the schooner a light whaleboat, pulled by four athletic men, shot from her side, and, rather dancing over than cutting through the waves crossed her course with a wonderful velocity. As the boats approached each other, the men, in obedience to signals from their officers, suspended their efforts, and for a few minutes they floated at rest, during which time there was the following dialogue:

"Is the old man mad?" exclaimed the young officer in the whale-boat, when his men had ceased rowing; "does he think that the bottom of the Ariel is made of iron, and that a rock can't knock a hole in it? or does he think that she is manned with alligators, who can't be drowned?"

A languid smile played for a moment round the handsome features of the young man, who was rather reclining than sitting in the stern sheets of the barge, as he replied:

"He knows your prudence too well, Captain Barnstable, to fear either the wreck of your vessel or the drowning of her crew. How near the bottom does your keel lie?"

"I am afraid to sound," returned Barnstable. "I have never the heart to touch a lead-line when I see the rocks coming up to breathe like so many porpoises."

"You are afloat!" exclaimed the other, with a vehemence that denoted an abundance of latent fire.

"Afloat!" echoed his friend; "ay! the little Ariel would float in air!" As he spoke he rose in the boat, and, lifting his leathern sea-cap from his head, stroked back the thick clusters of black locks which shadowed his sunburnt countenance, while he viewed his little vessel with the complacency of a seaman who was proud of her qualities. "But it's close work, Mr. Griffith, when a man rides to a single anchor in a place like this, and at such a nightfall. What are the orders?"

"I shall put into the surf and let go a grapnel; you will take Mr. Merry into your whale-boat and try to drive her through the breakers on the beach."

"Beach!" retorted Barnstable; "do you call a perpendicular rock of a hundred feet in height a beach?"

"We shall not dispute about terms," said Griffith, smiling, "but you must manage to get on the shore; we have seen the signal from the land, and know that the pilot, whom we have so long expected, is ready to come off."

Barnstable shook his head with a grave air, as he muttered to himself, "This is droll navigation; first we run into an unfrequented bay that is full of rocks and sandpits, and shoals, and then we get off our pilot. But how am I to know him?"

"Merry will give you the pass-word, and tell you where to look for him. I would land myself, but my orders forbid it. If you meet with difficulties, show three oar-blades in a row, and I will pull into your assistance. Three oars on end and a pistol will bring the fire of my muskets, and the signal repeated from the barge will draw a shot from the ship."

"I thank you, I thank you," said Barnstable, carelessly; "I believe I can fight my own battles against all the enemies we are likely to fall in with on this coast. But the old man is surely mad. I would—"

"You would obey his orders if he were here, and you will now please to obey mine," said Griffith, in a tone that the friendly expression of his eye contradicted. "Pull in and keep a lookout for a small man in a drab pea-jacket; Merry will give you the word; if he answer it, bring him off to the barge."

The young men now nodded familiarly and kindly to each other, and the boy who was called Mr. Merry having changed his place from the barge to the whale-boat, Barnstable threw himself into his seat, and, making a signal with his hand, his men again bent to their oars. The light vessel shot away from her companion, and dashed in boldly toward the rocks; after skirting the shore for some distance in quest of a favorable place, she was suddenly turned, and, dashing over the broken waves, was run upon a spot where a landing could be effected in safety.

In the meantime the barge followed these movements, at some distance, with a more measured progress, and when the whale-boat was observed to be drawn up alongside of a rock, the promised grapnel was cast into the water, and her crew deliberately proceeded to get their fire-arms in a state for immediate service. Everything appeared to be done in obedience to strict orders that must have been previously communicated; for the young man, who has been introduced to the reader by the name of Griffith, seldom spoke, and then only in the pithy expressions that are apt to fall from those who are sure of obedience.

When the boat had brought up to her grapnel, he sank back at his length on the cushioned seats of the barge, and, drawing his hat over his eyes in a listless manner, he continued for many minutes apparently absorbed in thoughts altogether foreign to his present situation. Occasionally he rose, and would first bend his looks in quest of his companions on the shore, and, then turning his expressive eyes toward the ocean, the abstracted and vacant air that so often usurped the place of animation and intelligence in his countenance, would give place to the anxious and intelligent look of a seaman gifted with an experience beyond his years. His weather-beaten and hardy crew, having made their dispositions for offence, sat in profound silence, with their hands thrust into the bosoms of their jackets, but with their eyes earnestly regarding every cloud that was gathering in the threatening atmosphere, and exchanging looks of deep care, whenever the boat rose higher than usual on one of those long, heavy ground-swells that were heaving in from the ocean with increasing rapidity and magnitude.

2

A horseman's coat shall hide
Thy taper shape and comeliness of side;
And with a bolder stride and looser air,
Mingled with men, a man thou must appear.

PRIOR

WHEN the whale-boat obtained the position we have described, the young lieutenant, who, in consequence of commanding a schooner, was usually addressed by the title of captain, stepped on the rocks, followed by the youthful midshipman, who had quitted the barge to aid in the hazardous duty of their expedition.

"This is, at best, but a Jacob's ladder we have to climb," said Barnstable, casting his eyes upward at the difficult ascent, "and it's by no means certain that we shall be well received, when we get up, though we should reach the top."

"We are under the guns of the frigate," returned the boy; "and you remember, sir, three oar-blades and a pistol, repeated from the barge, will draw her fire."

"Yes, on our own heads. Boy, never be so foolish as to trust a long shot. It makes a great smoke and some noise, but it's a terrible uncertain manner of throwing old iron about. In such a business as this, I would sooner trust Tom Coffin and his harpoon to back me, than the best broadside that ever rattled out of the three decks of a ninety-gun ship. Come, gather your limbs together, and try if you can walk on *terra firma*, Master Coffin."

The seaman who was addressed by this dire appellation arose slowly from the place where he was stationed as cockswain of the boat, and seemed to ascend high in the air by the gradual evolution of numberless folds in his body. When erect, he stood nearly six feet and as many inches in his shoes, though, when elevated in his most perpendicular attitude, there was a forward inclination about his head and shoulders that appeared to be the consequence of habitual confinement in limited lodgings. His whole frame was destitute of the rounded outlines of a well-formed man, though his enormous hands furnished a display of bones and sinews which gave indication of gigantic strength. On his head he wore a little, low, brown hat of wool, with an arched top, that threw an expression of solemnity and hardness over his harsh visage, the sharp prominent features of which were completely encircled by a set of black whiskers that began to be frizzled a little with age. One of his hands grasped, with a sort of instinct, the staff of a bright harpoon, the lower end of which he placed firmly on the rock, as, in obedience to the order of his commander, he left the place where, considering his vast dimensions, he had been established in an incredibly small space.

As soon as Captain Barnstable received this addition to his strength, he gave a few precautionary orders to the men in the boat, and proceeded to the difficult task of ascending the rocks. Notwithstanding the great daring and personal agility of Barnstable, he would have been completely baffled in this attempt but for the assistance he occasionally received from his cockswain, whose prodigious strength and great length of limbs enabled him to make exertions which it would have been useless for most men to attempt. When within a few feet of the summit, they availed themselves of a projecting rock to pause for consultation and breath, both of which seemed necessary for their further movements.

"This will be but a bad place for a retreat, if we should happen to fall in with enemies," said Barnstable. "Where are we to look for this pilot, Mr. Merry, or how are we to know him? and what certainty have you that he will not betray us?"

"The question you are to put to him is written on this bit of paper," returned the boy, as he handed the other the word of recognition; "we made the signal on the point of the rock at yon headland, but, as he must have seen our boat, he will follow us to this place. As to his betraying us, he seems to have the confidence of Captain Munson, who has kept a bright lookout for him ever since we made the land."

"Ay," muttered the lieutenant, "and I shall have a bright lookout kept on him now we are *on* the land. I like not this business of hugging the shore so closely, nor have I much faith in any traitor. What think you of it, Master Coffin?"

The hardy old seaman, thus addressed, turned his grave visage on his commander, and replied with a becoming gravity:

"Give me plenty of sea-room and good canvas, where there is no occasion for pilots at all, sir. For my part, I was born on board a chebacco-man, and never could see the use of more land than now and then a small island to raise a few vegetables, and to dry your fish. I'm sure the sight of it always makes me feel uncomfortable, unless we have the wind dead off-shore."

"Ah! Tom, you are a sensible fellow," said Barnstable, with an air half comic, half serious. "But we must be moving. The sun is just touching those clouds to seaward, and God keep us from riding out this night at anchor in such a place as this!"

Laying his hand on a projection of the rock above him, Barnstable swung himself forward, and, following this movement with a desperate leap or two, he stood at once on the brow of the cliff. His cockswain very deliberately raised the midshipman after his officer, and, proceeding with more caution, but less exertion, he soon placed himself by his side.

When they reached the level land that lay above the cliffs, and began to inquire, with curious and wary eyes, into the surrounding scenery, the adventurers discovered a cultivated country, divided in the usual manner by hedges and walls. Only one habitation for man, however, and that a small dilapidated cottage, stood within a mile of them, most of the dwellings being placed, as far as convenience would permit, from the fogs and damps of the ocean.

"Here seems to be neither anything to apprehend, nor the object of our search," said Barnstable, when he had taken the whole view in his survey; "I fear we have landed to no purpose, Mr. Merry. What say you, Long Tom; see you what we want?"

"I see no pilot, sir," returned the cockswain; "but it's an ill wind that blows luck to nobody; there is a mouthful of fresh meat stowed away under that row of bushes, that would make a double ration to all hands in the Ariel."

The midshipman laughed, as he pointed out to Barnstable the object of the cockswain's solicitude, which proved to be a fat ox, quietly ruminating under a hedge near them.

"There's many a hungry fellow aboard of us," said the boy, merrily, "who would be glad to second Long Tom's motion, if the time and business would permit us to slay the animal."

"It is but a lubber's blow, Mr. Merry," returned the cockswain, without a muscle of his hard face yielding, as he struck the end of his harpoon violently against the earth, and then made a motion toward poising the weapon; "let Captain Barnstable but say the word, and I'll drive the iron through him to the quick; I've sent it to the seizing in many a whale, that hadn't a jacket of such blubber as that fellow wears."

"Pshaw! you are not on a whaling voyage, where everything that offers is game," said Barnstable, turning himself pettishly away from the beast, as if he distrusted his own forbearance; "but stand fast! I see some one approaching behind the hedge. Look to your arms, Mr. Merry—the first thing we hear may be a shot."

"Not from that cruiser," cried the thoughtless lad; "he is a younker, like myself, and would hardly dare run down upon such a formidable force as we muster."

"You say true, boy," returned Barnstable, relinquishing the grasp he held on his pistol. "He comes on with caution, as if afraid. He is small, and is in drab, though I should hardly call it a pea-jacket—and yet he may be our man. Stand you both here, while I go and hail him."

As Barnstable walked rapidly toward the hedge, that in part concealed the stranger, the latter stopped suddenly, and seemed to be in doubt whether to advance or to retreat. Before he had decided on either, the active sailor was within a few feet of him.

"Pray, sir," said Barnstable, "what water have we in this bay?"

The slight form of the stranger started with an extraordinary emotion at this question, and he shrunk aside involuntarily, as if to conceal his features, before he answered, in a voice that was barely audible:

"I should think it would be the water of the German Ocean."

"Indeed! you must have passed no small part of your short life in the study of geography, to be so well informed," returned the lieutenant; "perhaps, sir, your cunning is also equal to telling me how long we shall sojourn together, if I make you a prisoner, in order to enjoy the benefit of your wit?"

To this alarming intimation, the youth who was addressed made no reply; but as he averted his face and concealed it with both hands, the offended sea-man, believing that a salutary impression had been made upon the fears of his auditor, was about to proceed with his interrogatories. The singular agitation of the stranger's frame, however, caused the lieutenant to continue silent a few moments longer, when, to his utter amazement, he discovered that what he had mistaken for alarm was produced by an endeavor, on the part of the youth, to suppress a violent fit of laughter.

"Now, by all the whales in the sea!" cried Barnstable, "but you are merry out of season, young gentleman. It's quite bad enough to be ordered to anchor in such a bay as this with a storm brewing before my eyes, without landing to be laughed at by a stripling who has not strength to carry a beard if he had one, when I ought to be getting an offing for the safety of both body and soul. But I'll know more of you and your jokes, if I take you into my own mess, and am giggled out of my sleep for the rest of the cruise."

As the commander of the schooner concluded, he approached the stranger with an air of offering some violence, but the other shrank back from his extended arm, and exclaimed, with a voice in which real terror had gotten the better of mirth: "Barnstable! dear Barnstable! would you harm me?"

The sailor recoiled several feet at this unexpected appeal, and, rubbing his eyes, he threw the cap from his head, before he cried:

"What do I hear! and what do I see! There lies the Ariel—and yonder is the frigate. Can this be Katherine Plowden?"

His doubts, if any doubts remained, were soon removed, for the stranger sank on the bank at her side, in an attitude in which female bashfulness was beautifully contrasted with her attire, and gave vent to her mirth in an uncontrollable burst of merriment.

From that moment, all thoughts of his duty, and the pilot, or even of the Ariel, appeared to be banished from the mind of the seaman, who sprang to her side, and joined in her mirth, though he hardly knew why or wherefore.

When the diverted girl had in some degree recovered her composure, she turned to her companion, who had sat good-naturedly by her side, content to be laughed at, and said:

"But this is not only silly, but cruel to others. I owe you an explanation of my unexpected appearance, and perhaps, also, of my extraordinary attire."

"I can anticipate everything," cried Barnstable; "you heard that we were on the coast, and have flown to redeem the promise you made me in America. But I ask no more; the chaplain of the frigate—"

"May preach as usual, and to as little purpose," interrupted the disguised female; "but no nuptial benediction shall be pronounced over me, until I have effected the object of this hazardous experiment. You are not usually selfish, Barnstable; would you have me forgetful of the happiness of others?"

"Of whom do you speak?"

"My poor, my devoted cousin. I heard that two vessels answering the description of the frigate and the Ariel were seen hovering on the coast, and I determined at once to have a communication with you. I have followed your movements for a week in this dress, but have been unsuccessful till now. Today I observed you to approach nearer to the shore than usual, and happily, by being adventurous, I have been successful."

"Ay, God knows we are near enough to the land! But does Captain Munson know of your wish to get on board his ship?"

"Certainly not—none know of it but yourself. I thought that if Griffith and you could learn our situation, you might be tempted to hazard a little to redeem us from our thraldom. In this paper I have prepared such an account as will, I trust, excite all your chivalry, and by which you may govern your movements."

"Our movements!" interrupted Barnstable. "You will pilot us in person."

"Then there's two of them!" said a hoarse voice near them.

The alarmed female shrieked as she recovered her feet, but she still adhered, with instinctive dependence, to the side of her lover. Barnstable, who recognized the tones of his cockswain, bent an angry brow on the sober visage that was peering at them above the hedge, and demanded the meaning of the interruption.

"Seeing you were hull-down, sir, and not knowing but the chase might lead you ashore, Mr. Merry thought it best to have a lookout kept. I told him that you were overhauling the mail-bags of the messenger for the news, but as he was an officer, sir, and I nothing but a common hand, I did as he ordered."

"Return, sir, where I commanded you to remain," said Barnstable; "and desire Mr. Merry to wait my pleasure."

The cockswain gave the usual reply of an obedient seaman; but, before he left the hedge, he stretched out one of his brawny arms toward the ocean, and said, in tones of solemnity suited to his apprehensions and character:

"I showed you how to knot a reef-point, and pass a gasket, Captain Barnstable, nor do I believe you could even take two half-hitches when you first came aboard of the Spalmacitty. These be things that a man is soon expert in, but it takes the time of his nat'ral life to larn to know the weather. There be streaked wind-galls in the offing that speak as plainly, to all that see them, and know God's language in the clouds, as ever you spoke through a trumpet, to shorten sail; besides, sir, don't you hear the sea moaning as if it knew the hour was at hand when it was to wake up from its sleep?"

"Ay, Tom," returned the officer, walking to the edge of the cliffs, and throwing a seaman's glance at the gloomy ocean, " 'tis a threatening night indeed; but this pilot must be had—and—"

"Is that the man?" interrupted the cockswain, pointing toward a man who was standing not far from them, an attentive observer of their proceedings, at the same time that he was narrowly watched himself by the young midshipman. "God send that he knows his trade well, for the bottom of a ship will need eyes to find its road out of this wild anchorage!"

"That must indeed be the man!" exclaimed Barnstable, at once recalled to his duty. He then held a short dialogue with his female companion, whom he left concealed by the hedge, and proceeded to address the stranger. When near enough to be heard, the commander of the schooner demanded:

"What water have you in this bay?"

The stranger, who seemed to expect this question, answered without the least hesitation:

"Enough to take all out in safety, who have entered with confidence."

"You are the man I seek," cried Barnstable; "are you ready to go off?"

"Both ready and willing," returned the pilot, "and there is need of haste. I would give the best hundred guineas that ever were coined for two hours more use of that sun which has left us, or for even half the time of this fading twilight."

"Think you our situation so bad?" said the lieutenant. "Follow this gentleman to the boat, then; I will join you by the time you can descend the cliffs. I believe I can prevail on another hand to go with us."

"Time is more precious now than any number of hands," said the pilot, throwing a glance of impatience from under his lowering brows, "and the consequences of delay must be visited on those who occasion it."

"And, sir, I will meet the consequences with those who have a right to inquire into my conduct," said Barnstable, haughtily.

With this warning and retort they separated; the young officer retracing his steps impatiently toward his mistress, muttering his indignation in suppressed execrations, and the pilot drawing the leather belt of his pea-jacket mechanically around his body, as he followed the midshipman and cockswain to their boat in moody silence.

Barnstable found the disguised female, who had announced herself as Katherine Plowden, awaiting his return with intense anxiety depicted on every feature of her intelligent countenance. As he felt the responsibility of his situation, notwithstanding his cool reply to the pilot, the young man hastily drew an arm of the apparent boy, forgetful of her disguise, through his own, and led her forward.

"Come, Katherine," he said, "the time urges to be prompt."

"What pressing necessity is there for immediate departure?" she inquired, checking his movements by withdrawing herself from his side.

"You heard the ominous prognostic of my cockswain on the weather, and I am forced to add my own testimony to his opinon. 'Tis a crazy night that threatens us, though I cannot repent of coming into the bay, since it has led to this interview."

"God forbid that we should either of us have cause to repent of it!" said Katherine, the paleness of anxiety chasing away the rich bloom that had mantled the animated face of the brunette. "But you have the paper—follow its directions, and come to our rescue; you will find us willing captives, if Griffith and yourself are our conquerors."

"What mean you, Katherine?" exclaimed her lover; "you at least are now in safety—'twould be madness to tempt your fate again. My vessel can and shall protect you, until your cousin is redeemed; and then, remember, I have a claim on you for life."

"And how would you dispose of me in the interval?" said the young maiden, retreating slowly from his advances.

"In the Ariel—by Heaven, you shall be her commander! I will bear that rank only in name."

"I thank you, thank you, Barnstable, but distrust my abilities to fill such a station," she said, laughing, though the color that again crossed her youthful features was like the glow of a summer's sunset, and even her mirthful eyes seemed to reflect their tints. "Do not mistake, saucy one. If I have done more than my sex will warrant, remember it was through a holy motive, and if I have more than a woman's enterprise, it must be—"

"To lift you above the weakness of your sex," he cried, "and to enable you to show your noble confidence in me."

"To fit me for, and to keep me worthy of being one day your wife." As she uttered these words she turned and disappeared, with a rapidity that eluded his attempt to detain her, behind an angle of the hedge, that was near them. For a moment, Barnstable remained motionless, through surprise, and when he sprang forward in pursuit, he was able only to catch a glimpse of her light form, in the gloom of the evening, as she again vanished in a little thicket at some distance.

Barnstable was about to pursue, when the air lighted with a sudden flash, and the bellowing report of a cannon rolled along the cliffs, and was echoed among the hills far inland.

"Ay, grumble away, old dotard!" the disappointed young sailor muttered to himself, while he reluctantly obeyed the signal; "you are in as great a hurry to get out of your danger as you were to run into it."

The quick reports of three muskets from the barge beneath where he stood urged him to quicken his pace, and, as he drew himself carelessly down the rugged and dangerous passes of the cliffs, his experienced eye beheld the well-known lights displayed from the frigate, which commanded "the recall of all her boats."

3

In such a time as this, it is not meet
That every nice offence should bear its
comment.

SHAKESPEARE

THE cliffs threw their dark shadows wide on the waters, and the gloom of the evening had so far advanced as to conceal the discontent that brooded over the ordinarily open brow of Barnstable as he sprang from the rocks into the boat, and took his seat by the side of the silent pilot.

"Shove off!" cried the lieutenant, in tones that his men knew must be obeyed. "A seaman's curse light on the folly that exposes planks and lives to such navigation; and all to burn some old timberman, or catch a Norway trader asleep! Give way, men, give way!"

Notwithstanding the heavy and dangerous surf that was beginning to tumble in upon the rocks in an alarming manner, the startled seamen succeeded in urging their light boat over the waves, and in a few seconds were without the point where danger was most to be apprehended. Barnstable had seemingly disregarded the breakers as they passed, but sat sternly eyeing the foam that rolled by them in successive surges, until the boat rose regularly on the long seas, when he turned his looks around the bay in quest of the barge.

"Ay, Griffith has tired of rocking in his pillowed cradle," he muttered, "and will give us a pull to the frigate, when we ought to be getting the schooner out of this hard-featured landscape. This is just such a place as one of your sighing lovers would dote on; a little land, a little water, and a good deal of rock. Damme, Long Tom, but I am more than half of your mind, that an island now and then is all the *terra firma* that a seaman needs."

"It's reason and philosophy, sir," returned the sedate cockswain; "and what land there is should always be a soft mud, or a sandy ooze, in order that an anchor might hold, and to make soundings sartin. I have lost many a deep sea, besides hand-leads by the dozen, on rocky bottoms; but give me the roadstead where a lead comes up light and an anchor heavy. There's a boat pulling athwart our fore-foot, Captain Barnstable; shall I run her aboard, or give her a berth, sir?"

"'Tis the barge!" cried the officer; "Ned has not deserted me, after all!"

A loud hail from the approaching boat confirmed this opinion, and, in a few seconds, the barge and whale-boat were again rolling by each other's side. Griffith was no longer reclining on the cushions of his seat, but spoke earnestly, and with a slight tone of reproach in his manner.

"Why have you wasted so many precious moments, when every minute threatens us with new dangers? I was obeying the signal, but I heard your oars, and pulled back to take out the pilot. Have you been successful?"

"There he is; and if he find his way out through the shoals, he will earn a right to his name. This bids fair to be a night when a man will need a spy-glass to find the moon. But when you hear that I have been on those rascally cliffs, you will be more ready to excuse my delay, Mr. Griffith."

"You have seen the true man, I trust, or we incur this hazard to an evil purpose."

"Ay, I have seen him that is a true man, and him that is not," replied Barnstable, bitterly; "you have the boy with you, Griffith—ask him what his young eyes have seen."

"Shall I?" cried the young midshipman, laughing; "then I have seen a little clipper, in disguise, outsail an old man-of-war's man in a hard chase, and I have seen a straggling rover in long-togs as much like my cousin—"

"Peace, gabbler!" exclaimed Barnstable in a voice of thunder; "would you detain the boats with your silly nonsense at a time like this? Away into the barge, sir, and if you find him willing to hear, tell Mr. Griffith what your foolish conjectures amount to at your leisure."

The boy stepped lightly from the whale-boat to the barge, whither the pilot had already preceded him, and, as he sank with a mortified air by the side of Griffith, he said, in a low voice:

"And that won't be long, I know, if Mr. Griffith thinks and feels on the coast of England as he thought and felt at home."

A silent pressure of his hand was the only reply that the young lieutenant made, before he paid the parting compliment to Barnstable, and directed his men to pull for their ship.

The boats were separating, and the splash of the oars was already heard, when the voice of the pilot was for the first time raised in earnest.

"Hold!" he cried; "hold water, I bid ye!"

The men ceased their efforts, at the commanding tones of his voice, and, turning toward the whale-boat, he continued:

"You will get your schooner under way immediately, Captain Barnstable, and sweep into the offing with as little delay as possible. Keep the ship well open from the northern headland, and, as you pass us, come within hail."

"This is a clean chart and plain sailing, Mr. Pilot," returned Barnstable; "but who is to justify my moving without orders, to Captain Munson? I have it in black and white, to run the Ariel into this feather-bed sort of a place, and I must at least have it by signal or word of mouth from my betters, before my cut-water curls another wave. The road may be as hard to find going out as it was coming in—and then I had daylight as well as your written directions to steer by."

"Would you lie there to perish on such a night?" said the pilot, sternly. "Two hours hence this heavy swell will break where your vessel now rides so quietly."

"There we think exactly alike; but, if I get drowned now, I am drowned according to orders; whereas, if I knock a plank out of the schooner's bottom, by following your directions, 'twill be a hole to let in mutiny, as well as sea-water. How do I know but the old man wants another pilot or two."

"That's philosophy," muttered the cockswain of the whale-boat, in a voice that was audible; "but it's a hard strain on a man's conscience to hold on in such an anchorage!"

"Then keep your anchor down, and follow it to the bottom," said the pilot to himself; "it's worse to contend with a fool than a gale of wind; but if—"

"No, no, sir—no fool neither," interrupted Griffith. "Barnstable does not deserve that epithet, though he certainly carries the point of duty to the extreme. Heave up at once, Mr. Barnstable, and get out of this bay as fast as possible."

"Ah! you don't give the order with half the pleasure with which I shall execute it; pull away, boys—the Ariel shall never lay her bones in such a hard bed, if I can help it."

As the commander of the schooner uttered these words with a cheering voice, his men spontaneously shouted, and the whale-boat darted away from her companion, and was soon lost in the gloomy shadows cast from the cliffs.

In the meantime, the oarsmen of the barge were not idle, but by strenuous efforts they forced the heavy boat rapidly through the water, and in a few minutes she ran alongside of the frigate. During this period the pilot, in a voice which had lost all the startling fierceness and authority it had manifested in his short dialogue with Barnstable, requested Griffith to repeat to him, slowly, the names of the officers that belonged to his ship. When the young lieutenant had complied with this request, he observed to his companion:

"All good men and true, Mr. Pilot; and though this business in which you are just now engaged may be hazardous to an Englishman, there are none with us who will betray you. We need your services, and, as we expect good faith from you, so shall we offer it to you in exchange."

"And how know you that I need its exercise?" asked the pilot, in a manner that denoted a cold indifference to the subject.

"Why, though you talk pretty good English, for a native," returned Griffith, "yet you have a small bur-r-r in your mouth that would prick the tongue of a man who was born on the other side of the Atlantic."

"It is but of little moment where a man is born, or how he speaks," returned the pilot, coldly, "so that he does his duty bravely, and in good faith."

It was perhaps fortunate for the harmony of this dialogue that the gloom, which had now increased to positive darkness, completely concealed the look of scornful irony that crossed the handsome features of the young sailor as he replied:

"True, true, so that he does his duty, as you say, in good faith. But, as Barnstable observed, you must know your road well to travel among these shoals on such a night as this. Know you what water we draw?"

" 'Tis a frigate's draught, and I shall endeavor to keep you in four fathoms; less than that would be dangerous."

"She's a sweet boat!" said Griffith; "and minds her helm as a marine watches the eye of his sergeant at a drill; but you must give her room in stays, for she fore-reaches, as if she would put out the wind's eye."

The pilot attended, with a practised ear, to this description of the qualities of the ship that he was about to attempt extricating from an extremely dangerous situation. Not a syllable was lost on him; and when Griffith had ended, he remarked, with the singular coldness that pervaded his manner:

"That is both a good and a bad quality in a narrow channel. I fear it will be the latter tonight, when we shall require to have the ship in leading-strings."

"I suppose we must feel our way with the lead?" said Griffith.

"We shall need both eyes and leads," returned the pilot, recurring insensibly to his soliloquizing tone of voice. "I have been both in and out in darker nights than this, though never with a heavier draught than a half-two."

"Then, by Heaven, you are not fit to handle that ship among these rocks and breakers!" exclaimed Griffith; "your men of a light draught never know their water; 'tis the deep keel only that finds a channel. Pilot! pilot! beware how you trifle with us ignorantly; for 'tis a dangerous experiment to play at hazards with an enemy."

"Young man, you know not what you threaten, nor whom," said the pilot, sternly, though his quiet manner still remained undisturbed; "you forget that you have a superior here, and that I have none."

"That shall be as you discharge your duty," cried Griffith; "for, if—"

"Peace!" interrupted the pilot, "we approach the ship, let us enter in harmony."

He threw himself back on the cushions when he had said this; and Griffith, though filled with the apprehensions of suffering, either by great ignorance or treachery on the part of his companion, smothered his feelings so far as to be silent, and they ascended the side of the vessel in apparent cordiality.

The frigate was already riding on lengthened seas, that rolled in from the ocean at each successive moment with increasing violence, though her top-sails still hung supinely from her yards; the air, which continued to breathe occasionally from the land, being unable to shake the heavy canvas of which they were composed.

The only sounds that were audible, when Griffith and the pilot had ascended to the gangway of the frigate, were produced by the sullen dashing of the sea against the massive bows of the ship, and the shrill whistle of the boatswain's mate, as he recalled the side-boys, who were placed on either side of the gangway, to do honor to the entrance of the first-lieutenant and his companion.

But though such a profound silence reigned among the hundreds who inhabited the huge fabric, the light produced by a dozen battle-lanterns, that were arranged in different parts of the decks, served not only to exhibit faintly the persons of the crew, but the mingled feeling of curiosity and care that dwelt on most of their countenances.

Large groups of men were collected in the gangways, around the mainmast, and on the booms of the vessel, whose faces were distinctly visible, while numerous figures, lying along the lower yards, or bending out of the tops, might be dimly traced in the background, all of whom expressed by their attitudes the interest they took in the arrival of the boat.

Though such crowds were collected in other parts of the vessel, the quarter-deck was occupied only by the officers, who were disposed according to their several ranks and were equally silent and attentive as the remainder of the crew. In front stood a small collection of young men, who, by their similarity of dress, were the equals and companions of Griffith, though his junior in rank. On the opposite side of the vessel was a larger assemblage of youths, who claimed Mr. Merry as their fellow. Around the capstan three or four figures were standing, one of whom wore a coat of blue, with the scarlet facings of a soldier, and another the black vestments of a ship's chaplain. Behind these, and nearer the passage to the cabin from which he had just ascended, stood the tall, erect form of the commander of the vessel.

After a brief salutation between Griffith and the junior officers, the former advanced, followed slowly by the pilot, to the place where he was expected by his veteran commander. The young man removed his hat entirely, as he bowed with a little more than his usual ceremony, and said:

"We have succeeded, sir, though not without more difficulty and delay than were anticipated."

"But you have not brought off the pilot," said the captain, "and, without him, all our risk and trouble have been in vain."

"He is here," said Griffith, stepping aside, and extending his arm toward the man that stood behind him, wrapped to the chin in his coarse pea-jacket, and his face shadowed by the falling rim of a large hat that had seen much and hard service.

"This!" exclaimed the captain; "then there is a sad mistake—this is not the man I would have seen, nor can another supply his place."

"I know not whom you expected, Captain Munson," said the stranger, in a low, quiet voice; "but if you have not forgotten the day when a very different flag from that emblem of tyranny that now hangs over yon taffrail was first spread to the wind, you may remember the hand that raised it."

"Bring here the light!" exclaimed the commander, hastily.

When the lantern was extended toward the pilot, and the glare fell strong on his features, Captain Munson started as he beheld the calm blue eye that met his gaze, and the composed but pallid countenance of the other. Involuntarily raising his hat, and baring his silver locks, the veteran cried:

"It is he! though so changed—"

"That his enemies did not know him," interrupted the pilot, quickly; then touching the other by the arm, as he led him aside, he continued, in a lower tone—"neither must his friends, until the proper hour shall arrive."

Griffith had fallen back to answer the eager questions of his messmates, and no part of this short dialogue was overheard by the officers, though it was soon perceived that their commander had discovered his error, and was satisfied that the proper man had been brought on board his vessel. For many minutes the two continued to pace a part of the quarter-deck, by themselves, engaged in deep and earnest discourse.

As Griffith had but little to communicate, the curiosity of his listeners was soon appeased, and all eyes were directed toward that mysterious guide, who was to conduct them from a situation already surrounded by perils, which each moment not only magnified in appearance, but increased in reality.

4

Behold the threaden sails,
Borne with the invisible and creeping winds,
Draw the huge bottoms through the
furrowed sea,
Breasting the lofty surge.

SHAKESPEARE

IT had been already explained to the reader that there were threatening symptoms in the appearance of the weather to create serious forebodings of evil in the breast of a seaman. When removed from the shadows of the cliffs, the night was not so dark but objects could be discerned at some little distance, and in the eastern horizon there was a streak of fearful light impending over the gloomy waters, in which the swelling outline formed by the rising waves was becoming each moment more distinct, and consequently more alarming. Several dark clouds overhung the vessel, whose towering masts apparently propped the black vapor, while a few stars were seen twinkling, with a sickly flame, in the streak of clear sky that skirted the ocean. Still, light currents of air occasionally swept across the bay, bringing with them the fresh odor from the shore, but their flitting irregularity too surely foretold them to be the expiring breath of the land-breeze. The roaring of the surf, as it rolled on the margin of the bay, produced a dull, monotonous sound, that was only interrupted, at times, by a hollow bellowing, as a larger wave than usual broke violently against some cavity in the rock. Everything, in short, united to render the scene gloomy and portentous, without creating instant terror, for the ship rose easily on the long billows, without even straightening the heavy cable that held her to her anchor.

The higher officers were collected around the capstan, engaged in earnest discourse about their situation and prospects, while some of the oldest and most favored seamen would extend their short walk to the hallowed precincts of the quarter-deck, to catch, with greedy ears, the opinions that fell from their superiors. Numberless were the uneasy glances that were thrown from both officers and men at their commander and the pilot, who still continued their secret communion in a distant part of the vessel. Once, an ungovernable curiosity, or the heedlessness of his years, led one of the youthful midshipmen near them, but a stern rebuke from his captain sent the boy, abashed and cowering, to hide his mortification among his fellows. This reprimand was received by the elder officers as an intimation that the consultation which they beheld was to be strictly inviolate; and, though it by no means suppressed the repeated expressions of their impatience, it effectually prevented an interruption to the communications, which all, however, thought unreasonably protracted for the occasion.

"This is no time to be talking over bearings and distances," observed the officer next in rank to Griffith; "but we should call the hands up, and try to kedge her off while the sea will suffer a boat to live."

" 'Twould be a tedious and bootless job to attempt warping a ship for miles against a head-beating sea," returned the first-lieutenant; "but the land breeze yet flutters aloft, and if our light sails would draw, with the aid of the ebb-tide we might be able to shove her from the shore."

"Hail the tops, Griffith," said the other, "and ask if they feel the air above; 'twill be a hint at least to set the old man and that lubberly pilot in motion."

Griffith laughed as he complied with the request, and when he received the customary reply to his call, he demanded in a loud voice:

"Which way have you the wind aloft?"

"We feel a light cat's-paw, now and then, from the land, sir," returned the sturdy captain of the top; "but our topsail hangs in the clew-lines, sir, without winking."

Captain Munson and his companion suspended their discourse while this question and answer were exchanged, and then resumed their dialogue as earnestly as if it had received no interruption.

"If it did wink, the hint would be lost on our betters," said the officer of the marines, whose ignorance of seamanship added greatly to his perception of the danger, but who, from pure idleness, made more jokes than any other man in the ship. "That pilot would not receive a delicate intimation through his ears, Mr. Griffith; suppose you try him by the nose."

"Faith, there was a flash of gunpowder between us in the barge," returned the first-lieutenant, "and he does not seem a man to stomach such hints as you advise. Although he looks so meek and quiet, I doubt whether he has paid much attention to the Book of Job."

"Why should he?" exclaimed the chaplain, whose apprehensions at least equalled those of the marine, and with a much more disheartening effect; "I am sure it would have been a great waste of time; there are so many charts of the coast, and books on the navigation of these seas, for him to study, that I sincerely hope he has been much better employed."

A loud laugh was created at this speech among the listeners, and it apparently produced the effect that was so long anxiously desired, by putting an end to the mysterious conference between their captain and the pilot. As the former came forward toward his expecting crew, he said, in the composed, steady manner that formed the principal trait in his character:

"Get the anchor, Mr. Griffith, and make sail on the ship; the hour has arrived when we must be moving."

The cheerful "Ay! ay! sir!" of the young lieutenant was hardly uttered, before the cries of half a dozen midshipmen were heard summoning the boatswain and his mates to their duty.

There was a general movement in the living masses that clustered around the mainmast, on the booms, and in the gangways, though their habits of discipline held the crew a moment longer in suspense. The silence was first broken by the sound of the boatswain's whistle, followed by the hoarse cry of "All hands, up anchor, ahoy!"—the former rising on the night air from its first low, mellow notes to a piercing shrillness that gradually died away on the waters; and the latter bellowing through every cranny of the ship, like the hollow murmurs of distant thunder.

The change produced by the customary summons was magical. Human beings sprang out from between the guns, rushed up the hatches, threw themselves with careless activity from the booms, and gathered from every quarter so rapidly, that, in an instant, the deck of the frigate was alive with men. The profound silence, that had hitherto been only interrupted by the low dialogue of the officers, was now changed for the stern orders of the lieutenants, mingled with the shriller cries of the midshipmen, and the hoarse bawling of the boatswain's crew, rising above the tumult of preparation and general bustle.

The captain and pilot alone remained passive in this scene of general exertion, for apprehension had even stimulated that class of officers which is called "idlers" to unusual activity, though frequently reminded by their more experienced messmates that, instead of aiding, they retarded the duty of the vessel. The bustle, however, gradually ceased, and, in a few minutes, the same silence pervaded the ship as before.

"We are brought-to, sir," said Griffith, who stood overlooking the scene, holding in one hand a short speaking-trumpet, and grasping with the other one of the shrouds of the ship, to steady himself in the position he had taken on a gun.

"Heave round, sir," was the calm reply.

"Heave round!" repeated Griffith, aloud.

"Heave round!" echoed a dozen eager voices at once, and the lively strains of a fife struck up a brisk air, to enliven the labor. The capstan was instantly set in motion, and the measured tread of the seamen was heard, as they stamped the deck in the circle of their march. For a few minutes no other sounds were heard, if we except the voice of an officer occasionally cheering the sailors, when it was announced that they "were short"; or, in other words, that the ship was nearly over her anchor.

"Heave and pull!" cried Griffith; when the quivering notes of the whistle were again succeeded by a general stillness in the vessel.

"What is to be done now, sir?" continued the lieutenant; "shall we trip the anchor? There seems not a breath of air; and, as the tide runs slack, I doubt whether the sea do not heave the ship ashore."

There was so much obvious truth in this conjecture, that all eyes turned from the light and animation afforded by the decks of the frigate, to look abroad on the waters, in a vain desire to pierce the darkness, as if to read the fate of their apparently devoted ship from the aspect of Nature.

"I leave all to the pilot," said the captain, after he had stood a short time by the side of Griffith, anxiously studying the heavens and the ocean. "What say you, Mr. Gray?"

The man who was thus first addressed by name was leaning over the bulwarks, with his eyes bent in the same direction as the others; but as he answered he turned his face toward the speaker, and the light from the deck fell full upon his quiet features, which exhibited a calmness bordering on the supernatural considering his station and responsibility.

"There is much to fear from this heavy ground-swell," he said, in the same unmoved tones as before; "but there is certain destruction to us if the gale that is brewing in the east finds us waiting its fury in this wild anchorage. All the hemp that was ever spun into cordage would not hold a ship an hour, chafing on these rocks, with a northeaster pouring its fury on her. If the powers of man can compass it, gentlemen, we must get an offing, and that speedily."

"You say no more, sir, than the youngest boy in the ship can see for himself," said Griffith. "Ha! here comes the schooner!"

The dashing of the long sweeps in the water was now plainly audible, and the little Ariel was seen through the gloom, moving heavily under their feeble impulse. As she passed slowly under the stern of the frigate, the cheerful voice of Barnstable was first heard, opening the communications between them.

"Here's a night for spectacles, Captain Munson!" he cried; "but I thought I heard your fife, sir. I trust, in God, you do not mean to ride it out here till morning?"

"I like the berth as little as yourself, Mr. Barnstable," returned the veteran seaman, in his calm manner, in which anxiety was, however, beginning to grow evident. "We are short; but are afraid to let go our hold of the bottom, lest the sea cast us ashore. How make you out the wind?"

"Wind!" echoed the other; "there is not enough to blow a lady's curl aside. If you wait, sir, till the land-breeze fills your sails, you will wait another moon. I believe I've got my egg-shell out of that nest of graycaps; but how it has been done in the dark, a better man than myself must explain."

"Take your directions from the pilot, Mr. Barnstable," returned his commanding officer, "and follow them strictly and to the letter."

A death-like silence, in both vessels, succeeded this order; for all seemed to listen eagerly to catch the words that fell from the man on whom even the boys now felt, depended their only hopes for safety. A short time was suffered to elapse, before his voice was heard, in the same low, but distinct tones as before:

"Your sweeps will soon be of no use to you," he said, "against the sea that begins to heave in; but your light sails will help them to get you out. So long as you can head east-and-by-north, you are doing well, and you can stand on until you open the light from that northern headland, when you can heave-to, and fire a gun; but if, as I dread, you are struck aback before you open the light, you may trust to your lead on the larboard tack; but beware, with your lead to the southward, for no lead will serve you there."

"I can walk over the same ground on one tack as on the other," said Barnstable, "and make both legs of a length."

"It will not do," returned the pilot. "If you fall off a point to starboard from east-and-by-north, in going large, you will find both rocks and points of shoals to bring you up; and beware, as I tell you, of the starboard tack."

"And how shall I find my way? You will let me trust to neither time, lead, nor log."

"You must trust to a quick eye and a ready hand. The breakers will only show you the dangers when you are not able to make out the bearings of the land. Tack in season, sir, and don't spare the lead when you head to port."

"Ay, ay," returned Barnstable, in a low, muttering voice. "This is a sort of blind navigation, with a vengeance, and all for no purpose that I can see. See! damme, eyesight is of about as much use now as a man's nose would be in reading the Bible."

"Softly, softly, Mr. Barnstable," interrupted his commander—for such was the anxious stillness in both vessels that even the rattling of the schooner's rigging was heard, as she rolled in the trough of the sea—"the duty on which Congress has sent us must be performed, at the hazard of our lives."

"I don't mind my life, Captain Munson," said Barnstable, "but there's a great want of conscience in trusting a vessel in such a place as this. However, it is a time to do, and not to talk. But if there be such danger to an easy draught of water, what will become of the frigate? Had I not better play jackal, and try and feel the way for you?"

"I thank you," said the pilot; "the offer is generous, but would avail us nothing. I have the advantage of knowing the ground well, and must trust to my memory and God's good favor. Make sail, make sail, sir, and, if you succeed, we will venture to break ground."

The order was promptly obeyed, and in a very short time the Ariel was covered with canvas. Though no air was perceptible on the decks of the frigate, the little schooner was so light that she succeeded in stemming her way over the rising waves, aided a little by the tide; and in a few minutes her low hull was just discernible in the streak of light along the horizon, with the dark outline of her sails rising above the sea, until their fanciful summits were lost in the shadows of the clouds.

Griffith had listened to the foregoing dialogue, like the rest of the junior officers, in profound silence; but when the Ariel began to grow indistinct to the eye, he jumped lightly from the gun to the deck, and cried:

"She slips off like a vessel from the stocks! Shall I trip the anchor, sir, and follow?"

"We have no choice," replied his captain. "You hear the question, Mr. Gray? Shall we let go the bottom?"

"It must be done, Captain Munson; we may want more drift than the rest of this tide to get us to a place of safety," said the pilot. "I would give five years from a life that I know will be short if the ship lay one mile farther seaward."

This remark was unheard by all except the commander of the frigate, who again walked aside with the pilot, where they resumed their mysterious communications. The words of assent were no sooner uttered, however, than Griffith gave forth from his trumpet the command to "heave away!" Again the strains of the fife were followed by the tread of the men at the capstan. At the same time that the anchor was heaving up the sails were loosened from the yards and opened to invite the breeze. In effecting this duty, orders were thundered through the trumpet of the first-lieutenant, and executed with the rapidity of thought. Men were to be seen, like spots in the dim light from the heavens, lying on every yard, or hanging as in air, while strange cries were heard issuing from every part of the rigging and each spar of the vessel. "Ready the fore-royal!" cried a shrill voice, as if from the clouds; "Ready the fore-yard!" uttered the hoarser tones of a seaman beneath him; "All ready aft, sir!" cried a third from another quarter; and in a few moments the order was given to "let fall."

The little light which fell from the sky was now excluded by the falling canvas, and a deeper gloom was cast athwart the decks of the ship, that served to render the brilliancy of the lanterns even vivid, while it gave to objects out-board a more appalling and dreary appearance than before.

Every individual, excepting the commander and his associate, was now earnestly engaged in getting the ship under way. The sounds of "We're away" were repeated by a burst from fifty voices, and the rapid evolutions of the capstan announced that nothing but the weight of the anchor was to be lifted. The hauling of cordage, the rattling of blocks, blended with the shrill calls of the boatswain and his mates, succeeded; and though to a landsman all would have appeared confusion and hurry, long practice and strict discipline enabled the crew to exhibit their ship under a cloud of canvas, from her deck to the trucks, in less time than we have consumed in relating it.

For a few minutes the officers were not disappointed by the results, for, though the heavy sails flapped lazily against the masts, the light duck on the loftier spars swelled outwardly, and the ship began sensibly to yield to their influence.

"She travels! she travels!" exclaimed Griffith, joyously. "Ah, the hussy; she has as much antipathy to the land as any fish that swims! It blows a little gale aloft yet?"

"We feel its dying breath," said the pilot, in low, soothing tones, but in a manner so sudden as to startle Griffith, at whose elbow they were unexpectedly uttered. "Let us forget, young man, everything but the number of lives that depend this night on your exertions and my knowledge."

"If you be but half as able to exhibit the one as I am willing to make the other, we shall do well," returned the lieutenant in the same tone. "Remember, whatever may be your feelings, that *we* are on the enemy's coast, and love it not enough to wish to lay our bones here."

With this brief explanation they separated, the vessel requiring the constant and close attention of the officers to her movements.

The exultation produced in the crew by the progress of their ship through the water was of short duration, for the breeze that had seemed to await their motions, after forcing the vessel for a quarter of a mile, fluttered for a few minutes amid their light canvas, and then left them entirely. The quartermaster, whose duty it was to superintend the helm, soon announced that he was losing the command of the vessel, as she was no longer obedient to her rudder. This ungrateful intelligence was promptly communicated to his commander by Griffith, who suggested the propriety of again dropping an anchor.

"I refer you to Mr. Gray," returned the captain; "he is the pilot, sir, and with him rests the safety of the vessel."

"Pilots sometimes lose ships as well as save them," said Griffith. "Know you the man well, Captain Munson, who holds all our lives in his keeping, and so coolly as if he cared but little for the venture?"

"Mr. Griffith, I do know him; he is, in my opinion, both competent and faithful. This much I tell you, to relieve your anxiety; more you must not ask. But is there not a shift of wind?"

"God forbid!" exclaimed the lieutenant; "if that northeaster catches us within the shoals, our case will be desperate indeed!"

The heavy rolling of the vessel caused an occasional expansion, and as sudden a reaction, in their sails, which left the oldest seaman in the ship in doubt which way the currents of air were passing, or whether there existed any that were not created by the flapping of their own canvas. The head of the ship, however, began to fall off from the sea, and notwithstanding the darkness, it soon became apparent that she was driving in bodily toward the shore.

During these few minutes of gloomy doubt, Griffith, by one of those sudden revulsions of the mind that connect the opposite extremes of feeling, lost his animated anxiety, and relapsed into the listless apathy that so often came over him, even in the most critical moments of trial and danger. He was standing with one elbow resting on his capstan, shading his eyes from the light of the battle-lantern that stood near him with one hand, when he felt a gentle pressure of the other, that recalled his recollection. Looking affectionately, though still recklessly, at the boy who stood at his side, he said:

"Dull music, Mr. Merry."

"So dull, sir, that I can't dance to it," returned the midshipman. "Nor do I believe there is a man in the ship who would not rather hear 'The girl I left behind me' than those execrable sounds."

"What sounds, boy? The ship is as quiet as the Quaker meeting in the Jerseys, before your good old grandfather used to break the charm of silence with his sonorous voice."

"Ah! laugh at my peaceable blood, if thou wilt, Mr. Griffith," said the arch youngster; "but remember, there is a mixture of it in all sorts of veins. I wish I could hear one of the old gentleman's chants now, sir; I could always sleep to them, like a gull in the surf. But he that sleeps tonight, with that lullaby, will make a nap of it."

"Sounds! I hear no sounds, boy, but the flapping aloft; even that pilot, who struts the quarter-deck like an admiral, has nothing to say."

"Is not that a sound to open a seaman's ear?"

"It is, in truth, a heavy roll of the surf, lad, but the night air carries it heavily to our ears. Know you not the sounds of the surf yet, younker?"

"I know it too well, Mr. Griffith, and do not wish to know it better. How fast are we tumbling in toward that surf, sir?"

"I think we hold our own," said Griffith, rousing again; "though we had better anchor. Luff, fellow, luff—you are broadside to the sea!"

The man at the wheel repeated his former intelligence, adding a suggestion that he thought the ship was "gathering stern-way."

"Haul up your courses, Mr. Griffith," said Captain Munson, "and let us feel the wind."

The rattling of the blocks was soon heard, and the enormous sheets of canvas that hung from the lower yards were instantly suspended "in the brails." When this change was effected, all on board stood silent and breathless, as if expecting to learn their fate by the result. Several contradictory opinions were at length hazarded among the officers, when Griffith seized the candle from the lantern, and, springing on one of the guns, held it on high, exposed to the action of the air. The little flame waved, with uncertain glimmering, for a moment, and then burned steadily, in a line with the masts. Griffith was about to lower his extended arm, when, feeling a slight sensation of coolness on his hand, he paused, and the light turned slowly toward the land, flared, flickered, and finally deserted the wick.

"Lose not a moment, Mr. Griffith," cried the pilot aloud; "clew up and furl everything but your three topsails, and let them be double-reefed. Now is the time to fulfil your promise."

The young man paused one moment in astonishment, as the clear, distinct tones of the stranger struck on his ears so unexpectedly; but, turning his eyes to seaward, he sprang on the deck, and proceeded to obey the order, as if life and death depended on his dispatch.

5

She rights! she rights, boys! ware off shore!

Song

THE extraordinary activity of Griffith, which communicated itself with promptitude to the crew, was produced by a sudden alteration in the weather. In place of the well-defined streak along the horizon, that has been already described, an immense body of misty light appeared to be moving in, with rapidity, from the ocean, while a distinct but distant roaring announced the sure approach of the tempest that had so long troubled the waters. Even Griffith, while thundering his orders through the trumpet, and urging the men, by his cries, to expedition, would pause for instants to cast anxious glances in the direction of the coming storm; and the faces of the sailors who lay on the yards were turned instinctively toward the same quarter of the heavens, while they knotted the reef points, or passed the gaskets that were to confine the unruly canvas to the prescribed limits.

The pilot alone, in that confused and busy throng, where voice rose above voice, and cry echoed cry, in quick succession, appeared as if he held no interest in the important stake. With his eyes steadily fixed on the approaching mist, and his arms folded together in composure, he stood calmly waiting the result.

The ship had fallen off, with her broadside to the sea, and was become unmanageable, and the sails were already brought into the folds necessary to her security, when the quick and heavy fluttering of canvas was thrown across the water, with all the gloomy and chilling sensations that such sounds produce where darkness and danger unite to appall the seaman.

"The schooner has it!" cried Griffith; "Barnstable has held on, like himself, to the last moment. God send that the squall leave him cloth enough to keep him from the shore!"

"His sails are easily handled," the commander observed, "and she must be over the principal danger. We are falling off before it, Mr. Gray; shall we try a cast of the lead?"

The pilot turned from his contemplative posture, and moved slowly across the deck before he returned any reply to this question—like a man who not only felt that everything depended on himself, but that he was equal to the emergency.

" 'Tis unnecessary," he at length answered; " 'twould be certain destruction to be taken aback; and it is difficult to say, within several points, how the wind may strike us."

" 'Tis difficult no longer," cried Griffith; "for here it comes, and in right earnest!"

The rushing sounds of the wind were now, indeed, heard at hand, and the words were hardly passed the lips of the young lieutenant, before the vessel bowed down heavily to one side, and then, as she began to move through the water, rose again majestically to her upright position, as if saluting, like a courteous champion, the powerful antagonist with which she was about to contend. Not another minute elapsed before the ship was throwing the waters aside, with a lively progress, and, obedient to her helm, was brought as near to the desired course as the direction of the wind would allow. The hurry and bustle on the yards gradually subsided, and the men slowly descended to the deck, all straining their eyes to pierce the gloom in which they were enveloped, and some shaking their heads in melancholy doubt, afraid to express the apprehensions they really entertained. All on board anxiously waited for the fury of the gale; for there were none so ignorant or inexperienced in that gallant frigate as not to know that as yet they only felt the infant effects of the wind. Each moment, however, it increased in power, though so gradual was the alteration that the relieved mariners began to believe that all their gloomy forebodings were not to be realized. During this short interval of uncertainty, no other sounds were heard than the whistling of the breeze, as it passed quickly through the mass of rigging that belonged to the vessel, and the dashing of the spray that began to fly from her bows, like the foam of a cataract.

"It blows fresh," cried Griffith, who was the first to speak in that moment of doubt and anxiety; "but it is no more than a cupful of wind after all. Give us elbow-room, and the right canvas, Mr. Pilot, and I'll handle the ship like a gentleman's yacht, in this breeze."

"Will she stay, think ye, under this sail?" said the low voice of the stranger.

"She will do all that man, in reason, can ask of wood and iron," returned the lieutenant; "but the vessel don't float the ocean that will tack under double-reefed topsails alone, against a heavy sea. Help her with the courses, pilot, and you shall see her come round like a dancing-master."

"Let us feel the strength of the gale first," returned the man who was called Mr. Gray, moving from the side of Griffith to the weather gangway of the vessel, where he stood in silence, looking ahead of the ship, with an air of singular coolness and abstraction.

All the lanterns had been extinguished on the deck of the frigate, when her anchor was secured, and, as the first mist of the gale had passed over, it was succeeded by a faint light that was a good deal aided by the glittering foam of the waters, which now broke in white curls around the vessel in every direction. The land could be faintly discerned, rising like a heavy bank of black fog above the margin of the waters, and was only distinguishable from the heavens by its deeper gloom and obscurity. The last rope was coiled, and deposited in its proper place by the seamen, and for several minutes the stillness of death pervaded the crowded decks. It was evident to every one that their ship was dashing at a prodigious rate through the waves; and as she was approaching, with such velocity, the quarter of the bay where the shoals and dangers were known to be situated, nothing but the habits of the most exact discipline could suppress the uneasiness of the officers and men within their own bosoms. At length the voice of Captain Munson was heard, calling to the pilot.

"Shall I send a hand into the chains, Mr. Gray," he said, "and try our water?"

Although this question was asked aloud, and the interest it excited drew many of the officers and men around him in eager impatience for his answer, it was unheeded by the man to whom it was addressed. His head rested on his hand as he leaned over the hammock-cloths of the vessel, and his whole air was that of one whose thoughts wandered from the pressing necessity of their situation. Griffith was among those who had approached the pilot; and after waiting a moment, from respect, to hear the answer to his commander's question, he presumed on his own rank, and, leaving the circle that stood at a little distance, stepped to the side of the mysterious guardian of their lives.

"Captain Munson desires to know whether you wish a cast of the lead?"

said the young officer, with a little impatience of manner. No immediate answer was made to this repetition of the question, and Griffith laid his hand
unceremoniously on the shoulder of the other, with an intent to rouse him
before he made another application for a reply, but the convulsive start of
the pilot held him silent in amazement.

"Fall back there," said the lieutenant, sternly, to the men, who were closing
around them in a compact circle; "away with you to your stations, and see all
clear for stays!" The dense mass of heads dissolved, at this order, like the
water of one of the waves commingling with the ocean, and the lieutenant and
his companion were left by themselves.

"This is not a time for musing, Mr. Gray," continued Griffith; "remember
our compact, and look to your charge—is it not time to put the vessel in stays?
Of what are you dreaming?"

The pilot laid his hand on the extended arm of the lieutenant, and grasped
it with a convulsive pressure, as he answered:

" 'Tis a dream of reality. You are young, Mr. Griffith, nor am I past the
noon of life; but, should you live fifty years longer, you can never see and
experience what I have encountered in my little period of three-and-thirty
years!"

A good deal astonished at this burst of feeling, so singular at such a moment, the young sailor was at a loss for a reply; but, as his duty was uppermost
in this thoughts, he still dwelt on the theme that most interested him.

"I hope much of your experience has been on this coast, for the ship travels
lively," he said, "and the daylight showed us so much to dread, that we do not
feel over-valiant in the dark. How much longer shall we stand on, upon this
tack?"

The pilot turned slowly from the side of the vessel, and walked toward the
commander of the frigate, as he replied, in a tone that seemed deeply agitated
by his melancholy reflections:

"You have your wish, then; much, very much of my early life was passed
on this dreaded coast. What to you is all darkness and gloom, to me is as light
as if a noonday sun shone upon it. But tack your ship, sir, tack your ship; I
would see how she works before we reach the point where she *must* behave
well, or we perish!"

Griffith gazed at him in wonder, while the pilot slowly paced the quarter-
deck, and then, rousing from his trance, gave forth the cheering order that
called each man to his station, to perform the desired evolution. The confident
assurances which the young officer had given to the pilot respecting the qualities of his vessel, and his own ability to manage her, were fully realized by the

result. The helm was no sooner put alee, than the huge ship bore up gallantly against the wind, and, dashing directly through the waves, threw the foam high into the air, as she looked boldly into the very eye of the wind: and then, yielding gracefully to its power, she fell off on the other tack, with her head pointed from those dangerous shoals that she had so recently approached with such terrifying velocity. The heavy yards swung round, as if they had been vanes to indicate the currents of the air; and in a few moments the frigate again moved, with stately progress, through the water, leaving the rocks and shoals behind her on one side of the bay, but advancing toward those that offered equal danger on the other.

During this time the sea was becoming more agitated, and the violence of the wind was gradually increasing. The latter no longer whistled amid the cordage of the vessel, but it seemed to howl, surlily, as it passed the complicated machinery that the frigate obtruded on its path. An endless succession of white surges rose above the heavy billows, and the very air was glittering with the light that was disengaged from the ocean. The ship yielded, each moment, more and more before the storm, and, in less than half an hour from the time that she had lifted her anchor, she was driven along with tremendous fury by the full power of the gale of wind. Still, the hardy and experienced mariners who directed her movements, held her to the course that was necessary to their preservation, and still Griffith gave forth, when directed by their unknown pilot, those orders that turned her in the narrow channel where alone safety was to be found.

So far, the performance of his duty appeared easy to the stranger, and he gave the required directions in those still, calm tones, that formed so remarkable a contrast to the responsibility of his situation. But when the land was becoming dim, in distance as well as darkness, and the agitated sea alone was to be discovered as it swept by them in foam, he broke in upon the monotonous roaring of the tempest with the sounds of his voice, seeming to shake off his apathy, and rouse himself to the occasion.

"Now is the time to watch her closely, Mr. Griffith," he cried: "here we get the true tide and the real danger. Place the best quartermaster of your ship in those chains, and let an officer stand by him, and see that he gives us the right water."

"I will take that office on myself," said the captain; "pass a light into the weather main-chains."

"Stand by your braces!" exclaimed the pilot, with startling quickness. "Heave away that lead!"

These preparations taught the crew to expect the crisis, and every officer and man stood in fearful silence, at his assigned station, awaiting the issue of the trial. Even the quartermaster at the con gave out his orders to the men at the wheel, in deeper and hoarser tones than usual, as if anxious not to disturb the quiet and order of the vessel.

While this deep expectation pervaded the frigate, the piercing cry of the leadsman, as he called, "By the mark, seven," rose above the tempest, crossed over the decks, and appeared to pass away to leeward, borne on the blast like the warnings of some water-spirit.

" 'Tis well," returned the pilot, calmly; "try it again."

The short pause was succeeded by another cry, "And a half five!"

"She shoals! she shoals!" exclaimed Griffith; "keep her a good full."

"Ay! you must hold the vessel in command, now," said the pilot, with those cool tones that are most appalling in critical moments, because they seem to denote most preparation and care.

The third call, "By the deep four!" was followed by a prompt direction from the stranger to tack.

Griffith seemed to emulate the coolness of the pilot, in issuing the necessary orders to execute this manœuvre.

The vessel rose slowly from the inclined position into which she had been forced by the tempest, and the sails were shaking violently, as if to release themselves from their confinement, while the ship stemmed the billows, when the well-known voice of the sailing-master was heard shouting from the fore-castle:

"Breakers! breakers, dead ahead!"

This appalling sound seemed yet to be lingering about the ship, when a second voice cried:

"Breakers on our lee-bow!"

"We are in a bight of the shoals, Mr. Gray," cried the commander. "She loses her way; perhaps an anchor might hold her."

"Clear away that best bower!" shouted Griffith, through his trumpet.

"Hold on!" cried the pilot, in a voice that reached the very hearts of all who heard him; "hold on everything."

The young man turned fiercely to the daring stranger who thus defied the discipline of his vessel, and at once demanded:

"Who is it that dares to countermand my orders? Is it not enough that you run the ship into danger, but you must interfere to keep her there? If another word—"

"Peace, Mr. Griffith," interrupted the captain, bending from the rigging, his gray locks blowing about in the wind, and adding a look of wildness to the haggard care that he exhibited by the light of his lantern; "yield the trumpet to Mr. Gray; he alone can save us."

Griffith threw his speaking-trumpet on the deck, and, as he walked proudly away, muttered, in bitterness of feeling:

"Then all is lost, indeed! and among the rest the foolish hopes with which I visited this coast."

There was, however, no time for reply; the ship had been rapidly running into the wind, and as the efforts of the crew were paralyzed by the contradictory orders they had heard, she gradually lost her way, and in a few seconds all her sails were taken aback.

Before the crew understood their situation, the pilot had applied the trumpet to his mouth, and, in a voice that rose above the tempest, he thundered forth his orders. Each command was given distinctly and with a precision that showed him to be master of his profession. The helm was kept fast, the head-yards swung up heavily against the wind, and the vessel was soon whirling round on her heel, with a retrograde movement.

Griffith was too much of a seaman not to perceive that the pilot had seized, with a perception almost intuitive, the only method that promised to extricate the vessel from her situation. He was young, impetuous and proud—but he was also generous. Forgetting his resentment and his mortification, he rushed forward among the men, and, by his presence and example, added certainty to the experiment. The ship fell off slowly before the gale, and bowed her yards nearly to the water, as she felt the blast pouring its fury on her broadside, while the surly waves beat violently against her stern, as if in reproach at departing from her usual manner of moving.

The voice of the pilot, however, was still heard, steady and calm, and yet so clear and high as to reach every ear; and the obedient seamen whirled the yards at his bidding, in despite of the tempest, as if they handled the toys of their childhood. When the ship had fallen off dead before the wind, her head-sails were shaken, her after-yards trimmed, and her helm shifted, before she had time to run upon the danger that had threatened, as well to leeward as to windward. The beautiful fabric, obedient to her government, threw her bows up gracefully toward the wind again, and, as her sails were trimmed, moved out from among the dangerous shoals in which she had been embayed, as steadily and swiftly as she had approached them.

A moment of breathless astonishment succeeded the accomplishment of this nice manœuvre, but there was no time for the usual expressions of surprise. The stranger still held the trumpet, and continued to lift his voice amid the howlings of the blast, whenever prudence or skill required any change in the management of the ship. For an hour longer there was a fearful struggle for their preservation, the channel becoming at each step more complicated, and the shoals thickening around the mariners on every side. The lead was cast rapidly, and the quick eye of the pilot seemed to pierce the darkness with a keenness of vision that exceeded human power. It was apparent to all in the vessel that they were under the guidance of one who understood the navigation thoroughly, and their exertions kept pace with their reviving confidence. Again and again the frigate appeared to be rushing blindly on shoals where the sea was covered with foam, and where destruction would have been as sudden as it was certain, when the clear voice of the stranger was heard warning them of the danger, and inciting them to their duty. The vessel was implicitly yielded to his government; and during those anxious moments when she was dashing the waters aside, throwing the spray over her enormous yards, each ear would listen eagerly for those sounds that had obtained a command over the crew, that can only be acquired under such circumstances, by great steadiness and consummate skill. The ship was recovering from the inaction of changing her course, in one of those critical tacks that she had made so often, when the pilot, for the first time, addressed the commander of the frigate, who still continued to superintend the all-important duty of the leadsman.

"Now is the pinch," he said, "and if the ship behaves well, we are safe; but, if otherwise, all we have yet done will be useless."

The veteran seaman whom he addressed, left the chains at this portentous notice, and, calling to his first lieutenant, required of the stranger an explanation of his warning.

"See you yon light on the southern headland?" returned the pilot; "you may know it from the star near it—by its sinking, at times, in the ocean. Now observe the hummock, a little north of it, looking like a shadow in the horizon —'tis a hill far inland. If we keep that light open from the hill, we shall do well; but if not, we shall surely go to pieces."

"Let us tack again!" exclaimed the lieutenant.

The pilot shook his head, as he replied:

"There is no more tacking or box-hauling to be done to-night. We have barely room to pass out of the shoals on this course; and, if we can weather the 'Devil's Grip,' we clear their uttermost point; but if not, as I said before, there is but an alternative."

"If we had beaten out the way we entered," exclaimed Griffith, "we should have done well."

"Say, also, if the tide would have let us do so," returned the pilot, calmly. "Gentlemen, we must be prompt; we have but a mile to go, and the ship ap-

pears to fly. That topsail is not enough to keep her up to the wind; we want both jib and mainsail."

" 'Tis a perilous thing to loosen canvas in such a tempest!" observed the doubtful captain.

"It must be done," returned the collected stranger; "we perish without it— see! the light already touches the edge of the hummock; the sea casts us to leeward!"

"It shall be done!" cried Griffith, seizing the trumpet from the hand of the pilot.

The orders of the lieutenant were executed almost as soon as issued; and, everything being ready, the enormous folds of the mainsails were trusted loose to the blast. There was an instant when the result was doubtful; the tremendous threshing of the heavy sail seemed to bid defiance to all restraint, shaking the ship to her centre; but art and strength prevailed, and gradually the canvas was distended, and, bellying as it filled, was drawn down to its usual place by the power of a hundred men. The vessel yielded to this immense addition of force, and bowed before it like a reed bending to a breeze. But the success of the measure was announced by a joyful cry from the stranger, that seemed to burst from his inmost soul.

"She feels it! she springs her luff! observe," he said, "the light opens from the hom-moc already: if she will only bear her canvas, we shall go clear!"

A report, like that of a cannon, interrupted his exclamation, and something resembling a white cloud was seen drifting before the wind from the head of the ship, till it was driven into the gloom far to leeward.

" 'Tis the jib, blown from the bolt ropes," said the commander of the frigate. "This is no time to spread light duck—but the mainsail may stand it yet."

"The sail would laugh at a tornado," returned the lieutenant; "but the mast springs like a piece of steel."

"Silence all!" cried the pilot. "Now, gentlemen, we shall soon know our fate. Let her luff—luff you can!"

This warning effectually closed all discourse; and the hardy mariners, knowing that they had already done all in the power of man to insure their safety, stood in breathless anxiety, awaiting the result. At a short distance ahead of them the whole ocean was white with foam, and the waves, instead of rolling on in regular succession, appeared to be tossing about in mad gambols. A single streak of dark billows, not half a cable's length in width, could be discerned running into this chaos of water; but it was soon lost to the eye amid the confusion of the disturbed element. Along this narrow path the vessel moved more heavily than before, being brought so near the wind as to keep her sails touching. The pilot silently proceeded to the wheel, and with his own hands, he undertook the steerage of the ship. No noise proceeded from the frigate to interrupt the horrid tumult of the ocean; and she entered the channel among the breakers, with the silence of a desperate calmness. Twenty times, as the foam rolled away to leeward, the crew were on the eve of uttering their joy, as they supposed the vessel past the danger; but breaker after breaker would still heave up before them, following each other into the general mass, to check their exultation. Occasionally the fluttering of the sails would be heard; and when the looks of the startled seamen were turned to the wheel, they beheld the stranger grasping the spokes, with his quick eye glancing from the water to the canvas. At length the ship reached a point where she appeared to be rushing directly into the jaws of destruction, when suddenly her course was changed, and her head receded rapidly from the wind. At the same instant the voice of the pilot was heard shouting:

"Square away the yards!—in mainsail!"

A general burst from the crew echoed "Square away the yards!" and, quick as thought, the frigate was seen gliding along the channel before the wind. The eye had hardly time to dwell on the foam, which seemed like clouds driving in the heavens, and directly the gallant vessel issued from her perils, and rose and fell on the heavy waves of the sea.

The seamen were yet drawing long breaths, and gazing behind them like men recovered from a trance, when Griffith approached the man who had so successfully conducted them through their perils. The lieutenant grasped the hand of the other, as he said:

"You have this night proved yourself a faithful pilot, and such a seaman as the world cannot equal."

The pressure of the hand was warmly returned by the unknown mariner, who replied:

"I am no stranger to the seas, and I may yet find my grave in them. But you, too, have deceived me; you have acted nobly, young man, and Congress—"

"What of Congress?" asked Griffith, observing him to pause.

"Why, Congress is fortunate if it has many such ships as this," said the stranger, coldly, walking away toward the commander.

Griffith gazed after him a moment in surprise; but, as his duty required his attention, other thoughts soon engaged his mind.

The vessel was pronounced to be in safety. The gale was heavy and increasing, but there was a clear sea before them, and, as she slowly stretched out into the bosom of the ocean, preparations were made for her security during its continuance. Before midnight everything was in order. A gun from the

Ariel soon announced the safety of the schooner also, which had gone out by another and an easier channel, that the frigate had not dared to attempt; when the commander directed the usual watch to be set and the remainder of the crew to seek their necessary repose.

The captain withdrew with the mysterious pilot to his own cabin. Griffith gave his last order, and, renewing his charge to the officer instructed with the care of the vessel, he wished him a pleasant watch, and sought the refreshment of his own cot. For an hour the young lieutenant lay musing on the events of the day. The remark of Barnstable would occur to him, in connection with the singular comment of the boy; and then his thoughts would recur to the pilot, who, taken from the hostile shores of Britain, and with her accent on his tongue, had served them so faithfully and so well. He remembered the anxiety of Captain Munson to procure this stranger, at the very hazard from which they had just been relieved, and puzzled himself with conjecturing why a pilot was to be sought at such a risk. His more private feelings would then resume their sway, and the recollection of America, his mistress and his home mingled with the confused images of the drowsy youth. The dashing of the billows against the side of the ship, the creaking of guns and bulkheads, with the roaring of the tempest, however, became gradually less and less distinct, until nature yielded to necessity, and the young man forgot even the romantic images of his love in the deep sleep of a seaman.

6

The letter! ay! the letter!
'Tis there a woman loves to speak her wishes;
It spares the blushes of the love-sick maiden,
And every word's a smile, each line a tongue.

Duo

THE slumbers of Griffith continued till late on the following morning, when he was awakened by the report of a cannon, issuing from the deck above him. He threw himself listlessly from his cot, and, perceiving the officer of marines near him as his servant opened the door of his state-room, he inquired, with some little interest in his manner, "if the ship was in chase of anything, that a gun was fired?"

" 'Tis no more than a hint to the Ariel," the soldier replied, "that there is bunting abroad for them to read. It seems as if all hands were asleep on board her, for we have shown her signals these ten minutes, and she takes us for a collier, I believe, by the respect she pays it."

"Say, rather, that she takes us for an enemy, and is wary," returned Griffith. "Brown Dick has played the English so many tricks himself that he is tender of his faith."

"Why, they have shown him a yellow flag over a blue one, with a cornet, and that spells Ariel, in every signal-book we have; surely he can't suspect the English of knowing how to read Yankee."

"I have known Yankees read more difficult English," said Griffith, smiling;

"but, in truth, I suppose that Barnstable has been, like myself, keeping a dead reckoning of his time, and his men have profited by the occasion. She is lying-to, I trust."

"Ay! like a cork in a mill-pond, and I dare say you are right. Give Barnstable plenty of sea room, a heavy wind, and but little sail, and he will send his men below, put that fellow he calls Long Tom at the tiller, and follow himself, and sleep as quietly as I ever could at church."

"Ah! yours is a somniferous orthodoxy, Captain Manual," said the young sailor, laughing, while he slipped his arms into the sleeves of a morning round-about, covered with the gilded trappings of his profession; "sleep appears to come most naturally to all you idlers. But give me a passage, and I will go up, and call the schooner down to us in the turning of an hour glass."

The indolent soldier raised himself from the leaning posture he had taken against the door of the state-room, and Griffith proceeded through the dark ward-room, up the narrow stairs that led him to the principal battery of the ship, and thence, by another and broader flight of steps, to the open deck.

The gale still blew strong, but steadily; the blue water of the ocean was rising in mimic mountains, that were crowned with white foam, which the wind at times lifted from its kindred element to propel in mist, through the air, from summit to summit. But the ship rode on these agitated billows with an easy and regular movement that denoted the skill with which her mechanical powers were directed. The day was bright and clear, and the lazy sun, who seemed unwilling to meet the toil of ascending to the meridian, was crossing the heavens with a southern inclination that hardly allowed him to temper the moist air of the ocean with his genial heat. At the distance of a mile, directly in the wind's eye, the Ariel was seen, obeying the signals which had caused the dialogue we have related. Her low, black hull was barely discernible, at moments, when she rose to the crest of a larger wave than common; but the spot of canvas that she exposed to the wind was to be seen, seeming to touch the water on either hand, as the little vessel rolled amid the seas. At times she was entirely hid from view, when the faint lines of her raking masts would be again discovered issuing, at it were, from the ocean, and continuing to ascend, until the hull itself would appear, thrusting its bows into the air, surrounded by foam, and apparently ready to take its flight into another element.

After dwelling a moment on the beautiful sight we have attempted to describe, Griffith cast his eye upward, to examine, with the keenness of a seaman, the disposition of things aloft, and then turned his attention to those who were on the deck of the frigate.

His commander stood, in his composed manner, patiently awaiting the execution of his order by the Ariel, and at his side was placed the stranger who had so recently acted such a conspicuous part in the management of the ship. Griffith availed himself of daylight and his situation to examine the appearance of this singular being more closely than the darkness and confusion of the preceding night had allowed. He was a trifle below the middle size in stature, but his form was muscular and athletic, exhibiting the finest proportions of manly beauty. His face appeared rather characterized by melancholy and thought, than by that determined decision which he had so powerfully displayed in the moments of their most extreme danger; but Griffith well knew that it could also exhibit looks of the fiercest impatience. At present, it appeared to the curious youth, when compared to the glimpses he had caught by the lights of their lanterns, like the ocean at rest, contrasted with the waters around him. The eyes of the pilot rested on the deck, or, when they did wander, it was with uneasy and rapid glances. The large pea-jacket that concealed most of his other attire, was as roughly made, and of materials as coarse, as that worn by the meanest seaman in the vessel; and yet, it did not escape the inquisitive gaze of the young lieutenant, that it was borne with an air of neatness and care that was altogether unusual in men of his profession. The examination of Griffith ended here, for the near approach of the Ariel attracted the attention of all on the deck of the frigate to the conversation that was about to pass between their respective commanders.

As the little schooner rolled along their stern, Captain Munson directed his subordinate to leave his vessel and repair on board the ship. As soon as the order was received, the Ariel rounded to, and, drawing ahead into the smooth water occasioned by the huge fabric that protected her from the gale, the whale-boat was again launched from her decks, and manned by the same crew that had landed on those shores which were now faintly discerned far to leeward, looking like blue clouds on the skirts of the ocean.

When Barnstable had entered his boat, a few strokes sent it, dancing over the waves, to the side of the ship. The little vessel was then veered off to a distance, where it rode in safety, under the care of a boat-keeper, and the officer and his men ascended the side of the lofty frigate.

The usual ceremonials of reception were rigidly observed by Griffith and his juniors, when Barnstable touched the deck; and, though every hand was ready to be extended toward the reckless seaman, none presumed to exceed the salutations of official decorum, until a short and private dialogue had taken place between him and the captain.

In the meantime, the crew of the whale-boat passed forward, and mingled with the seamen of the frigate, with the exception of the cockswain, who established himself in one of the gangways, where he stood in the utmost composure, fixing his eyes aloft, and shaking his head, in evident dissatisfaction, as he studied the complicated mass of rigging above him. This spectacle soon attracted to his side some half-dozen youths, with Mr. Merry at their head, who endeavored to entertain their guest in a manner that should most conduce to the indulgence of their own waggish propensities.

The conversation between Barnstable and his superior soon ended; when the former, beckoning to Griffith, passed the wondering group who had collected around the capstan, awaiting his leisure to greet him more cordially, and led the way to the ward-room with the freedom of one who felt himself no stranger. As this unsocial manner formed no part of the natural temper or ordinary deportment of the man, the remainder of the officers suffered their first-lieutenant to follow him alone, believing that duty required that their interview should be private. Barnstable was determined that it should be so, at all events; for he seized the lamp from the mess-table, and entered the state-room of his friend, closing the door behind them, and turning the key. When they were both within its narrow limits—pointing to the only chair the little apartment contained, with a sort of instinctive deference to his companion's rank—the commander of the schooner threw himself carelessly on a sea-chest; and, placing the lamp on the table, he opened the discourse as follows:

"What a night we had of it! Twenty times I thought I could see the sea breaking over you; and I had given you over as drowned men, or, what is worse, as men driven ashore, to be led to the prison-ships of these islanders, when I saw your lights in answer to my gun. Had you hoisted the conscience of a murderer, you wouldn't have relieved him more than you did me, by showing that bit of tallow and cotton, tipped with flint and steel. But, Griffith, I have a tale to tell of a different kind—"

"Of how you slept when you found yourself in deep water, and how your crew strove to outdo their commander, and how all succeeded so well, that there was a gray head on board here that began to shake with displeasure," interrupted Griffith; "truly, Dick, you will get into lubberly habits on board that bubble in which you float about, where all hands go to sleep as regularly as the inhabitants of a poultry-yard go to roost."

"Not so bad, not half so bad, Ned," returned the other, laughing; "I keep as sharp a discipline as if we wore a flag. To be sure, forty men can't make as much parade as three or four hundred; but, as for making or taking in sail, I am your better any day."

"Ay, because a pocket-handkerchief is sooner opened and shut than a table-cloth. But I hold it to be unseamanlike to leave any vessel without human eyes, and those open, to watch whether she goes east or west, north or south."

"And who is guilty of such a dead man's watch?"

"Why, they say aboard here, that, when it blows hard, you seat the man you call Long Tom by the side of the tiller, tell him to keep her head to sea, and then pipe all hands to their nightcaps, where you all remain, comfortably stowed in your hammocks, until you are awakened by the snoring of your helmsman."

" 'Tis a damned scandalous insinuation," cried Barnstable, with an indignation that he in vain attempted to conceal. "Who gives currency to such a libel, Mr. Griffith?"

"I had it of the marine," said his friend, losing the archness that had instigated him to worry his companion, in the vacant air of one who was careless of everything; "but I don't believe half of it myself—I have no doubt you all had your eyes open last night, whatever you might have been about this morning."

"Ah! this morning! There was an oversight, indeed! But I was studying a new signal-book, Griffith, that has a thousand times more interest for me than all the bunting you can show, from the head to the heel of your masts."

"What! have you found out the Englishman's private talk?"

"No, no," said the other, stretching forth his hand, and grasping the arm of his friend. "I met last night one on those cliffs, who has proved herself what I always believed her to be, and loved her for—a girl of quick thought and bold spirit."

"Of whom do you speak?"

"Of Katherine—"

Griffith started from his chair involuntarily at the sound of this name, and the blood passed quickly through the shades of his countenance, leaving it now pale as death, and then burning as if oppressed by a torrent from his heart. Struggling to overcome an emotion, which he appeared ashamed to betray, even to the friend he most loved, the young man soon recovered himself so far as to resume his seat, when he asked, gloomily:

"Was she alone?"

"She was; but she left with me this paper, and this invaluable book, which is worth a library of all other works."

The eye of Griffith rested vacantly on the treasure that the other valued so highly, but his hand seized eagerly the open letter which was laid on the table for his perusal. The reader will at once understand that it was in the handwriting of a female, and that it was the communication Barnstable had received from his betrothed on the cliffs. Its contents were as follows:

"Believing that Providence may conduct me where we shall meet, or whence I may be able to transmit to you this account, I have prepared a short statement of the situation of Cecilia Howard and myself; not, however, to urge you and Griffith to any rash or foolish hazards, but that you may both sit down, and, after due consultation, determine what is proper for our relief.

"By this time, you must understand the character of Colonel Howard too well to expect he will ever consent to give his niece to a rebel. He has already sacrificed to his loyalty, as he calls it (but I whisper to Cecilia, 'tis his treason), not only his native country, but no small part of his fortune also. In the frankness of my disposition (you know my frankness, Barnstable, but too well!) I confessed to him, after the defeat of the mad attempt Griffith made to carry off Cecilia, in Carolina, that I had been foolish enough to enter into some weak promise to the brother officer who had accompanied the young sailor in his traitorous visits to the plantation. Heigho! I sometimes think it would have been better for us all, if your ship had never been chased into the river, or, after she was there, if Griffith had made no attempt to renew his acquaintance with my cousin. The colonel received the intelligence as such a guardian would hear that his ward was about to throw away thirty thousand dollars and herself on a traitor to his king and country. I defended you stoutly: said that you had no king, as the tie was dissolved; that America was your country, and that your profession was honorable; but it would not all do. He called you a rebel; that I was used to. He said you were a traitor; that, in his vocabulary, amounts to the same thing. He even hinted that you were a coward; and that I knew to be false, and did not hesitate to tell him so. He used fifty opprobrious terms that I cannot remember; but among others were the beautiful epithets of 'disorganizer,' 'leveller,' 'democrat,' and 'Jacobin' (I hope he did not mean a monk!). In short, he acted Colonel Howard in a rage. But as his dominion does not, like that of his favorite kings, continue from generation to generation, and one short year will release me from his power, and leave me mistress of my own actions—that is, if your fine promises are to be believed—I bore it all very well, being resolved to suffer anything but martyrdom, rather than abandon Cecilia. She, dear girl, has much more to distress her than I can have; she is not only the ward of Colonel Howard, but his niece, and his sole heir. I am persuaded this last circumstance makes no difference in either her conduct or her feelings; but he appears to think it gives him a right to tyrannize over her on all occasions. After all, Colonel Howard is a gentleman when you do not put him in a passion, and, I believe, a thoroughly honest man; and Cecilia even loves him. But a man who is driven from his country, in his sixtieth year, with the loss of near half his fortune, is not apt to canonize those who compel the change.

"It seems that when the Howards lived on this island, a hundred years ago, they dwelt in the county of Northumberland. Hither, then, he brought us, when political events, and his dread of becoming the uncle to a rebel, induced him to abandon America, as he says, forever. We have been here now three months, and for two-thirds of that time have lived in tolerable comfort, but latterly the papers have announced the arrival of the ship and your schooner in France; and from that moment as strict a watch has been kept over us as if we had meditated a renewal of the Carolina flight. The colonel on his arrival here, hired a building, that is, part house, part abbey, part castle, and all prison; because it is said to have once belonged to an ancestor of his. In this delightful dwelling there are many cages that will secure more uneasy birds than we are. About a fortnight ago an alarm was given in a neighboring village which is situated on the shore, that two American vessels, answering your description, had been seen hovering along the coast; and, as people in this quarter dream of nothing but that terrible fellow, Paul Jones, it was said that he was on board one of them. But I believe that Colonel Howard suspects who you really are. He was very minute in his inquiries, I hear; and since then has established a sort of garrison in the house, under the pretence of defending it against marauders, like those who are said to have laid my Lady Selkirk under contribution.

"Now understand me, Barnstable; on no account would I have you risk yourself on shore; neither must there be blood spilt, if you love me; but that you may know what sort of a place we are confined in, and by whom surrounded, I will describe both our prison and the garrison. The whole building is of stone, and not to be attempted with slight means. It has windings and turnings, both internally and externally, that would require more skill than I possess to make intelligible; but the rooms we inhabit are in the upper or third floor of a wing, that you may call a tower if you are in a romantic mood, but which, in truth, is nothing but a wing. Would to God I could fly with it! If any accident should bring you in sight of the dwelling, you will know our rooms by the three smoky vanes that whiffle about its pointed roof, and also by the windows in that story being occasionally open. Opposite to our windows, at the distance of half a mile, is a retired, unfrequented ruin, concealed, in a great measure, from observation by a wood, and affording none of the best accommodations, it is true, but shelter in some of its vaults or apartments. I have prepared according to the explanations you once gave me on this subject, a set of small signals of differently-colored silks, and a little dictionary of all the phrases that I could imagine as useful to refer to, properly numbered to correspond with the key and the flags, all of which I shall send you with this letter. You must prepare your own flags, and of course, I retain mine, as well as a copy of the key and book. If opportunity should ever offer, we can have, at least a pleasant discourse together; you from the top of the old tower in the ruins, and I from the east window of my dressing-room! But now for the garrison. In addition to the commandant, Colonel Howard, who retains all the fierceness of his former military profession, there is, as his second in authority, that bane of Cecilia's happiness, Kit Dillon, with his long Savannah face, scornful eyes of black, and skin of the same color. This gentleman, you know, is a distant relative of the Howards, and wishes to be more nearly allied. He is poor, it is true, but then, as the colonel daily remarks, he is a good and loyal subject, and no rebel. When I asked why he was not in arms in these stirring times, contending for the prince he loves so much, the colonel answers that it is not his profession; that he has been educated for the law, and was destined to fill one of the highest judicial stations in the colonies, and that he hoped he should yet live to see him sentence certain nameless gentlemen to condign punishment. This was consoling, to be sure; but I bore it. However, he left Carolina with us, and here he is, and here he is likely to continue unless you can catch him, and anticipate his judgment on himself. The colonel has long desired to see this gentleman the husband of Cecilia, and since the news of your being on the coast, the siege has nearly amounted to a storm. The consequences are, that my cousin at first kept her room, and then the colonel kept her there, and even now she is precluded from leaving the wing we inhabit. In addition to these two principal jailers, we have four men-servants, two black and two white; and an officer and twenty soldiers from the neighboring town are billeted on us, by particular desire, until the coast is declared free from pirates!—yes, that is the musical name they give you—and when their own people land, and plunder, and rob, and murder the men and insult the women, they are called heroes! It's a fine thing to be able to invent names and make dictionaries—and it must be your fault if mine has been framed for no purpose. I declare, when I recollect all the insulting and cruel things I hear in this country of my own and her people, it makes me lose my temper and forget my sex; but do not let my ill-humor urge you to anything rash; remember your life, remember their prisons, remember your reputation, but do not, do not forget your

"KATHERINE PLOWDEN.

"P.S.—I had almost forgotten to tell you, that in the signal-book you will find a more particular description of our prison, where it stands, and a drawing of the grounds, etc."

When Griffith concluded this epistle, he returned it to the man to whom it was addressed, and fell back in his chair, in an attitude that denoted deep reflection.

"I knew she was here, or I should have accepted the command offered to me by our commissioners in Paris," he at length uttered; "and I thought that some lucky chance might throw her in my way, but this is bringing us close, indeed! This intelligence must be acted on, and that promptly. Poor girl! what does she not suffer in such a situation?"

"What a beautiful hand she writes!" exclaimed Barnstable; " 'tis as clear, and as pretty, and as small, as her own delicate fingers. Griff, what a log-book she would keep!"

"Cecilia Howard touch the coarse leaves of a log-book!" cried the other, in amazement; but perceiving Barnstable to be poring over the contents of his mistress's letter, he smiled at their mutual folly, and continued silent. After a short time spent in cool reflection, Griffith inquired of his friend the nature and circumstances of his interview with Katherine Plowden. Barnstable related it, briefly, as it occurred, in the manner already known to the reader.

"Then," said Griffith, "Merry is the only one, besides ourselves, who knows of this meeting, and he will be too chary of the reputation of his kinswoman to mention it."

"Her reputation needs no shield, Mr. Griffith," cried her lover; " 'tis as spotless as the canvas about your head, and—"

"Peace, dear Richard; I entreat your pardon; my words may have conveyed more than I intended; but it is important that our measures should be secret, as well as prudently concerted."

"We must get them both off," returned Barnstable, forgetting his displeasure the moment it was exhibited, "and that, too, before the old man takes it into his wise head to leave the coast. Did you ever get a sight of his instructions, or does he keep silent?"

"As the grave. This is the first time we have left port that he has not conversed freely with me on the nature of the cruise; but not a syllable has been exchanged between us on the subject since we sailed from Brest."

"Ah! that is your Jersey bashfulness," said Barnstable; "wait till I come alongside him, with my Eastern curiosity, and I pledge myself to get it out of him in an hour."

" 'Twill be diamond cut diamond, I doubt," said Griffith, laughing; "you will find him as acute at evasion as you can possibly be at a cross-examination."

"At any rate, he gives me a chance today; you know, I suppose, that he sent for me to attend a consultation of his officers on important matters?"

"I did not," returned Griffith, fixing his eyes intently on the speaker; "what has he to offer?"

"Nay, that you must ask your pilot; for, while talking to me, the old man would turn and look at the stranger every minute, as if watching for signals how to steer."

"There is a mystery about that man, and our connection with him, that I cannot fathom," said Griffith. "But I hear the voice of Manual calling for me; we are wanted in the cabin. Remember, you do not leave the ship without seeing me again."

"No, no, my dear fellow; from the public we must retire to another private consultation."

The young men arose, and Griffith, throwing off the roundabout in which he had appeared on deck, drew on a coat of more formal appearance, and, taking a sword carelessly in his hand, they proceeded together along the passage already described to the gun-deck, where they entered, with the proper ceremonials, into the principal cabin of the frigate.

7

Sempronius, speak.

Cato

THE arrangements for the consultation were brief and simple. The veteran commander of the frigate received his orders with punctilious respect; and pointing to the chairs that were placed around the table, which was a fixture in the centre of his cabin, he silently seated himself, and his example was followed by all without ceremony. In taking their stations, however, a quiet but rigid observance was paid to the rights of seniority and rank. On the right of the captain was placed Griffith, as next in authority; and opposite to him was seated the commander of the schooner. The officer of marines, who was included in the number, held the next situation in point of precedence, the same order being observed at the bottom of the table, which was occupied by a hard-featured, square-built, athletic man, who held the office of sailing-master. When order was restored, after the short interruption of taking their places, the officer who had required the advice of his inferiors, opened the business on which he demanded their opinions.

"My instructions direct me, gentlemen," he said, "after making the coast of England, to run the land down—"

The hand of Griffith was elevated respectfully for silence, and the veteran paused, with a look that inquired the reason of his interruption.

"We are not alone," said the lieutenant, glancing his eye toward the part of the cabin where the pilot stood, leaning on one of the guns, in an attitude of easy indulgence.

The stranger moved not at this direct hint; neither did his eye change from his close survey of the chart that lay near him on the deck. The captain dropped his voice to tones of cautious respect, as he replied:

" 'Tis only Mr. Gray. His services will be necessary on the occasion, and therefore nothing need be concealed from him."

Glances of surprise were exchanged among the young men; but Griffith bowing his silent acquiescence in the decision of his superior, the latter proceeded:

"I was ordered to watch for certain signals from the headlands that we made, and was furnished with the best of charts, and such directions as enabled us to stand into the bay we entered last night. We have now obtained a pilot, and one who has proved himself a skilful man; such a one, gentlemen, as no officer need hesitate to rely on, in any emergency, either on account of his integrity or his knowledge."

The veteran paused and turned his looks on the countenances of the listeners, as if to collect their sentiments on this important point. Receiving no other reply than the one conveyed by the silent inclinations of the heads of his hearers, the commander resumed his explanations, referring to an open paper in his hand:

"It is known to you all, gentlemen, that the unfortunate question of retaliation has been much agitated between the two governments, our own and that of the enemy. For this reason, and for certain political purposes, it has become an object of solicitude with our commissioners in Paris to obtain a few individuals of character from the enemy, who may be held as a check on their proceedings, while at the same time it brings the evils of war, from our own shores, home to those who have caused it. An opportunity now offers to put this plan in execution, and I have collected you in order to consult on the means."

A profound silence succeeded this unexpected communication of the object of their cruise. After a short pause the captain added, addressing himself to the sailing-master:

"What course would you advise me to pursue, Mr. Boltrope?"

The weather-beaten seaman who was thus called on to break through the difficulties of a knotty point with his opinion, laid one of his short, bony hands on the table, and began to twirl an inkstand with great industry, while with the other he conveyed a pen to his mouth, which was apparently masticated with all the relish that he could possibly have felt had it been a leaf from the famous Virginian weed. But perceiving that he was expected to answer, after looking first to his right hand and then to his left, he spoke as follows, in a hoarse, thick voice, in which the fogs of the ocean seemed to have united with sea-damps and colds to destroy everything like melody:

"If this matter is ordered, it is to be done, I suppose," he said; "for the old rule runs, 'Obey orders, if you break owners'; though the maxim which says, 'One hand for the owner, and t'other for yourself,' is quite as good, and has saved many a hearty fellow from a fall that would have balanced the purser's books. Not that I mean a purser's books are not as good as any other man's; but that, when a man is dead, his account must be closed, or there will be a false muster. Well, if the thing is to be done, the next question is, *how* is it to be done? There is many a man that knows there is too much canvas on a ship, who can't tell how to shorten sail. Well, then, if the thing is really to be done, we must either land a gang to seize them, or we must show false lights and sham colors to lead them off to the ship. As for landing, Captain Munson, I can only speak for one man, and that is myself, which is to say that, if you run the ship with her jib-boom into the King of England's parlor windows, why, I'm consenting, nor do I care how much of his crockery is cracked in so doing; but, as to putting the print of my foot on one of his sandy beaches, if I do, that is, always speaking for only one man, and saving your presence, may I hope to be d——d!"

The young men smiled as the tough old seaman uttered his sentiments so frankly, rising with his subject to that which with him was the climax of all discussion; but his commander, who was but a more improved scholar from the same rough school, appeared to understand his arguments entirely, and, without altering a muscle of his rigid countenance, he required the opinion of the junior lieutenant.

The young man spoke firmly, but modestly, though the amount of what he said was not much more distinct than that uttered by the master, and was very much to the same purpose, with the exception that he appeared to entertain no personal reluctance to trusting himself on dry ground.

The opinions of the others grew gradually more explicit and clear as they ascended in the scale of rank, until it came to the turn of the captain of the marines to speak. There was a trifling exhibition of professional pride about the soldier in delivering his sentiments on a subject that embraced a good deal more of his peculiar sort of duty than ordinarily occurred in the usual operations of the frigate.

"It appears to me, sir, that the success of this expedition depends altogether upon the manner in which it is conducted." After this lucid opening, the soldier hesitated a moment, as if to collect his ideas for a charge that should look down all opposition, and proceeded: "The landing, of course, will be effected on a fair beach, under cover of the frigate's guns, and, could it possibly be done, the schooner should be anchored in such a manner as to throw in a flanking fire on the point of debarkation. The arrangements for the order of march must a good deal depend on the distance to go over; though I should think, sir, an advanced party of seamen, to act as pioneers for the column of marines, should be pushed a short distance in front, while the baggage and baggage-guard might rest upon the frigate until the enemy was driven into the interior, when it could advance without danger. There should be flank-guards, under the orders of two of the oldest midshipmen; and a light corps might be formed of the topmen to co-operate with the marines. Of course, sir, Mr. Griffith will lead, in person, the musket-men and boarders, armed with their long pikes, whom I presume he will hold in reserve, as I trust my military claims and experience entitle me to the command of the main body."

"Well done, field-marshal!" cried Barnstable, with a glee that seldom regarded time or place; "you should never let salt-water mould your buttons; but in Washington's camp, ay! and in Washington's tent, you should swing your hammock in future. Why, sir, do you think we are about to invade England?"

"I know that every military movement should be executed with precision, Captain Barnstable," returned the marine. "I am too much accustomed to hear the sneers of the sea-officers to regard what I know proceeds from ignorance. If Captain Munson is disposed to employ me and my command in this expedition, I trust he will discover that marines are good for something more than to mount guard and pay salutes." Then, turning haughtily from his antagonist, he continued to address himself to their common superior, as if disdaining further intercourse with one who, from the nature of the case, must be unable to comprehend the force of what he said. "It will be prudent, Captain Munson, to send out a party to reconnoitre, before we march; and, as it may be necessary to defend ourselves in case of a repulse, I would beg leave to recommend that a corps be provided with intrenching tools, to accompany the expedition. They would be extremely useful, sir, in assisting to throw up fieldworks; though, I doubt not, tools might be found in abundance in this country, and laborers impressed for the service, on an emergency."

This was too much for the risibility of Barnstable, who broke forth in a fit of scornful laughter, which no one saw proper to interrupt; though Griffith, on turning his head, to conceal the smile that was gathering on his own face, perceived the fierce glance which the pilot threw at the merry seaman, and wondered at its significance and impatience. When Captain Munson thought that the mirth of the lieutenant was concluded, he mildly desired his reasons for amusing himself so exceedingly with the plans of the marine.

" 'Tis a chart for a campaign!" cried Barnstable, "and should be sent off express to Congress, before the Frenchmen are brought into the field!"

"Have you any better plan to propose, Mr. Barnstable?" inquired the patient commander.

"Better! ay, one that will take no time, and cause no trouble, to execute it," cried the other; " 'tis a seaman's job, sir, and must be done with a seaman's means."

"Pardon me, Captain Barnstable," interrupted the marine whose jocular vein was entirely absorbed in his military pride; "if there be service to be done on shore, I claim it as my right to be employed."

"Claim what you will, soldier; but how will you carry on the war with a parcel of fellows who don't know one end of a boat from the other?" returned the reckless sailor. "Do you think that a barge or a cutter is to be beached in the same manner you ground firelock, by word of command? No, no, Captain Manual—I honor your courage, for I have seen it tried, but d——e if—"

"You forget we wait for your project, Mr. Barnstable," said the veteran.

"I crave your patience, sir, but no project is necessary. Point out the bearings and the distance of the place where the men you want are to be found, and I will take the heel of the gale, and run in to the land, always speaking for good water and no rocks. Mr. Pilot, you will accompany me, for you carry as true a map of the bottom of these seas in your head as ever was made of dry ground. I will look out for good anchorage; or, if the wind should blow off-shore, let the schooner stand off and on, till we should be ready to take the broad sea again. I would land, out of my whale-boat, with Long Tom and a boat's crew, and, finding out the place you will describe, we shall go up and take the men you want, and bring them aboard. It's all plain sailing; though, as it is a well-peopled country, it may be necessary to do our shorework in the dark."

"Mr. Griffith, we only wait for your sentiments," proceeded the captain, "when, by comparing opinions, we may decide on the most prudent course."

The first-lieutenant had been much absorbed in thought during the discussion of the subject, and might have been, on that account, better prepared to give his opinion with effect. Pointing to the man who yet stood behind him, leaning on a gun, he commenced by asking:

"Is it your intention that man shall accompany the party?"

"It is."

"And from him you expect the necessary information, sir, to guide your movements?"

"You are altogether right."

"If, sir, he has but a moiety of the skill on the land that he possesses on the water, I will answer for his success," returned the lieutenant, bowing slightly to the stranger, who received the compliment by a cold inclination of his head. "I must desire the indulgence of both Mr. Barnstable and Captain Manual," he continued, "and claim the command as of right belonging to my rank."

"It belongs naturally to the schooner," exclaimed the impatient Barnstable.

"There may be enough for us all to do," said Griffith, elevating a finger to the other, in a manner, and with an impressive look, that was instantly comprehended. "I neither agree wholly with the one nor the other of those gentlemen. 'Tis said that, since our appearance on the coast, the dwellings of many of the gentry are guarded by small detachments of soldiers from the neighboring towns."

"Who says it?" asked the pilot, advancing among them with a suddenness that caused a general silence.

"I say it, sir," returned the lieutenant, when the momentary surprise had passed away.

"Can you vouch for it?"

"I can."

"Name a house, or an individual, that is thus protected."

Griffith gazed at the man who thus forgot himself in the midst of a consultation like the present, and, yielding to his native pride, hesitated to reply. But mindful of the declarations of his captain, and the recent service of the pilot, he at length said, with a little embarrassment of manner:

"I know it to be the fact, in the dwelling of a Colonel Howard who resides but a few leagues to the north of us."

The stranger started at the same, and then, raising his eye keenly to the face of the young man, appeared to study his thoughts in his varying countenance. But the action, and the pause that followed, were of short continuance. His lip slightly curled, whether in scorn or with a concealed smile would have been difficult to say, so closely did it resemble both, and, as he dropped quietly back to his place at the gun, he said:

" 'Tis more than probable you are right, sir; and, if I might presume to advise Captain Munson, it would be to lay great weight on your opinion."

Griffith turned, to see if he could comprehend more meaning in the manner of the stranger than his words expressed, but his face was again shaded by his hand, and his eyes were once more fixed on the chart with the same vacant abstraction as before.

"I have said, sir, that I agree wholly neither with Mr. Barnstable nor Captain Manual," continued the lieutenant, after a short pause. "The command of this party is mine, as the senior officer, and I must beg leave to claim it. I certainly do not think the preparation Captain Manual advises, necessary; neither would I undertake the duty with as little caution as Mr. Barnstable proposes. If there are soldiers to be encountered, we should have soldiers to oppose them; but as it must be sudden boatwork, and regular evolutions must give place to a seaman's bustle, a sea-officer should command. Is my request granted, Captain Munson?"

The veteran replied, without hesitation: "It is, sir; it was my intention to offer you the service, and I rejoice to see you accept it so cheerfully."

Griffith with difficulty concealed the satisfaction with which he listened to his commander, and a radiant smile illumined his pale features, when he observed:

"With me then, sir, let the responsibility rest. I request that Captain Manual, with twenty men, may be put under my orders, if that gentleman does not dislike the duty." The marine bowed, and cast a glance of triumph at Barnstable. "I will take my own cutter, with her tried crew, go on board the schooner, and when the wind lulls we will run in to the land, and then be governed by circumstances."

The commander of the schooner threw back the triumphant look of the marine, and exclaimed in his joyous manner:

" 'Tis a good plan, and done like a seaman, Mr. Griffith. Ay, ay, let the schooner be employed; and, if it be necessary, you shall see her anchored in one of their duck-ponds, with her broadside to bear on the parlor-windows of the best house in the island! But twenty marines! they will cause a jam in my little craft."

"Not a man less than twenty would be prudent," returned Griffith. "More service may offer than that we seek."

Barnstable well understood his allusion, but still he replied:

"Make it all seamen, and I will give you room for thirty. But these soldiers never know how to stow away their arms and legs, unless at a drill. One will take the room of two sailors; they swing their hammocks athwart-ships, heads to leeward, and then turn out wrong end uppermost at the call. Why, damn it, sir, the chalk and rotten-stone of twenty soldiers will choke my hatches!"

"Give me the launch, Captain Munson!" exclaimed the indignant marine, "and we will follow Mr. Griffith in an open boat, rather than put Captain Barnstable to so much inconvenience."

"No, no, Manual," cried the other, extending his muscular arm across the table, with an open palm, to the soldier; "you would all become so many Jonahs in uniform, and I doubt whether the fish could digest your cartridge boxes and bayonet belts. You shall go with me, and learn, with your own eyes, whether we keep the cat's watch aboard the Ariel that you joke about."

The laugh was general, at the expense of the soldier, if we except the pilot and the commander of the frigate. The former was a silent and apparently an abstracted, but, in reality, a deeply interested listener to the discourse; and there were moments when he bent his looks on the speakers, as if he sought more in their characters than was exhibited by the gay trifling of the moment. Captain Munson seldom allowed a muscle of his wrinkled features to disturb their repose; and if he had not the real dignity to repress the untimely mirth of his officers, he had too much good nature to wish to disturb their harmless enjoyments. He expressed himself satisfied with the proposed arrangements, and beckoned to his steward to place before them the usual beverage, with which all their consultations concluded.

The sailing-master appeared to think that the same order was to be observed in their potations as in council, and, helping himself to an allowance which retained its hue even in its diluted state, he first raised it to the light, and then observed:

"This ship's water is nearly the color of rum itself; if it only had its flavor, what a set of hearty dogs we should be!—Mr. Griffith, I find you are willing to haul your land-tacks aboard. Well, it's natural for youth to love the earth; but there is one man, and he is sailing-master of this ship, who saw land enough, last night, to last him a twelvemonth. But, if you will go, here's a good land-fall, and a better offing to you. Captain Munson, my respects to you. I say, sir, if we should keep the ship more to the south'ard, it's my opinion, and that's but one man's, we should fall in with some of the enemy's homeward-bound West Indiamen, and find wherewithal to keep the life in us when we see fit to go ashore ourselves."

As the tough old sailor made frequent application of the glass to his mouth with one hand, and kept a firm hold of the decanter with the other, during this speech, his companions were compelled to listen to his eloquence, or depart with their thirst unassuaged. Barnstable, however, quite coolly dispossessed the tar of the bottle, and, mixing for himself a more equal potation, observed in the act:

"That is the most remarkable glass of grog you have, Boltrope, that I ever sailed with; it draws as little water as the Ariel, and is as hard to find the bottom. If your spirit-room enjoys the same sort of engine to replenish it, as you pump out your rum, Congress will sail this frigate cheaply."

The other officers helped themselves with still greater moderation, Griffith barely moistening his lips, and the pilot rejecting the offered glass altogether. Captain Munson continued standing, and his officers, perceiving that their presence was no longer necessary, bowed, and took their leave. As Griffith was retiring last, he felt a hand laid lightly on his shoulder, and, turning, perceived that he was detained by the pilot.

"Mr. Griffith," he said, when they were quite alone with the commander of the frigate, "the occurrences of the last night should teach us confidence in each other; without it, we go on a dangerous and fruitless errand."

"Is the hazard equal?" returned the youth. "I am known to all to be the man I seem—am in the service of my country—belong to a family, and enjoy a name that is a pledge for my loyalty to the cause of America—and yet I trust myself on hostile ground, in the midst of enemies, with a weak arm, and under circumstances where treachery would prove my ruin. Who and what is the man who thus enjoys your confidence, Captain Munson? I ask the question less for myself than for the gallant men who will fearlessly follow wherever I lead."

A shade of dark displeasure crossed the features of the stranger, at one part of this speech, and at its close he sank into deep thought. The commander, however, replied:

"There is a show of reason in your question, Mr. Griffith—and yet you are not the man to be told that implicit obedience is what I have a right to expect. I have not your pretensions, sir, by birth or education, and yet Congress has not seen proper to overlook my years and services. I command this frigate—"

"Say no more," interrupted the pilot. "There is reason in his doubts, and they shall be appeased. I like the proud and fearless eye of the young man, and, while he dreads a gibbet from my hands, I will show him how to repose a noble confidence. Read this, sir, and tell me if you distrust me now?"

While the stranger spoke he thrust his hand into the bosom of his dress, and drew forth a parchment, decorated with ribbons, and bearing a massive seal, which he opened and laid on the table before the youth. As he pointed with his finger impressively to different parts of the writing his eye kindled with a look of unusual fire, and there was a faint tinge discernible on his pallid features when he spoke. "See!" he said, "royalty itself does not hesitate to bear witness in my favor, and that is not a name to occasion dread to an American."

Griffith gazed with wonder at the fair signature of the unfortunate Louis, which graced the bottom of the parchment; but when his eye obeyed the signal of the stranger, and rested on the body of the instrument, he started back from the table, and fixing his animated eyes on the pilot he cried, while a glow of fiery courage flitted across his countenance:

"Lead on! I'll follow you to death!"

A smile of gratified exultation struggled around the lips of the stranger, who took the arm of the young man and led him into a state-room, leaving the commander of the frigate standing in his unmoved and quiet manner a spectator of, but hardly an actor in, the scene.

8

Fierce bounding, forward sprang the ship,
Like a greyhound starting from the slip,
To seize his flying prey.

Lord of the Isles

ALTHOUGH the subject of the consulta-
tion remained a secret with those whose opinions were required, yet enough
of the result leaked out among the subordinate officers to throw the whole
crew into a state of eager excitement. The rumor spread itself along the decks
of the frigate, with the rapidity of an alarm, that an expedition was to attempt
the shore on some hidden service, dictated by the Congress itself; and conjectures were made respecting its force and destination, with all that interest
which might be imagined would exist among the men whose lives or liberties
were to abide the issue. A gallant and reckless daring, mingled with the desire
of novelty, however, was the prevailing sentiment among the crew, who
would have received with cheers the intelligence that their vessel was commanded to force the passage of the united British fleet. A few of the older and
more prudent of the sailors were exceptions to this thoughtless hardihood, and
one or two, among whom the cockswain of the whale-boat was the most conspicuous, ventured to speak doubtingly of all sorts of land service, as being
of a nature never to be attempted by seamen.

Captain Manual had his men paraded in the weather gangway; and after a
short address, calculated to inflame their military ardor and patriotism, ac-

quainted them that he required twenty volunteers, which was in truth half their number, for a dangerous service. After a short pause, the company stepped forward, like one man, and announced themselves as ready to follow him to the end of the world. The marine cast a look over his shoulder, at this gratifying declaration, in quest of Barnstable; but, observing that the sailor was occupied with some papers on a distant part of the quarter-deck, he proceeded to make a most impartial division among the candidates for glory, taking care, at the same time, to cull his company in such a manner as to give himself the flower of his men, and consequently to leave the ship the refuse.

While this arrangement was taking place, and the crew of the frigate was in this state of excitement, Griffith ascended to the deck, his countenance flushed with unusual enthusiasm, and eyes beaming with a look of animation and gayety, that had long been strangers to the face of the young man. He was giving forth the few necessary orders to the seamen he was to take with him from the ship, when Barnstable again motioned him to follow, and led the way once more to the state-room.

"Let the wind blow its pipe out," said the commander of the Ariel, when they were seated; "there will be no landing on the eastern coast of England till the sea goes down. But this Kate was made for a sailor's wife! See, Griffith, what a set of signals she has formed, out of her own cunning head."

"I hope your opinion may prove true, and that you may be the happy sailor who is to wed her," returned the other. "The girl has indeed discovered surprising art in this business! Where could she have learned the method and system so well?"

"Where! why, where she learned better things; how to prize a whole-hearted seaman, for instance. Do you think that my tongue was jammed in my mouth, all the time we used to sit by the side of the river in Carolina, and that we found nothing to talk about?"

"Did you amuse your mistress with treatises on the art of navigation, and the science of signals?" said Griffith, smiling.

"I answered her questions, Mr. Griffith, as any civil man would to a woman he loved. The girl has as much curiosity as one of my own towns-women who has weathered cape forty without a husband, and her tongue goes like a dog-vane in a calm, first one way and then another. But here is her dictionary. Now own, Griff, in spite of your college learning and sentimentals, that a woman of ingenuity and cleverness is a very good sort of a help-mate."

"I never doubted the merits of Miss Plowden," said the other, with a droll gravity that often mingled with his deeper feelings, the result of a sailor's habits, blended with native character. "But this indeed surpasses all my expectations! Why, she has, in truth, made a most judicious selection of phrases. 'No. 168.**** indelible'; '169.**** end only with life'; '170.**** I fear your's misleads me'; '171–' "

"Pshaw!" exclaimed Barnstable, snatching the book from before the laughing eyes of Griffith; "what folly to throw away our time now on such nonsense! What think you of this expedition to the land?"

"That it may be the means of rescuing the ladies, though it fail in making the prisoners we anticipate."

"But this pilot! you remember that he holds us by our necks, and can run us all up to the yard-arm of some English ship whenever he chooses to open his throat at their threats or bribes."

"It would have been better that he should have cast the ship ashore, when he had her entangled in the shoals; it would have been our last thought to suspect him of treachery then," returned Griffith. "I follow him with confidence, and must believe that we are safer with him than we should be without him."

"Let him lead to the dwelling of his fox-hunting ministers of state," cried Barnstable, thrusting his book of signals into his bosom; "but here is a chart that will show us the way to the port we wish to find. Let my foot once more touch *terra firma,* and you may write craven against my name if that laughing vixen slips her cable before my eyes, and shoots into the wind's eye again, like a flying-fish chased by a dolphin. Mr. Griffith, we must have the chaplain with us to the shore."

"The madness of love is driving you into the errors of the soldier. Would you lie by to hear sermons, with a flying party like ours?"

"Nay, nay, we must lay-to for nothing that is not unavoidable; but there are so many tacks in such a chase, when one has time to breathe, that we might as well spend our leisure in getting that fellow to splice us together. He has a handy way with a prayer-book, and could do the job as well as a bishop; and I should like to be able to say that this is the last time that these two saucy names, which are written at the bottom of this letter, should ever be seen sailing in the company of each other."

"It will not do," said his friend, shaking his head, and endeavoring to force a smile which his feelings suppressed; "it will not do, Richard; we must yield our own inclinations to the service of our country; nor is this pilot a man who will consent to be led from his purpose."

"Then let him follow his purpose alone," cried Barnstable. "There is no human power, always saving my superior officer, that shall keep me from throwing abroad these tiny signals, and having a private talk with my dark-eyed Kate. But for a paltry pilot! he may luff and bear away as he pleases, while I shall steer as true as a magnet for that old ruin, where I can bring my eyes to bear on that romantic wing and three smoky vanes. Not that I'll forget my duty; no, I'll help you catch the Englishmen; but, when that is done, hey! for Katherine Plowden and my true love!"

"Hush, madcap! the ward-room holds long ears, and our bulkheads grow thin by wear. I must keep you and myself to our duty. This is no children's game that we play; it seems the commissioners at Paris have thought proper to employ a frigate in the sport!"

Barnstable's gayety was a little repressed by the grave manner of his companion; but after reflecting a moment, he started on his feet, and made the usual movements for departure.

"Whither?" asked Griffith, gently detaining his impatient friend.

"To old Moderate; I have a proposal to make that may remove every difficulty."

"Name it to me, then; I am in his counsel, and may save you the trouble and mortification of a refusal."

"How many of those gentry does he wish to line his cabin with?"

"The pilot has named no less than six, all men of rank and consideration with the enemy. Two of them are peers, two more belong to the Commons' House of Parliament, one is a general, and the sixth, like ourselves, is a sailor, and holds the rank of captain. They muster at a hunting-seat near the coast, and, believe me, the scheme is not without its plausibility."

"Well, then, there are two apiece for us. You follow the pilot, if you will; but let me sheer off for this dwelling of Colonel Howard, with my cockswain and boat's crew. I will surprise his house, release the ladies, and, on my way back, lay my hands on two of the first lords I fall in with. I suppose, for our business, one is as good as another."

Griffith could not repress a faint laugh, while he replied:

"Though they are said to be each other's peers, there is, I believe, some difference even in the quality of lords. England might thank us for ridding her of some among them. Neither are they to be found, like beggars, under every hedge. No, no, the men we seek must have something better than their nobility to recommend them to our favor. But let us examine more closely into this plan and map of Miss Plowden; something may occur that shall yet bring the place within our circuit, like a contingent duty of the cruise."

Barnstable reluctantly relinquished his own wild plan to the more sober judgment of his friend, and they passed an hour together, inquiring into the practicability, and consulting on the means, of making their public duty subserve the purposes of their private feelings.

The gale continued to blow heavily during the whole of that morning; but towards noon the usual indications of better weather became apparent. During these few hours of inaction in the frigate, the marines, who were drafted for service on the land, moved through the vessel with a busy and stirring air, as if they were about to participate in the glory and danger of the campaign their officers had planned, while the few seamen who were to accompany the expedition steadily paced the deck, with their hands thrust into the bosom of their neat blue jackets, or occasionally stretched toward the horizon, as their fingers traced, for their less experienced shipmates, the signs of an abatement in the gale among the driving clouds. The last lagger among the soldiers had appeared, with his knapsack on his back, in the lee gangway, where his comrades were collected, armed and accoutred for the strife, when Captain Munson ascended to the quarter-deck, accompanied by the stranger and his first lieutenant. A word was spoken by the latter in a low voice to a midshipman, who skipped gayly along the deck, and presently the shrill call of the boatswain was heard, preceding the hoarse cry of:

"Away there, you Tigers, away!"

A smart roll of the drum followed, and the marines paraded, while six seamen who belonged to the cutter that owned so fierce a name, made their preparations for lowering their little bark from the quarter of the frigate into the troubled sea. Everything was conducted in the most exact order, and with a coolness and skill that bade defiance to the turbulence of the angry elements. The marines were safely transported from the ship to the schooner, under the favoring shelter of the former, though the boat appeared, at times, to be seeking the cavities of the ocean, and again to be riding in the clouds, as she passed from one vessel to the other.

At length it was announced that the cutter was ready to receive the officers of the party. The pilot walked aside, and held private discourse for a few moments with the commander, who listened to his sentences with marked and singular attention. When their conference was ended, the veteran bared his gray head to the blasts, and offered his hand to the other with a seaman's frankness, mingled with the deference of an inferior. This compliment was courteously returned by the stranger, who turned quickly on his heel, and directed the attention of those who awaited his movements, by a significant gesture, to the gangway.

"Come, gentlemen, let us go," said Griffith, starting from a reverie, and bowing his hasty compliments to his brethren in arms.

When it appeared that his superiors were ready to enter the boat, the boy, who by nautical courtesy was styled Mr. Merry, and who had been ordered to be in readiness, sprang over the side of the frigate and glided into the cutter with the activity of a squirrel. But the captain of the marines paused, and cast a meaning glance at the pilot, whose place it was to precede him. The stranger, as he lingered on the deck, was examining the aspect of the heavens, and seemed unconscious of the expectations of the soldier, who gave vent to his impatience, after a moment's detention, by saying:

"We wait for you, Mr. Gray."

Aroused by the sound of his name, the pilot glanced his quick eye on the speaker, but, instead of advancing, he gently bent his body, as he again signed toward the gangway with his hand. To the astonishment not only of the soldier, but of all who witnessed this breach of naval etiquette, Griffith bowed low, and entered the boat with the same promptitude as if he were preceding an admiral. Whether the stranger became conscious of his want of courtesy, or was too indifferent to surrounding objects to note occurrences, he immediately followed himself, leaving to the marine the post of honor. The latter, who was distinguished for his skill in all matters of naval or military etiquette, thought proper to apologize at a fitting time to the first-lieutenant for suffering his senior officer to precede him into a boat, but never failed to show a becoming exultation, when he recounted the circumstance, by dwelling on the manner in which he had brought down the pride of the haughty pilot.

Barnstable had been several hours on board his little vessel, which was every way prepared for their reception; and, as soon as the heavy cutter of the frigate was hoisted on her deck, he announced that the schooner was ready to sail. It has been already intimated, that the Ariel belonged to the smallest class of sea-vessels; and, as the symmetry of her construction reduced even that size in appearance, she was peculiarly well adapted to the sort of service in which she was about to be employed. Notwithstanding her lightness rendered her nearly as buoyant as a cork, and at times she actually seemed to ride on the foam, her low decks were perpetually washed by the heavy seas that dashed against her frail sides, and she tossed and rolled in the hollows of the waves in a manner that compelled even the practised seamen who trod her decks to move with guarded steps. Still she was trimmed and cleared with an air of nautical neatness and attention that afforded the utmost possible room for her dimensions; and, though in miniature, she wore the trappings of war as proudly as if the metal she bore was of a more fatal and dangerous character. The murderous gun, which, since the period of which we are writing, has been universally adopted in all vessels of inferior size, was then in the infancy of its invention, and was known to the American mariner only by reputation, under the appalling name of a "smasher." Of a vast calibre, though short and easily managed, its advantages were even in that early day beginning to be appreciated, and the largest ships were thought to be unusually well provided with the means of offence, when they carried two or three cannon of this formidable invention among their armament. At a later day, this weapon has been improved and altered, until its use has become general in vessels of a certain size, taking its appellation from the Carron, on the banks of which river it was first moulded. In place of these carronades, six light brass cannon were firmly lashed to the bulwarks of the Ariel, their brazen throats blackened by the sea-water, which so often broke harmlessly over these engines of destruction. In the centre of the vessel, between her two masts, a gun of the same metal, but of nearly twice the length of the other, was mounted on a carriage of a new and singular construction, which admitted of its being turned in any direction, so as to be of service in most of the emergencies that occur in naval warfare.

The eye of the pilot examined this armament closely, and then turned to the well-ordered decks, the neat and compact rigging, and the hardy faces of the fine young crew, with manifest satisfaction. Contrary to what had been his practice during the short time he had been with them, he uttered his gratification freely and aloud.

"You have a tight boat, Mr. Barnstable," he said, "and a gallant-looking crew. You promise good service, sir, in time of need, and that hour may not be far distant."

"The sooner the better," returned the reckless sailor; "I have not had an opportunity of scaling my guns since we quitted Brest, though we passed several of the enemy's cutters coming up the Channel, with whom our bull-dogs longed for a conversation. Mr. Griffith will tell you, pilot, that my little sixes can speak, on occasions, with a voice nearly as loud as the frigate's eighteens."

"But not to as much purpose," observed Griffith; " 'vox et præterea nihil,' as we said at the school."

"I know nothing of your Greek and Latin, Mr. Griffith," retorted the commander of the Ariel; "but if you mean that those seven brass playthings won't throw a round shot as far as any gun of their size and height above the water, or won't scatter grape and cannister with any blunderbuss in your ship, you may possibly find an opportunity that will convince you to the contrary before we part company."

"They promise well," said the pilot, who was evidently ignorant of the good understanding that existed between the two officers, and wished to conciliate all under his directions; "and I doubt not they will argue the leading points of a combat with good discretion. I see that you have christened them—I suppose for their respective merits! They are indeed expressive names!"

" 'Tis the freak of an idle moment," said Barnstable, laughing, as he glanced his eyes to the cannon, above which were painted the several quaint names of "boxer," "plumper," "grinder," "scatterer," "exterminator," and "nail-driver."

"Why have you thrown the mid-ship gun without the pale of your baptism?" asked the pilot; "or do you know it by the usual title of the 'old woman'?"

"No, no, I have no such petticoat terms on board me," cried the other; "but move more to starboard, and you will see its style painted on the cheeks of the carriage; it's a name that need not cause them to blush either."

" 'Tis a singular epithet, though not without some meaning!"

"It has more than you perhaps dream of, sir. That worthy seaman whom you see leaning against the foremast, and who would serve, on occasion, for a spare spar himself, is the captain of that gun, and more than once has decided some warm disputes with John Bull, by the manner in which he has wielded it. No marine can trail his musket more easily than my cockswain can train his nine-pounder on an object; and thus from their connection, and some resemblance there is between them in length, it has got the name which you perceive it carries—that of 'Long Tom.' "

The pilot smiled as he listened, but, turning away from the speaker, the deep reflection that crossed his brow but too plainly showed that he trifled only from momentary indulgence; and Griffith intimated to Barnstable that, as the gale was sensibly abating, they would pursue the object of their destination.

Thus recalled to his duty, the commander of the schooner forgot the delightful theme of expatiating on the merits of his vessel, and issued the necessary order to direct their movements. The little schooner slowly obeyed the impulse of her helm, and fell off before the wind, when the folds of her square sail, though limited by a prudent reef, were open to the blasts, and she shot away from her consort like a meteor dancing across the waves. The black mass of the frigate's hull soon sunk in the distance; and, long before the sun had fallen below the hills of England, her tall masts were barely distinguishable by the small cloud of sail that held the vessel to her station. As the ship disappeared, the land seemed to issue out of the bosom of the deep; and so rapid was their progress, that the dwellings of the gentry, the humbler cottages, and even the dim lines of the hedges, became gradually more distinct to the eyes of the bold mariners, until they were beset with the gloom of the evening, when the whole scene faded from their view in the darkness of the hour, leaving only the faint outline of the land visible in the tract before them, and the sullen billows of the ocean raging with appalling violence in their rear.

Still the little Ariel held on her way, skimming the ocean like a waterfowl seeking its place of nightly rest, and shooting in toward the land as fearlessly as if the dangers of the preceding night were already forgotten. No shoals or rocks appeared to arrest her course, and we must leave her gliding into the dark streak that was thrown from the high and rocky cliffs that lined a basin of bold entrance, where the mariners often sought and found a refuge from the dangers of the German Ocean.

9

Sirrah! how dare you leave your
barley-broth
To come in armor thus, against your king?

Drama

THE large irregular building inhabited by
Colonel Howard well deserved the name it had received from the pen of
Katherine Plowden. Notwithstanding the confusion in its orders, owing to
the different ages in which its several parts had been erected, the interior was
not wanting in that appearance of comfort which forms the great characteristic of English domestic life. Its dark and intricate mazes of halls, galleries,
and apartments, were all well provided with good and substantial furniture;
and, whatever might have been the purposes of their original construction,
they were now peacefully appropriated to the service of a quiet and well-
ordered family.

There were divers portentous traditions of cruel separations and blighted
loves, which always linger, like cobwebs, around the walls of old houses, to
be heard here also, and which, doubtless, in abler hands, might easily have
been wrought up into scenes of high interest and delectable pathos. But our
humbler efforts must be limited by an attempt to describe man as God has
made him, vulgar and unseemly as he may appear to sublimated faculties, to
the possessors of which enviable qualifications we desire to say, at once, that
we are determined to eschew all things supernaturally refined, as we would

the devil. To all those, then, who are tired of the company of their species we would bluntly insinuate, that the sooner they throw aside our pages, and seize upon those of some more highly-gifted bard, the sooner will they be in the way of quitting earth, if not of attaining heaven. Our business is solely to treat of man, and this fair scene on which he acts, and that not in his subtleties and metaphysical contradictions, but in his palpable nature, that all may understand our meaning as well as ourselves—whereby we manifestly reject the prodigious advantage of being thought a genius, by perhaps foolishly refusing the mighty aid of incomprehensibility to establish such a character.

Leaving the gloomy shadows of the cliffs, under which the little Ariel has been seen to steer, and the sullen roaring of the surf along the margin of the ocean, we shall endeavor to transport the reader to the dining-parlor of St. Ruth's Abbey, taking the evening of the same day as the time for introducing another collection of those personages whose acts and characters it has become our duty to describe.

The room was not of very large dimensions, and every part was glittering with the collected light of half a dozen candles, aided by the fierce rays that glanced from the grate, which held a most cheerful fire of sea-coal. The mouldings of the dark oak wainscoting threw back upon the massive table of mahogany streaks of strong light, which played among the rich fluids that were sparkling on the board, in mimic halos. The outline of this picture of comfort was formed by damask curtains of a deep red, and enormous oak chairs, with leathern backs and cushioned seats, as if the apartment were hermetically sealed against the world and its chilling cares.

Around the table, which still stood in the center of the floor, were seated three gentlemen, in the easy enjoyment of their daily repast. The cloth had been drawn and the bottle was slowly passing among them, as if those who partook of its bounty well knew that neither the time nor the opportunity would be wanting for their deliberate indulgence in its pleasures.

At one end of the table an elderly man was seated, who performed whatever little acts of courtesy the duties of a host would appear to render necessary, in a company where all seemed to be equally at their ease and at home. This gentleman was in the decline of life, though his erect carriage, quick movements, and steady hand, equally denoted that it was an old age free from the usual infirmities. In his dress, he belonged to that class whose members always follow fashions of the age anterior to the one in which they live, whether from disinclination to sudden changes of any kind, or from the recollections of a period which, with them, has been hallowed by scenes and feelings that the chilling evening of life can neither revive nor equal. Age might possibly have thrown its blighting frosts on his thin locks, but art had labored to conceal the ravages with the nicest care. An accurate outline of powder covered not only the parts where the hair actually remained, but wherever nature had prescribed that hair should grow. His countenance was strongly marked in features, if not in expression, exhibiting, on the whole, a look of noble integrity and high honor, which was a good deal aided in its effect by the lofty, receding forehead, that rose like a monument above the whole, to record the character of the aged veteran. A few streaks of branching red mingled with a swarthiness of complexion, that was rendered more conspicuous by the outline of the unsullied white, which nearly surrounded his prominent features.

Opposite to the host, who it will at once be understood was Colonel Howard, was the thin yellow visage of Mr. Christopher Dillon, that bane to the happiness of her cousin, already mentioned by Miss Plowden.

Between these two gentlemen was a middle-aged, hard-featured man, attired in the livery of King George, whose countenance emulated the scarlet of his coat, and whose principal employment, at the moment, appeared to consist in doing honor to the cheer of his entertainer.

Occasionally a servant entered or left the room in silence, giving admission, however, through the opened door, to the rushing sounds of the gale, as the wind murmured amid the angles and high chimneys of the edifice.

A man, in the dress of a rustic, was standing near the chair of Colonel Howard, between whom and the master of the mansion a dialogue had been maintained, which closed as follows. The colonel was the first to speak, after the curtain is drawn from between the eyes of the reader and the scene.

"Said you, farmer, that the Scotchman beheld the vessel with his own eyes?"

The answer was a simple negative.

"Well, well," continued the colonel, "you can withdraw."

The man made a rude attempt at a bow, which being returned by the old soldier with formal grace, he left the room. The host, turning to his companions, resumed the subject.

"If those rash boys have really persuaded the silly dotard who commands the frigate to trust himself within the shoals on the eve of such a gale as this, their case must have been hopeless indeed! Thus may rebellion and disaffection ever meet with the just indignation of Providence! It would not surprise me, gentlemen, to hear that my native land had been engulfed by earthquakes, or swallowed by the ocean, so awful and inexcusable has been the weight of her transgressions! And yet it was a proud and daring boy who held the second station in that ship! I knew his father well, and a gallant gentleman he was, who, like my own brother, the parent of Cecilia, preferred to serve his master on the ocean rather than on the land. His son inherited the bravery of his high spirit, without its loyalty. One would not wish to have such a youth drowned, either."

This speech, which partook much of the nature of a soliloquy, especially toward its close, called for no immediate reply; but the soldier, having held his glass to the candle, to admire the rosy hue of its contents, and then sipped of the fluid so often that nothing but a clear light remained to gaze at, quietly replaced the empty vessel on the table, and, as he extended an arm toward the blushing bottle, he spoke, in the careless tones of one whose thoughts were dwelling on another theme:

"Ay, true enough, sir; good men are scarce, and, as you say, one cannot but mourn his fate, though his death be glorious; quite a loss to his majesty's service, I dare say, it will prove."

"A loss to the service of his majesty!" echoed the host—"his death glorious! no, Captain Borroughcliffe, the death of no rebel can be glorious; and how he can be a loss to his majesty's service, I am myself quite at a loss to understand."

The soldier, whose ideas were in that happy state of confusion that renders it difficult to command the one most needed, but who still, from long discipline, had them under a wonderful control for the disorder of his brain, answered, with great promptitude:

"I mean, the loss of his example, sir. It would have been so appalling to others to have seen the young man executed instead of shot in battle."

"He is drowned, sir."

"Ah! that is the next thing to being hanged; that circumstance had escaped me."

"It is by no means certain, sir, that the ship and schooner that the drover saw are the vessels you take them to have been," said Mr. Dillon, in a harsh, drawling tone of voice. "I should doubt their daring to venture so openly on the coast, and in the direct track of our vessels-of-war."

"These people are our countrymen, Christopher, though they are rebels," exclaimed the colonel. "They are a hardy and brave nation. When I had the honor to serve his majesty, some twenty years since, it was my fortune to face the enemies of my king in a few small affairs, Captain Borroughcliffe; such as the siege of Quebec, and the battle before its gates, a trifling occasion at Ticonderoga, and that unfortunate catastrophe of General Braddock—with a few others. I must say, sir, in favor of the colonists, that they played a manful game on the latter day; and this gentleman who now heads the rebels sustained a gallant name among us for his conduct in that disastrous business. He was a discreet, well-behaved young man, and quite a gentleman. I have never denied that Mr. Washington was very much of a gentleman."

"Yes!" said the soldier, yawning, "he was educated among his majesty's troops, and he could hardly be otherwise. But I am quite melancholy about this unfortunate drowning, Colonel Howard. Here will be an end of my vocation, I suppose; and I am far from denying that your hospitality has made these quarters most agreeable to me."

"Then, sir, the obligation is only mutual," returned the host, with a polite inclination of his head; "but gentlemen who, like ourselves, have been made free of the camp, need not bandy idle compliments about such trifles. If it were my kinsman, Dillon, now, whose thoughts run more on Coke upon Littleton than on the gayeties of a mess-table and a soldier's life, he might think such formalities as necessary as his hard words are to a deed. Come, Borroughcliffe, my dear fellow, I believe we have given an honest glass to each of the royal family (God bless them all!), let us swallow a bumper to the memory of the immortal Wolfe."

"An honest proposal, my gallant host, and such a one as a soldier will never decline," returned the captain, who roused himself with the occasion. "God bless them all! say I, in echo; and if this gracious queen of ours ends as famously as she has begun, 'twill be such a family of princes as no other army of Europe can brag of around a mess-table."

"Ay, ay, there is some consolation in that thought in the midst of this dire rebellion of my countrymen. But I'll vex myself no more with the unpleasant recollections; the arms of my sovereign will soon purge that wicked land of the foul stain."

"Of that there can be no doubt," said Borroughcliffe, whose thoughts still continued a little obscured by the sparkling madeira that had long lain ripening under a Carolinian sun; "these Yankees fly before his majesty's regulars, like so many dirty clowns in a London mob before a charge of the horse-guards."

"Pardon me, Captain Borroughcliffe," said his host, elevating his person to more than its usual erect attitude; "they may be misguided, deluded, and betrayed, but the comparison is unjust. Give them arms, and give them discipline, and he who gets an inch of their land from them, plentiful as it is, will find a bloody day on which to take possession."

"The veriest coward in Christendom would fight in a country where wine brews itself into such a cordial as this," returned the cool soldier. "I am a living proof that you mistook my meaning; for had not those loose-flapped gentlemen they call Vermontese and Hampshire-granters (God grant them his blessing for the deed!) finished two-thirds of my company, I should not have been at this day under your roof, a recruiting instead of a marching officer; neither should I have been bound up in a covenant, like the law of Moses, could Burgoyne have made head against their long-legged marchings and counter-marchings. Sir, I drink their healths, with all my heart; and with such a bottle of golden sunshine before me, rather than displease so good a friend, I will go through Gates' whole army, regiment by regiment, company by company, or, if you insist on the same, even man by man, in a bumper."

"On no account would I tax your politeness so far," returned the colonel, abundantly mollified by this ample concession; "I stand too much your debtor, Captain Borroughcliffe, for so freely volunteering to defend my house against the attacks of my piratical, rebellious, and misguided countrymen, to think of requiring such a concession."

"Harder duty might be performed, and no favors asked, my respectable host," returned the soldier. "Country quarters are apt to be dull, and the liquor is commonly execrable; but in such a dwelling as this a man can rock himself in the very cradle of contentment. And yet there is one subject of complaint that I should disgrace my regiment did I not speak of—for it is incumbent on me, both as a man and a soldier, to be no longer silent."

"Name it sir, freely, and its cause shall be as freely redressed," said the host, in some amazement.

"Here we three sit, from morning to night," continued the soldier, "bachelors all, well provisioned, and better liquored, I grant you, but like so many well-fed anchorites, while two of the loveliest damsels in the island pine in solitude within a hundred feet of us, without tasting the homage of our sighs. This, I will maintain, is a reproach both to your character, Colonel Howard, as an old soldier, and to mine as a young one. As to our old friend Coke on top of Littleton here, I leave him to the quiddities of the law to plead his own cause."

The brow of the host contracted for a moment, and the sallow cheek of Dillon, who had sat during the dialogue in a sullen silence, appeared to grow even livid; but gradually the open brow of the veteran resumed its frank expression, and the lips of the other relaxed into a Jesuitical sort of a smile, that was totally disregarded by the captain, who amused himself with sipping his wine while he waited for an answer, as if he analyzed each drop that crossed his palate.

After an embarrassing pause of a moment, Colonel Howard broke the silence.

"There is reason in Borroughcliffe's hint, for such I take it to be—"

"I meant it for a plain, matter-of-fact complaint," interrupted the soldier.

"And you have cause for it," continued the colonel. "It is unreasonable, Christopher, that the ladies should allow their dread of these piratical countrymen of ours to exclude us from their society, though prudence may require that they remain secluded in their apartments. We owe the respect to Captain Borroughcliffe, that at least we admit him to the sight of the coffee-urn in an evening."

"That is precisely my meaning," said the captain; "as for dining with them, why, I am well provided for here; but there is no one knows how to set hot water a-hissing in so professional a manner as a woman. So forward, my dear and honored colonel, and lay your injunctions on them that they command your humble servant and Mr. Coke unto Littleton to advance and give the countersign of gallantry."

Dillon contracted his disagreeable features into something that was intended for a satirical smile before he spoke as follows:

"Both the veteran Colonel Howard and the gallant Captain Borroughcliffe may find it easier to overcome the enemies of his majesty in the field than to shake a woman's caprice. Not a day has passed, these three weeks, that I have not sent my inquiries to the door of Miss Howard, as became her father's kinsman, with a wish to appease her apprehensions of the pirates; but little has she deigned me in reply, more than such thanks as her sex and breeding could not well dispense with."

"Well, you have been as fortunate as myself, and why you should be more so I see no reason," cried the soldier, throwing a glance of cool contempt at the other; "fear whitens the cheek, and ladies best love to be seen when the roses flourish rather than the lilies."

"A woman is never so interesting, Captain Borroughcliffe," said the gallant host, "as when she appears to lean on man for support; and he who does not feel himself honored by the trust is a disgrace to his species."

"Bravo! my honored sir, a worthy sentiment, and spoken like a true soldier; but I have heard much of the loveliness of the ladies of the Abbey since I have been in my present quarters, and I feel a strong desire to witness beauty encircled by such loyalty as could induce them to flee their native country, rather than to devote their charms to the rude keeping of the rebels." The colonel looked grave, and for a moment fierce; but the expression of his displeasure soon passed away in a smile of forced gayety, and, as he cheerfully rose from his seat, he cried:

"You shall be admitted this very night, and this instant, Captain Borroughcliffe. We owe it, sir, to your services here, as well as in the field, and those froward girls shall be humored no longer. Nay, it is nearly two weeks since I have seen my ward myself; nor have I laid eyes on my niece but twice in all that time. Christopher, I leave the captain under your good care while I go seek admission into the cloisters; we call that part of the building the cloisters, because it holds our nuns, sir! You will pardon my early absence from the table, Captain Borroughcliffe."

"I beg it may not be mentioned; you leave an excellent representative behind you, sir," cried the soldier, taking in the lank figure of Mr. Dillon in a sweeping glance that terminated with a settled gaze on his decanter. "Make my devoirs to the recluses, and say all that your own excellent wit shall suggest as an apology for my impatience. Mr. Dillon, I meet you in a bumper to their healths, and in their honor."

The challenge was coldly accepted; and while these gentlemen still held their glasses to their lips Colonel Howard left the apartment, bowing low, and uttering a thousand excuses to his guest as he proceeded, and even offering a very unnecessary apology to the same effect to his habitual inmate, Mr. Dillon.

"Is fear so very powerful within these old walls," said the soldier, when the door closed behind their host, "that your ladies deem it necessary to conceal themselves before even an enemy is known to have landed?"

Dillon coldly replied:

"The name of Paul Jones is terrific to all on this coast, I believe; nor are the ladies of St. Ruth singular in their apprehensions."

"Ah! the pirate has bought himself a desperate name since the affair of Flamborough Head. But let him look to't, if he trusts himself in another Whitehaven expedition, while there is a detachment of the —th in the neighborhood, though the men shall be nothing better than recruits."

"Our last accounts leave him safe in the court of Louis," returned his companion; "but there are men as desperate as himself, who sail the ocean under the rebel flag, and from one or two of them we have had much reason to apprehend the vengeance of disappointed men. It is they that we hope are lost in this gale."

"Hum! I hope they were dastards, or your hopes are a little unchristian, and—"

He would have proceeded, but the door opened and his orderly entered, and announced that a sentinel had detained three men, who were passing along the highway near the Abbey, and who, by their dress, appeared to be seamen.

"Well, let them pass," cried the captain; "what, have we nothing to do better than to stop passengers, like footpads, on the king's highway? Give them of your canteens, and let the rascals pass! Your orders were to give the alarm if any hostile party landed on the coast, not to detain peaceable subjects on their lawful business."

"I beg your honor's pardon," returned the sergeant; "but these men seemed lurking about the grounds for no good, and as they kept carefully aloof from the place where our sentinel was posted, until to-night, Downing thought it looked suspiciously, and detained them."

"Downing is a fool, and it may go hard with him for his officiousness. What have you done with the men?"

"I took them to the guard-room in the east wing, your honor."

"Then feed them; and hark ye, sirrah! liquor them well, that we hear no complaints, and let them go."

"Yes, sir; yes, your honor shall be obeyed; but there is a straight, soldierly-looking fellow among them, that I think might be persuaded to enlist, if he were detained till morning. I doubt, sir, by his walk, but he has served already."

"Ha! what say you?" cried the captain, pricking up his ears like a hound who hears a well-known cry, "served, think ye, already?"

"There are signs about him, your honor, to that effect. An old soldier is seldom deceived in such a thing; and considering his disguise, for it can be no other, and the place where we took him, there is no danger of a have-us corpses until he is tied to us by the laws of the kingdom."

"Peace, you knave!" said Borroughcliffe, rising and making a devious route toward the door; "you speak in the presence of my lord chief justice that is to be, and should not talk lightly of the laws. But still you say reason; give me your arm, sergeant, and lead the way to the east wing; my eyesight is good for nothing in such a dark night. A soldier should always visit his guard before the tattoo beats."

After emulating the courtesy of their host, Captain Borroughcliffe retired on this patriotic errand, leaning on his subordinate in a style of most familiar condescension. Dillon continued at the table, endeavoring to express the rancorous feelings of his breast by a satirical smile of contempt, that was necessarily lost on all but himself, as a large mirror threw back the image of his morose and unpleasant features.

But we must precede the veteran colonel in his visits to the "cloisters."

10

And kindness like their own
Inspired those eyes, affectionate and glad,
That seemed to love whate'er they looked
*   upon;*
Whether with Hebe's mirth her features
*   shone,*
Or if a shade more pleasing them o'ercast—
Yet so becomingly th' expression past,
That each succeeding look was lovelier than
*   the last.*
                              Gertrude of Wyoming

THE western wing of St. Ruth House, or Abbey, as the building was indiscriminately called, retained but few vestiges of the uses to which it had been originally devoted. The upper apartments were small and numerous, extending on either side of a long, low, and dark gallery, and might have been the dormitories of the sisterhood who were said to have once inhabited that portion of the edifice; but the ground-floor had been modernized, as it was then called, about a century before, and retained just enough of its ancient character to blend the venerable with what was thought comfortable in the commencement of the reign of the third George. As this wing had been appropriated to the mistress of the mansion, ever since the building had changed its spiritual character for one of a more carnal nature, Colonel Howard continued the arrangement when he became the temporary possessor of St. Ruth, until, in the course of events, the apartments which had been appropriated for the accommodation and convenience of his niece were eventually converted into her prison. But as the severity of the old veteran was as often marked by an exhibition of his virtues as of his foibles, the confinement and his displeasure constituted the sole subjects of complaint that were given to the young lady. That our readers may be better qualified to judge of the nature of their imprisonment, we shall transport them, without further circumlocution, into the presence of the two females, whom they must be already prepared to receive.

The withdrawing-room of St. Ruth's was an apartment which, tradition said, had formerly been the refectory of the little bevy of fair sinners who sought a refuge within its walls from the temptations of the world. Their number was not large; nor their entertainments very splendid, or this limited space could not have contained them. The room, however, was of fair dimensions, and an air of peculiar comfort, mingled with chastened luxury, was thrown around it by the voluminous fold of the blue damask curtains that nearly concealed the sides where the deep windows were placed, and by the dark leathern hangings, richly stamped with cunning devices in gold, that ornamented the two others. Massive couches in carved mahogany, with chairs of a similar material and fashion, all covered by the same rich fabric that composed the curtains, together with a Turkey carpet, over the shaggy surface of which all the colors of the rainbow were scattered in bright confusion, united to relieve the gloomy splendor of the enormous mantel, deep, heavy cornices, and the complicated carvings of the massive woodwork which cumbered the walls. A brisk fire of wood was burning on the hearth, in compliment to the wilful prejudice of Miss Plowden, who had maintained, in her most vivacious manner, that sea-coal was "only tolerable for blacksmiths and Englishmen." In addition to the cheerful blaze from the hearth, two waxen lights, in candlesticks of massive silver, were lending their aid to enliven the apartment. One of these was casting its rays brightly along the confused colors of the carpet on which it stood, flickering before the active movements of the form that played around it with light and animated inflections. The posture of this young lady was infantile in grace, and, with one ignorant of her motives, her employment would have been obnoxious to the same construction. Divers small square pieces of silk, strongly contrasted to each other in color, lay on every side of her, and were changed, as she kneeled on the floor, by her nimble hands, into as many different combinations, as if she was humoring the fancies of her sex, or consulting the shades of her own dark but rich complexion in the shop of a mercer. The close satin dress of this young female served to display her small figure in its true proportions, while her dancing eyes of jet black shamed the dyes of the Italian manufacturer by their superior radiancy. A few ribbons of pink, disposed about her person with an air partly studied, and yet carelessly coquettish, seemed rather to reflect than lend the rich bloom that mantled around her laughing countenance, leaving to the eye no cause to regret that she was not fairer.

Another female figure, clad in virgin white, was reclining on the end of a distant couch. The seclusion in which they lived might have rendered this female a little careless of her appearance, or, what was more probable, the comb had been found unequal to its burden; for her tresses, which rivalled the hue and gloss of the raven, had burst from their confinement, and dropping over her shoulders, fell along her dress in rich profusion, finally resting on the damask of the couch, in dark folds, like glittering silk. A small hand, which seemed to blush at its own naked beauties, supported her head, embedded in the volumes of her hair, like the fairest alabaster set in the deepest ebony. Beneath the dark profusion of her curls, which, notwithstanding the sweeping train that fell about her person, covered the summit of her head, lay a low, spotless forehead of dazzling whiteness, that was relieved by two arches so slightly and truly drawn that they appeared to have been produced by the nicest touches of art. The fallen lids and long silken lashes concealed the eyes that rested on the floor as if their mistress mused in melancholy. The remainder of the features of this maiden were of a kind that is most difficult to describe, being neither regular nor perfect in their several parts, yet harmonizing and composing a whole that formed an exquisite picture of female delicacy and loveliness. There might or there might not have been a tinge of slight red in her cheeks, but it varied with each emotion of her bosom, even as she mused in quiet, now seeming to steal insidiously over her glowing temples, and then leaving her face an almost startling paleness. Her stature, as she reclined, seemed above the medium height of womanhood, and her figure was rather delicate than full, though the little foot that rested on the damask cushion before her displayed a rounded outline that any of her sex might envy.

"Oh! I'm as expert as if I were signal-officer to the lord high admiral of this realm!" exclaimed the laughing female on the floor, clapping her hands together in girlish exultation. "I do long, dear Cecilia, for an opportunity to exhibit my skill."

While her cousin was speaking, Miss Howard raised her head, with a faint smile, and, as she turned her eyes toward the other, a spectator might have been disappointed, but could not have been displeased, by the unexpected change the action produced in the expression of her countenance. Instead of the piercing black eyes that the deep color of her tresses would lead him to expect, he would have beheld two large, mild, blue orbs, that seemed to float in a liquid so pure as to be nearly invisible, and which were more remarkable for their tenderness and persuasion, than for the vivid flashes that darted from the quick glances of her companion.

"The success of your mad excursion to the seaside, my cousin, has bewildered your brain," returned Cecilia; "but I know not how to conquer your disease, unless we prescribe salt-water for the remedy, as in some other cases of madness."

"Ah! I am afraid your nostrum would be useless," cried Katherine; "it has failed to wash out the disorder from the sedate Mr. Richard Barnstable, who has had the regimen administered to him through many a hard gale, but who continues as fair a candidate for Bedlam as ever. Would you think it, Cicely, the crazy one urged me, in ten minutes' conversation we held together on the cliff, to accept of his schooner as a shower-bath!"

"I can think that your hardihood might encourage him to expect much, but surely he could not have been serious in such a proposal!"

"Oh! to do the wretch justice, he did say something of a chaplain to consecrate the measure, but there was boundless impudence in the thought. I have not, nor shall I forget it, or forgive him for it, these six-and-twenty years. What a fine time he must have had of it, in his little Ariel, among the monstrous waves we saw tumbling in upon the shore to-day, coz! I hope they will wash his impudence out of him! I do think the man cannot have a dry thread about him, from sun to sun. I must believe it as a punishment for his boldness, and, be certain, I shall tell him of it. I will form half a dozen signals this instant to joke at his moist condition, in very revenge."

Pleased with her own thoughts, and buoyant with the secret hope that her adventurous undertaking would be finally crowned with complete success, the gay girl shook her black locks in infinite mirth, and tossed the mimic flags gayly around her person, as she was busied in forming new combinations, in order to amuse herself with her lover's disastrous situation. But the features of her cousin clouded with the thoughts that were excited by her remarks, and she replied, in a tone that bore some little of the accents of reproach:

"Katherine! Katherine! can you jest when there is so much to apprehend? Forget you what Alice Dunscombe told us of the gale this morning, and that she spoke of two vessels, a ship and a schooner, that had been seen venturing with fearful temerity within the shoals, only six miles from the Abbey, and that, unless God in His gracious providence had been kind to them, there was but little doubt that their fate would be a sad one? Can you, that know so well who and what these daring mariners are, be merry about the self-same winds that cause their danger?"

The thoughtless, laughing girl was recalled to her recollection by this remonstrance, and every trace of mirth vanished from her countenance, leaving a momentary death-like paleness crossing her face, as she clasped her hands before her, and fastened her keen eyes vacantly on the splendid pieces of silk that now lay unheeded around her. At this critical moment the door of the room slowly opened, and Colonel Howard entered the apartment with an air that displayed a droll mixture of stern indignation with a chivalric and habitual respect to the sex.

"I solicit your pardon, young ladies, for the interruption," he said; "I trust, however, that an old man's presence can never be entirely unexpected in the drawing-room of his wards."

As he bowed, the colonel seated himself on the end of the couch, opposite to the place where his niece had been reclining, for Miss Howard had risen at his entrance, and continued standing until her uncle had comfortably disposed of himself. Throwing a glance which was not entirely free from self-condemnation around the comfortable apartment, the veteran proceeded, in the same tone as before:

"You are not without the means of making any guest welcome nor do I see the necessity of such constant seclusion from the eyes of the world as you thus rigidly practise."

Cecilia looked timidly at her uncle, with surprise, before she returned an answer to his remark.

"We certainly owe much to your kind attention, dear sir," she at length uttered; "but is our retirement altogether voluntary?"

"How can it be otherwise! are you not mistress of this mansion? In selecting the residence where your—and, permit me to add, my ancestors, so long dwelt in credit and honor, I have surely been less governed by any natural pride that I might have entertained on such a subject, than by a desire to consult your comfort and happiness. Everything appears to my aged eyes as if we ought not to be ashamed to receive our friends within these walls. The cloisters of St. Ruth, Miss Howard, are not entirely bare, neither are their tenants wholly unworthy to be seen."

"Open then the portals of the Abbey, sir, and your niece will endeavor to do proper credit to the hospitality of its master."

"That was spoken like Harry Howard's daughter, frankly and generously!"

cried the old soldier, insensibly edging himself near to his niece. "If my brother had devoted himself to the camp, instead of the sea, Cecilia, he would have made one of the bravest and ablest generals in his majesty's service—poor Harry! He might have been living at this very day, and at this moment leading the victorious troops of his sovereign through the revolted colonies in triumph. But he is gone, Cicely, and has left you behind him as his dear representative, to perpetuate our family, and to possess what little has been left to us from the ravages of the times."

"Surely, dear sir," said Cecilia, taking his hand, which had unconsciously approached her person, and pressing it to her lips, "we have no cause to complain of our lot in respect to fortune, though it may cause us bitter regret that so few of us are left to enjoy it."

"No, no, no," said Katherine, in a low, hurried voice; "Alice Dunscombe is and must be wrong; Providence would never abandon brave men to so cruel a fate!"

"Alice Dunscombe is here to atone for her error, if she has fallen into one," said a quiet, subdued voice, in which the accents of a provincial dialect, however, were slightly perceptible, and which, in its low tones, wanted that silvery clearness that gave so much feminine sweetness to the words of Miss Howard, and which even rang melodiously in the ordinarily vivacious strains of her cousin.

The surprise created by these sudden interruptions caused a total suspension of the discourse. Katherine Plowden, who had continued kneeling in the attitude before described, arose, and, as she looked about her in momentary confusion, the blood again mantled her face with the fresh and joyous springs of life. The other speaker advanced steadily into the middle of the room; and after returning, with steady civility, the low bow of Colonel Howard, seated herself on the opposite couch. The manner of her entrance, her reception, and her attire, sufficiently denoted that the presence of this female was neither unusual nor unwelcome. She was dressed with marked simplicity, though with a studied neatness, that more than compensated for the absence of ornaments. Her age might not have much exceeded thirty, but there was an adoption of customs in her attire that indicated she was not unwilling to be thought older. Her fair flaxen hair was closely confined by a dark bandeau, such as was worn in a nation farther north by virgins only, over which a few curls strayed in a manner that showed the will of their mistress alone restrained their luxuriance. Her light complexion had lost much of its brilliancy, but enough still remained to assert its original beauty and clearness. To this description might be added fine, mellow, blue eyes; beautifully white, though large teeth; a regular set of features, and a person that was clad in a dark lead-colored silk, which fitted her full but gracefully-moulded form with the closest exactness.

Colonel Howard paused a moment after this lady was seated, and then turning himself to Katherine with an air that became stiff and constrained by attempting to seem extremely easy, he said:

"You no sooner summon Miss Alice, but she appears, Miss Plowden—ready and (I am bold to say, Miss Alice) able to defend herself against all charges, that her worst enemies can allege against her."

"I have no charges to make against Miss Dunscombe," said Katherine, pettishly, "nor do I wish to have dissensions created between me and my friends, even by Colonel Howard."

"Colonel Howard will studiously avoid such offences in future," said the veteran, bowing; and turning stiffly to the others, he continued: "I was just conversing with my niece as you entered, Miss Alice, on the subject of her immuring herself like one of the veriest nuns who ever inhabited these cloisters. I tell her, madam, that neither her years nor my fortune, nor, indeed, her own—for the child of Harry Howard was not left penniless—require that we should live as if the doors of the world were closed against us, or there was no other entrance to St. Ruth's but through those antiquated windows. Miss Plowden, I feel it to be my duty to inquire why those pieces of silk are provided in such an unusual abundance and in so extraordinary a shape?"

"To make a gala dress for the ball you are about to give, sir," said Katherine, with a saucy smile that was only checked by the reproachful glance of her cousin. "You have taste in a lady's attire, Colonel Howard; will not this bright yellow form a charming relief to my brown face, while this white and black relieve one another, and this pink contrasts so sweetly with black eyes? Will not the whole form a turban fit for an empress to wear?"

As the arch maiden prattled on in this unmeaning manner, her rapid fingers entwined the flags in a confused mass, which she threw over her head in a form not unlike the ornament for which she intimated it was intended. The veteran was by far too polite to dispute a lady's taste, and he renewed the dialogue with his slightly awakened suspicion completely quieted by her dexterity and artifice. But, although it was not difficult to deceive Colonel Howard in matters of female dress, the case was very different with Alice Dunscombe. This lady gazed with a steady eye and reproving countenance on the fantastical turban, until Katherine threw herself by her side, and endeavored to lead her attention to other subjects by her playful motions and whispered questions.

"I was observing, Miss Alice," continued the colonel, "that, although the

times had certainly inflicted some loss on my estate, yet we were not so much reduced as to be unable to receive our friends in a manner that would not disgrace the descendants of the ancient possessors of St. Ruth. Cecilia, here, my brother Harry's daughter, is a young lady that any uncle might be proud to exhibit, and I would have her, madam, show your English dames that we rear no unworthy specimens of the parent stock on the other side of the Atlantic."

"You have only to declare your pleasure, my good uncle," said Miss Howard, "and it shall be executed."

"Tell us how we can oblige you, sir," continued Katherine, "and if it be in any manner that will relieve the tedium of this dull residence, I promise you at least one cheerful assistant to your scheme."

"You speak fair," cried the colonel, "and like two discreet and worthy girls. Well, our first step shall be to send a message to Dillon and the captain, and invite them to attend your coffee. I see the hour approaches."

Cecilia made no reply, but looked distressed, and dropped her mild eyes to the carpet; but Miss Plowden took it upon herself to answer.

"Nay, sir, that would be for them to proceed in the matter; as your proposal was that the first step should be ours, suppose we all adjourn to your part of the house, and do the honors of the tea-table in your drawing-room instead of our own? I understand, sir, that you have had an apartment fitted up for that purpose in some style; a woman's tastes might aid your designs, however."

"Miss Plowden, I believe I intimated to you some time since," said the displeased colonel, "that so long as certain suspicious vessels were known to hover on this coast, I should desire that you and Miss Howard would confine yourselves to this wing."

"Do not say that we confine ourselves," said Katherine; "but let it be spoken in plain English, that you confine us here."

"Am I a jailer, madam, that you apply such epithets to my conduct? Miss Alice must form strange conclusions of our manners, if she receives her impressions from your very singular remarks. I—"

"All measures adopted from a dread of the ship and schooner that ran within the Devil's Grip, yester-eve, may be dispensed with now," interrupted Miss Dunscombe, in a melancholy, reflecting tone. "There are few living who know the dangerous paths that can conduct even the smallest craft in safety from the land, with daylight and fair winds; but when darkness and adverse gales oppose them, their chance for safety lies wholly in God's kindness."

"There is truly much reason to believe they are lost," returned the veteran, in a voice in which no exultation was apparent.

"They are not lost!" exclaimed Katherine, with startling energy, leaving her seat and walking across the room to join Cecilia, with an air that seemed to elevate her little figure to the height of her cousin. "They are skilful and they are brave, and what gallant sailors can do will they do, and successfully; besides, in what behalf would a just Providence sooner exercise its merciful power, than to protect the daring children of an oppressed country, while contending against tyranny and countless wrongs?"

The conciliating disposition of the colonel deserted him, as he listened. His own black eyes sparkled with a vividness unusual for his years, and his courtesy barely permitted the lady to conclude, ere he broke forth:

"What sin, madam, what damning crime, would sooner call down the just wrath of Heaven on the transgressors, than the act of foul rebellion? It was this crime, madam, that deluged England in blood in the reign of the first Charles; it is this crime that has dyed more fields red than all the rest of man's offences united; it has been visited on our race as a condign punishment, from the days of the deservedly devoted Absalom down to the present time; in short, it lost Heaven forever to some of the most glorious of its angels, and there is much reason to believe that it is the one unpardonable sin named in the holy gospels."

"I know not that you have authority for believing it to be the heavy enormity that you mention, Colonel Howard," said Miss Dunscombe, anticipating the spirited reply of Katherine, and willing to avert it; she hesitated an instant, and then drawing a heavy, shivering sigh, she continued in a voice that grew softer as she spoke: "'tis indeed a crime of magnitude, and one that throws the common backslidings of our lives, speaking by comparison, into the sunshine of his favor. Many there are who sever the dearest ties of this life, by madly rushing into its sinful vortex: for I fain think the heart grows hard with the sight of human calamity, and becomes callous to the miseries its owner inflicts; especially where we act the wrongs on our own kith and kin, regardless who or how many that are dear to us suffer by our evil deeds. It is, besides, Colonel Howard, a dangerous temptation to one little practised in the great world, to find himself suddenly elevated into the seat of power; and if it do not lead to the commission of great crimes, it surely prepares the way to it, by hardening the heart."

"I hear you patiently, Miss Alice," said Katherine, dancing her little foot, in affected coolness; "for you neither know of whom nor to whom you speak. But Colonel Howard has not that apology.—Peace, Cecilia, for I must speak! Believe them not, dear girl; there is not a wet hair on their heads. For you, Colonel Howard, who must recollect that the sister's son of the mothers of both your niece and myself is on board that frigate, there is an appearance of cruelty in using such language."

"I pity the boy! from my soul I pity him!" exclaimed the veteran; "he is a child, and has followed the current that is sweeping our unhappy colonies down the tide of destruction. But there are others in that vessel who have no excuse of ignorance to offer. There is a son of my old acquaintance, and the bosom friend of my brother Harry, Cecilia's father, dashing Hugh Griffith, as we called him. The urchins left home together, and were rated on board one of his majesty's vessels on the same day. Poor Harry lived to carry a broad pennant in the service, and Hugh died in command of a frigate. This boy, too! he was nurtured on board his father's vessel, and learned, from his majesty's discipline, how to turn his arms against his king. There is something shockingly unnatural in that circumstance, Miss Alice; 'tis the child inflicting a blow on the parent. 'Tis such men as these, with Washington at their head, who maintain the bold front that this rebellion wears."

"There are men, who have never worn the servile livery of Britain, sir, whose names are as fondly cherished in America as any that she boasts of," said Katherine, proudly; "ay, sir, and those who would gladly oppose the bravest officers in the British fleet."

"I contend not against your misguided reason," said Colonel Howard, rising with cool respect. "A young lady who ventures to compare rebels with gallant gentlemen engaged in their duty to their prince, cannot escape the imputation of possessing a misguided reason. No man—I speak not of women, who cannot be supposed so well versed in human nature—but no man who has reached the time of life that entitles him to be called by that name, can consort with these disorganizers, who would destroy everything that is sacred—these levellers, who would pull down the great to exalt the little—these Jacobins, who—who—"

"Nay, sir, if you are at a loss for opprobrious epithets," said Katherine, with provoking coolness, "call on Mr. Christopher Dillon for assistance; he waits your pleasure at the door."

Colonel Howard turned in amazement, forgetting his angry declamations at this unexpected intelligence, and beheld, in reality, the sombre visage of his kinsman, who stood holding the door in his hand, apparently as much surprised at finding himself in the presence of the ladies as they themselves could be at his unusual visit.

11

*Prithee, Kate, let's stand aside, and see the
end of this controversy.*

SHAKESPEARE

DURING the warm discussions of the pre-
ceding chapter, Miss Howard had bowed her pale face to the arm of the
couch, and sat an unwilling and distressed listener to the controversy; but
now that another, and one whom she thought an unauthorized, intruder on
her privacy was announced, she asserted the dignity of her sex as proudly,
though with something more of discretion, than her cousin could possibly
have done. Rising from her seat, she inquired:

"To what are we indebted for so unexpected a visit from Mr. Dillon? Surely
he must know that we are prohibited going to the part of the dwelling where
he resides, and I trust Colonel Howard will tell him that common justice requires we should be permitted to be private."

The gentleman replied, in a manner in which malignant anger was sufficiently mingled with calculating humility:

"Miss Howard will think better of my intrusion when she knows that I
come on business of importance to her uncle."

"Ah! that may alter the case, Kit; but the ladies must have the respect that
is due to their sex. I forgot, somehow, to have myself announced; but that
Borroughcliffe leads me deeper into my madeira than I have been accustomed
to go since the time when my poor brother Harry, with his worthy friend,

Hugh Griffith—the devil seize Hugh Griffith, and all his race—your pardon, Miss Alice—what is your business with me, Mr. Dillon?"

"I bear a message from Captain Borroughcliffe. You may remember that, according to your suggestions the sentinels were to be changed every night, sir."

"Ay! ay! we practised that in our campaign against Montcalm; 'twas necessary to avoid the murders of their Indians, who were sure, Miss Alice, to shoot down a man at his post, if he were placed two nights running in the same place."

"Well, sir, your prudent precautions have not been thrown away," continued Dillon, moving farther into the apartment, as if he felt himself becoming a more welcome guest as he proceeded; "the consequences are, that we have already made three prisoners."

"Truly it has been a most politic scheme!" exclaimed Katherine Plowden, with infinite contempt. "I suppose, as Mr. Christopher Dillon applauds it so highly, that it has some communion with the law! and that the redoubtable garrison of St. Ruth are about to reap the high glory of being most successful thief-takers!"

The sallow face of Dillon actually became livid as he replied, and his whole frame shook with the rage he vainly endeavored to suppress.

"There may be a closer communion with the law, and its ministers, perhaps, than Miss Plowden can desire," he said; "for rebellion seldom finds favor in any Christian code."

"Rebellion!" exclaimed the colonel; "and what has this detention of three vagabonds to do with rebellion, Kit? Has the damnable poison found its way across the Atlantic?—your pardon, Miss Alice—but this is a subject on which you can feel with me; I know your sentiments on the allegiance that is due to our anointed sovereign. Speak, Mr. Dillon, are we surrounded by another set of demons? If so, we must give ourselves to the work, and rally round our prince; for this island is the main pillar of his throne."

"I cannot say that there is any appearance, at present, of an intention to rise in this island," said Dillon, with demure gravity; "though the riots in London warrant any precautionary measures on the part of his majesty's ministers, even to a suspension of the *habeas corpus*. But you have had your suspicions concerning two certain vessels that have been threatening the coast, for several days past, in a most piratical manner?"

The little foot of Katherine played rapidly on the splendid carpet, but she contented herself with bestowing a glance of the most sovereign contempt on the speaker, as if she disdained any further reply. With the colonel, however, this was touching a theme that lay nearest his heart, and he answered in a manner worthy of the importance of the subject:

"You speak like a sensible man and a loyal subject, Mr. Dillon. The *habeas corpus*, Miss Alice, was obtained in the reign of King John, along with Magna Charta, for the security of the throne, by his majesty's barons; some of my own blood were of the number, which alone would be a pledge that the dignity of the crown was properly consulted. As to our piratical countrymen, Christopher, there is much reason to think that the vengeance of an offended Providence has already reached them. Those who know the coast well tell me, that without a better pilot than an enemy would be likely to procure, it would be impossible for any vessel to escape the shoals among which they entered, on a dark night, and with an adverse gale; the morning has arrived, and they are not to be seen?"

"But be they friends, or be they enemies, sir," continued Dillon, respectfully, "there is much reason to think that we have now in the Abbey those who can tell us something of their true character; for the men we have detained carry with them the appearance of having just landed, and wear not only the dress, but the air of seamen."

"Of seamen?" echoed Katherine, a deadly paleness chasing from her cheek the bloom which indignation had heightened.

"Of seamen, Miss Plowden," repeated Dillon, with malignant satisfaction, but concealing it under an air of submissive respect.

"I thank you, sir, for so gentle a term," replied the young lady, recollecting herself, and recovering her presence of mind in the same instant; "the imagination of Mr. Dillon is so apt to conjure the worst that he is entitled to our praise for so far humoring our weakness as not to alarm us with the apprehensions of their being pirates."

"Nay, madam, they may yet deserve that name," returned the other, coldly; "but my education has instructed me to hear the testimony before I pronounce sentence."

"Ah! that the boy has found in his Coke upon Littleton," cried the colonel; "the law is a salutary corrective to human infirmities, Miss Alice; and, among other things, it teaches patience to a hasty temperament. But for this cursed, unnatural rebellion, madam, the young man would at this moment have been diffusing its blessings from a judicial chair, in one of the colonies—ay! and I pledge myself to all alike, black and white, red and yellow, with such proper distinctions as Nature has made between the officer and the private. Keep a good heart, kinsman; we shall yet find a time; the royal arms have many hands, and things look better at the last advices. But come, we will proceed to the guard-room, and put these stragglers to the question; run away, I'll venture to predict, from one of his majesty's cruisers, or, perhaps, honest subjects engaged in supplying the service with men. Come, Kit, come, let us go, and—"

"Are we then to lose the company of Colonel Howard so soon?" said Katherine, advancing to her guardian, with an air of blandishment and pleasantry. "I know that he too soon forgets the hasty language of our little disputes to part in anger, if, indeed, he will even quit us till he has tasted of our coffee."

The veteran turned to the speaker of this unexpected address, and listened with profound attention. When she had done, he replied with a good deal of softness in his tones:

"Ah! provoking one! you know me too well to doubt my forgiveness; but duty must be attended to, though even a young lady's smiles tempt me to remain. Yes, yes, child—you, too, are the daughter of a very brave and worthy seaman; but you carry your attachment to that profession too far, Miss Plowden—you do, indeed you do."

Katherine might have faintly blushed; but the slight smile which mingled with the expression of her shame, gave to her countenance a look of additional archness, and she laid her hand lightly on the sleeve of her guardian, to detain him, as she replied:

"Yet why leave us, Colonel Howard? It is long since we have seen you in the cloisters, and you know you come as a father; tarry, and you may yet add confessor to the title."

"I know thy sins already, girl," said the worthy colonel, unconsciously yielding to her gentle efforts to lead him back to his seat; "they are, deadly rebellion in your heart to your prince, a most inveterate propensity to salt-water, and a great disrespect to the advice and wishes of an old fellow whom your father's will and the laws of the realm have made the guardian of your person and fortune."

"Nay, say not the last, dear sir," cried Katherine; "for there is not a syllable you have ever said to me on that foolish subject that I have forgotten. Will you resume your seat again? Cecilia, Colonel Howard consents to take his coffee with us."

"But you forget the three men, honest Kit, there, and our respectable guest, Captain Borroughcliffe."

"Let honest Kit stay there, if he please; you may send a request to Captain Borroughcliffe to join our party; I have a woman's curiosity to see the soldier; and as for the three men—" she paused, and affected to muse a moment, when she continued, as if struck by an obvious thought: "yes, and the men can be brought in and examined here; who knows but they may have been wrecked in the gale, and need our pity and assistance, rather than deserve your suspicions?"

"There is a solemn warning in Miss Plowden's conjecture, that should come home to the breasts of all who live on this wild coast," said Alice Dunscombe; "I have known many a sad wreck among the hidden shoals, and when the wind has blown but a gentle gale, compared to last night's tempest. The wars, and the uncertainties of the times, together with man's own wicked passions, have made great havoc with those who know well the windings of the channels among the 'Ripples.' Some there were who could pass, as I have often heard, within a fearful distance of the 'Devil's Grip,' the darkest night that ever shadowed England; but all are now gone of that daring set, either by the hand of death, or, what is even as mournful, by unnatural banishment from the land of their fathers."

"This war has then probably drawn off most of them, for your recollections must be quite recent, Miss Alice," said the veteran; "as many of them were engaged in the business of robbing his majesty's revenue, the country is in some measure requited for the former depredations by their present services, and at the same time it is happily rid of their presence. Ah! madam, ours is a glorious constitution, where things are so nicely balanced, that, as in the physical organization of a healthy, vigorous man, the baser parts are purified in the course of things by its own wholesome struggles."

The pale features of Alice Dunscombe became slightly tinged with red as the colonel proceeded, nor did the faint glow entirely leave her pallid face until she had said:

"There might have been some who knew not how to respect the law of the land, for such are never wanting; but there were others who, however guilty they might be in many respects, need not charge themselves with that mean crime, and yet who could find the passages that lie hid from common eyes, beneath the rude waves, as well as you could find the way through the halls and galleries of the Abbey, with a noonday sun shining upon its vanes and high chimneys."

"It is your pleasure, Colonel Howard, that we examine the three men, and ascertain whether they belong to the number of these gifted pilots?" said Christopher Dillon, who was growing uneasy at his awkward situation, and who hardly deemed it necessary to conceal the look of contempt which he cast at the mild Alice while he spoke; "perhaps we may gather information enough from them to draw a chart of the coast that may gain us credit with my lords of the Admiralty."

This unprovoked attack on their unresisting and unoffending guest brought the rich blood to the very temples of Miss Howard, who rose, and addressed herself to her kinsman with a manner that could not easily be mistaken, any more than it could be condemned:

"If Mr. Dillon will comply with the wishes of Colonel Howard, as my cousin has expressed them, we shall not, at least, have to accuse ourselves of unnecessarily detaining men who probably are more unfortunate than guilty."

When she concluded, Cecilia walked across the apartment and took a seat by the side of Alice Dunscombe, with whom she began to converse in a low, soothing tone of voice. Mr. Dillon bowed with a deprecating humility, and having ascertained that Colonel Howard chose to give an audience, where he sat, to the prisoners, he withdrew to execute his mission, secretly exulting at any change that promised to lead to a renewal of an intercourse that might terminate more to his advantage than the lofty beauty whose favor he courted was, at present, disposed to concede.

"Christopher is a worthy, serviceable, good fellow," said the colonel when the door closed, "and I hope to live yet to see him clad in ermine. I would not be understood literally, but figuratively; for furs would but ill comport with the climate of the Carolinas. I trust I am to be consulted by his majesty's ministers when the new appointments shall be made for the subdued colonies, and he may safely rely on my good word being spoken in his favor. Would he not make an excellent and independent ornament of the bench, Miss Plowden?"

Katherine compressed her lips a little as she replied:

"I must profit by his own discreet rules, and see testimony to that effect, before I decide, sir. But listen!" The young lady's color changed rapidly, and her eyes became fixed in a sort of feverish gaze on the door. "He has at least been active; I hear the heavy tread of men already approaching."

"Ah! it is he certainly; justice ought always to be prompt as well as certain, to make it perfect; like a drumhead court-martial, which, by-the-way, is as summary a sort of government as heart could wish to live under. If his majesty's ministers could be persuaded to introduce into the revolted colonies—"

"Listen!" interrupted Katherine, in a voice which bespoke her deep anxiety; "they draw near!"

The sound of footsteps was, in fact, now so audible as to induce the colonel to suspend the delivery of his plan for governing the recovered provinces. The long, low gallery, which was paved with a stone flagging, soon brought the footsteps of the approaching party more distinctly to their ears, and presently a low tap at the door announced their arrival. Colonel Howard arose, with the air of one who was to sustain the principal character in the ensuing interview, and bade them enter. Cecilia and Alice Dunscombe merely cast careless looks at the opening door, indifferent to the scene; but the quick eye of Katherine embraced, at a glance, every figure in the group. Drawing a long, quivering breath, she fell back on the couch, and her eyes again lighted with their playful expression as she hummed a low, rapid air, with a voice in which even the suppressed tones were liquid melody.

Dillon entered, preceding the soldier, whose gait had become more steady, and in whose rigid eye a thoughtful expression had taken the place of its former vacant gaze. In short, something had manifestly restored to him a more complete command of his mental powers, although he might not have been absolutely sobered. The rest of the party continued in the gallery, while Mr. Dillon presented the renovated captain to the colonel, where the latter did him the same kind office with the ladies.

"Miss Plowden," said the veteran, for she offered first in the circle, "this is my friend Captain Borroughcliffe; he has long been ambitious of this honor, and I have no doubt his reception will be such as to leave him no cause to repent he has been at last successful."

Katherine smiled, and answered with ambiguous emphasis:

"I know not how to thank him sufficiently for the care he has bestowed on our poor persons."

The soldier looked steadily at her for a moment, with an eye that seemed to threaten a retaliation in kind, ere he replied:

"One of those smiles, madam, would be an ample compensation for services that are more real than such as exist only in intention."

Katherine bowed with more complacency than she usually bestowed on those who wore the British uniform; and they proceeded to the next.

"This is Miss Alice Dunscombe, Captain Borroughcliffe, daughter of a worthy clergyman who was formerly the curate of this parish, and a lady who does us the pleasure of giving us a good deal of her society, though far less than we all wish for."

The captain returned the civil inclination of Alice, and the colonel proceeded:

"Miss Howard, allow me to present Captain Borroughcliffe, a gentleman who, having volunteered to defend St. Ruth in these critical times, merits all the favor of its mistress."

Cecilia gracefully rose and received her guest with sweet complacency. The soldier made no reply to the customary compliments that she uttered, but stood an instant gazing at her speaking countenance, and then, laying his hand involuntarily on his breast, bowed nearly to his sword-hilt.

These formalities duly observed, the colonel declared his readiness to receive the prisoners. As the door was opened by Dillon, Katherine cast a cool and steady look at the strangers, and beheld the light glancing along the arms of the soldiers who guarded them. But the seamen entered alone; while the rattling of arms and the heavy dash of the muskets on the stone pavement announced that it was thought prudent to retain a force at hand to watch these secret intruders on the grounds of the Abbey.

12

Falstaff: *Food for powder, they'll fill a pit as well as better.*

THE three men who now entered the apartment appeared to be nothing daunted by the presence into which they were ushered, though clad in the coarse and weatherbeaten vestments of seamen who had been exposed to recent and severe duty. They silently obeyed the direction of the soldier's finger and took their stations in a distant corner of the room, like men who knew the deference due to rank, at the same time that the habits of their lives had long accustomed them to encounter the vicissitudes of the world. With this slight preparation Colonel Howard began the business of examinations.

"I trust ye are all good and loyal subjects," the veteran commenced, with a considerate respect for innocence, "but the times are such that even the most worthy characters become liable to suspicion, and, consequently, if our apprehensions should prove erroneous, you must overlook the mistake, and attribute it to the awful condition into which rebellion has plunged this empire. We have much reason to fear that some project is about to be undertaken on the coast by the enemy, who has appeared, we know, with a frigate and schooner; and the audacity of the rebels is only equalled by their shameless and wicked disrespect for the rights of the sovereign."

While Colonel Howard was uttering his apologetic preamble, the prisoners fastened their eyes on him with much interest; but when he alluded to the apprehended attack, the gaze of two of them became more keenly attentive, and, before he concluded, they exchanged furtive glances of deep meaning. No reply was made, however, and after a short pause, as if to allow time for his words to make a proper impression, the veteran continued:

"We have no evidence, I understand, that you are in the smallest degree connected with the enemies of this country; but as you have been found out of the king's highway, or, rather, on a by-path, which I must confess is frequently used by the people of the neighborhood, but which is nevertheless nothing but a by-path, it becomes no more than what self-preservation requires of us to ask you a few such questions as I trust will be satisfactorily answered. To use your own nautical phrases, 'From whence came ye, pray?' and 'Whither are ye bound?' "

A low, deep voice replied:

"From Sunderland last, and bound overland to Whitehaven."

This simple and direct answer was hardly given, before the attention of the listeners was called to Alice Dunscombe, who uttered a faint shriek, and rose from her seat involuntarily, while her eyes seemed to roll fearfully and perhaps a little wildly round the room.

"Are you ill, Miss Alice?" said the sweet, soothing tones of Cecilia Howard; "you are, indeed you are; lean on me, that I may lead you to your apartment."

"Did you hear it, or was it only fancy?" she answered, her cheek blanched to the whiteness of death, and her whole frame shuddering as if in convulsions; "say, did you hear it too?"

"I have heard nothing but the voice of my uncle, who is standing near you, anxious, as we all are, for your recovery from this dreadful agitation."

Alice still gazed wildly from face to face. Her eye did not rest satisfied with dwelling on those who surrounded her, but surveyed, with a sort of frantic eagerness, the figures and appearance of the three men, who stood in humble patience, the silent and unmoved witnesses of this extraordinary scene. At length she veiled her eyes with both her hands, as if to shut out some horrid vision, and then, removing them, she smiled languidly, as she signed for Cecilia to assist her from the room. To the polite and assiduous offers of the gentlemen, she returned no other thanks than those conveyed in her looks and gestures; but when the sentinels who paced the gallery were passed, and the ladies were alone, she breathed a long, shivering sigh, and found an utterance.

" 'Twas like a voice from the silent grave!" she said, "but it could be no more than mockery. No, no, 'tis a just punishment for letting the image of the creature fill the place that should be occupied only with the Creator. Ah! Miss Howard, Miss Plowden, ye are both young—in the pride of your beauty and loveliness—but little do ye know, and less do ye dread, the temptations and errors of a sinful world."

"Her thoughts wander!" whispered Katherine, with anxious tenderness; "some awful calamity has affected her intellect!"

"Yes, it must be; my sinful thoughts have wandered, and conjured sounds that it would have been dreadful to hear in truth, and within these walls," said Alice, more composedly, smiling with a ghastly expression, as she gazed at the two beautiful solicitous maidens who supported her yielding person. "But the moment of weakness is passed, and I am better; aid me to my room, and return, that you may not interrupt the reviving harmony between yourselves and Colonel Howard. I am now better—nay, I am quite restored."

"Say not so, dear Miss Alice," returned Cecilia; "your face denies what your kindness to us induces you to utter; ill, very ill, you are, nor shall even your own commands induce me to leave you."

"Remain, then," said Miss Dunscombe, bestowing a look of grateful affection on her lovely supporter; "and while our Katherine returns to the drawing-room, to give the gentlemen their coffee, you shall continue with me, as my gentle nurse."

By this time they had gained the apartment, and Katherine, after assisting her cousin to place Alice on her bed, returned to do the honors of the drawing-room. Colonel Howard ceased his examination of the prisoners, at her entrance, to inquire, with courtly solicitude, after the invalid; and, when his questions were answered, he again proceeded, as follows:

"This is what the lads would call plain sailing, Borroughcliffe: they are out of employment in Sunderland, and have acquaintances and relatives in White-haven, to whom they are going for assistance and labor. All very probable, and perfectly harmless."

"Nothing more so, my respectable host," returned the jocund soldier; "but it seemeth a grievous misfortune that a trio of such flesh and blood should need work wherewithal to exercise their thews and sinews, while so many of the vessels of his majesty's fleet navigate the ocean in quest of the enemies of Old England."

"There is truth in that; much truth in your remark," cried the colonel. "What say you, my lads, will you fight the Frenchmen and the Don—ay! and even my own rebellious and infatuated countrymen? Nay, by Heaven, it is not a trifle that shall prevent his Majesty from possessing the services of three such heroes. Here are five guineas apiece for you the moment that you put foot on board the Alacrity cutter; and that can easily be done, as she lies at anchor this very night, only two short leagues to the south of this, in a small port, where she is riding out the gale as snugly as if she were in a corner of this room."

One of the men affected to gaze at the money with longing eyes, while he asked, as if weighing the terms of the engagement:

"Whether the Alacrity was called a good sea-boat, and was thought to give a comfortable berth to her crew?"

"Comfortable!" echoed Borroughcliffe; "for that matter, she is called the bravest cutter in the navy. You have seen much of the world, I dare say; did you ever see such a place as the marine arsenal at Carthagena, in old Spain?"

"Indeed I have, sir," returned the seaman, in a cool, collected tone.

"Ah! you have! well, did you ever meet with a house in Paris that they call the Tuileries? because it's a dog-kennel to the Alacrity."

"I have even fallen in with the place you mention, sir," returned the sailor; "and must own the berth quite good enough for such as I am, if it tallies with your description."

"The deuce take these blue-jackets!" muttered Borroughcliffe, addressing himself unconsciously to Miss Plowden, near whom he happened to be at the time; "they run their tarry countenances into all the corners of the earth, and abridge a man most lamentably in his comparisons. Now, who the devil would have thought that fellow had ever put his sea-green eyes on the palace of King Louis?"

Katherine heeded not his speech, but sat eyeing the prisoners with a confused and wavering expression of countenance, while Colonel Howard renewed his discourse by exclaiming:

"Come, come, Borroughcliffe, let us give the lads no tales for a recruit, but good, plain, honest English—God bless the language, and the land for which it was first made, too! There is no necessity to tell these men, if they are, what they seem to be, practical seamen, that a cutter of ten guns contains all the room and accommodations of a palace."

"Do you allow nothing for English oak and English comfort, mine host?" said the immovable captain; "do you think, good sir, that I measure fitness and propriety by square and compass, as if I were planning Solomon's Temple anew? All I mean to say is, that the Alacrity is a vessel of singular compactness and magical arrangement of room. Like the tent of that handsome brother of the fairy in the Arabian Nights, she is big or she is little, as occasion needeth; and now hang me if I don't think I have uttered more in her favor than her commander would say to help me to a recruit, though no lad in the three kingdoms should appear willing to try how a scarlet coat would suit his boorish figure."

"That time has not yet arrived, and God forbid that it ever should, while the monarch needs a soldier in the field to protect his rights!—But what say ye, my man? you have heard the recommendation that Captain Borroughcliffe has given to the Alacrity, which is altogether true—after making some allowances for language. Will ye serve? shall I order you a cheering glass a man, and lay by the gold till I hear from the cutter that you are enrolled under the banners of the best of kings?"

Katherine Plowden, who hardly seemed to breathe, so close and intent was the interest with which she regarded the seamen, fancied she observed lurking smiles on their faces; but if her conjectures were true, their disposition to be merry went no further, and the one who had spoken hitherto replied, in the same calm manner as before:

"You will excuse us if we decline shipping in the cutter, sir; we are used to distant voyages and large vessels, whereas the Alacrity is kept at coast duty and is not of a size to lay herself alongside of a Don, or a Frenchman with a double row of teeth."

"If you prefer that sort of sport, you must to the right-about for Yarmouth; there you will find ships that will meet anything that swims," said the colonel.

"Perhaps the gentlemen would prefer abandoning the cares and dangers of the ocean for a life of ease and gayety," said the captain. "The hand that has long dallied with the marlinspike may be easily made to feel a trigger, as gracefully as a lady touches the keys of her piano. In short, there is and there is not a great resemblance between the life of a sailor and that of a soldier. There are no gales of wind, nor short allowances, nor reefing topsails, nor shipwrecks, among soldiers; and, at the same time, there is just as much, or ever more, grog-drinking, jollifying, care-killing fun around a canteen and an open knapsack, than there is on the end of a mess-chest, with a full can and a Saturday-night breeze. I crossed the ocean several times, and I must own that a ship, in good weather, is very much the same as a camp or comfortable barracks; mind, I say only in very good weather."

"We have no doubt that all you say is true, sir," observed the spokesman of the three; "but what to you may seem a hardship, to us is pleasure. We have faced too many a gale to mind a capful of wind, and should think ourselves always in the calm latitudes in one of your barracks, where there is nothing to do but to eat our grub, and to march a little fore and aft a small piece of green earth. We hardly know one end of a musket from the other."

"No!" said Borroughcliffe, musing; and then, advancing with a quick step toward them, he cried, in a spirited manner, "Attention! right! dress!"

The speaker, and the seaman next him, gazed at the captain in silent wonder; but the third individual of the party, who had drawn himself a little aside, as if willing to be unnoticed, or perhaps pondering on his condition, involuntarily started at this unexpected order, and, erecting himself, threw his head to the right as promptly as if he had been on a parade-ground.

"Oho! ye are apt scholars, gentlemen, and ye can learn, I see," continued Borroughcliffe—"I feel it to be proper that I detain these men till to-morrow morning, Colonel Howard; and yet I would give them better quarters than the hard benches of the guard-room."

"Act your pleasure, Captain Borroughcliffe," returned the host, "so you do but your duty to our royal master. They shall not want for cheer, and they can have a room over the servants' offices in the south side of the Abbey."

"Three rooms, my colonel, three rooms must be provided, though I give up my own."

"There are several empty apartments there, where blankets might be taken, and the men placed for safe-keeping, if you deem it necessary; though, to me, they seem like good, loyal tars, whose greatest glory it would be to serve their prince, and whose chief pleasure would consist in getting alongside of a Don or a Monsieur."

"We shall discuss these matters anon," said Borroughcliffe, dryly. "I see Miss Plowden begins to look grave at our abusing her patience so long, and I know that cold coffee is, like withered love, but a tasteless sort of a beverage. Come, gentlemen, *en avant!* you have seen the Tuileries, and must have heard a little French. Mr. Christopher Dillon, know you where these three small apartments are 'situate, lying, and being,' as your parchments read?"

"I do, sir," said the complying lawyer, "and shall take much pleasure in guiding you to them. I think your decision that of a prudent and sagacious officer, and much doubt whether Durham Castle, or some other fortress, will be thought too big to hold them, ere long."

As this speech was uttered while the men were passing from the room, its effect on them was unnoticed; but Katherine Plowden, who was left for a few moments by herself, sat and pondered over what she had seen and heard with a thoughtfulness of manner that was not usual to her gay and buoyant spirits. The sounds of the retiring footsteps, however, gradually grew fainter, and the return of her guardian alone recalled the recollection of the young lady to the duties of her situation.

While engaged in the little offices of the tea-table, Katherine threw many furtive glances at the veteran; but, although he seemed to be musing, there was nothing austere or suspicious in his frank open countenance.

"There is much useless trouble taken with these wandering seamen, sir," said Katherine at length; "it seems to be the particular province of Mr. Christopher Dillon to make all that come in contact with him excessively uncomfortable."

"And what has Kit to do with the detention of the men?"

"What! why, has he not undertaken to stand godfather to their prisons? —by a woman's patience, I think, Colonel Howard, this business will gain a pretty addition to the names of St. Ruth. It is already called a house, an abbey, a place, and by some a castle; let Mr. Dillon have his way for a month, and it will add jail to the number."

"Kit is not so happy as to possess the favor of Miss Plowden; but still Kit is a worthy fellow, and a good fellow, and a sensible fellow; ay! and, what is more valuable than all these put together, Miss Katherine, Mr. Christopher Dillon is a faithful and loyal subject to his prince. His mother was my cousin-german, madam, and I cannot say how soon I may call him my nephew. The Dillons are of good Irish extraction, and I believe that even Miss Plowden will admit that the Howards have some pretensions to a name."

"Ah! it is those very things called names that I most allude to," said Katherine quickly. "But an hour since you were indignant, my dear guardian, because you suspected that I insinuated you ought to write jailer behind the name of Howard, and even now you submit to have the office palmed upon you."

"You forget, Miss Katherine Plowden, that it is the pleasure of one of his majesty's officers to detain these men."

"But I thought that the glorious British constitution, which you so often mention," interrupted the young lady, spiritedly, "gives liberty to all who touch these blessed shores; you know, sir, that out of twenty blacks that you brought with you, how few remain; the rest having fled on the wings of the spirit of British liberty!"

This was touching a festering sore in the colonel's feelings, and his provoking ward well knew the effects her observation was likely to produce. Her guardian did not break forth in a violent burst of rage, or furnish those manifestations of his ire that he was wont to do on less important subjects; but he arose, with all his dignity concentrated in a look, and, after making a violent effort to restrain his feelings within the bounds necessary to preserve the decorum of his exit, he ventured a reply.

"That the British constitution is glorious, madam, is most true. That this island is the sole refuge where liberty has been able to find a home, is also true. The tyranny and oppression of the Congress, which are grinding down the colonies to the powder of desolation and poverty, are not worthy the sacred name. Rebellion pollutes all that it touches, madam. Although it often commences under the sanction of holy liberty, it ever terminates in despotism. The annals of the world, from the time of the Greeks and Romans down to the present day, abundantly prove it. There was that Julius Cæsar—he was one of your people's men, and he ended a tyrant. Oliver Cromwell was another—a rebel, a demagogue, and a tyrant. The gradations, madam, are as inevitable as from childhood to youth, and from youth to age. As for the little affair that you have been pleased to mention of the—of the—of my private concerns, I can only say that the affairs of nations are not to be judged of by domestic incidents, any more than domestic occurrences are to be judged of by national politics." The colonel, like many a better logician, mistook his antithesis for argument and paused a moment to admire his own eloquence; but the current of his thoughts, which always flowed in torrents on this subject, swept him along in its course, and he continued: "Yes, madam, here, and here alone, is true liberty to be found. With this solemn asseveration, which is not lightly made, but which is the result of sixty years' experience, I leave you, Miss Plowden; let it be a subject of deep reflection with you, for I too well understand your treacherous feelings not to know that your political errors encourage your personal foibles; reflect, for your own sake, if you love not only your own happiness but your respectability and standing in the world. As for the black hounds that you spoke of they are a set of rebellious, mutinous, ungrateful rascals; and if ever I meet one of the damned——"

The colonel had so far controlled his feelings as to leave the presence of the lady before he broke out into the bitter invectives we had recorded, and Katherine stood a minute, pressing her forefinger on her lips, listening to his voice as it grumbled along the gallery, until the sounds were finally excluded by the closing of a distant door. The wilful girl then shook her dark locks, and a smile of arch mischief blended with an expression of regret in her countenance, as she spoke to herself, while with hurried hands she threw her tea equipage aside in a confused pile:

"It was, perhaps, a cruel experiment, but it has succeeded. Though prisoners ourselves, we are at least left free for the remainder of this night. These mysterious sailors must be examined more closely. If the proud eye of Edward Griffith was not glaring under the black wig of one of them, I am no judge of features; and where has Master Barnstable concealed his charming visage! for neither of the others could be he. But now for Cecilia."

Her light form glided from the room, while she was yet speaking; and flitting along the dimly-lighted passages, it disappeared in one of those turnings that led to the more secret apartments of the Abbey.

13

*How! Lucia, wouldst thou have me sink
        away
In pleasing dreams, and lose myself in love?*

Cato

THE reader must not imagine that the world stood still during the occurrence of scenes we have related. By the time the three seamen were placed in as many different rooms, and a sentinel was stationed in the gallery common to them all, in such a manner as to keep an eye on his whole charge at once, the hour had run deep into the night. Captain Borroughcliffe obeyed a summons from the colonel, who made him an evasive apology for the change in their evening's amusement, and challenged his guest to a renewal of the attack on the madeira. This was too grateful a theme to be lightly discussed by the captain; and the Abbey clock had given forth as many of its mournful remonstrances as the division of the hours would permit, before they separated. In the meantime Mr. Dillon became invisible; though a servant, when questioned by the host on the subject, announced that he "believed Mr. Christopher had chosen to ride over to ——, to be in readiness to join the hunt, on the morning, with the dawn." While the gentlemen were thus indulging themselves in the dining-parlor, and laughing over the tales of other times and hard campaigns, two very different scenes occurred in other parts of the building.

When the quiet of the Abbey was only interrupted by the howling of the wind, or by the loud and prolonged laughs which echoed through the passages from the joyous pair, who were thus comfortably established by the side of the bottle, a door was gently opened on one of the galleries of the "cloisters," and Katherine Plowden issued from it, wrapped in a close mantle, and holding in her hand a chamber-lamp, which threw its dim light faintly along the gloomy walls in front, leaving all behind her obscured in darkness. She was, however, soon followed by two other female figures, clad in the same manner, and provided with similar lights. When all were in the gallery, Katherine drew the door softly to, and proceeded in front to lead the way.

"Hist!" said the low, tremulous voice of Cecilia, "they are yet up in the other parts of the house; and, if it be as you suspect, our visit would betray them, and prove the means of their certain destruction."

"Is the laugh of Colonel Howard in his cups so singular and unknown to your ear, Cecilia, that you know it not?" said Katherine, with a little spirit; "or do you forget that on such occasions he seldom leaves himself ears to hear, or eyes to see with? But follow me; it is as I suspect—it must be as I suspect; and unless we do something to rescue them, they are lost, unless they have laid a deeper scheme than is apparent."

"It is a dangerous road ye both journey," added the placid tones of Alice Dunscombe; "but ye are young, and ye are credulous."

"If you disapprove of our visit," said Cecilia, "it cannot be right, and we had better return."

"No, no; I have said naught to disapprove of your present errand. If God has put the lives of those in your custody whom ye have taught yourselves to look up to with love and reverence, such as woman is bound to yield to one man, He has done it for no idle purpose. Lead us to their doors, Katherine; let us relieve our doubts, at least."

The ardent girl did not wait for a second bidding, but she led them with light and quick steps along the gallery, until they reached the termination, where they descended to the basement-floor by a flight of narrow steps; and, carefully opening a small door, emerged into the open air. They now stood on a small plat of grass, which lay between the building and the ornamental garden, across which they moved rapidly, concealing their lights, and bending their shrinking forms before the shivering blasts that poured their fury upon them from the ocean. They soon reached a large but rough addition to the buildings, that concealed its plain architecture behind the more labored and highly-finished parts of the edifice, into which they entered through a massive door that stood ajar, as if to admit them.

"Chloe has been true to my orders," whispered Katherine, as they passed out of the chilling air; "now, if all the servants are asleep, our chance to escape unnoticed amounts to certainty."

It became necessary to go through the servants' hall, which they effected unobserved, as it had but one occupant, an aged black man, who, being posted with his ear within two feet of a bell, in this attitude had committed himself to a deep sleep. Gliding through this hall they entered divers long and intricate passages, all of which seemed as familiar to Katherine as they were unknown to her companions, until they reached another flight of steps, which they ascended. They were now near their goal, and stopped to examine whether any or what difficulties were likely to be opposed to their further progress.

"Now, indeed, our case seems hopeless," whispered Katherine, as they stood, concealed by the darkness, in one end of an extremely long, narrow passage; "here is the sentinel in the building, instead of being, as I had supposed, under the windows; what is to be done now?"

"Let us return," said Cecilia, in the same manner; "my influence with my uncle is great, even though he seems unkind to us at times. In the morning I will use it to persuade him to free them, on receiving their promise to abandon all such attempts in future."

"In the morning it will be too late," returned Katherine; "I saw that demon Kit Dillon mount his horse, under the pretense of riding to the great hunt of to-morrow, but I know his malicious eye too well to be deceived in his errand. He is silent, that he may be sure; and if to-morrow comes and finds Griffith within these walls, he will be condemned to a scaffold."

"Say no more," said Alice Dunscombe, with singular emotion; "some lucky circumstance may aid us with this sentinel."

As she spoke, she advanced: they had not proceeded far before the stern voice of the soldier challenged the party.

" 'Tis no time to hesitate," whispered Katherine—"We are the ladies of the Abbey, looking to our domestic affairs," she continued, aloud, "and think it a little remarkable that we are to encounter armed men while going through our own dwelling."

The soldier respectfully presented his musket, and replied:

"My orders are to guard the doors of these three rooms, ladies; we have prisoners in them, and, as for anything else, my duty will be to serve you in all my power."

"Prisoners!" exclaimed Katherine, in affected surprise; "does Captain Borroughcliffe make St. Ruth's Abbey a jail? Of what offences are the poor men guilty?"

"I know not, my lady; but, as they are sailors, I suppose they have run from his majesty's service."

"This is singular, truly! and why are they not sent to the county prison?"

"This must be examined into," said Cecilia, dropping the mantle from before her face. "As mistress of this house, I claim a right to know whom its walls contain; you will oblige me by opening the doors, for I see you have the keys suspended from your belt."

The sentinel hesitated. He was greatly awed by the presence and beauty of the speakers, but a still voice reminded him of his duty. A lucky thought, however, interposed to relieve him from his dilemma, and at the same time to comply with the request, or rather order, of the lady. As he handed her the keys, he said:

"Here they are, my lady; my orders are to keep the prisoners in, not to keep any one out. When you are done with them, you will please return them to me, if it be only to save a poor fellow's eye; for unless the door is kept locked, I shall not dare to look about me for a moment."

Cecilia promised to return the keys, and she had applied one of them to a lock with a trembling hand, when Alice Dunscombe arrested her arm, and addressed the soldier.

"Say you there are three?—are they men in years?"

"No, my lady, all good, serviceable lads, who couldn't do better than to serve his majesty, or, as it may prove, worse than to run from their colors."

"But are their years and appearance similar? I ask; for I have a friend who has been guilty of some boyish tricks, and has tried the seas, I hear, among other foolish hazards."

"There is no boy here. In the far room on the left is a smart, soldier-looking chap, of about thirty, who the captain thinks has carried a musket before now; on him I am charged to keep a particular eye. Next to him is as pretty a looking youth as eyes could wish to see, and it makes one feel mournful to think what he must come to, if he has really deserted his ship. In the room near you is a smaller, quiet little body, who might make a better preacher than a sailor, or a soldier either, he has such a gentle way with him."

Alice covered her eyes with her hand a moment, and then, recovering herself, proceeded:

"Gentleness may do more for the unfortunate men than fear; here is a guinea: withdraw to the far end of the passage, where you can watch them as well as here, while we enter, and endeavor to make them confess who and what they really are."

The soldier took the money and, after looking about him in a little uncertainty, he at length complied, as it was obviously true they could only escape by passing him, near the flight of steps. When he was beyond hearing, Alice Dunscombe turned to her companions, and a slight glow appeared in feverish spots on her cheeks, as she addressed them:

"It would be idle to attempt to hide from you, that I expect to meet the individual whose voice I must have heard in reality to-night, instead of only imaginary sounds, as I vainly, if not wickedly, supposed. I have many reasons for changing my opinion, the chief of which is, that he is leagued with the rebellious Americans in this unnatural war. Nay, chide me not, Miss Plowden; you will remember that I found my being on this island.—I come here on no vain or weak errand, Miss Howard, but to spare human blood." She paused, as if struggling to speak calmly. "But no one can witness the interview except our God."

"Go, then," said Katherine, secretly rejoicing at her determination, "while we inquire into the characters of the others."

Alice Dunscombe turned the key; and, gently opening the door, she desired her companions to tap for her, as they returned, and then instantly disappeared in the apartment.

Cecilia and her cousin proceeded to the next door, which they opened in silence, and entered cautiously into the room. Katherine Plowden had so far examined into the arrangements of Colonel Howard as to know that, at the same time he ordered blankets to be provided for the prisoners, he had not thought it necessary to administer any further to the accommodations of men who had apparently made their beds and pillows of planks for the greater part of their lives.

The ladies accordingly found the youthful sailor whom they sought, with his body rolled in the shaggy covering, extended at his length along the naked boards, and buried in a deep sleep. So timid were the steps of his visitors, and so noiseless was their entrance, that they approached even to his side without disturbing his slumbers. The head of the prisoner lay rudely pillowed on a billet of wood, one hand protecting his face from its rough surface, and the other thrust into his bosom, where it rested, with a relaxed grasp, on the handle of a dirk. Although he slept, and that heavily, yet his rest was unnatural and perturbed. His breathing was hard and quick, and something like the low, rapid murmurings of a confused utterance mingled with his respiration. The moment had now arrived when the character of Cecilia Howard appeared to undergo an entire change. Hitherto she had been led by her cousin, whose activity and enterprise seemed to qualify her so well for the office of guide;

but now she advanced before Katherine, and, extending her lamp in such a manner as to throw the light across the face of the sleeper, she bent to examine his countenance, with keen and anxious eyes.

"Am I right?" whispered her cousin.

"May God, in his infinite compassion, pity and protect him!" murmured Cecilia, her whole frame involuntarily shuddering, as the conviction that she beheld Griffith flashed across her mind. "Yes, Katherine, it is he, and presumptuous madness has driven him here. But time presses; he must be awakened, and his escape effected at every hazard."

"Nay, then, delay no longer, but rouse him from his sleep."

"Griffith! Edward Griffith!" said the soft tones of Cecilia. "Griffith, awake!"

"Your call is useless, for they sleep nightly among tempests and boisterous sounds," said Katherine; "but I have heard it said that the smallest touch will generally cause one of them to stir."

"Griffith!" repeated Cecilia, laying her fair hand timidly on his own.

The flash of lightning is not more nimble than the leap that the young man made to his feet, which he no sooner gained than his dirk gleamed in the light of the lamps as he brandished it fiercely with one hand, while with the other he extended a pistol, in a menacing attitude, toward only his disturbers.

"Stand back!" he exclaimed; "I am your prisoner as a corpse!"

The fierceness of his front, and the glaring eyeballs, that rolled wildly around him, appalled Cecilia, who shrank back in fear, dropping her mantle from her person, but still keeping her mild eyes fastened on his countenance with a confiding gaze that contradicted her shrinking attitude, as she replied:

"Edward, it is I, Cecilia Howard, come to save you from destruction; you are known even through your ingenious disguise."

The pistol and the dirk fell together on the blanket of the young sailor, whose looks instantly lost their disturbed expression in a glow of pleasure.

"Fortune at length favors me!" he cried. "This is kind, Cecilia; more than I deserve, and much more than I expected. But you are not alone?"

" 'Tis my cousin Kate; to her piercing eyes you owe your detection, and she has kindly consented to accompany me, that we might urge you to—nay, that we might, if necessary, assist you to fly. For 'tis cruel folly, Griffith, thus to tempt your fate."

"Have I tempted it, then, in vain!—Miss Plowden, to you I must appeal for an answer and a justification."

Katherine looked displeased; but, after a moment's hesitation, she replied:

"Your servant, Mr. Griffith; I perceive that the erudite Captain Barnstable has not only succeeded in spelling through my scrawl, but he has also given it to all hands for perusal."

"Now you do both him and me injustice," said Griffith; "it surely was not treachery to show me a plan in which I was to be a principal actor."

"Ah! doubtless your excuses are as obedient to your calls as your men," returned the young lady; "but how comes it that the hero of the Ariel sends a deputy to perform a duty that is so peculiarly his own? Is he wont to be second in rescues?"

"Heaven forbid that you should think so meanly of him for a moment! We owe you much, Miss Plowden; but we may have other duties. You know that we serve our common country, and have a superior with us, whose beck is our law."

"Return, then, Mr. Griffith, while you may to the service of our bleeding country," said Cecilia; "and after the joint efforts of her brave children have expelled the intruders from her soil, let us hope there shall come a time when Katherine and myself may be restored to our native homes."

"Think you, Miss Howard, to how long a period the mighty arm of the British king may extend that time? We shall prevail—a nation fighting for its dearest rights must ever prevail; but 'tis not the work of a day, for a people, poor, scattered, and impoverished as we have been to beat down a power like that of England; surely you forget that, in bidding me to leave you with such expectations, Miss Howard, you doom me to an almost hopeless banishment!"

"We must trust to the will of God," said Cecilia; "if He ordain that America is to be free only after protracted sufferings, I can aid her but with my prayers; but you have an arm and an experience, Griffith, that might do her better service. Waste not your usefulness, then, in visionary schemes for private happiness, but seize the moments as they offer, and return to your ship, if indeed it is yet in safety, and endeavor to forget this mad undertaking, and, for a time, the being who has led you to the adventure."

"This is a reception that I had not anticipated," returned Griffith; "for though accident, and not intention, has thrown me into your presence this evening, I did hope that, when I again saw the frigate, it would be in your company, Cecilia."

"You cannot justly reproach me, Mr. Griffith, with your disappointment, for I have not uttered or authorized a syllable that could induce you or any one to believe that I would consent to quit my uncle."

"Miss Howard will not think me presumptuous if I remind her that there was a time when she did not think me unworthy to be intrusted with her person and happiness."

A rich bloom mantled on the face of Cecilia, as she replied:

"Nor do I now, Mr. Griffith; but you do well to remind me of my former weakness, for the recollection of its folly and imprudence only adds to my present strength."

"Nay," interrupted her eager lover, "if I intended a reproach, or harbored a boastful thought, spurn me from you forever, as unworthy of your favor."

"I acquit you of both much easier than I can acquit myself of the charge of weakness and folly," continued Cecilia; "but there are many things that have occurred since we last met to prevent a repetition of such inconsiderate rashness on my part. One of them is," she added, smiling sweetly, "that I have numbered twelve additional months to my age, and a hundred to my experience. Another, and perhaps a more important one, is, that my uncle then continued among the friends of his youth, surrounded by those whose blood mingles with his own; but here he lives a stranger; and, though he finds some consolation in dwelling in a building where his ancestors have dwelt before him, yet he walks as an alien through its gloomy passages, and would find the empty honor but a miserable compensation for the kindness and affection of one whom he has loved and cherished from her infancy."

"And yet he is opposed to you in your private wishes, Cecilia, unless my besotted vanity has led me to believe what it would now be madness to learn was false; and, in your opinions of public things, you are quite as widely separated. I should think there could be but little happiness dependent on a connection where there is no one feeling entertained in common."

"There is, and an all-important one," said Miss Howard; "'tis our love. He is my kind, my affectionate, and, unless thwarted by some evil cause, my indulgent uncle and guardian—and I am his brother Harry's child. This tie is not easily to be severed, Mr. Griffith; though, as I do not wish to see you crazed, I shall not add that your besotted vanity has played you false; but surely, Edward, it is possible to feel a double tie, and so to act as to discharge our duties to both. I never, never can or will consent to desert my uncle, a stranger as he is in the land whose rule he upholds so blindly. You know not this England, Griffith; she receives her children from the colonies with cold and haughty distrust, like a jealous step-mother, who is wary of the favors that she bestows on her fictitious offspring."

"I know her in peace, and I know her in war," said the young sailor, proudly, "and can add that she is a haughty friend, and a stubborn foe; but she grapples now with those who ask no more of her than an open sea and an enemy's favors. But this determination will be melancholy tidings for me to convey to Barnstable."

"Nay," said Cecilia, smiling, "I cannot vouch for others who have no uncles, and who have an extra quantity of ill-humor and spleen against this country, its people, and its laws, although profoundly ignorant of them all."

"Is Miss Howard tired of seeing me under the tiles of St. Ruth?" asked Katherine. "But hark! are there not footsteps approaching along the gallery?"

They listened, in breathless silence, and soon heard distinctly the approaching tread of more than one person. Voices were quite audible, and before they had time to consult on what was best to be done, the words of the speakers were distinctly heard at the door of their own apartment.

"Ay! he has a military air about him, Peters, that will make him a prize. Come, open the door."

"This is not his room, your honor," said the alarmed soldier; "he quarters in the last room in the gallery."

"How know you that, fellow? Come, produce the key, and open the way for me; I care not who sleeps here; there is no saying but I may enlist them all three."

A single moment of dreadful incertitude succeeded, when the sentinel was heard saying in reply to this peremptory order:

"I thought your honor wanted to see the one with the black stock, and so left the rest of the keys at the other end of the passage; but——"

"But nothing, you loon; a sentinel should always carry his keys about him like a jailer; follow, then, and let me see the lad who dresses so well to the right."

As the heart of Katherine began to beat less vehemently, she said:

" 'Tis Borroughcliffe, and too drunk to see that we have left the key in the door; but what is to be done? We have but a moment for consultation."

"As the day dawns," said Cecilia, quickly, "I shall send here, under the pretence of conveying you food, my own women——"

"There is no need of risking anything for my safety," interrupted Griffith; "I hardly think we shall be detained, and, if we are, Barnstable is at hand with a force that would scatter these recruits to the four winds of heaven."

"Ah! that would lead to bloodshed, and scenes of horror!" exclaimed Cecilia.

"Listen!" cried Katherine, "they approach again!"

A man now stopped, once more, at their door, which was opened softly, and the face of the sentinel was thrust into the apartment.

"Captain Borroughcliffe is on his rounds, and for fifty of your guineas I would not leave you here another minute."

"But one word more," said Cecilia.

"Not a syllable, my lady, for my life!" returned the man; "the lady from the next room waits for you, and in mercy to a poor fellow go back where you came from."

The appeal was unanswerable, and they complied, Cecilia saying, as they left the room:

"I shall send you food in the morning, young man, and directions how to take the remedy necessary to your safety."

In the passage they found Alice Dunscombe, with her face concealed in her mantle; and it would seem, by the heavy sighs that escaped her, deeply agitated, by the interview which she had just encountered.

But as the reader may have some curiosity to know what occurred to distress this unoffending lady so sensibly, we shall detain the narrative to relate the substance of that which passed between her and the individual whom she sought.

14

As when a lion in his den,
Hath heard the hunter's cries,
And rushes forth to meet his foes,
So did the Douglas rise.

PERCY

ALICE DUNSCOMBE did not find the second of the prisoners buried, like Griffith, in sleep, but he was seated on one of the old chairs that were in the apartment, with his back to the door, and apparently looking through the small window, on the dark and dreary scenery over which the tempest was yet sweeping in its fury. Her approach was unheeded, until the light from her lamp glared across his eyes, when he started from his musing posture, and advanced to meet her. He was the first to speak.

"I expected this visit," he said, "when I found that you recognized my voice; and I felt a deep assurance in my breast that Alice Dunscombe would never betray me."

His listener, though expecting this confirmation of her conjectures, was unable to make an immediate reply, but she sank into the seat he had abandoned, and waited a few moments as if to recover her powers.

"It was, then, no mysterious warning! no airy voice that mocked my ears; but a dread reality!" she at length said. "Why have you thus braved the indignation of the laws of your country? On what errand of fell mischief has your ruthless temper again urged you to embark?"

"This is strong and cruel language, coming from you to me, Alice Duns-combe," returned the stranger, with cool asperity, "and the time has been when I should have been greeted, after a shorter absence, with milder terms."

"I deny it not; I cannot, if I would, conceal my infirmity from myself or you; I hardly wish it to continue unknown to the world. If I have once es-teemed you—if I have plighted to you my troth, and in my confiding folly forgot my higher duties, God has amply punished me for the weakness in your own evil deeds."

"Nay, let not our meeting be embittered with useless and provoking re-criminations," said the other; "for we have much to say before you communi-cate the errand of mercy on which you have come hither. I know you too well, Alice, not to see that you perceive the peril in which I am placed, and are willing to venture something for my safety. Your mother—does she yet live?"

"She has gone in quest of my blessed father," said Alice, covering her pale face with her hands; "they have left me alone, truly; for he who was to have been all to me, was first false to his faith, and has since become unworthy of my confidence."

The stranger became singularly agitated, his usually quiet eye glancing hastily from the floor to the countenance of his companion, as he paced the room with hurried steps; at length he replied:

"There is much, perhaps, to be said in explanation that you do not know. I left the country, because I found in it nothing but oppression and injustice, and I could not invite you to become the bride of a wanderer, without either name or fortune. But I have now the opportunity of proving my truth. You say you are alone; be so no longer, and try how far you were mistaken in be-lieving that I should one day supply the place to you of both father and mother."

There is something soothing to a female ear in the offer of even protracted justice, and Alice spoke with less of acrimony in her tones, during the re-mainder of their conference, if not with less of severity in her language.

"You talk not like a man whose very life hangs but on a thread that the next minute may snap asunder. Whither would you lead me? is it to the Tower at London?"

"Think not I have weakly exposed my person without a sufficient protec-tion," returned the stranger, with cool indifference; "there are many gallant men who only wait my signal to crush the paltry force of this officer like a worm beneath my feet."

"Then has the conjecture of Colonel Howard been true, and the manner in which the enemy's vessels have passed the shoals is no longer a mystery! You have been their pilot?"

"I have."

"What! would ye pervert the knowledge gained in the spring-time of your guileless youth to the foul purpose of bringing desolation to the doors of those you once knew and respected? John! John! is the image of the maiden, whom in her morning of beauty and simplicity I believe you did love, so faintly impressed that it cannot soften your hard heart to the misery of those among whom she has been born, and who compose her little world?"

"Not a hair of theirs shall be touched, not a thatch shall blaze, nor shall a sleepless night befall the vilest among them—and all for your sake, Alice! England comes to this contest with a seared conscience and bloody hands, but all shall be forgotten for the present, when both opportunity and power offer to make her feel our vengeance even in her vitals. I come on no such errand."

"What, then, has led you blindly into snares, where all your boasted aid would avail you nothing; for, should I call aloud your name even here, in the dark and dreary passages of this obscure edifice, the cry would echo through the country ere the morning, and a whole people would be found in arms to punish your audacity."

"My name has been sounded, and that in no gentle strains," returned the pilot, scornfully, "when a whole people have quailed at it—the craven, cowardly wretches flying before the man they had wronged. I have lived to bear the banners of the new Republic proudly in sight of the three kingdoms, when practised skill and equal arms have in vain struggled to pluck it down. Ay! Alice, the echoes of my guns are still roaring among your eastern hills, and would render my name more appalling than inviting to your sleeping yeomen."

"Boast not of the momentary success that the arm of God has yielded to your unhallowed efforts," said Alice; "for a day of severe and heavy retribution must follow; nor flatter yourself with the idle hope that your name, terrible as ye have rendered it to the virtuous, is sufficient of itself to drive the thoughts of home, and country, and kin, from all who hear it. Nay, I know not that even now, in listening to you, I am not forgetting a solemn duty, which would teach me to proclaim your presence, that the land might know that her unnatural son is a dangerous burden in her bosom."

The pilot turned quickly in his short walk; and, after reading her countenance, with the expression of one who felt his security, he said in gentler tones:

"Would that be Alice Dunscombe? would that be like the mild, generous

girl whom I knew in my youth? But I repeat, the threat would fail to intimi-
date, even if you were capable of executing it. I have said that it is only needful
to make the signal to draw around me a force sufficient to scatter these dogs of
soldiers to the four winds of heaven."

"Have you calculated your power justly, John?" said Alice, unconsciously
betraying her deep interest in his safety. "Have you reckoned the probability
of Mr. Dillon's arriving, accompanied by an armed band of horsemen with
this morning's sun? for it's no secret in the Abbey that he is gone in quest of
such assistance."

"Dillon!" exclaimed the pilot, starting; "who is he? and on what suspicion
does he seek this addition to your guard?"

"Nay, John, look not at me, as if you would know the secrets of my heart.
It was not I who prompted him to such a step; you cannot for a moment
think that I would betray you! But too surely he has gone; and, as the night
wears rapidly away, you should be using the hour of grace to effect your own
security."

"Fear not for me, Alice," returned the pilot, proudly, while a faint smile
struggled around his compressed lips; "and yet I like not this movement either.
How call you his name? Dillon! is he a minion of King George?"

"He is, John, what you are not, a loyal subject of his sovereign lord the
king; and, though a native of the revolted colonies, he has preserved his virtue
uncontaminated amid the corruptions and temptations of the times."

"An American! and disloyal to the liberties of the human race! By Heaven,
he had better not cross me; for, if my arm reach him, it shall hold him forth
as a spectacle of treason to the world!"

"And has not the world enough of such a spectacle in yourself? Are ye not,
even now, breathing your native air, though lurking through the mists of the
island, with desperate intent against its peace and happiness?"

A dark and fierce expression of angry resentment flashed from the eyes of
the pilot, and even his iron frame seemed to shake with emotion, as he answered:

"Call you his dastardly and selfish treason, aiming, as it does, to aggrandize
a few, at the expense of millions, a parallel case to the generous ardor that im-
pels a man to fight in the defence of sacred liberty? I might tell you that I am
armed in the common cause of my fellow-subjects and countrymen; that,
though an ocean divided us in distance, yet we are a people of the same blood,
and children of the same parents, and that the hand which oppresses one
inflicts an injury on the other. But I disdain all such narrow apologies. I was
born on this orb, and I claim to be a citizen of it. A man with a soul not to be

limited by the arbitrary boundaries of tyrants and hirelings, but one who has the right as well as the inclination to grapple with oppression, in whose name soever it is exercised, or in whatever hollow and specious shape it founds its claim to abuse our race."

"Ah! John, John, though this may sound like reason to rebellious ears, to mine it seemeth only as the ravings of insanity. It is vain ye build up your new and disorganizing systems of rule, or rather misrule, which are opposed to all that the world has ever yet done, or ever will see done, in peace and happiness. What avail your subtleties and false reasonings against the heart? It is the heart which tells us where our home is, and how to love it."

"You talk like a weak and prejudiced woman, Alice," said the pilot, more composedly; "and one who would shackle nations with the ties that bind the young and feeble of your own sex together."

"And by what holier and better bond can they be united!" said Alice. "Are not the relations of domestic life of God's establishing, and have not the nations grown from families, as branches spread from the stem, till the tree overshadows the land? 'Tis an ancient and sacred tie that binds man to his nation; neither can it be severed without infamy."

The pilot smiled disdainfully, and, throwing open the rough exterior of his dress, he drew forth, in succession, several articles, while a glowing pride lighted his countenance as he offered them singly to her notice.

"See, Alice!" he said; "call you this infamy? This broad sheet of parchment is stamped with a seal of no mean importance, and it bears the royal name of the princely Louis also! And view this cross! decorated as it is with jewels, the gift of the same illustrious hand; it is not apt to be given to the children of infamy, neither is it wise or decorous to stigmatize a man who has not been thought unworthy to consort with princes and nobles by the opprobrious name of the 'Scotch Pirate.' "

"And have ye not earned the title, John, by ruthless deeds and bitter animosity? I could kiss the bawbles ye show me, if they were a thousand times less splendid, had they been laid upon your breast by the hands of your lawful prince; but now they appear to my eyes as indelible blots upon your attainted name. As for your associates, I have heard of them: and it seemeth that a queen might be better employed than encouraging by her smiles the disloyal subjects of other monarchs, though even her enemies. God only knows when His pleasure may suffer a spirit of disaffection to rise up among the people of her own nation, and then the thought that she has encouraged rebellion may prove both bitter and unwelcome."

"That the royal and lovely Antoinette has deigned to repay my services with a small portion of her gracious approbation is not among the least of my boasts," returned the pilot, in affected humility, while secret pride was manifested even in his lofty attitude. "But venture not a syllable in her dispraise, for you know not whom you censure. She is less distinguished by her illustrious birth and elevated station, than by her virtues and loveliness. She lives the first of her sex in Europe—the daughter of an emperor, the consort of the most powerful king, and the smiling and beloved patroness of a nation who worship at her feet. Her life is above all reproach, as it is above all earthly punishment, were she so lost as to merit it; and it has been the will of Providence to place her far beyond the reach of all human misfortunes."

"Has it placed her above human errors, John? Punishment is the natural and inevitable consequence of sin; and unless she can say more than has ever fallen to the lot of humanity to say truly, she may be made to feel the chastening arm of One to whose eyes all her pageantry and power are as vacant as the air she breathes—so insignificant must it seem when compared to his own just rule! But if you vaunt that you have been permitted to kiss the hem of the robes of the French queen, and have been the companion of high-born and flaunting ladies, clad in their richest array, can ye yet say to yourself, that amid them all ye have found one whose tongue has been bold to tell you the truth, or whose heart has sincerely joined in her false professions?"

"Certainly none have met me with the reproaches that I have this night received from Alice Dunscombe, after a separation of six long years," returned the pilot.

"If I have spoken to you the words of holy truth, John, let them not be the less welcome, because they are strangers to your ears. Oh! think that she who has thus dared to use the language of reproach to one whose name is terrible to all who live on the border of this island, is led to the rash act by no other motive than interest in your eternal welfare."

"Alice! Alice! you madden me with these foolish speeches! Am I a monster to frighten unprotected women and helpless children? What mean these epithets, as coupled with my name? Have you, too, lent a credulous ear to the vile calumnies which the policy of your rulers has ever attempted to destroy the fair fame of those who oppose them, and those chiefly who oppose them with success? My name may be terrible to the officers of the royal fleet, but where and how have I earned a claim to be considered formidable to the helpless and unoffending?"

Alice Dunscombe cast a furtive and timid glance at the pilot, which spoke even stronger than her words, as she replied:

"I know not that all which is said of you and your deeds is true. I have often prayed, in bitterness and sorrow, that a tenth part of that which is laid to your charge may not be heaped on your devoted head at the great and final account. But, John, I have known you long and well, and Heaven forbid that, on this solemn occasion, which may be the last of our earthly interviews, I should be found wanting in Christian duty, through a woman's weakness! I have often thought, when I have heard the gall of bitter reproach and envenomed language hurled against your name, that they who spoke so rashly, little understood the man they vituperated. But, though ye are at times, and I may say almost always, as mild and even as the smoothest sea over which ye have ever sailed, yet God has mingled in your nature a fearful mixture of fierce passions, which, roused, are more like the southern waters when troubled with the tornado. It is difficult for me to say how far this evil spirit may lead a man who has been goaded by fancied wrongs to forget his country and home, and who is suddenly clothed with power to show his resentments."

The pilot listened with rooted attention, and his piercing eye seemed to reach the seat of those thoughts which she but half expressed; still, he retained the entire command of himself, and answered, more in sorrow than in anger:

"If anything could convert me to your own peaceful and unresisting opinions, Alice, it would be the reflections that offer themselves at this conviction, that even you have been led, by the base tongues of my dastardly enemies, to doubt my honor and conduct. What is fame, when a man can be thus traduced to his nearest friends? But no more of these childish reflections; they are unworthy of myself, my office, and the sacred cause in which I have enlisted!"

"Nay, John, shake them not off," said Alice, unconsciously laying her hand on his arm; "they are as the dew to the parched herbage, and may freshen the feelings of your youth, and soften the heart that has grown hard, if hard it be, more by unnatural indulgence, than its own base inclinations."

"Alice Dunscombe," said the pilot, approaching her with solemn earnestness, "I have learned much this night, though I came not in quest of such knowledge. You have taught me how powerful is the breath of the slanderer, and how frail is the tenure by which we hold our good names. Full twenty time have I met the hirelings of your prince in open battle, fighting ever manfully under that flag which was first raised to the breeze by my own hands, and which, I thank my God, I have never yet seen lowered an inch; but with no one act of cowardice or private wrong in all that service can I reproach myself; and yet, how am I rewarded? The tongue of the vile calumniator is keener than the sword of the warrior, and leaves a more indelible scar!"

"Never have ye uttered a truer sentiment, John, and God send that ye may encourage such thoughts to your own eternal advantage!" said Alice, with engaging interest. "You say that you have risked your own precious life in twenty combats, and observe how little of Heaven's favor is bestowed on the abettors of rebellion! They tell me that the world has never witnessed a more desperate and bloody struggle than this last, for which your name has been made to sound to the farthermost ends of the isle."

" 'Twill be known wherever naval combats are spoken of!" interrupted the pilot, the melancholy which had begun to lower in his countenance giving place to a look of proud exultation.

"And yet its fancied glory cannot shield your name from wrong, nor are the rewards of the victor equal, in a temporal sense, to those which the vanquished has received. Know you that our gracious monarch, deeming your adversary's cause so sacred, has extended to him his royal favor?"

"Ay! he has dubbed him knight!" exclaimed the pilot, with a scornful and bitter laugh; "let him be again furnished with a ship, and me with another opportunity, and I promise him an earldom, if being again vanquished can constitute a claim!"

"Speak not so rashly, nor vaunt yourself of possessing a protecting power that may desert you, John, when you most need it, and least expect the change," returned his companion; "the battle is not always to the strong, neither is the race to the swift."

"Forget you, my good Alice, that your words will admit of a double meaning? Has the battle been with the strong? Though you say not well in denying the race to the swift. Yes, yes, often and again have the dastards escaped me by their prudent speed! Alice Dunscombe, you know not the thousandth part of the torture that I have been made to feel, by high-born miscreants, who envy the merit they cannot equal, and detract from the glory of deeds that they dare not attempt to emulate. How have I been cast upon the ocean, like some unworthy vessel that is commissioned to do a desperate deed, and then to bury itself in the ruin it has made! How many malignant hearts have triumphed as they beheld my canvas open, thinking that it was spread to hasten me to a gibbet, or to a tomb in the bosom of the ocean; but I have disappointed them!"

The eyes of the pilot no longer gazed with their piercing and settled meaning; but they flashed with a fierce and wild pleasure, as he continued, in a louder voice:

"Yes, bitterly have I disappointed them! Oh! the triumph over my fallen enemies has been tame to this heartfelt exultation which places me immeasurably above those false and craven hypocrites! I begged, I implored the Frenchmen for the meanest of their craft, which possessed but the common qualities of a ship-of-war; I urged the policy and necessity of giving me such a force, for even then I promised to be found in harm's way; but envy and jealousy robbed me of my just dues, and of more than half my glory. They call me pirate! If I have claim to the name, it was furnished more by the paltry outfit of my friends than by any act toward my enemies!"

"And do not these recollections prompt you to return to your allegiance, to your prince and native land, John?" said Alice in a subdued voice.

"Away with the silly thought!" interrupted the pilot, recalled to himself as if by a sudden conviction of the weakness he had betrayed; "it is ever thus where men are made conspicuous by their works—but to your visit—I have the power to rescue myself and companions from this paltry confinement, and yet I would not have it done with violence for your sake. Bring you the means of doing it in quiet?"

"When the morning arrives you will all be conducted to the apartment where we first met. This will be done at the solicitation of Miss Howard, under the plea of compassion and justice, and with the professed object of inquiring into your situations. Her request will not be refused; and while your guard is stationed at the door, you will be shown, by another entrance, through the private apartments of the wing, to a window whence you can easily leap to the ground, where a thicket is at hand; afterward we shall trust your safety to your own discretion."

"And if this Dillon, of whom you have spoken, should suspect the truth, how will you answer to the law for aiding our escape?"

"I believe he little dreams who is among the prisoners," said Alice, musing, "though he may have detected the character of one of your companions. But it is private feeling rather than public spirit that urges him on."

"I have suspected something of this," returned the pilot, with a smile that crossed those features where ungovernable passions had so lately been exhibited, with an effect that might be likened to the last glimmering of an expiring conflagration, serving to render the surrounding ruin more obvious. "This young Griffith has led me from my direct path with his idle imprudence, and it is right that his mistress should incur some risk. But with you, Alice, the case is different; here you are only a guest, and it is unnecessary that you should be known in the unfortunate affair. Should my name get abroad, this recreant American, this Colonel Howard, will find all the favor he has purchased by advocating the cause of tyranny necessary to protect him from the displeasure of the ministry."

"I fear to trust so delicate a measure to the young discretion of my amiable friend," said Alice, shaking her head.

"Remember that she has her attachment to plead in her excuse; but dare you say to the world that you still remember, with gentle feelings, the man whom you stigmatize with such opprobrious epithets?"

A slight color gleamed over the brow of Alice Dunscombe, as she uttered, in a voice that was barely audible:

"There is no longer a reason why the world should know of such a weakness, though it did exist." And, as the faint glow passed away, leaving her face pale nearly as the hue of death, her eyes kindled with unusual fire, and she added: "They can but take my life, John; and that I am ready to lay down in your service!"

"Alice!" exclaimed the softened pilot, "my kind, my gentle Alice—"

The knock of the sentinel at the door was heard at this critical moment. Without waiting for a reply to his summons, the man entered the apartment, and, in hurried language, declared the urgent necessity that existed for the lady to retire. A few brief remonstrances were uttered by both Alice and the pilot, who wished to comprehend more clearly each other's intentions relative to the intended escape; but the fear of personal punishment rendered the soldier obdurate, and a dread of exposure at length induced the lady to comply. She arose, and was leaving the apartment with lingering steps, when the pilot, touching her hand, whispered to her impressively:

"Alice, we meet again before I leave this island forever?"

"We meet in the morning, John," she returned, in the same tone of voice, "in the apartments of Miss Howard."

He dropped her hand and she glided from the room, when the impatient sentinel closed the door, and silently turned the key on his prisoner. The pilot remained in a listening attitude, until the light footsteps of the retiring pair were no longer audible, when he paced his confined apartment with perturbed steps, occasionally pausing to look out at the driving clouds, and the groaning oaks that were trembling and rocking their broad arms in the fitful gusts of the gale. In a few minutes the tempest in his own passions had gradually subsided to the desperate and still calmness that made him the man he was; when he again seated himself where Alice had found him, and began to muse on the events of the times, from which the transition to projecting schemes of daring enterprise and mighty consequences was but the usual employment of his active and restless mind.

15

Sir Andrew:

*I have no exquisite reason for't, but I've
reason good enough.*

Twelfth Night

THE countenance of Captain Borroughcliffe,
when the sentinel admitted him to the apartment he had selected, was in that
state of doubtful illumination, when looks of peculiar cunning blend so nicely
with the stare of vacancy, that the human face is rendered not unlike an April
day, now smiling and inviting, and at the next moment clouded and dreary.
It is quite apparent that the soldier had an object for his unexpected visit, by
the importance of his air, and the solemnity of the manner with which he entered on the business. He waved his hand for the sentinel to retire, with lofty
dignity, and continued balancing his body, during the closing of the door,
and while a sound continued audible to his confused faculties, with his eyes
fixed in the direction of the noise, with that certain sort of wise look that in
many men supplies the place of something better. When the captain felt himself secure from interruption, he moved round with quick and military precision, in order to face the man of whom he was in quest. Griffith had been
sleeping, though uneasily, and with watchfulness; and the pilot had been
calmly awaiting the visit which it seemed he had anticipated; but their associate, who was no other than Captain Manual, of the marines, was discovered
in a very different condition from either. Though the weather was cool, and

the night tempestuous, he had thrown aside his pea-jacket, with most of his disguise, and was sitting ruefully on his blanket, wiping, with one hand, the large drops of sweat from his forehead, and occasionally grasping his throat with the other, with a kind of convulsed mechanical movement. He stared wildly at his visitor, though his entrance produced no other alteration in these pursuits than a more diligent application of his handkerchief, and a more frequent grasping of his naked neck, as if he were willing to ascertain, by actual experiment, what degree of pressure the part was able to sustain, without exceeding a given quantity of inconvenience.

"Comrade, I greet ye!" said Borroughcliffe, staggering to the side of his prisoner, where he seated himself with an entire absence of ceremony; "comrade, I greet ye! Is the kingdom in danger, that gentlemen traverse the island in the uniform of the regiment of *incognitus, incognitu, 'torum*—damme, how I forget my Latin! Say, my fine fellow, are you one of these *'torums?*"

Manual breathed a little hard, which, considering the manner he had been using his throat, was a thing to be expected; but, swallowing his apprehensions, he answered with more spirit than his situation rendered prudent, or the occasion demanded.

"Say what you will of me, and treat me as you please, I defy any man to call me Tory with truth."

"You are no *'torum!* Well, then, the war-office has got up a new dress! Your regiment must have earned their facings in storming some water-battery, or perhaps it has done duty as marines. Am I right?"

"I'll not deny it," said Manual, more stoutly; "I have served as a marine for two years, though taken from the line of—"

"The army," said Borroughcliffe, interrupting a most damning confession of which "State line" the other belonged to. "I kept a dog-watch myself, once, on board the fleet of my Lord Howe; but it is a service that I do not envy any man. Our afternoon parades were dreadfully unsteady, for it's a time, you know, when a man wants solid ground to stand on. However, I purchased my company with some prize-money that fell in my way, and I always remember the marine service with gratitude. But this is dry work. I have put a bottle of sparkling madeira in my pocket, with a couple of glasses, which we will discuss, while we talk over more important matters. Thrust your hand into my right pocket; I have been used to dress to the front so long, that it comes mighty awkward to me to make this backward motion, as if it were into a cartridge box."

Manual, who had been at a loss how to construe the manner of the other, perceived at once a good deal of plain English in this request, and he dislodged one of Colonel Howard's dusty bottles, with a dexterity that denoted the earnestness of his purpose. Borroughcliffe had made a suitable provision of glasses; and, extracting the cork in a certain scientific manner, he tendered to his companion a bumper of the liquor, before another syllable was uttered by either of the expectants. The gentlemen concluded their draughts with a couple of smacks, that sounded not unlike the pistols of two practised duellists, though certainly a much less alarming noise, when the entertainer renewed the discourse.

"I like one of your musty-looking bottles, that is covered with dust and cobwebs, with a good Southern tan on it," he said. "Such liquor does not abide in the stomach, but it gets into the heart at once, and becomes blood in the beating of a pulse. But how soon I knew you! That sort of knowledge is the freemasonry of our craft. I knew you to be the man you are, the moment I laid eyes on you in what we call our guard-room; but I thought I would humor the old soldier who lives here, by letting him have the formula of the examination, as a sort of deference to his age and former rank. But I knew you the instant I saw you. I have seen you before!"

The theory of Borroughcliffe, in relation to the incorporation of wine with the blood might have been true in the case of the marine, whose whole frame appeared to undergo a kind of magical change by the experiment of drinking, which, the reader will understand, was diligently persevered in, while a drop remained in the bottle. The perspiration no longer rolled from his brow, neither did his throat manifest that uneasiness which had rendered such constant external application necessary; but he settled down into an air of cool but curious interest, which, in some measure, was the necessary concomitant of his situation.

"We may have met before, as I have been much in service, and yet I know not where you could have seen me," said Manual. "Were you ever a prisoner of war?"

"Hum! not exactly such an unfortunate devil; but a sort of conventional non-combatant. I shared the hardships, the glory, the equivocal victories (where we killed and drove countless numbers of rebels—who were not), and woe is me! the capitulation of Burgoyne. But let that pass—which was more than the Yankees would allow us to do. You know not where I could have seen you? I have seen you on parade, in the field, in battle and out of battle, in camp, in barracks, in short, everywhere but in a drawing-room. No, no; I have never seen you before this night in a drawing-room!"

Manual stared in a good deal of wonder and some uneasiness, at these confident assertions which promised to put his life in no little jeopardy; and it is to be supposed that the peculiar sensation about the throat was revived, as he made a heavy draft, before he said:

"You will swear to this—can you call me by name?"

"I will swear to it in any court in Christendom," said the dogmatical soldier; "and your name is—is—Fugleman!"

"If it is I'll be damned!" exclaimed the other, with exulting precipitation.

"Swear not!" said Borroughcliffe, with a solemn air; "for what mattereth an empty name! Call thyself by what appellation thou wilt, I know thee. Soldier is written on thy martial front; thy knee bendeth not; nay, I even doubt if the rebellious member bow in prayer—"

"Come, sir," interrupted Manual, a little sternly; "no more of this trifling, but declare your will at once. Rebellious member, indeed! These fellows will call the skies of America rebellious heavens shortly!"

"I like thy spirit, lad," returned the undisturbed Borroughcliffe; "it sits as gracefully on a soldier as his sash and gorget; but it is lost on an old campaigner. I marvel, however, that thou takest such umbrage at my slight attack on thy orthodoxy. I fear the fortress must be weak, where the outworks are defended with such a waste of unnecessary courage!"

"I know not why or wherefore you have paid me this visit, Captain Borroughcliffe," said Manual, with a laudible discretion, which prompted him to reconnoitre the other's views a little, before he laid himself more open; "if captain be your rank, and Borroughcliffe be your name. But this I do know, that if it be only to mock me in my present situation, it is neither soldier-like nor manly, and it is what, in other circumstances, might be attended by some hazard."

"Hum!" said the other, with his immovable coolness; "I see you set the wine down as nothing, though the king drinks not as good; for the plain reason that the sun of England cannot find its way through the walls of Windsor Castle as easily as the sun of Carolina can warm a garret covered with cedar shingles. But I like your spirit more and more. So draw yourself up in battle array, and let us have another charge at this black bottle, when I shall lay before your military eyes a plan of the whole campaign."

Manual first bestowed an inquiring glance on his companion; when, discovering no other expression than foolish cunning, which was fast yielding before the encroaching footsteps of stupid inebriety, he quietly placed himself in the desired position. The wine was drunk, when Borroughcliffe proceeded to open his communications more unreservedly.

"You are a soldier and I am a soldier. That you are a soldier, my orderly could tell; for the dog has both seen a campaign, and smelt villainous saltpetre, when compounded according to a wicked invention; but it required the officer to detect the officer. Privates do not wear such linen as this, which seemeth to me an unreasonably cool attire for the season; nor velvet stocks, with silver buckles; nor is there often the odorous flavor of sweet-scented pomatum to be discovered around their greasy locks. In short, thou art both soldier and officer."

"I confess it," said Manual; "I hold the rank of captain, and shall expect the treatment of one."

"I think I have furnished you with wine fit for a general," returned Borroughcliffe; "but have your own way. Now, it would be apparent to men whose faculties had not been rendered clear by such cordials as this dwelling aboundeth with, that when you officers journey through the island, clad in the uniform *incognitorum*, which, in your case, means the marine corps, that something is in the wind of more than usual moment. Soldiers owe their allegiance to their prince, and, next to him, to war, women, and wine. Of war, there is none in the realm; of women, plenty; but wine, I regret to say—that is, good wine, grows both scarce and dear. Do I speak to the purpose, comrade?"

"Proceed," said Manual, whose eyes were not less attentive than his ears, in a hope to discover whether his true character were understood.

"*En avant!* in plain English, forward march! Well, the difficulty lies between women and wine; which, when the former are pretty and the latter rich, is a very agreeable sort of an alternative. That it is not wine of which you are in quest, I must believe, my comrade captain, or you would not go on the adventure in such shabby attire. You will excuse me, but who would think of putting anything better than their port before a man in a pair of tarred trousers! No! no! Hollands, green-and-yellow Hollands, is a potation good enough to set before one of the present bearing."

"And yet I have met with him who has treated me to the choicest of the south-side madeira!"

"Know you the very side the precious fluid comes? That looks more in favor of the wine. But, after all, woman, dear, capricious woman, who one moment fancies she sees a hero in regimentals, and the next a saint in a cassock; and who always sees something admirable in a suitor, whether he be clad in tow or velvet—woman is at the bottom of this mysterious masquerading. Am I right, comrade?"

By this time Manual had discovered that he was safe, and he returned to the conversation with a revival of all his ready wits, which had been strangely paralyzed by his previous disorder in the region of the throat. First bestowing a wicked wink on his companion, and a look that would have outdone the wisest aspect of Solomon, he replied:

"Ah! woman has much to answer for!"

"I knew it," exclaimed Borroughcliffe; "and this confession only confirms me in the good opinion I have always entertained of myself. If his Majesty has any particular wish to close this American business, let him have a certain convention burnt and a nameless person promoted, and we shall see! But answer, as you love truth; is it a business of holy matrimony, or a mere dalliance with the sweets of Cupid?"

"Of honest wedlock," said Manual, with an air as serious as if Hymen already held him in his fetters.

" 'Tis honest! Is there money?"

"Is there money?" repeated Manual, with a sort of contemptuous echo. "Would a soldier part with his liberty but with his life, unless the chains were made of gold?"

"That's the true military doctrine!" cried the other; "faith, you have some discretion in your amphibious corps, I find! But why this disguise? are the 'seniors grave,' as well as 'potent and reverend?' Why this disguise, I again ask?"

"Why this disguise?" repeated Manual, coolly. "Is there any such thing as love in your regiment without disguise? With us it is a regular symptom of the disease."

"A most just and discreet description of the passion, my amphibious comrade!" said the English officer; "and the symptoms in your case are attended by some very malignant tokens. Does your mistress love tar?"

"No, but she loveth me; and, of course, whatever attire I choose to appear in."

"Still discreet and sagacious! and yet only a most palpable feint to avoid my direct attack. You have heard of such a place as Gretna Green, a little to the north of this, I dare say, my aquatic comrade. Am I right?"

"Gretna Green!" said Manual, a little embarrassed by his ignorance; "some parade-ground, I suppose?"

"Ay, for those who suffer under the fire of Master Cupid. A parade-ground! well, there is some artful simplicity in that! But all will not do with an old campaigner. It is a difficult thing to impose on an old soldier, my water-battery. Now listen and answer; and you shall see what it is to possess a discernment—therefore deny nothing. You are in love?"

"I deny nothing," said Manual, comprehending at once that this was the safest course.

"Your mistress is willing, and the money is ready, but the old people say, halt!"

"I am still mute."

" 'Tis prudent. You say march—Gretna Green is the object; and your flight is to be by water!"

"Unless I can make my escape by water, I shall never make it," said Manual, with another sympathetic movement with his hand to his throat.

"Keep mute; you need tell me nothing. I can see into a mystery that is as deep as a well, to-night. Your companions are hirelings; perhaps your shipmates; or men to pilot you on this expedition!"

"One is my shipmate, and the other is our pilot," said Manual, with more truth than usual.

"You are well provided. One thing more, and I shall become mute in my turn. Does she whom you seek lie in this house?"

"She does not; she lies but a short distance from this place; and I should be a happy fellow could I but once more put foot—"

"Eyes on her. Now listen, and you shall have your wish. You possess the ability to march yet, which, considering the lateness of the hour, is no trifling privilege; open that window—is it possible to descend from it?"

Manual eagerly complied, but he turned from the place in disappointment.

"It would be certain death to attempt the leap. The devil only could escape from it."

"So I should think," returned Borroughcliffe, dryly. "You must be content to pass for that respectable gentleman for the rest of your days, in St. Ruth's Abbey. For through that identical hole must you wing your flight on the pinions of love."

"But how? The thing is impossible."

"In imagination only. There is some stir, a good deal of foolish apprehension, and a great excess of idle curiosity, among certain tenants of this house, on your account. They fear the rebels, who, we all know, have not soldiers enough to do their work neatly at home, and who, of course, would never think of sending any here. You wish to be snug—I wish to serve a brother in distress. Through that window you must be supposed to fly—no matter how; while by following me you can pass the sentinel, and retire peaceably, like any other mortal, on your own two stout legs."

This was a result that exceeded all that Manual had anticipated from their amicable but droll dialogue; and the hint was hardly given before he threw on the garments that agitation had before rendered such encumbrances; and, in less time than we have taken to relate it, the marine was completely equipped for his departure. In the meantime, Captain Borroughcliffe raised himself to an extremely erect posture, which he maintained with the inflexibility of a rigid martinet. When he found himself established on his feet, the soldier intimated to his prisoner that he was ready to proceed. The door was instantly opened by Manual, and together they entered the gallery.

"Who comes there?" cried the sentinel, with a vigilance and vigor that he intended should compensate for his previous neglect of duty.

"Walk straight, that he may see you," said Borroughcliffe, with much philosophy.

"Who goes there?" repeated the sentinel, throwing his musket to a poise, with a rattling round that echoed along the naked walls.

"Walk crooked," added Borroughcliffe, "that if he fire he may miss."

"We shall be shot at, with this folly," muttered Manual. "We are friends, and your officer is one of us."

"Stand, friends—advance, officer, and give the countersign," said the sentinel.

"That is much easier said than done," returned his captain; "forward, Mr. Amphibious, you can walk like a postman—move to the front, and proclaim the magical word, 'loyalty'; 'tis a standing countersign, ready furnished to my hands by mine host, the colonel; your road is then clear before you—but hark—"

Manual made an eager step forward, when recollecting himself, he returned, and added: "My assistants, the seamen! I can do nothing without them."

"Lo! the keys are in the doors, ready for my admission," said the Englishman; "turn them, and bring out your forces."

Quick as thought, Manual was in the room of Griffith, to whom he briefly communicated the situation; when he reappeared in the passage, and then proceeded on a similar errand to the room of the pilot.

"Follow, and behave as usual," he whispered; "say not a word, but trust all to me."

The pilot arose, and obeyed these instructions without asking a question, with the most admirable coolness.

"I am now ready to proceed," said Manual, when they had joined Borroughcliffe.

During the short time occupied in these arrangements, the sentinel and his captain had stood looking at each other with great military exactitude, the former ambitious of manifesting his watchfulness, the latter awaiting the return of the marine. The captain now beckoned to Manual to advance and give the countersign.

"Loyalty," whispered Manual when he approached the sentinel. But the soldier had been allowed time to reflect; and, as he well understood the situation of his officer, he hesitated to allow the prisoner to pass. After a moment's pause, he said:

"Advance, friends." At this summons the whole party moved to the point of his bayonet, when the man continued: "The prisoners have the countersign, Captain Borroughcliffe, but I dare not let them pass."

"Why not?" asked the captain; "am I not here, sirrah? do you not know me?"

"Yes, sir, I know your honor and respect your honor; but I was posted here by my sergeant, and ordered not to let these men pass out on any account."

"That's what I call good discipline," said Borroughcliffe, with an exulting laugh; "I knew the lad would not mind me any more than that he would obey the orders of that lamp. Here are no slaves of the lamp, my amphibious comrade; drill ye your marines in this consummate style to niceties?"

"What means this trifling?" said the pilot, sternly.

"Ah! I thought I should turn the laugh on you," cried Manual, affecting to join in the mirth; "we know all these things well, and we practise them in our corps; but though the sentinel cannot know you, the sergeant will; so let him be called, and orders be given through him to the man on post, that we may pass out."

"Your throat grows uneasy, I see," said Borroughcliffe; "you crave another bottle of the generous fluid. Well, it shall be done. Sentinel, you can throw up yon window, and give a call to the sergeant."

"The outcry will ruin us," said the pilot in a whisper to Griffith.

"Follow me," said the young sailor. The sentinel was turning to execute the orders of his captain as Griffith spoke, when, springing forward, in an instant he wrenched the musket from his hands; a heavy blow with its butt felled the astonished soldier to the floor; then, poising his weapon, Griffith exclaimed:

"Forward! we can clear our own way now!"

"On!" said the pilot, leaping lightly over the prostrate soldier, a dagger gleaming in one hand, and a pistol presented in the other.

Manual was by his side in an instant, armed in a similar manner; and the three rushed together from the building, without meeting any one to oppose their flight.

Borroughcliffe was utterly unable to follow; and so astounded was he by this sudden violence, that several minutes passed before he was restored to the use of his speech, a faculty which seldom deserted him. The man had recov-

ered his senses and his feet, however; and the two stood gazing at each other in mute condolence. At length the sentinel broke the silence:

"Shall I give the alarm, your honor?"

"I rather think not, Peters. I wonder if there be any such thing as gratitude or good-breeding in the marine corps?"

"I hope your honor will remember that I did my duty, and that I was disarmed while executing your orders."

"I can remember nothing about it, Peters, except that it is rascally treatment, and such as I shall yet make this amphibious aquatic gentleman answer for. But lock the door—look as if nothing had happened, and—"

"Ah! your honor, that is not so easily done as your honor may please to think. I have not any doubt but there is the print of the breech of a musket stamped on my back and shoulders, as plainly to be seen as that light."

"Then look as you please; but hold your peace, sirrah. Here is a crown to buy a plaster. I heard the dog throw away your musket on the stairs—go seek it, and return to your post; and when you are relieved, act as if nothing had happened. I take the responsibility on myself."

The man obeyed; and, when he was once more armed, Borroughcliffe, a good deal sobered by the surprise, made the best of his way to his own apartment, muttering threats and execrations against the "corps of the marines and the whole race," as he called them, "of aquatic amphibii."

16

Away! away! the covey's fled the cover,
Put forth the dogs, and let the falcon fly—
I'll spend some leisure in the keen pursuit,
Nor longer waste my hours in sluggish quiet.

THE soldier passed the remainder of the night in the heavy sleep of a bacchanalian, and awoke late on the following morning, only when aroused by the entrance of his servant. When the customary summons had induced the captain to unclose his eyelids, he arose in his bed, and, after performing the usual operation of a diligent friction on his organs of vision, he turned sternly to his man, and remarked, with an ill-humor that seemed to implicate the innocent servant in the fault which his master condemned:

"I thought, sirrah, that I ordered Sergeant Drill not to let a drumstick touch a sheepskin while we quartered in the dwelling of this hospitable old colonel! Does the fellow despise my commands? or does he think the roll of a drum, echoing through the crooked passages of St. Ruth, a melody that is fit to disturb the slumbers of its inmates?"

"I believe, sir," returned the man, "it was the wish of Colonel Howard himself that on this occasion the sergeant should turn out the guard by the roll of the drum."

"The devil it was! I see the old fellow loves to tickle the drum of his own ear now and then with familiar sounds; but have you had a muster of the cattle from the farm-yard too, as well as a parade of the guard? I hear the trampling of feet, as if the old Abbey were a second ark, and all the beasts of the field were coming aboard of us!"

" 'Tis nothing but the party of dragoons from ——, who are wheeling in the court-yard, sir, where the colonel has gone out to receive them."

"Court-yard! light dragoons!" repeated Borroughcliffe, in amazement; "and has it come to this, that twenty stout fellows of the —th are not enough to guard such a rookery as this old Abbey, against the ghosts and northeast storms, but we must have horse to re-enforce us? Hum! I suppose some of these booted gentlemen have heard of this South Carolina madeira."

"Oh, no, sir!" cried his man; "it is only the party that Mr. Dillon went to seek last evening, after you saw fit, sir, to put the three pirates in irons."

"Pirates in irons!" said Borroughcliffe, again passing his hands over his eyes, though in a more reflecting manner than before; "ha! oh! I remember to have put three suspicious-looking rascals in the black hole, or some such place; but what can Mr. Dillon, or the light dragoons have to do with these fellows?"

"That we do not know, sir; but it is said below, sir, as some suspicions had fallen on their being conspirators and rebels from the colonies, and that they were great officers and Tories in disguise; some said that one was General Washington, and others that it was only three members of the Yankee Parliament, come over to get our good old English fashions to set themselves up with."

"Washington! Members of Congress! Go—go, simpleton, and learn how many these troopers muster and what halt they make; but stay, place my clothes near me. Now, do as I bid you, and if the dragoon-officer inquire for me, make my respects, and tell him I shall be with him soon. Go, fellow, go!"

When the man left the room, the captain, while he proceeded with the business of the toilet, occasionally gave utterance to the thoughts that crowded on his recollection, after the manner of a soliloquy:

"Ay! my commission to a half-pay ensigncy, that some of these lazy fellows, who must have a four-legged beast to carry them to the wars, have heard of the 'south side.' South side! I believe I must put an advertisement in the London *Gazette*, calling that amphibious soldier to an account. If he be a true man, he will not hide himself under his incognito, but will give me a meeting. If that should fail, damme, I'll ride across to Yarmouth, and call out the first of the mongrel breed that I fall in with. 'Sdeath! was ever such an insult practised on a gentleman and a soldier before? Would that I only knew his name! Why, if the tale should get abroad, I shall be the standing joke of the mess-table until some greater fool than myself can be found. It would cost me at least six duels to get rid of it. No, no; not a trigger will I pull in my own regiment about the silly affair; but I'll have a crack at some marine in very revenge; for that is no more than reasonable. That Peters! if the scoundrel should dare whisper anything of the manner in which he was stamped with the breech of a musket! I can't flog him for it; but if I don't make it up to him the first time he gives me a chance, I am ignorant of the true art of balancing regimental accounts."

By the time the recruiting officer had concluded this soliloquy, which affords a very fair exposition of the current of his thoughts, he was prepared to meet the new-comers, and he accordingly descended to the court-yard, as in duty bound, to receive them in his proper person. Borroughcliffe encountered his host in earnest conversation with a young man in cavalry uniform, in the principal entrance of the Abbey, and was greeted by the former with:

"A good-morning to you, my worthy guard and protector! here is rare news for your royal ears. It seems that our prisoners are enemies of the king in disguise; and, Cornet Fitzgerald—Captain Borroughcliffe, of the —th, permit me to make you acquainted with Mr. Fitzgerald, of the —th light dragoons." While the soldiers exchanged their salutations the old man continued: "The cornet has been kind enough to lead down a detachment of his troop to escort the rogues up to London, or some other place, where they will find enough good and loyal officers to form a court-martial that can authorize their execution as spies. Christopher Dillon, my worthy kinsman Kit, saw into their real characters at a glance; while you and I, like two unsuspecting boys, thought the rascals would have made fit men to serve the king. But Kit has an eye and a head that few enjoy like him, and I would that he might receive his dues at the English bar."

"It is to be desired, sir," said Borroughcliffe, with a grave aspect that was produced chiefly by his effort to give effect to his sarcasm, but a little, also, by the recollection of the occurrences that were yet to be explained; "but what reason has Mr. Christopher Dillon to believe that the three seamen are more or less than they seem?"

"I know not what; but a good and sufficient reason, I will venture my life," cried the colonel; "Kit is a lad for reasons, which you know is the foundation of his profession, and knows how to deliver them manfully in the proper place; but you know, gentlemen, that the members of the bar cannot assume the open and bold front that becomes a soldier, without often endangering the cause in which they are concerned. No, no; trust me, Kit has his reasons, and in good time will he deliver them."

"I hope, then," said the captain, carelessly, "that it may be found that we have had a proper watch on our charge, Colonel Howard; I think you told me the windows were too high for an escape in that direction, for I had no sentinel outside of the building."

"Fear nothing, my worthy friend," cried his host; "unless your men have slept, instead of watching, we have them safe; but, as it will be necessary to convey them away before any of the civil authority can lay hands on them, let us proceed to the rear and unkennel the dogs. A party of the horse might proceed at once with them to ——, while we are breaking our fasts. It would be no very wise thing to allow the civilians to deal with them, for they seldom have a true idea of the nature of the crime."

"Pardon me, sir," said the young officer of horse; "I was led to believe, by Mr. Dillon, that we might meet with a party of the enemy in some little force, and that I should find a pleasanter duty than that of constable; besides, sir, the laws of the realm guarantee to the subject a trial of his peers, and it is more than I dare do to carry the men to the barracks, without first taking them before a magistrate."

"Ay! you speak of loyal and dutiful subjects," said the colonel; "and, as respects them, doubtless, you are right; but such privileges are withheld from enemies and traitors."

"It must first be proved that they are such, before they can receive the treatment or the punishment that they merit," returned the young man, a little positively, who felt the more confidence, because he had only left the Temple the year before. "If I take charge of the men at all, it will be only to transfer them safely to the city authority."

"Let us go and see the prisoners," cried Borroughcliffe, with a view to terminate a discussion that was likely to wax warm, and which he knew to be useless; "perhaps they may quietly enroll themselves under the banners of our sovereign, when all other interference, save that of wholesome discipline, will become unnecessary."

"Nay, if they are of a rank in life to render such a step probable," returned the cornet, "I am well content that the matter should be settled. I trust, however, that Captain Borroughcliffe will consider that the —th light dragoons has some merit in this affair, and that we are far short of our numbers in the second squadron."

"We shall not be difficult at a compromise," returned the captain, "there is one apiece for us, and a toss of a guinea shall determine who has the third man. Sergeant! follow to deliver over your prisoners, and relieve your sentry."

As they proceeded, in compliance with this arrangement, to the building in the rear, Colonel Howard, who made one of the party, observed:

"I dispute not the penetration of Captain Borroughcliffe, but I understand from Mr. Christopher Dillon that there is reason to believe one of these men, at least, to be of a class altogether above that of a common soldier; in which case your plans may fall to the ground."

"And who does he deem the gentleman to be?" asked Borroughcliffe—"a Bourbon in disguise, or a secret representative of the rebel Congress?"

"Nay, nay: he said nothing more; my kinsman Kit keeps a close mouth whenever Dame Justice is about to balance her scales. There are men who may be said to have been born to be soldiers; of which number I should call the Earl Cornwallis, who makes such head against the rebels in the two Carolinas; others seem to be intended by Nature for divines and saints on earth, such as their graces of York and Canterbury; while another class appear as if it were impossible for them to behold things unless with discriminating, impartial, and disinterested eyes; to which, I should say, belong my Lord Chief Justice Mansfield, and my kinsman, Mr. Christopher Dillon. I trust, gentlemen, that, when the royal arms have crushed this rebellion, his majesty's ministers will see the propriety of extending the dignity of the peerage to the colonies, as a means of reward to the loyal, and a measure of policy to prevent further disaffection, in which case I hope to see my kinsman decorated with the ermine of justice bordering the mantle of a peer."

"Your expectations, my excellent sir, are right reasonable; as I doubt not your kinsman will become at some future day, that which he is not at present, unhappily for his deserts, right honorable," said Borroughcliffe. "But be of good heart, sir; from what I have seen of his merits, I doubt not that the law will yet have its revenue in due season, and that we shall be properly edified and instructed how to attain elevation in life, by the future exaltation of Mr. Christopher Dillon; though by what title he is to be then known, I am at a loss to say."

Colonel Howard was too much occupied with his own *ex-parte* views of the war and things in general, to observe the shrewd looks that were exchanged between the soldiers; but he answered with perfect simplicity:

"I have reflected much on that point, and have come to the opinion that, as he has a small estate on that river, he should cause his first barony to be known by the title of 'Pedee.'"

"Barony!" echoed Borroughcliffe; "I trust the new nobles of a new world will disdain the old, worn-out distinctions of a hackneyed universe—eschew all baronies, mine host, and cast earldoms and dukedoms to the shades. The immortal Locke has unlocked his fertile mind to furnish you with appellations suited to the originality of your condition and the nature of your country. Ah! here comes the Cacique of Pedee, in his proper person!"

As Borroughcliffe spoke, they were ascending the flight of stone steps which led to the upper apartments, where the prisoners were still supposed to be confined; and, at the same moment, the sullen, gloomy features of Dillon were seen as he advanced along the lower passage, with an expression of malicious exultation hovering above his dark brow, that denoted his secret satisfaction. As the hours passed away, the period had come round when the man who had been present at the escape of Griffith and his friends, was again posted to perform the duty of sentinel. As this soldier well knew the situation of his trust, he was very coolly adjusted, with his back against the wall, endeavoring to compensate himself for his disturbed slumbers during the night, when the sounds of the approaching footsteps warned him to assume the appearance of watchfulness.

"How, now, fellow!" cried Borroughcliffe; "what have you to say to your charge?"

"I believe the men sleep, your honor; for I have heard no noises from the rooms since I relieved the last sentinel."

"The lads are weary, and are right to catch what sleep they can in their comfortable quarters," returned the captain. "Stand to your arms, sirrah! and throw back your shoulders; and do not move like a crab, or a train-band corporal; do you not see an officer of horse coming up? Would you disgrace your regiment?"

"Ah! your honor, Heaven only knows whether I shall ever get my shoulders even again."

"Buy another plaster," said Borroughcliffe, slipping a shilling into his hand; "observe, you know nothing but your duty."

"Which is, your honor—"

"To mind me, and be silent. But here comes the sergeant with his guard; he will relieve you."

The rest of the party stopped at the other end of the gallery, to allow a few files of soldiers who were led by the orderly to pass them, when they all moved toward the prisoners in a body. The sentinel was relieved in due military style; when Dillon placed his hand on one of the doors, and said, with a malicious sneer:

"Open here first, Mr. Sergeant; this cage holds the man we most want."

"Softly, softly, my lord chief-justice, and most puissant cacique," said the captain; "the hour has not yet come to empanel a jury of fat yeomen, and no man must interfere with my boys but myself."

"The rebuke is harsh, I must observe, Captain Borroughcliffe," said the colonel; "but I pardon it because it is military. No, no, Kit; these nice points must be left to martial usages. Be not impatient, my cousin; I doubt not the hour will come when you shall hold the scales of justice, and satisfy your loyal longings on many a traitor. Zounds! I could almost turn executioner myself in such a cause!"

"I can curb my impatience, sir," said Dillon, with hypocritical meekness, and great self-command, though his eyes were gleaming with savage exultation. "I beg pardon of Captain Borroughcliffe, if, in my desire to render the civil authority superior to the military, I have trespassed on your customs."

"You see, Borroughcliffe!" exclaimed the colonel, exultingly, "the lad is ruled by an instinct in all matters of law and justice. I hold it to be impossible that a man thus endowed can ever become a disloyal subject. But our breakfast waits, and Mr. Fitzgerald has breathed his horse this cool morning; let us proceed at once to the examination."

Borroughcliffe motioned to the sergeant to open the door, and the whole party entered the vacant room.

"Your prisoner has escaped!" cried the cornet, after a single moment employed in making sure of the fact.

"Never! it must not, shall not be!" cried Dillon, quivering with rage, as he glanced his eyes furiously around the apartment; "here has been treachery, and foul treason to the king!"

"By whom committed, Mr. Christopher Dillon?" said Borroughcliffe, knitting his brow, and speaking in a suppressed tone. "Dare you, or any man living, charge treason to the —th?"

A very different feeling from rage appeared now to increase the shivering propensities of the future judge, who at once perceived it was necessary to moderate his passion; and he returned, as it were by magic, to his former plausible and insinuating manner, as he replied:

"Colonel Howard will understand the cause of my warm feelings, when I tell him that this very room contained, last night, that disgrace to his name and country, as well as traitor to his king, Edward Griffith, of the rebel navy."

"What!" exclaimed the colonel, starting, "has that recreant youth dared to pollute the threshold of St. Ruth with his footstep? But you dream, Kit; there would be too much hardihood in the act."

"It appears not, sir," returned the other; "for, though in this very apartment he most certainly was, he is here no longer. And yet from this window, though open, escape would seem to be impossible, even with much assistance."

"If I thought that the contumelious boy had dared to be guilty of such an act of gross impudence," cried the colonel, "I should be tempted to resume my arms, in my old age, to punish his effrontery. What! is it not enough that he entered my dwelling in the colony, availing himself of the distraction of the times, with an intent to rob me of my choicest jewel—ay? gentlemen, even of my brother Harry's daughter—but that he must also invade this hallowed island with a like purpose, thus thrusting his treason, as it were, into the presence of his abused prince! No, no, Kit, thy loyalty misleads thee; he has never dared to do the deed!"

"Listen, sir, and you shall be convinced," returned the pliant Christopher. "I do not wonder at your unbelief; but as a good testimony is the soul of justice, I cannot resist its influence. You know that two vessels, corresponding in appearance to the two rebel cruisers that annoyed us so much in the Carolinas, have been seen on the coast for several days, which induced us to beg the protection of Captain Borroughcliffe. Three men are found, the day succeeding that on which we hear that these vessels came within the shoals, stealing through the grounds of St. Ruth, in sailors' attire. They are arrested, and in the voice of one of them, sir, I immediately detected that of the traitor Griffith. He was disguised, it is true, and cunningly so; but when a man has devoted his whole life to the business of investigating truth," he added, with an air of much modesty, "it is difficult to palm any disguise on his senses."

Colonel Howard was strongly impressed with the probability of these conjectures, and the closing appeal confirmed him immediately in his kinsman's opinion, while Borroughcliffe listened with deep interest to the speakers, and more than once bit his lip with vexation. When Dillon concluded, the soldier exclaimed:

"I'll swear there was a man among them who has been used to the drill."

"Nothing more probable, my worthy friend," said Dillon; "for, as the landing was never made without some evil purpose, rely on it, he came not unguarded or unprotected. I dare say, the three were all officers, and one of them might have been of the marines. That they had assistance is certain, and it was because I felt assured they had a force secreted at hand, that I went in quest of the re-enforcement."

There was so much plausibility, and, in fact, so much truth in all this, that conviction was unwillingly admitted by Borroughcliffe, who walked aside a moment, to conceal the confusion which, in spite of his ordinary inflexibility of countenance, he felt was manifesting itself in his rubric visage, while he muttered:

"The amphibious dog! he was a soldier, but a traitor and an enemy. No doubt he will have a marvellous satisfaction in delighting the rebellious ears of his messmates by rehearsing the manner in which he poured cold water down the back of one Borroughcliffe, of the —th, who was amusing him, at the same time, by pouring good, rich, south-side madeira down his own rebellious throat. I have a good mind to exchange my scarlet coat for a blue-jacket, on purpose to meet the sly rascal on the other element, where we can discuss the matter over again. Well, sergeant, do you find the other two?"

"They are gone together, your honor," returned the orderly who just then re-entered from an examination of the other apartments; "and, unless the evil one helped them off, it's a mysterious business to me."

"Colonel Howard," said Borroughcliffe, gravely, "your precious south-side cordial must be banished from the board, regularly with the cloth, until I have my revenge; for satisfaction of this insult is mine to claim, and I seek it this instant. Go, Drill; detain a guard for the protection of the house, and feed the rest of your command, then beat the general, and we will take the field. Ay! my worthy veteran host, for the first time since the days of the unlucky Charles Stuart, there shall be a campaign in the heart of England."

"Ah! rebellion, rebellion! accursed, unnatural, unholy rebellion, caused the calamity then and now!" exclaimed the colonel.

"Had I not better take a hasty refreshment for my men and their horses?" asked the cornet, "and then make a sweep for a few miles along the coast? It may be my luck to encounter the fugitives, or some part of their force."

"You have anticipated my very thoughts," returned Borroughcliffe. "The Cacique of Pedee may close the gates of St. Ruth, and, by barring the windows, and arming the servants, he can make a very good defence against an attack, should they think proper to assail our fortress; after he has repulsed them, leave it to me to cut off their retreat."

Dillon but little relished this proposal; for he thought an attempt to storm the Abbey would be the most probable course adopted by Griffith, in order to rescue his mistress; and the jurist had none of the spirit of a soldier in his composition. In truth, it was this deficiency that had induced him to depart in person, the preceding night, in quest of the re-enforcement, instead of sending an express on the errand. But the necessity of devising an excuse for a change in this dangerous arrangement was obviated by Colonel Howard, who explained, as soon as Borroughcliffe concluded his plan:

"To me, Captain Borroughcliffe, belongs, of right, the duty of defending St. Ruth, and it shall be no boy's play to force my works; but Kit would rather try his chance in the open field, I know. Come, let us to our breakfast, and then he shall mount, and act as a guide to the horse, along the difficult passes of the seashore."

"To breakfast then let it be," cried the captain; "I distrust not my new commander of the fortress; and in the field the cacique forever! We follow you, my worthy host."

This arrangement was hastily executed in all its parts. The gentlemen swallowed their meal in the manner of men who ate only to sustain nature, and as a duty; after which the whole house became a scene of bustling activity. The troops were mustered and paraded; Borroughcliffe, setting apart a guard for the building, placed himself at the head of the remainder of his little party, and they moved out of the courtyard in open order, and at quick time. Dillon joyfully beheld himself mounted on one of the best of Colonel Howard's hunters, where he knew that he had the control, in a great measure, of his own destiny; his bosom throbbing with a powerful desire to destroy Griffith, while he entertained a lively wish to effect his object without incurring any personal risk. At his side was the young cornet, seated with practised grace in his saddle, who, after giving time for the party of foot-soldiers to clear the premises, glanced his eye along the few files he led, and then gave the word to move. The little division of horse wheeled briskly into open column, and, the officer touching his hat to Colonel Howard, they dashed through the gateway together, and pursued their route towards the sea-side at a hand-gallop.

The veteran lingered a few minutes, while the clattering of hoofs was to be heard, or the gleam of arms was visible, to hear and gaze on sounds and sights that he still loved; after which, he proceeded, in person, and not without a secret enjoyment of the excitement, to barricade the doors and windows, with an undaunted determination of making, in case of need, a stout defence.

St. Ruth lay but a short two miles from the ocean, to which the numerous roads led, through the grounds of the Abbey, which extended to the shore. Along one of these paths Dillon conducted his party, until, after a few minutes of hard riding, they approached the cliffs, when, posting his troops under cover of a little copse, the cornet advanced with his guide to the verge of the perpendicular rocks, whose bases were washed by the foam that still whitened the waters from the surges of the subsiding sea.

The gale had broken before the escape of the prisoners; and, as the power of the eastern tempest had gradually diminished, a light current from the south, that blew directly along the land, prevailed; and, though the ocean still rolled in fearful billows, their surfaces were smooth, and they were becoming, at each moment, less precipitous and more regular. The eyes of the horsemen were cast in vain over the immense expanse of water that was glistening brightly under the rays of the sun, which had just risen from its bosom, in quest of some object, or distant sail, that might confirm their suspicions, or relieve their doubts. But everything of that description appeared to have avoided the dangerous navigation during the violence of the late tempest, and Dillon was withdrawing his eyes in disappointment from the vacant view, when, as they fell toward the shore, he beheld that which caused him to exclaim:

"There they go! and by Heaven, they will escape!"

The cornet looked in the direction of the other's finger, when he beheld, at a short distance from the land, and apparently immediately under his feet, a little boat that looked like a dark shell upon the water, rising and sinking amid the waves, as if the men it obviously contained were resting on their oars in idle expectation.

" 'Tis they!" continued Dillon; "or, what is more probable, it is their boat waiting to convey them to their vessel; no common business would induce seamen to lie in this careless manner within such a narrow distance of the surf."

"And what is to be done? They cannot be made to feel horse where they are; nor would the muskets of the foot be of any use. A light three-pounder would do its work handsomely on them!"

The strong desire which Dillon entertained to intercept, or rather to destroy, the party, rendered him prompt at expedients. After a moment of musing, he replied:

"The runaways must yet be on the land; and by scouring the coast, and posting men at proper intervals, their retreat can easily be prevented; in the meantime I will ride under the spur to —— Bay, where one of his majesty's cutters now lies at anchor. It is but half an hour of hard riding, and I can be on board of her. The wind blows directly in her favor; and, if we can once bring her down behind that headland, we shall infallibly cut off or sink these midnight depredators."

"Off, then!" cried the cornet, whose young blood was boiling for a skirmish; "you will at least drive them to the shore, where I can deal with them."

The words were hardly uttered before Dillon, after galloping furiously along the cliffs, and turning short into a thick wood that lay in his route, was out of sight. The loyalty of this gentleman was altogether of a calculating nature, and was intimately connected with what he considered his fealty to himself. He believed that the possession of Miss Howard's person and fortune were advantages that would much more than counter-balance any elevation that he was likely to obtain by the revolution of affairs in his native colony. He considered Griffith as the only natural obstacle to his success; and he urged his horse forward with a desperate determination to work the ruin of the young sailor before another sun had set. When a man labors in an evil cause, with such feelings, and with such incentives, he seldom slights or neglects his work; and Mr. Dillon, accordingly, was on board the Alacrity several minutes short of the time in which he had promised to perform the distance.

The plain old seaman who commanded the cutter listened to his tale with cautious ears, and examined into the state of the weather, and other matters connected with his duty, with the slow and deliberate decision of one who had never done much to acquire a confidence in himself, and who had been but niggardly rewarded for the little he had actually performed.

As Dillon was urgent, however, and the day seemed propitious, he at length decided to act as he was desired, and the cutter was accordingly gotten under way.

A crew of something less than fifty men moved with no little of their commander's deliberation; but as the little vessel rounded the point behind which she had been anchored, her guns were cleared, and the usual preparations were completed for immediate and actual service.

Dillon, sorely against his will, was compelled to continue on board, in order to point out the place where the unsuspecting boatmen were expected to be entrapped. Everything being ready, when they had gained a safe distance from the land, the Alacrity was kept away before the wind, and gliding along the shore with a swift and easy progress, that promised a speedy execution of the business in which her commander had embarked.

17

Polonius: *Very like a whale.*

SHAKESPEARE

NOTWITHSTANDING the object of their expedition was of a public nature, the feelings which had induced both Griffith and Barnstable to accompany the pilot with so much willingness, it will easily be seen, were entirely personal. The short intercourse that he had maintained with his associates enabled the mysterious leader of their party to understand the characters of his two principal officers so thoroughly as to induce him, when he landed with the purpose of reconnoitring to ascertain whether the objects of his pursuit still held their determination to assemble at the appointed hour, to choose Griffith and Manual as his only associates, leaving Barnstable in command of his own vessel, to await their return and to cover their retreat. A good deal of argument, and some little of the authority of his superior officer, was necessary to make Barnstable quietly acquiesce in this arrangement; but as his good sense told him that nothing should be unnecessarily hazarded until the moment to strike the final blow had arrived, he became gradually more resigned; taking care, however, to caution Griffith to reconnoitre the Abbey while his companion was reconnoitring —— house. It was the strong desire of Griffith to comply with this injunction, which carried them a little out of their proper path, and led to the consequences that we have partly related. The evening of that day was the time when the pilot intended to complete his enterprise, thinking to entrap his game while enjoying the festivities that usually succeeded their sports; and an early hour in the morning was appointed, when Barnstable should appear at the nearest point to the Abbey to take off his countrymen, in order that they might be as little as possible subjected to the gaze of their enemies by daylight. If they failed to arrive at the appointed time, his instructions were to return to his schooner, which lay snugly embayed in a secret and retired haven, that but few ever approached either by land or water.

While the young cornet still continued gazing at the whale-boat (for it was the party from the schooner that he saw), the hour expired for the appearance of Griffith and his companions; and Barnstable reluctantly determined to comply with the letter of his instructions, and leave them to their own sagacity and skill to regain the Ariel. The boat had been suffered to ride in the edge of the surf, since the appearance of the sun; and the eyes of her crew were kept anxiously fixed on the cliffs, though in vain, to discover the signal that was to call them to the place of landing. After looking at his watch for the twentieth time, and as often casting glances of uneasy dissatisfaction toward the shore, the lieutenant exclaimed:

"A charming prospect this, Master Coffin, but rather too much poetry in it for your taste; I believe you relish no land that is of a harder consistency than mud!"

"I was born on the waters, sir," returned the cockswain, from his snug abode, where he was bestowed with his usual economy of room, "and it's according to all things for a man to love his native soil. I'll not deny, Captain Barnstable, but I would rather drop my anchor on a bottom that won't broom a keel, though, at the same time, I harbor no great malice against dry land."

"I shall never forgive it myself, if any accident has befallen Griffith in this excursion," rejoined the lieutenant; "his pilot may be a better man on the water than on *terra firma*, Long Tom."

The cockswain turned his solemn visage, with an extraordinary meaning, toward his commander, before he replied:

"For as long a time as I have followed the waters, sir, and that has been ever since I've drawn my rations, seeing that I was born while the boat was crossing Nantucket shoals, I've never known a pilot come off in greater need than the one we fell in with when we made that stretch or two on the land, in the dog-watch of yesterday."

"Ay! the fellow has played his part like a man; the occasion was great, and it seems that he was quite equal to his work."

"The frigate's people tell me, sir, that he handled the ship like a top," continued the cockswain; "but she is a ship that is a nateral inimy of the bottom!"

"Can you say as much for this boat, Master Coffin?" cried Barnstable; "keep her out of the surf, or you'll have us rolling in upon the beach, presently, like an empty water-cask; you must remember that we cannot all wade, like yourself, in two-fathom water."

The cockswain cast a cool glance at the crests of foam that were breaking over the tops of the billows, within a few yards of where their boat was riding, and called aloud to his men:

"Pull a stroke or two; away with her into dark water."

The drop of the oars resembled the movements of a nice machine, and the light boat skimmed along the water like a duck, that approaches to the very brink of some imminent danger, and then avoids it, at the most critical moment, apparently without an effort. While this necessary movement was making, Barnstable arose and surveyed the cliffs with keen eyes, and then, turning once more, in disappointment from his search, he said:

"Pull more from the land, and let her run down at an easy stroke to the schooner. Keep a lookout at the cliffs, boys; it is possible that they are stowed in some of the holes in the rocks, for it's no daylight business they are on."

The order was promptly obeyed, and they had glided along for nearly a mile in this manner, in the most profound silence, when suddenly the stillness was broken by a heavy rush of air, and a dash of the water, seemingly at no great distance from them.

"By Heaven, Tom," cried Barnstable, starting, "there is the blow of a whale!"

"Ay, ay, sir," returned the cockswain, with undisturbed composure; "here is his spout not half a mile to seaward; the easterly gale has driven the creater to leeward, and he begins to find himself in shoal water. He's been sleeping, while he should have been working to windward!"

"The fellow takes it coolly, too; he's in no hurry to get an offing!"

"I rather conclude, sir" said the cockswain, rolling over his tobacco in his mouth, very composedly, while his little sunken eyes began to twinkle with pleasure at the sight, "the gentleman has lost his reckoning, and don't know which way to head to take himself back into blue water."

" 'Tis a fin-back!" exclaimed the lieutenant; "he will soon make headway, and be off."

"No, sir, 'tis a right whale," answered Tom; "I saw his spout; he threw up a pair of as pretty rainbows as a Christian would wish to look at. He's a raal oil-butt, that fellow!"

Barnstable laughed, turned himself away from the tempting sight, and tried to look at the cliffs; and then unconsciously bent his longing eyes again on the sluggish animal, who was throwing his huge carcass, at times, for many feet from the water, in idle gambols. The temptation for sport, and the recollection of his early habits, at length prevailed over his anxiety in behalf of his friends, and the young officer inquired of his cockswain:

"Is there any whale-line in the boat, to make fast to that harpoon which you bear about with you in fair weather or foul?"

"I never trust the boat from the schooner without part of a shot, sir," returned the cockswain; "there is something nateral in the sight of a tub to my old eyes."

Barnstable looked at his watch, and again at the cliffs, when he exclaimed, in joyous tones:

"Give strong way, my hearties! There seems nothing better to be done; let us have a stroke of a harpoon at this impudent rascal!"

The men shouted spontaneously, and the old cockswain suffered his solemn visage to relax into a small laugh, while the whale-boat sprang forward like a courser for the goal. During the few minutes they were pulling toward their game, Long Tom arose from his crouching attitude in the stern-sheets, and transferred his huge form to the bows of the boat, where he made such preparations to strike the whale as the occasion required. The tub, containing about half of a whale-line, was placed at the feet of Barnstable, who had been preparing an oar to steer with in place of the rudder, which was unshipped, in order that if necessary the boat might be whirled round when not advancing.

Their approach was utterly unnoticed by the monster of the deep, who continued to amuse himself with throwing the water in two circular spouts high into the air, occasionally flourishing the broad flukes of his tail with a graceful but terrific force, until the hardy seamen were within a few hundred feet from him, when he suddenly cast his head downward, and, without an apparent effort, reared his immense body for many feet above the water, waving his tail violently, and producing a whizzing noise that sounded like the rushing of winds.

The cockswain stood erect, poising his harpoon, ready for the blow; but when he beheld the creature assume this formidable attitude, he waved his hand to his commander, who instantly signed to his men to cease rowing. In this situation the sportsmen rested for a few moments, while the whale struck several blows on the water in rapid succession, the noise of which re-echoed along the cliffs, like the hollow reports of so many cannon. After this wanton exhibition of his terrible strength, the monster sank again into his native element, and slowly disappeared from the eyes of his pursuers.

"Which way did he head, Tom?" cried Barnstable, the moment the whale was out of sight.

"Pretty much up and down, sir," returned the cockswain, whose eye was gradually brightening with the excitement of the sport; "he'll soon run his nose against the bottom if he stands long on that course, and will be glad to get another snuff of pure air. Send her a few fathoms to starboard, sir, and I promise we shall not be out of his track."

The conjecture of the experienced old seaman proved true; for in a few moments the water broke near them, and another spout was cast into the air, when the huge animal rushed for half his length in the same direction, and fell on the sea with a turbulence and foam equal to that which is produced by the launching of a vessel for the first time into its proper element. After this evolution the whale rolled heavily, and seemed to rest from further efforts.

His slightest movements were closely watched by Barnstable and his cockswain, and when he was in a state of comparative rest, the former gave a signal to his crew to ply their oars once more. A few long and vigorous strokes sent the boat directly up to the broadside of the whale, with its bows pointing toward one of the fins, which was at times, as the animal yielded sluggishly to the action of the waves, exposed to view. The cockswain poised his harpoon with much precision, and then darted it from him with a violence that buried the iron in the blubber of their foe. The instant the blow was made Long Tom shouted with singular earnestness:

"Starn all!"

"Stern all!" echoed Barnstable; when the obedient seamen, by united efforts, forced the boat in a backward direction, beyond the reach of any blow from their formidable antagonist. The alarmed animal, however, meditated no such resistance; ignorant of his own power, and of the insignificance of his enemies, he sought refuge in flight. One moment of stupid surprise succeeded the entrance of the iron, when he cast his huge tail into the air with a violence that threw the sea around him into increased commotion, and then disappeared with the quickness of lightning amid a cloud of foam.

"Snub him!" shouted Barnstable; "hold on, Tom, he rises already."

"Ay, ay, sir," replied the composed cockswain, seizing the line, which was running out of the boat with a velocity that rendered such a manœuvre rather hazardous, and causing it to yield more gradually round the large loggerhead that was placed in the bows of the boat for that purpose. Presently the line stretched forward, and rising to the surface with tremulous vibrations, it indicated the direction in which the animal might be expected to reappear. Barnstable had cast the bows of the boat toward that point, before the terrified and wounded victim rose once more to the surface, whose time was, however, no longer wasted in his sports, but who cast the waters aside, as he forced his way with prodigious velocity along the surface. The boat was dragged violently in his wake, and cut through the billows with a terrific rapidity, that at moments appeared to bury the slight fabric in the ocean. When Long Tom beheld his victim throwing his spouts on high again, he pointed with exultation to the jetting fluid, which was streaked with the deep red of blood, and cried.

"Ay, I've touched the fellow's life! it must be more than two feet of blubber that stops my iron from reaching the life of any whale that ever sculled the ocean!"

"I believe you have saved yourself the trouble of using the bayonet you have rigged for a lance," said his commander, who entered into the sport with all the ardor of one whose youth had been chiefly passed in such pursuits. "Feel your line, Master Coffin; can we haul alongside of our enemy? I like not the course he is steering, as he tows us from the schooner."

" 'Tis the creater's way, sir," said the cockswain; "you know they need the air in their nostrils, when they run, the same as a man—but lay hold, boys, and let's haul up to him."

The seaman now seized the whale-line, and slowly drew their boat to within a few feet of the tail of the fish, whose progress became sensibly less rapid, as he grew weak with the loss of blood. In a few minutes he stopped running, and appeared to roll uneasily on the water, as if suffering the agony of death.

"Shall we pull in and finish him, Tom?" cried Barnstable; "a few sets from your bayonet will do it."

The cockswain stood examining his game with cool discretion, and replied to his interrogator:

"No, sir, no—he's going into his flurry; there's no occasion for disgracing ourselves by using a soldier's weapon in taking a whale. Starn off, sir, starn off, the creater's in his flurry!"

The warning of the prudent cockswain was promptly obeyed, and the boat cautiously drew off to a distance, leaving to the animal a clear space while under its dying agonies. From a state of perfect rest, the terrible monster threw its tail on high, as when in sport, but its blows were trebled in rapidity and violence, till all was hid from view by a pyramid of foam, that was deeply dyed with blood. The roarings of the fish were like the bellowing of a herd of bulls; and to one who was ignorant of the fact, it would have appeared as if a thousand monsters were engaged in deadly combat, behind the bloody mist that obstructed the view. Gradually, these efforts subsided, and when the discolored water again settled down to the long and regular swell of the ocean, the fish was seen, exhausted, and yielding passively to his fate. As life departed, the enormous black mass rolled to one side; and, when the white and glistening skin of the belly became apparent, the seamen well knew that their victory was achieved.

"What's to be done now?" said Barnstable as he stood and gazed with a diminished excitement at their victim; "he will yield no food, and his carcass will probably drift to land, and furnish our enemies with the oil."

"If I had but the creater in Boston Bay," said the cockswain, "it would prove the making of me; but such is my luck forever! Pull up, at any rate, and let me get my harpoon and line—the English shall never get them while old Tom Coffin can blow."

"Don't speak too fast," said the strokesman of the boat; "whether he get your iron or not, here he comes in chase!"

"What mean you, fellow?" cried Barnstable.

"Captain Barnstable can look for himself," returned the seaman, "and tell whether I speak truth."

The young sailor turned and saw the Alacrity bearing down before the wind, with all her sails set, as she rounded a headland but a short half league to windward of the place where the boat lay.

"Pass that glass to me," said the captain, with steady composure. "This promises us work in one of two ways; if she be armed, it has become our turn to run; if not, we are strong enough to carry her."

A very brief survey made the experienced officer acquainted with the true character of the vessel in sight; and, replacing the glass with much coolness, he said:

"That fellow shows long arms and ten teeth, besides King George's pennant from his topmast-head. Now, my lads, you are to pull for your lives; for, whatever may be the notions of Master Coffin on the subject of his harpoon, I have no inclination to have my arms pinioned by John Bull, though his majesty himself put on the irons."

The men well understood the manner and meaning of their commander; and, throwing aside their coats, they applied themselves in earnest to their task. For half an hour a profound silence reigned in the boat, which made an amazing progress. But many circumstances conspired to aid the cutter; she had a fine breeze, with smooth water, and a strong tide in her favor; and at the expiration of the time we have mentioned, it was but too apparent that the distance between the pursued and pursuers was lessened nearly half. Barnstable preserved his steady countenance, but there was an expression of care gathering around his dark brow, which indicated that he saw the increasing danger of their situation.

"That fellow has long legs, Master Coffin," he said, in a cheerful tone; "your whale-line must go overboard, and the fifty oar must be handled by your delicate hands."

Tom arose from his seat, and, proceeding forward, he cast the tub and its contents together into the sea, when he seated himself at the bow oar, and bent his athletic frame with amazing vigor to the task.

"Ah! there is much of your philosophy in that stroke, Long Tom," cried his commander. "Keep it up, boys; and if we gain nothing else, we shall at least gain time for deliberation. Come, Master Coffin, what think you? We have three resources before us; let us hear which is your choice; first, we can turn and fight and be sunk; secondly, we can pull to the land, and endeavor to make good our retreat to the schooner in that manner; and, thirdly, we can head to the shore, and possibly, by running under the guns of that fellow, get the wind of him, and keep the air in our nostrils, after the manner of the whale. D——n the whale! but for the tow the black rascal gave us, we should have been out of sight of this rover!"

"If we fight," said Tom, with quite as much composure as his commander manifested, "we shall be taken or sunk; if we land, sir, I shall be taken, for one man, as I never could make any headway on dry ground, and if we try to get the wind of him by pulling under the cliffs, we shall be cut off by a parcel of lubbers that I can see running along their edges, hoping, I dare say, that they shall be able to get a skulking shot at a boat's crew of honest sea-faring men."

"You speak with as much truth as philosophy, Tom," said Barnstable, who saw his slender hopes of success curtailed by the open appearance of the horse and foot on the cliffs. "These Englishmen have not slept the last night, and I fear Griffith and Manual will fare but badly. That fellow brings a capful of wind down with him—'tis just his play, and he walks like a race-horse. Ha! he begins to be in earnest!"

While Barnstable was speaking, a column of white smoke was seen issuing from the bows of the cutter; and, as the report of a cannon was wafted to their ears, the shot was seen skipping from wave to wave, tossing the water in spray, and flying to a considerable distance beyond them.

The seamen cast cursory glances in the direction of the passing ball, but it produced no manifest effect in either their conduct or appearance. The cockswain, who scanned its range with an eye of more practice than the rest, observed: "That's a lively piece for its metal, and it speaks with a good clear voice; but if they should hear it aboard the Ariel, the man who fired it will be sorry it wasn't born dumb."

"You are the prince of philosophers, Master Coffin!" cried Barnstable; "there is some hope in that; let the Englishmen talk away, and, my life on it, the Ariel don't believe it is thunder; hand me a musket—I'll draw another shot."

The piece was given to Barnstable, who discharged it several times, as if to taunt their enemies; and the scheme was completely successful. Goaded by the insults, the cutter discharged gun after gun at the little boat, throwing the shot frequently so near as to wet her crew with the spray, but without injuring them in the least. The failure of these attempts of the enemy excited the mirth of the reckless seamen, instead of creating any alarm; and whenever a shot came nearer than common, the cockswain would utter some such expression as:

"A ground swell, a long shot, and a small object make a clean target"; or, "A man must squint straight to hit a boat."

As, notwithstanding their unsuccessful gunnery, the cutter was constantly gaining on the whale-boat, there was a prospect of a speedy termination of the chase, when the report of a cannon was thrown back like an echo from one of the Englishman's discharges, and Barnstable and his companions had the pleasure of seeing the Ariel stretching slowly out from the little bay where she had passed the night, with the smoke of the gun of defiance curling above her taper masts.

A loud and simultaneous shout of rapture was given by the lieutenant and all his boat's crew at this cheering sight, while the cutter took in all her light sails, and, as she hauled up on a wind, she fired a whole broadside at the successful fugitives. Many stands of grape, with several round shot, flew by the boat, and fell upon the water near them, raising a cloud of foam, but without doing any injury.

"She dies in a flurry," said Tom, casting his eyes at the little vortex into which the boat was then entering.

"If her commander be a true man," cried Barnstable, "he'll not leave us on so short an acquaintance. Give way my souls! give way! I would see more of this loquacious cruiser."

The temptation for exertion was great, and it was not disregarded by the men; in a few minutes the whale boat reached the schooner, when the crew of the latter received their commander and his companions with shouts and cheers that rang across the waters and reached the ears of the disappointed spectators on the verge of the cliffs.

18

Thus guided on their course they bore,
Until they neared the main-land shore;
When frequent on the hollow blast
Wild shouts of merriment were cast.

Lord of the Isles

THE joyful shouts and hearty cheers of the Ariel's crew continued for some time after her commander had reached her deck. Barnstable answered the congratulations of his officers by cordial shakes of the hand; and, after waiting for the ebullition of delight among the seamen to subside a little, he beckoned with an air of authority for silence.

"I thank you, my lads, for your good will," he said, when all were gathered around him in deep attention; "they have given us a tough chase, and, if you had left us another mile to go, we had been lost. That fellow is a king's cutter; and, though his disposition to run to leeward is a good deal mollified, yet he shows signs of fight. At any rate, he is stripping off some of his clothes, which looks as if he were game. Luckily for us, Captain Manual has taken all the marines ashore with him (though what he has done with them, or himself, is a mystery), or we should have had our decks lumbered with live cattle; but, as it is, we have a good working breeze, tolerably smooth water, and a dead match! There is a sort of national obligation on us to whip that fellow; and therefore, without more words about the matter, let us turn to and do it, that we may get our breakfasts."

To this specimen of marine eloquence the crew cheered as usual, the young men burning for the combat, and the few old sailors who belonged to the schooner shaking their heads with infinite satisfaction, and swearing by sundry strange oaths that their captain "could talk, when there was need of such thing, like the best dictionary that ever was launched."

During this short harangue, and the subsequent comments, the Ariel had been kept, under a cloud of canvas, as near to the wind as she could lie; and, as this was her best sailing, she had stretched swiftly out from the land to a distance whence the cliffs and the soldiers, who were spread along their summits, were plainly visible. Barnstable turned his glass repeatedly, from the cutter to the shore, as different feelings predominated in his breast, before he again spoke.

"If Mr. Griffith is stowed away among those rocks," he at length said, "he shall see as pretty an argument discussed, in as few words, as he ever listened to, provided the gentlemen in yonder cutter have not changed their minds as to the road they intend to journey. What think you, Mr. Merry?"

"I wish with all my heart and soul, sir," returned the fearless boy, "that Mr. Griffith was safe aboard us; it seems the country is alarmed, and God knows what will happen if he is taken! As to the fellow to windward, he'll find it easier to deal with the Ariel's boat than with her mother; but he carries a broad sail; I question if he means to show play."

"Never doubt him, boy," said Barnstable; "he is working off the shore, like a man of sense, and, besides, he has his spectacles on, trying to make out what tribe of Yankee Indians we belong to. You'll see him come to the wind presently, and send a few pieces of iron down this way, by way of letting us know where to find him. Much as I like your first lieutenant, Mr. Merry, I would rather leave him on the land this day than see him on my decks. I want no fighting captain to work this boat for me! But tell the drummer, sir, to beat to quarters."

The boy, who was staggering under the weight of his melodious instrument, had been expecting this command, and, without waiting for the midshipman to communicate the order, he commenced that short rub-a-dub air that will at any time rouse a thousand men from the deepest sleep, and cause them to fly to their means of offence with a common soul. The crew of the Ariel had been collected in groups studying the appearance of the enemy, cracking their jokes, and waiting only for this usual order to repair to the guns; and, at the first tap of the drum, they spread with steadiness to the different parts of the little vessel, where their various duties called them. The cannon were surrounded by small parties of vigorous and athletic young men; the few marines were drawn up in array with muskets; the officers appeared in their boarding-caps, with pistols stuck in their belts, and naked sabres in their hands. Barnstable paced his little quarter-deck with a firm tread, dangling a speaking-trumpet by its lanyard on his forefinger, or occasionally applying the glass to his eye, which, when not in use, was placed under one arm, while his sword was resting against the foot of the mainmast; a pair of heavy ship's pistols were thrust into his belt also; and piles of muskets, boarding-pikes, and naked sabres, were placed on different parts of the deck. The laugh of the seamen was heard no longer; and those who spoke uttered their thoughts only in low and indistinct whispers.

The English cutter held her way from the land, until she got an offing of more than two miles, when she reduced her sails to a yet smaller number; and, heaving into the wind, she fired a gun in a direction opposite to that which pointed to the Ariel.

"Now I would wager a quintal of codfish, Master Coffin," said Barnstable, "against the best cask of porter that was ever brewed in England, that fellow believes a Yankee schooner can fly in the wind's eye! If he wishes to speak to us, why don't he give his cutter a little sheet and come down?"

The cockswain had made his arrangements for the combat with much more method and philosophy than any other man in the vessel. When the drum beat to quarters, he threw aside his packet, vest, and shirt, with as little hesitation as if he stood under an American sun, and with all the discretion of a man who had engaged in an undertaking that required the free use of his utmost powers. As he was known to be a privileged individual in the Ariel, and one whose opinions, in all matters of seamanship, were regarded as oracles by the crew, and were listened to by his commander with no little demonstration of respect, the question excited no surprise. He was standing at the breech of his long gun with his brawny arms folded on a breast that had been turned to the color of blood by long exposure, his grizzled locks fluttering in the breeze, and his tall form towering far above the heads of all near him.

"He hugs the wind, sir, as if it was his sweetheart," was his answer; "but he'll let go his hold soon; and, if he don't we can find a way to make him fall to leeward."

"Keep a good full!" cried the commander in a stern voice; "and let the vessel go through the water. That fellow walks well, Long Tom; but we are too much for him on a bowling; though, if he continue to draw ahead in this manner, it will be night before we can get alongside him."

"Ay, ay, sir," returned the cockswain; "them cutters carries a press of canvas when they seem to have but little; their gaffs are all the same as young booms, and spread a broad head to their mainsails. But it's no hard matter to knock a few cloths out of their bolt-ropes, when she will both drop astern and to leeward."

"I believe there is good sense in your scheme this time," said Barnstable; "for I am anxious about the frigate's people—though I hate a noisy chase. Speak to him, Tom, and let us see if he will answer."

"Ay, ay, sir," cried the cockswain, sinking his body in such a manner as to let his head fall to a level with the cannon that he controlled, when, after divers orders, and sundry movements to govern the direction of the piece, he applied a match, with a rapid motion, to the priming. An immense body of white smoke rushed from the muzzle of the cannon, followed by a sheet of vivid fire, until, losing its power, it yielded to the wind, and, as it rose from the water, spread like a cloud, and, passing through the masts of the schooner, was driven far to leeward, and soon blended in the mists which were swiftly scudding before the fresh breezes of the ocean.

Although many curious eyes were watching this beautiful sight from the cliffs, there was too little of novelty in the exhibition to attract a single look of the crew of the schooner from the more important examination of the effect of the shot on their enemy. Barnstable sprang lightly on a gun, and watched the instant when the ball would strike, with keen interest, while Long Tom threw himself aside from the line of the smoke with similar intention; holding one of his long arms extended toward his namesake, with a finger on the vent, and supporting his frame by placing the hand of the other on the deck, as his eyes glanced through an opposite port-hole, in an attitude that most men might have despaired of imitating with success.

"There go the chips!" cried Barnstable. "Bravo! Master Coffin, you never planted iron in the ribs of an Englishman with more judgment. Let him have another piece of it; and, if he likes the sport, we'll play a game of long bowls with him!"

"Ay, ay, sir," returned the cockswain, who, the instant he witnessed the effects of his shot, had returned to supcrintcnd thc reloading of his gun; "if he holds on half an hour longer, I'll dub him down to our own size, when we can close and make an even fight of it."

The drum of the Englishman was now, for the first time, heard rattling across the waters, and echoing the call to quarters, that had already proceeded from the Ariel.

"Ah! you have sent him to his guns!" said Barnstable; "we shall now hear more of it; wake him up, Tom—wake him up."

"We shall start him on end, or put him to sleep altogether, shortly," said the deliberate cockswain, who never allowed himself to be at all hurried, even by his commander. "My shot are pretty much like a shoal of porpoises, and commonly sail in each other's wake. Stand by—heave her breech forward —so; get out of that, you damned young reprobate, and let my harpoon alone!"

"What are you at there, Master Coffin?" cried Barnstable; "are you tongue-tied?"

"Here's one of the boys skylarking with my harpoon in the lee-scuppers, and by-and-by, when I shall want it most, there'll be a no-man's land to hunt for it in."

"Never mind the boy, Tom; send him aft here to me, and I'll polish his behavior; give the Englishman some more iron."

"I want the little villain to pass up my cartridges," returned the angry old seaman; "but if you'll be so good, sir, as to hit him a crack or two, now and then, as he goes by you to the magazine, the monkey will learn his manners, and the schooner's work will be all the better done for it.—A young herring-faced monkey! to meddle with a tool ye don't know the use of. If your parents had spent more of their money on your edication, and less on your outfit, you'd ha' been a gentleman to what ye are now."

"Hurrah! Tom, hurrah!" cried Barnstable, a little impatiently; "is your namesake never to open his throat again?"

"Ay, ay, sir; all ready," grumbled the cockswain; "depress a little; so—so; a damned young baboon-behaved curmudgeon; overhaul that forward fall more; stand by with your match—but I'll pay him!—fire!" This was the actual commencement of the fight; for as the shot of Tom Coffin travelled, as he had intimated, very much in the same direction, their enemy found the sport becoming too hot to be endured in silence, and the report of the second gun from the Ariel was instantly followed by that of the whole broadside of the Alacrity. The shot of the cutter flew in a very good direction, but her guns were too light to give them efficiency at that distance; and as one or two were heard to strike against the bend of the schooner, and fall back innocuously, into the water, the cockswain, whose good humor became gradually restored as the combat thickened, remarked with his customary apathy:

"Them count for no more than love-taps—does the Englishman think that we are firing salutes?"

"Stir him up, Tom! every blow you give him will help to open his eyes," cried Barnstable, rubbing his hands with glee, as he witnessed the success of his efforts to close.

Thus far the cockswain and his crew had the fight, on the part of the Ariel, altogether to themselves, the men who were stationed at the smaller and shorter guns standing in perfect idleness by their sides; but in ten or fifteen minutes the commander of the Alacrity, who had been staggered by the weight of the shot that had struck him, found that it was no longer in his power to retreat, if he wished it; when he decided on the only course that was left for a brave man to pursue, and steered boldly in such a direction as would soonest bring him in contact with his enemy, without exposing his vessel to be raked by his fire. Barnstable watched each movement of his foe with eagle eyes, and when the vessel had got within a lessened distance, he gave the order for a general fire to be opened. The action now grew warm and spirited on both sides. The power of the wind was counteracted by the constant explosion of the cannon; and, instead of driving rapidly to leeward, a white canopy of curling smoke hung above the Ariel, or rested on the water, lingering in her wake, so as to mark the path by which she was approaching to a closer and still deadlier struggle. The shouts of the young sailors as they handled their instruments of death, became more animated and fierce, while the cockswain pursued his occupation with the silence and skill of one who labored in a regular vocation. Barnstable was unusually composed and quiet, maintaining the grave deportment of a commander on whom rested the fortunes of the contest, at the same time that his dark eyes were dancing with the fire of suppressed animation.

"Give it them!" he occasionally cried, in a voice that might be heard amid the bellowing of the cannon; "never mind their cordage, my lads; drive home their bolts, and make your marks below their ridge-ropes."

In the meantime the Englishman played a manful game.

He had suffered a heavy loss by the distant cannonade, which no metal he possessed could retort upon his enemy; but he struggled nobly to repair the error in judgment with which he had begun the contest. The two vessels gradually drew nigher to each other, until they both entered into the common cloud created by their fire, which thickened and spread around them in such a manner as to conceal their dark hulls from the gaze of the curious and interested spectators on the cliffs. The heavy reports of the cannon were now mingled with the rattling of muskets and pistols, and streaks of fire might be seen glancing like flashes of lightning through the white cloud which enshrouded the combatants; and many minutes of painful uncertainty followed, before the deeply-interested soldiers, who were gazing at the scene, discovered on whose banners victory had alighted.

We shall follow the combatants into their misty wreath, and display to the reader the events as they occurred.

The fire of the Ariel was much the most quick and deadly, both because she had suffered less, and her men were less exhausted; and the cutter stood desperately on to decide the combat, after grappling, hand to hand. Barnstable anticipated her intention, and well understood her commander's reason for adopting this course; but he was not a man to calculate coolly his advantages, when pride and daring invited him to a more severe trial. Accordingly, he met the enemy half-way, and, as the vessels rushed together, the stern of the schooner was secured to the bows of the cutter, by the joint efforts of both parties. The voice of the English commander was now plainly to be heard, in the uproar, calling to his men to follow him.

"Away there, boarders! repel boarders on the starboard quarter!" shouted Barnstable through his trumpet.

This was the last order that the gallant young sailor gave with this instrument; for, as he spoke, he cast it from him, and, seizing his sabre, flew to the spot where the enemy was about to make his most desperate effort. The shouts, execrations, and tauntings of the combatants now succeeded to the roar of the cannon, which could be used no longer with effect, though the fight was still maintained with spirited discharges of the small-arms.

"Sweep him from his decks!" cried the English commander, as he appeared on his own bulwarks, surrounded by a dozen of his bravest men, "drive the rebellious dogs into the sea!"

"Away there, marines!" retorted Barnstable, firing his pistol at the advancing enemy, "leave not a man of them to sup his grog again."

The tremendous and close volley that succeeded this order nearly accomplished the command of Barnstable to the letter, and the commander of the Alacrity, perceiving that he stood alone, reluctantly fell back on the deck of his own vessel, in order to bring on his men once more.

"Board her! graybeards and boys, idlers and all!" shouted Barnstable, springing in advance of his crew. A powerful arm arrested the movement of the dauntless seaman, and before he had time to recover himself, he was drawn violently back to his own vessel by the irresistible grasp of his cockswain.

"The fellow's in his flurry," said Tom, "and it wouldn't be wise to go within reach of his flukes; but I'll just step ahead and give him a set with my harpoon."

Without waiting for a reply, the cockswain reared his tall frame on the bulwarks, and was in the act of stepping on board of his enemy, when a sea separated the vessels, and he fell with a heavy dash of the waters into the ocean. As twenty muskets and pistols were discharged at the instant he appeared, the crew of the Ariel supposed his fall to be occasioned by his wounds, and were rendered doubly fierce by the sight, and the cry of their commander to — "Revenge Long Tom! board her! Long Tom or death!"

They threw themselves forward in irresistible numbers, and forced a passage, with much bloodshed, to the forecastle of the Alacrity. The Englishman was overpowered, but still remained undaunted—he rallied his crew, and bore up most gallantly to the fray. Thrusts of pikes and blows of sabres were becoming close and deadly, while muskets and pistols were constantly discharged by those who were kept at a distance by the pressure of the throng of closer combatants.

Barnstable led his men in advance, and became a mark of peculiar vengeance to his enemies, as they slowly yielded before his vigorous assaults. Chance had placed the two commanders on opposite sides of the cutter's deck, and the victory seemed to incline toward either party, wherever these daring officers directed the struggle in person. But the Englishman, perceiving that the ground he maintained in person was lost elsewhere, made an effort to restore the battle, by changing his position, followed by one or two of his best men. A marine, who preceded him, levelled his musket within a few feet of the American commander, and was about to fire, when Merry glided among the combatants, and passed his dirk into the body of the man, who fell at the blow; shaking his piece with horrid imprecations, the wounded soldier prepared to deal his vengeance on his youthful assailant, when the fearless boy leaped within its muzzle, and buried his own keen weapon in his heart.

"Hurrah!" shouted the unconscious Barnstable, from the edge of the quarter-deck, where, attended by a few men, he was driving all before him. "Revenge!—Long Tom and victory!"

"We have them!" exclaimed the Englishman; "handle your pikes! we have them between two fires."

The battle would probably have terminated very differently from what previous circumstances had indicated, had not a wild-looking figure appeared in the cutter's channels at that moment, issuing from the sea, and gaining the deck at the same instant. It was Long Tom, with his iron visage rendered fierce by his previous discomfiture, and his grizzled locks drenched with the briny element from which he had risen, looking like Neptune with his trident. Without speaking he poised his harpoon, and, with a powerful effort, pinned the unfortunate Englishman to the mast of his own vessel.

"Starn all!" cried Tom, by a sort of instinct, when the blow was struck; and, catching up the musket of the fallen marine, he dealt out terrible and fatal blows with its butt on all who approached him, utterly disregarding the use of the bayonet on its muzzle. The unfortunate commander of the Alacrity brandished his sword with frantic gestures, while his eyes rolled in horrid wildness, when he writhed for an instant in his passing agonies, and then, as his head dropped lifeless upon his gored breast, he hung against the spar, a spectacle of dismay to his crew. A few of the Englishmen stood chained to the spot in silent horror at the sight, but most of them fled to their lower deck, or hastened to conceal themselves in the secret parts of the vessel, leaving to the Americans the undisputed possession of the Alacrity.

Two-thirds of the cutter's crew suffered either in life or limbs by this short struggle; nor was the victory obtained by Barnstable without paying the price of several valuable lives. The first burst of conquest was not, however, the moment to appreciate the sacrifice, and loud and reiterated shouts proclaimed the exultation of the conquerors. As the flush of victory subsided, however, recollection returned, and Barnstable issued such orders as humanity and his duty rendered necessary. While the vessels were separating, and the bodies of the dead and wounded were removing, the conqueror paced the deck of his prize, as if lost in deep reflection. He passed his hand frequently across his blackened and blood-stained brow, while his eyes would rise to examine the vast canopy of smoke that was hovering above the vessels like a dense fog exhaling from the ocean. The result of his deliberations was soon announced to the crew.

"Haul down all your flags," he cried; "set the Englishman's colors again, and show the enemy's jack above our ensign in the Ariel."

The appearance of the whole channel-fleet within half gun-shot would not have occasioned more astonishment among the victors than this extraordinary mandate. The wondering seamen suspended their several employments to gaze at the singular change that was making in the flags, those symbols that were viewed with a sort of reverence; but none presumed to comment openly on the procedure except Long Tom, who stood on the quarter-deck of the prize, straightening the pliable iron of the harpoon which he had recovered with as much care and diligence as if it were necessary to the maintenance of their conquest. Like the others, however, he suspended his employment when he heard this order, and manifested no reluctance to express his dissatisfaction at the measure.

"If the Englishmen grumble at the fight, and think it not fair play," muttered the cockswain, "let us try it over again, sir; as they are somewhat short of hands they can send a boat to the land, and get off a gang of them lazy riptyles, the soldiers, who stand looking at us like so many red lizards crawling on a beach, and we'll give them another chance; but damme, if I see the use of whipping them, if this is to be the better end of the matter."

"What's that you're grumbling there, like a dead northeaster, you horse-mackerel?" said Barnstable; "where are our friends and countrymen who are on the land? are we to leave them to swing on gibbets or rot in dungeons?"

The cockswain listened with great earnestness, and, when his commander had spoken, he struck the palm of his broad hand against his brawny thigh, with a report like a pistol, and answered:

"I see how it is, sir; you reckon the red-coats have Mr. Griffith in tow. Just run the schooner into shoal water, Captain Barnstable, and drop an anchor, where we can get the long gun to bear on them, and give me the whale-boat with five or six men to back me—they must have long legs if they get an offing before I run them aboard!"

"Fool! do you think a boat's crew could contend with fifty armed soldiers?"

"Soldiers!" echoed Tom, whose spirits had been strongly excited by the conflict, snapping his fingers with ineffable disdain; "that for all the soldiers that were ever rigged, one whale could kill a thousand of them; and here stands the man that has killed his round hundred of whales!"

"Pshaw! you grampus, do you turn braggart in your old age?"

"It's no bragging, sir, to speak a log-book truth; but if Captain Barnstable thinks that old Tom Coffin carries a speaking-trumpet for a figure-head, let him pass the word forrard to man the boats."

"No, no, my old master at the marlinspike," said Barnstable, kindly; "I know thee too well, thou brother of Neptune! but shall we not throw the bread-room dust in those Englishmen's eyes by wearing their bunting awhile till something may offer to help our captured countrymen?"

The cockswain shook his head and cogitated a moment, as if struck with sundry new ideas, when he answered:

"Ay, ay, sir; that's blue-water philosophy—as deep as the sea. Let the rip-tyles clew up the corners of their mouths to their eyebrows now; when they come to hear the raal Yankee truth of the matter, they will sheet them down to their leather neckcloths!"

With this reflection the cockswain was much consoled, and the business of repairing damages and securing the prize proceeded without further interruption on his part. The few prisoners who were unhurt were rapidly transferred to the Ariel. While Barnstable was attending to this duty, an unusual bustle drew his eyes to one of the hatchways, where he beheld a couple of his marines dragging forward a gentleman, whose demeanor and appearance indicated the most abject terror. After examining the extraordinary appearance of this individual for a moment, in silent amazement, the lieutenant exclaimed:

"Who have we here? some amateur in fights! an inquisitive wonder-seeking non-combatant, who has volunteered to serve his king, and perhaps draw a picture, or write a book, to serve himself! Pray, sir, in what capacity did you serve in this vessel?"

The captive ventured a sidelong glance at his interrogator, in whom he expected to encounter Griffith, but, perceiving that it was a face he did not know, he felt a revival of confidence that enabled him to reply:

"I came by accident; being on board the cutter at the time her late commander determined to engage you. It was not in his power to land me, as I trust you will not hesitate to do; your conjecture of my being a non-combatant—"

"Is perfectly true," interrupted Barnstable; "it requires no spy-glass to read that name written on you from stem to stern; but for certain weighty reasons—"

He paused to turn at a signal given him by young Merry, who whispered eagerly in his ear:

" 'Tis Mr. Dillon, kinsman of Colonel Howard; I've seen him often, sailing in the wake of my cousin Cicely."

"Dillon!" exclaimed Barnstable, rubbing his hands with pleasure; "what, Kit of that name! he with 'the Savannah face, eyes of black, and skin of the same color?" He's grown a little whiter with fear; but he's a prize, at this moment, worth twenty Alacrities!"

These exclamations were made in a low voice, and at some little distance from the prisoner, whom he now approached and addressed.

"Policy, and consequently duty, require that I should detain you for a short time, sir; but you shall have a sailor's welcome to whatever we possess, to lessen the weight of captivity."

Barnstable precluded any reply, by bowing to his captive, and turning away to superintend the management of his vessels. In a short time it was announced that they were ready to make sail, when the Ariel and her prize were brought close to the wind, and commenced beating slowly along the land, as if intending to return to the bay whence the latter had sailed that morning. As they stretched in to the shore on the first tack, the soldiers on the cliffs rent the air with their shouts and acclamations, to which Barnstable, pointing to the assumed symbols that were fluttering in the breeze from his masts, directed his crew to respond in the most cordial manner. As the distance, and the want of boats, prevented any further communication, the soldiers, after gazing at the receding vessels for a time, disappeared from the cliffs, and were soon lost from the sight of the adventurous mariners. Hour after hour was consumed in the tedious navigation, against an adverse tide, and the short day was drawing to a close, before they approached the mouth of their destined haven. While making one of their numerous stretches, to and from the land, the cutter, in which Barnstable continued, passed the victim of their morning's sport, riding on the water, the waves curling over his huge carcass, as on some rounded rock, and already surrounded by the sharks, who were preying on his defenceless body.

"See! Master Coffin," cried the lieutenant, pointing out the object to his cockswain as they glided by it, "the shovel-nosed gentlemen are regaling daintily; you have neglected the Christian's duty of burying your dead."

The old seaman cast a melancholy look at the dead whale, and replied:

"If I had the creature in Boston Bay, or on the Sandy Point of Munny Moy, 'twould be the making of me! But riches and honor are for the great and the larned, and there's nothing left for poor Tom Coffin to do, but to veer and haul on his own rolling tackle, that he may ride out the rest of the gale of life without springing any of his old spars."

"How now, Long Tom!" cried the officer; "these rocks and cliffs will ship-wreck you on the shoals of poetry yet; you grow sentimental!"

"Them rocks might wrack any vessel that struck them," said the literal cockswain; "and as for poetry, I wants none better than the good old song of Captain Kidd; but it's enough to raise solemn thoughts in a Cape Poge Indian, to see an eighty-barrel whale devoured by sharks—'tis an awful waste of property! I've seen the death of two hundred of the creaters, though it seems to keep the rations of poor old Tom as short as ever."

The cockswain walked aft, while the vessel was passing the whale, and seating himself on the taffrail, with his face resting gloomily on his bony hand, he fastened his eyes on the object of his solicitude, and continued to gaze at it with melancholy regret, while it was to be seen glistening in the sun-beams, as it rolled its glittering side of white into the air, or the rays fell un-reflected on the black and rougher coat of the back of the monster. In the meantime, the navigators diligently pursued their way for the haven we have mentioned, into which they steered with every appearance of the fearlessness of friends, and the exultation of conquerors.

A few eager and gratified spectators lined the edges of the small bay, and Barnstable concluded his arrangement for deceiving the enemy, by admonish-ing his crew that they were now about to enter on a service that would re-quire their utmost intrepidity and sagacity.

19

Our trumpet called you to this gentle parle.

King John

As Griffith and his companions rushed from the offices of St. Ruth into the open air they encountered no one to intercept their flight, or communicate the alarm. Warned by the experience of the earlier part of the same night they avoided the points where they knew the sentinels were posted, though fully prepared to bear down all resistance, and were soon beyond the probability of immediate detection. They proceeded for the distance of half a mile with rapid strides, and, with the stern and sullen silence of men who expected to encounter immediate danger, resolved to breast it with desperate resolution; but, as they plunged into a copse, that clustered around the ruin which has been already mentioned, they lessened their exertions to a more deliberate pace, and a short but guarded dialogue ensued.

"We have had a timely escape," said Griffith; "I would much rather have endured captivity than have been the cause of introducing confusion and bloodshed into the peaceful residence of Colonel Howard."

"I would, sir, that you had been of this opinion some hours earlier," returned the pilot, with a severity in his tones that even conveyed more meaning than his words.

"I may have forgotten my duty, sir, in my anxiety to inquire into the condition of a family in whom I feel a particular interest," returned Griffith, in a manner in which pride evidently struggled with respect; "but this is not a time for regrets; I apprehend that we follow you on an errand of some moment, where actions would be more acceptable than any words of apology. What is your pleasure now?"

"I much fear that our project will be defeated," said the pilot, gloomily; "the alarm will spread with the morning fogs, and there will be musterings of the yeomen, and consultations of the gentry, that will drive all thoughts of amusement from their minds. The rumor of the descent will, at any time, force sleep from the shores of this island to at least ten leagues inland."

"Ay, you have probably passed some pleasant nights with your eyes open, among them, yourself, Master Pilot," said Manual; "they may thank the Frenchman Thurot, in the old business of '56, and our own dare-devil, the bloody Scotchman, as the causes of their quarters being so often beaten up. After all, Thurot, with his fleet, did no more than bully them a little, and the poor fellow was finally extinguished by a few small cruisers, like a drummer's boy under a grenadier's cap; but honest Paul sang a different tune for his countrymen to dance to, and—"

"I believe you will shortly dance yourself, Manual," interrupted Griffith, quickly, "and in very pleasure that you have escaped an English prison."

"Say, rather, an English gibbet," continued the elated marine; "for had a court-martial or a court-civil discussed the manner of our entrance into this island, I doubt whether we should have fared better than the dare-devil himself, honest—"

"Pshaw!" exclaimed the impatient Griffith; "enough of this nonsense, Captain Manual; we have other matters to discuss now. What course have you determined to pursue, Mr. Gray?"

The pilot started, like a man roused from a deep musing, at this question, and, after a pause of a moment, he spoke in a low tone of voice, as if still under the influence of deep and melancholy feeling:

"The night has already run into the morning watch, but the sun is backward to show himself in this latitude in the heart of winter. I must depart, my friends, to rejoin you some ten hours hence; it will be necessary to look deeper into our scheme before we hazard anything, and no one can do the service but myself. Where shall we meet again?"

"I have reason to think that there is an unfrequented ruin at no great distance from us," said Griffith; "perhaps we might find both shelter and privacy among its deserted walls."

"The thought is good," returned the pilot, "and 'twill answer a double purpose. Could you find the place where you put the marines in ambush, Captain Manual?"

"Has a dog a nose, and can he follow a clean scent?" exclaimed the marine; "do you think, Signor Pilota, that a general ever puts his forces into an ambuscade where he can't find them himself? 'Fore God! I knew well enough where the rascals lay snoring on their knapsacks, some half an hour ago, and I would have given the oldest majority in Washington's army to have had them where a small intimation from myself could have brought them in line ready dressed for a charge. I know not how you fared, gentlemen, but with me the sight of twenty such vagabonds would have been a joyous spectacle; we would have tossed that Captain Borroughcliffe and his recruits on the point of our bayonets as the devil would pitch—"

"Come, come, Manual," said Griffith, a little angrily, "you constantly forget our situation and our errand; can you lead your men hither without discovery before the day dawns?"

"I want but the shortest half hour that a bad watch ever travelled over to do it in."

"Then follow, and I will appoint a place of secret rendezvous," rejoined Griffith; "Mr. Gray can learn our situation at the same time."

The pilot was seen to beckon, through the gloom of the night, for his companions to move forward; when they proceeded, with cautious steps, in quest of the desired shelter. A short search brought them in contact with a part of the ruinous walls, which spread over a large surface, and which in places reared their black fragments against the sky, casting a deeper obscurity across the secret recesses of the wood.

"This will do," said Griffith, when they had skirted for some distance the outline of the crumbling fabric; "bring up your men to this point, where I will meet you, and conduct them to some more secret place, for which I shall search during your absence."

"A perfect paradise, after the cable-tiers of the Ariel!" exclaimed Manual; "I doubt not but a good spot might be selected among these trees for a steady drill—a thing my soul has pined after for six long months."

"Away, away!" cried Griffith; "here is no place for idle parades; if we find shelter from discovery and capture until you shall be needed in a deadly struggle, 'twill be well."

Manual was slowly retracing his steps to the skirts of the wood, when he suddenly turned and asked:

"Shall I post a small picket, a mere corporal's guard, in the open ground in front, and make a chain of sentinels to our works?"

"We have no works—we want no sentinels," returned his impatient commander; "our security is only to be found in secrecy. Lead up your men under the cover of the trees, and let those three bright stars be your landmarks —bring them in a range with the northern corner of the wood—"

"Enough, Mr. Griffith," interrupted Manual; "a column of troops is not to be steered like a ship, by compass, and bearings, and distances—trust me, sir, the march shall be conducted with proper discretion, though in a military manner."

Any reply or expostulation was prevented by the sudden disappearance of the marine, whose retreating footsteps were heard for several moments, as he moved at a deliberate pace through the underwood. During this short interval, the pilot stood reclining against the corner of the ruins in profound silence; but when the sounds of Manual's march were no longer audible, he advanced from under the deeper shadows of the wall, and approached his youthful companion.

"We are indebted to the marine for our escape," he said; "I hope we are not to suffer by his folly."

"He is what Barnstable calls a rectangular man," returned Griffith, "and will have his way in matters of his profession, though a daring companion in a hazardous expedition. If we can keep him from exposing us by his silly parade, we shall find him a man who will do his work like a soldier, sir, when need happens."

" 'Tis all I ask; until the last moment, he and his command must be torpid; for if we are discovered, any attempt of ours, with some twenty bayonets and a half-pike or two, would be useless against the force that would be brought to crush us."

"The truth of your opinion is too obvious," returned Griffith; "those fellows will sleep a week at a time in a gale at sea, but the smell of the land wakes them up, and I fear 'twill be hard to keep them close during the day."

"It must be done, sir, by the strong hand of force," said the pilot sternly, "if it cannot be done by admonition; if we had no more than the recruits of that drunken martinet to cope with, it would be no hard task to drive them into the sea; but I learned in my prison that horse are expected on the shore with the dawn; there is one they call Dillon, who is on the alert to do us mischief."

"The miscreant!" muttered Griffith. "Then you also have had communion, sir, with some of the inmates of St. Ruth?"

"It behooves a man who is embarked in a perilous enterprise to seize all opportunities to learn his hazard," said the pilot, evasively; "if the report be true, I fear we have but little hopes of succeeding in our plans."

"Nay, then, let us take the advantage of the darkness to regain the schooner;

the coasts of England swarm with hostile cruisers, and a rich trade is flowing into the bosom of this island from the four quarters of the world; we shall not seek long for a foe worthy to contend with, nor for the opportunities to cut up the Englishman in his sinews of war—his wealth."

"Griffith," returned the pilot, in his still, low tones, that seemed to belong to a man who never knew ambition, nor felt human passion, "I grow sick of this struggle between merit and privileged rank. It is in vain that I scour the waters which the King of England boastingly calls his own, and capture his vessels in the very mouths of his harbors, if my reward is to consist only of violated promises, and hollow professions: but your proposition is useless to me; I have at length obtained a ship of a size sufficient to convey my person to the shores of honest, plain-dealing America; and I would enter the hall of Congress, on my return, attended by a few of the legislators of this learned isle, who think they possess the exclusive privilege to be wise, and virtuous, and great."

"Such a retinue might doubtless be grateful both to your own feelings and those who would receive you," said Griffith, modestly; "but would it effect the great purposes of our struggle? or is it an exploit, when achieved, worth the hazard you incur?"

Griffith felt the hand of the pilot on his own, pressing it with a convulsive grasp, as he replied, in a voice, if possible, even more desperately calm than his former tones:

"There is glory in it, young man; if it be purchased with danger, it shall be rewarded by fame! It is true, I wear your republican livery, and call the Americans my brothers; but it is because you combat in behalf of human nature. Were your cause less holy, I would not shed the meanest drop that flows in English veins, to serve it; but now, it hallows every exploit that is undertaken in its favor, and the names of all who contend for it shall belong to posterity. Is there no merit in teaching these proud islanders that the arm of liberty can pluck them from the very empire of their corruption and oppression?"

"Then let me go and ascertain what we most wish to know; you have been seen there, and might attract—"

"You little know me," interrupted the pilot: "the deed is my own. If I succeed, I shall claim the honor, and it is proper that I incur the hazard; if I fail, it will be buried in oblivion, like fifty others of my schemes, which, had I power to back me, would have thrown this kingdom in consternation, from the lookouts on the boldest of its headlands to those on the turrets of Windsor Castle. But I was born without the nobility of twenty generations to corrupt my blood and deaden my soul, and am not trusted by the degenerate wretches who rule the French marine."

" 'Tis said that ships of two decks are building from our own oak," said Griffith; "and you have only to present yourself in America, to be employed most honorably."

"Ay! the republics cannot doubt the man who has supported their flag, without lowering it an inch, in so many bloody conflicts! I do go there, Griffith, but my way lies on this path: my pretended friends have bound my hands often, but my enemies, never—neither shall they now. Ten hours will determine all I wish to know, and with you I trust the safety of the party till my return: be vigilant, but be prudent."

"If you should not appear at the appointed hour," exclaimed Griffith, as he beheld the pilot turning to depart, "where am I to seek, and how serve you?"

"Seek me not, but return to your vessel; my earliest years were passed on this coast, and I can leave the island should it be necessary, as I entered it, aided by this disguise and my own knowledge; in such an event, look to your charge, and forget me entirely."

Griffith could distinguish the silent wave of his hand when the pilot concluded, and the next instant he was left alone. For several minutes the young man continued where he had been standing, musing on the singular endowments and restless enterprise of the being with whom chance had thus unexpectedly brought him in contact, and with whose fate and fortune his own prospects had, by the intervention of unlooked-for circumstances, become intimately connected. When the reflections excited by recent occurrences had passed away, he entered within the sweeping circle of the ruinous walls, and, after a very cursory survey of the state of the dilapidated building, he was satisfied that it contained enough secret places to conceal his men, until the return of the pilot should warn them that the hour had come when they must attempt the seizure of the devoted sportsmen, or darkness should again facilitate their return to the Ariel. It was now about the commencement of that period of deep night which seamen distinguish as the morning watch, and Griffith ventured to the edge of the little wood, to listen if any sounds or tumult indicated that they were pursued. On reaching a point where his eye could faintly distinguish distant objects, the young man paused, and bestowed a close and wary investigation on the surrounding scene.

The fury of the gale had sensibly abated, but a steady current of sea-air was rushing through the naked branches of the oaks, lending a dreary and mournful sound to the gloom of the dim prospect. At the distance of a short half-mile, the confused outline of the pile of St. Ruth rose proudly against the streak of light which was gradually increasing above the ocean, and there were moments when the young seaman even fancied he could discern the bright caps that topped the waves of his own disturbed element. The long, dull roar of the surf, as it tumbled heavily on the beach, or dashed with un-broken violence against the hard boundary of rocks, was borne along by the blasts distinctly to his ears. It was a time and a situation to cause the young seaman to ponder deeply on the changes and chances of his hazardous profes-sion. Only a few short hours had passed since he was striving with his utmost skill, and with all his collected energy, to guide the enormous fabric, in which so many of his comrades were now quietly sleeping on the broad ocean, from that very shore on which he now stood in cool indifference to the danger. The recollection of home, America, his youthful and enduring passion, and the character and charms of his mistress, blended in a sort of wild and feverish confusion, which was not, however, without its pleasures, in the ardent fancy of the young man; and he was slowly approaching, step by step, toward the Abbey, when the sound of footsteps, proceeding evidently from the measured tread of disciplined men, reached his ears. He was instantly recalled to his recollection by this noise, which increased as the party deliberately ap-proached; and in a few moments he was able to distinguish a line of men marching in order toward the edge of the wood, from which he had so re-cently issued. Retiring rapidly under the deeper shadow of the trees, he waited until it was apparent the party intended to enter under its cover also, when he ventured to speak.

"Who comes? and what errand?" he cried.

"A skulker, and to burrow like a rabbit, or jump from hole to hole like a wharf-rat!" said Manual, sulkily; "here have I been marching, within half musket-shot of the enemy, without daring to pull a trigger even on their out-posts, because our muzzles are plugged with that universal extinguisher of gunpowder, called prudence. 'Fore God! Mr. Griffith, I hope you may never feel the temptation to do an evil deed, which I felt just now, to throw a volley of small shot into that dog-kennel of a place, if it were only to break its windows and let in the night air upon the sleeping sot who is dozing away the fumes of some good, old, south-side—harkye, Mr. Griffith, one word in your ear."

A short conference took place between the two officers, apart from the men, at the close of which, as they rejoined the party, Manual might be heard urging his plans on the reluctant ears of Griffith in the following words:

"I could carry the old dungeon without waking one of the snorers; and consider, sir, we might get a stock of as rich cordial from its cellars as ever oiled the throat of a gentleman!"

" 'Tis idle, 'tis idle," said Griffith impatiently; "we are not robbers of hen-roosts, nor wine-gaugers, to be prying into the vaults of the English gentry, Captain Manual; but honorable men, employed in the sacred cause of liberty and our country. Lead your party into the ruin, and let them seek their rest; we may have work for them with the dawn."

"Evil was the hour when I quitted the line of the army, to place a soldier under the orders of an awkward squad of tarry jackets!" muttered Manual, as he proceeded to execute an order that was delivered with an air of authority that he knew must be obeyed. "As pretty an opportunity for a surprise and a forage thrown away, as ever crossed the path of a partisan! but, by all the rights of man! I'll have an encampment in some order.—Here, you sergeant, detail a corporal and three men for a picket, and station them in the skirts of this wood. We shall have a sentinel in advance of our position, and things shall be conducted with some air of discipline."

Griffith heard this order with great inward disgust; but, as he anticipated the return of the pilot before the light could arrive to render this weak exposure of their situation apparent, he forbore exercising his power to alter the arrangement. Manual had, therefore, the satisfaction of seeing his little party quartered, as he thought, in a military manner, before he retired with Griffith and his men into one of the vaulted apartments of the ruin, which, by its open and broken doors, invited their entrance. Here the marines disposed themselves to rest, while the two officers succeeded in passing the tedious hours, without losing their characters for watchfulness by conversing with each other, or, at whiles, suffering their thoughts to roam in the very different fields which fancy would exhibit to men of such different characters. In this manner hour after hour passed, in listless quiet, or sullen expectation, until the day had gradually advanced, and it became dangerous to keep the sentinels and picket in a situation where they were liable to be seen by any straggler who might be passing near the wood. Manual remonstrated against any alteration, as being entirely unmilitary, for he was apt to carry his notions of tactics to extremes whenever he came in collision with a sea officer; but in this instance his superior was firm, and the only concession the captain could obtain was the permission to place a solitary sentinel within a few feet of the vault, though under cover of the crumbling walls of the building itself. With this slight deviation in their arrangements, the uneasy party remained for several hours longer, impatiently awaiting the period when they should be required to move.

The guns first fired from the Alacrity had been distinctly audible, and were pronounced by Griffith, whose practised ear detected the metal of the piece that was used, as not proceeding from the schooner. When the rapid though distant rumbling of the spirited cannonade became audible, it was with difficulty that Griffith could restrain either his own feelings or the conduct of his companions within those bounds that prudence and their situation required. The last gun was, however, fired, and not a man had left the vault, and conjectures as to the result of the fight succeeded to those which had been made on the character of the combatants during the action. Some of the marines would raise their heads from the fragments which served them as pillows on which they were seeking disturbed and stolen slumbers, and after listening to the cannon would again compose themselves to sleep, like men who felt no concern in a contest in which they did not participate. Others, more alive to events, and less drowsy, lavishly expended their rude jokes on those who were engaged in the struggle, or listened with a curious interest to mark the progress of the battle, by the uncertain index of its noise. When the fight had been some time concluded, Manual indulged his ill-humor more at length:

"There has been a party of pleasure within a league of us, Mr. Griffith," he said, "at which, but for our present subterraneous quarters, we might have been guests, and thus laid some claim to the honor of sharing the victory. But it is not too late to push the party on as far as the cliffs, where we shall be in sight of the vessels, and we may possibly establish a claim to our share of the prize-money."

"There is but little wealth to be gleaned from the capture of a king's cutter," returned Griffith; "and there would be less honor were Barnstable encumbered with our additional and useless number."

"Useless!" repeated Manual; "there is much good service to be got out of twenty-three well-drilled and well-chosen marines; look at those fellows, Mr. Griffith, and then tell me if you think them an encumbrance in the hour of need."

Griffith smiled, and glanced his eye over the sleeping group—for when the firing had ceased the whole party had again sought their repose—and he could not help admiring the athletic and sinewy limbs that lay scattered around the gloomy vault, in every posture that ease or whim dictated. From the stout frames of the men, his glance was directed to the stack of fire-arms, from whose glittering tubes and polished bayonets strong rays of light were reflected, even in that dark apartment. Manual followed the direction of his eyes, and the expression of his countenance, with inward exultation; but he had the forbearance to await his reply before he manifested his feelings more openly.

"I know them to be true men," said Griffith, "when needed, but—hark! what says he?"

"Who goes there? what noise is that?" repeated the sentinel, who was placed at the entrance of the vault.

Manual and Griffith sprang at the same instant from their places of rest, and stood, unwilling to create the slightest sounds, listening with most intense anxiety to catch the next indication of the cause of the guardian's alarm. A short stillness like that of death succeeded, during which Griffith whispered:

" 'Tis the pilot! his hour has been long passed."

The words were hardly spoken when the clashing of steel in fierce and sudden contact was heard, and at the next instant the body of the sentinel fell heavily along the stone steps that led to the open air, and rolled lifelessly to their feet, with the bayonet that had caused his death projecting from a deep wound in his breast.

"Away, away! sleepers, away!" shouted Griffith.

"To arms!" cried Manual, in a voice of thunder.

The alarmed marines, suddenly aroused from their slumbers at these thrilling cries, sprang on their feet in a confused cluster, and at that fatal moment a body of living fire darted into the vault, which reëchoed with the reports of twenty muskets. The uproar, the smoke, and the groans which escaped from many of his party, could not restrain Griffith another instant; his pistol was fired through the cloud which concealed the entrance of the vault, and he followed the leaden messenger, trailing a half-pike, and shouted to his men:

"Come on! follow, my lads; they are nothing but soldiers."

Even while he spoke, the ardent young seaman was rushing up the narrow passage; but as he gained the open space, his foot struck the writhing body of the victim of his shot, and he was precipitated headlong into a group of armed men.

"Fire! Manual, fire!" shouted the infuriated prisoner; "fire, while you have them in a cluster."

"Ay, fire, Mr. Manual," said Borroughcliffe, with great coolness, "and shoot your own officer. Hold him up, boys! hold him up in front; the safest place is nighest to him."

"Fire!" repeated Griffith, making desperate efforts to release himself from the grasp of five or six men; "fire, and disregard me."

"If he do, he deserves to be hung," said Borroughcliffe; "such fine fellows are not sufficiently plenty to be shot at like wild beasts in chains. Take him from before the mouth of the vault, boys, and spread yourselves to your duty."

At the time Griffith issued from the cover, Manual was mechanically employed in placing his men in order; and the marines, accustomed to do everything in concert and array, lost the moment to advance. The soldiers of Borroughcliffe reloaded their muskets, and fell back behind different portions of the wall, where they could command the entrance to the vault with their fire, without much exposure to themselves. This disposition was very coolly reconnoitred by Manual in person, through some of the crevices in the wall, and he hesitated to advance against the force he beheld while so advantageously posted. In this situation several shots were fired by either party without effect, until Borroughcliffe, perceiving the inefficacy of that mode of attack, summoned the garrison of the vault to a parley.

"Surrender to the forces of his majesty, King George the Third," he cried, "and I promise you quarter."

"Will you release your prisoner, and give us free passage to our vessels?" asked Manual; "the garrison to march out with all the honors of war, and officers to retain their side-arms?"

"Inadmissible," returned Borroughcliffe, with great gravity; "the honor of his majesty's arms, and the welfare of the realm, forbid such a treaty; but I offer you safe quarter and honorable treatment."

"Officers to retain their side-arms, your prisoner to be released, and the whole party to return to America on parole, not to serve until exchanged?"

"Not granted," said Borroughcliffe. "The most that I can yield is a good potation of the generous south-side; and, if you are the man I take you for, you will know how to prize such an offer."

"In what capacity do you summon us to yield? as men entitled to the benefit of the laws of arms, or as rebels to your king?"

"Ye are rebels all, gentlemen," returned the deliberate Borroughcliffe, "and as such you must yield; though so far as good treatment and good fare goes, you are sure of it while in my power; in all other respects you lie at the mercy of his most gracious majesty."

"Then let his majesty show his gracious face, and come and take us, for I'll be—"

The asseveration of the marine was interrupted by Griffith, whose blood had sensibly cooled, and whose generous feelings were awakened in behalf of his comrades, now that his own fate seemed decided.

"Hold, Manual," he cried, "make no rash oaths. Captain Borroughcliffe, I am Edward Griffith, a lieutenant in the navy of the United American States, and I pledge you my honor to a parole—"

"Release him," said Borroughcliffe.

Griffith advanced between the two parties and spoke so as to be heard by both:

"I propose to descend to the vault and ascertain the loss and present strength of Captain Manual's party; if the latter be not greater than I apprehend, I shall advise him to surrender on the usual conditions of civilized nations."

"Go," said the soldier; "but stay; is he a half-and-half—an amphibious—pshaw! I mean a marine?"

"He is, sir, a captain in that corps—"

"The very man," interrupted Borroughcliffe; "I thought I recollected the liquid sound of his voice. It will be well to speak to him of the good fare of St. Ruth; and you may add, that I know my man; I shall besiege instead of storming him, with the certainty of a surrender when his canteen is empty. The vault he is in holds no such beverage as the cellars of the Abbey."

Griffith smiled, in spite of the occasion and his vexation; and, making a slight inclination of his head, he passed into the vault, giving notice to his friends, by his voice, in order to apprise them who approached.

He found six of the marines, including the sentinel, lying dead on the ragged pavement, and four others wounded, but stifling their groans, by order of their commander, that they might not inform the enemy of his weakness. With the remainder of his command, Manual had intrenched himself behind the fragment of a wall that intersected the vault, and, regardless of the dismaying objects before him, maintained as bold a front, and as momentous an air, as if the fate of a walled town depended on his resolution and ingenuity.

"You see, Mr. Griffith," he cried, when the young sailor approached this gloomy but really formidable arrangement, "that nothing short of artillery can dislodge me; as for that drinking Englishman above, let him send down his men by platoons of eight or ten, and I'll pile them up on those steps, four and five deep!"

"But artillery can and will be brought, if it should be necessary," said Griffith; "and there is not the least chance of your eventual escape; it may be possible for you to destroy a few of the enemy, but you are too humane to wish to do it unnecessarily."

"No doubt," returned Manual, with a grim smile; "and yet methinks I could find present pleasure in shooting seven of them—yes, just seven, which is one more than they have struck off my roster."

"Remember your own wounded," added Griffith; "they suffer for want of aid, while you protect a useless defence."

A few smothered groans from the sufferers seconded this appeal, and Manual yielded, though with a very ill grace, to the necessity of the case.

"Go, then, and tell him that we will surrender as prisoners of war," he said, "on the conditions that he grants me my side-arms, and that suitable care shall be taken of the sick—be particular to call them sick—for some lucky accident may yet occur before the compact is ratified, and I would not have him learn our loss."

Griffith, without waiting for a second bidding, hastened to Borroughcliffe with his intelligence.

"His side-arms!" repeated the soldier, when the other had done; "what are they, I pray thee, a marline-spike? For if his equipments be no better than thine own, my worthy prisoner, there is little need to quarrel about their ownership."

"Had I but ten of my meanest men, armed with such half-pikes, and Captain Borroughcliffe and his party were put at deadly strife with us," retorted Griffith, "he might find occasion to value our weapons more highly."

"Four such fiery gentlemen as yourself would have routed my command," returned Borroughcliffe, with undisturbed composure. "I trembled for my ranks when I saw you coming out of the smoke like a blazing comet from behind a cloud! and I shall never think of somersets without returning inward thanks to their inventor. But our treaty is made; let your comrades come forth and pile their arms."

Griffith communicated the result to the captain of marines, when the latter led the remnant of his party out of his sunken fortress into the open air.

The men, who had manifested throughout the whole business that cool subordination and unyielding front, mixed with the dauntless spirit that to this day distinguishes the corps of which they were members, followed their commander in sullen silence, and stacked their arms, with as much regularity and precision as if they had been ordered to relieve themselves after a march. When this necessary preliminary had been observed, Borroughcliffe unmasked his forces, and our adventurers found themselves once more in the power of the enemy, and under circumstances which rendered the prospect of a speedy release from their captivity nearly hopeless.

20

Falstaff:

If your father will do me any honor, so;
If not, let him kill the next Percy himself;
I look to be either earl or duke, I can assure
you.

King Henry IV, Part I

MANUAL cast sundry discontented and sullen looks from his captors to the remnant of his own command, while the process of pinioning the latter was conducted, with much discretion, under the direction of Sergeant Drill, when, meeting in one of his dissatisfied glances with the pale and disturbed features of Griffith, he gave vent to his ill-humor by saying:

"This results from neglecting the precautions of military discipline. Had the command been with me, who, I may say without boasting, have been accustomed to the duties of the field, proper pickets would have been posted, and, instead of being caught like so many rabbits in a burrow to be smoked out with brimstone, we should have had an open field for the struggle; or we might have possessed ourselves of these walls, which I could have made good, for two hours at least, against the best regiment that ever wore King George's facings."

"Defend the outworks before retreating to the citadel!" cried Borroughcliffe; "'tis the game of war, and shows science; but had you kept closer to your burrow, the rabbits might now have all been frisking about in that pleas-

ant abode. The eyes of a timid hind were greeted this morning, while journeying near this wood, with a passing sight of armed men in strange attire; and,
as he fled with an intent of casting himself into the sea, as fear will sometimes
urge one of his kind to do, he luckily encountered me on the cliffs, who hu-
manely saved his life, by compelling him to conduct us hither. There is often
wisdom in science, my worthy contemporary in arms, but there is sometimes
safety in ignorance."

"You have succeeded, sir, and have a right to be pleasant," said Manual, seating himself gloomily on a fragment of the ruin, and fastening his looks on the
melancholy spectacle of the lifeless bodies at his feet; "but these men have been
my own children, and you will excuse me if I cannot retort your pleasantries.
Ah! Captain Borroughcliffe, you are a soldier, and know how to value merit. I
took those very fellows, who sleep on these stones so quietly, from the hand of
Nature, and made them the pride of our art. They were no longer men, but
brave lads, who ate and drank, wheeled and marched, loaded and fired,
laughed, or were sorrowful, spoke or were silent, only at my will. As for soul,
there was but one among them all, and that was in my keeping! Groan, my
children, groan freely now; there is no longer a reason to be silent. I have
known a single musket-bullet cut the buttons from the coats of five of them
in a row, without razing the skin of a man! I could ever calculate, with certainty, how many it would be necessary to expend in all regular service; but
this accursed banditti business has robbed me of the choicest of my treasures.
You stand at ease now, my children; groan, it will soften your anguish."

Borroughcliffe appeared to participate, in some degree, in the feelings of
his captive, and he made a few appropriate remarks in the way of condolence,
while he watched the preparations that were making by his own men to move.
At length his orderly announced that substitutes for barrows were provided
to sustain the wounded, and inquired if it were his pleasure to return to their
quarters.

"Who has seen the horse?" demanded the captain; "which way did they
march? Have they gained any tidings of the discovery of this party of the
enemy?"

"Not from us, your honor," returned the sergeant; "they had ridden along
the coast before we left the cliffs, and it was said their officer intended to scour
the shore for several miles, and spread the alarm."

"Let him; it is all such gay gallants are good for.—Drill, honor is almost as
scarce an article with our arms just now as promotion. We seem but the
degenerate children of the heroes of Poictiers. You understand me, sergeant?"

"Some battle fou't by his majesty's troops against the French, your honor," returned the orderly, a little at a loss to comprehend the expression of his officer's eye.

"Fellow, you grow dull on victory," exclaimed Borroughcliffe; "come hither, I would give you orders. Do you think, Mister Drill, there is more honor, or likely to be more profit, in this little morning's amusement than you and I can stand under?"

"I should not, your honor; we have both pretty broad shoulders—"

"That are not weakened by undue burdens of this nature," interrupted the captain significantly; "if we let the news of this affair reach the ears of those hungry dragoons, they would charge upon us open-mouthed, like a pack of famished beagles, and claim at least half the credit, and certainly all the profit."

"But, your honor, there was not a man of them even—"

"No matter, Drill; I've known troops that have been engaged, and have suffered, cheated out of their share of victory by a well-worded despatch. You know, fellow, that in the smoke and confusion of a battle a man can only see what passes near him, and common prudence requires that he only mention in his official letters what he knows can't be easily contradicted. Thus your Indians, and, indeed, all allies, are not entitled to the right of a general order, any more than to the right of a parade. Now, I dare say, you have heard of a certain battle of Blenheim?"

"Lord! your honor, 'tis the pride of the British army, that and the Culloden! 'Twas when the great Corporal John beat the French king and all his lords and nobility, with half his nation in arms to back him."

"Ay! there is a little of the barrack readings in the account, but it is substantially true; know you how many French were in the field that day, Mister Drill?"

"I have never seen the totals of their muster, sir, in print; but, judging by the difference betwixt the nations, I should suppose some hundreds of thousands."

"And yet, to oppose this vast army, the duke had only ten or twelve thousand well-fed Englishmen! You look astounded, sergeant!"

"Why, your honor, that does seem rather an over-match for an old soldier to swallow; the random shot would sweep away so small a force."

"And yet the battle was fought, and the victory won. But the Duke of Marlborough had a certain Mr. Eugene, with some fifty or sixty thousand High-Dutchers, to back him. You never heard of Mr. Eugene?"

"Not a syllable, your honor. I always thought that Corporal John—"

"Was a gallant and great general; you thought right, Mister Drill. So would a certain nameless gentleman be also, if his majesty would sign a commission to that effect. However, a majority is on the high-road to a regiment, and with even a regiment a man is comfortable! In plain English, Mister Drill, we must get our prisoners into the Abbey with as little noise as possible, in order that the horse may continue their gambols along the coast, without coming to devour our meal. All the fuss must be made at the War Office—for that trifle you may trust me; I think I know who holds a quill that is as good in its way as the sword he wears. Drill is a short name, and can easily be written within the folds of a letter."

"Lord, your honor!" said the gratified halberdier, "I'm sure such an honor is more—but your honor can ever command me."

"I do; and it is to be close, and to make your men keep close, until it shall be time to speak, when I pledge myself there shall be noise enough." Borroughcliffe shook his head, with a grave air, as he continued: "It has been a devil of a bloody fight, sergeant! look at the dead and wounded; a wood on each flank—supported by a ruin in the centre. Oh! ink—ink can be spilt on the details with great effect. Go, fellow, and prepare to march."

Thus enlightened on the subject of his commander's ulterior views, the non-commissioned agent of the captain's wishes proceeded to give suitable instructions to the rest of the party, and to make the more immediate preparations for a march. The arrangements were soon completed. The bodies of the slain were left unsheltered, the seclusion of the ruin being deemed a sufficient security against the danger of any discovery, until darkness should favor their removal, in conformity with Borroughcliffe's plan to monopolize the glory. The wounded were placed on rude litters, composed of the muskets and blankets of the prisoners, when the conquerors and vanquished moved together in a compact body from the ruin, in such a manner as to make the former serve as a mask to conceal the latter from the curious gaze of any casual passenger. There was but little, indeed, to apprehend on this head, for the alarm and the terror, consequent on the exaggerated reports that flew through the country, effectually prevented any intruders on the usually quiet and retired domains of St. Ruth.

The party was emerging from the wood, when the crackling of branches, and rustling of dried leaves, announced, however, that an interruption of some sort was about to occur.

"If it should be one of their rascally patrols!" exclaimed Borroughcliffe, with very obvious displeasure, "they trample like a regiment of cavalry! but, gentlemen, you will acknowledge, yourselves, that we were retiring from the field of battle when we met the reinforcement, if it should prove to be such."

"We are not disposed, sir, to deny you the glory of having achieved your victory single-handed," said Griffith, glancing his eyes uneasily in the direction of the approaching sounds, expecting to see the pilot issue from the thicket in which he seemed to be entangled, instead of any detachment of his enemies.

"Clear the way, Cæsar!" cried a voice at no great distance from them; "break through the accursed vines on my right, Pompey—press forward, my fine fellows, or we may be too late to smell even the smoke of the fight."

"Hum!" ejaculated the captain, with his philosophic indifference of manner entirely re-established, "this must be a Roman legion just awoke from a trance of some seventeen centuries, and that the voice of a centurion. We will halt, Mister Drill, and view the manner of an ancient march!"

While the captain was yet speaking, a violent effort disengaged the advancing party from the thicket of brambles in which they had been entangled, when two blacks, each bending under a load of fire-arms, preceded Colonel Howard into the clear space where Borroughcliffe had halted his detachment. Some little time was necessary to enable the veteran to arrange his disordered dress, and to remove the perspiring effects of the unusual toil from his features, before he could observe the addition to the captain's numbers.

"We heard you fire," cried the old soldier, making, at the same time, the most diligent application of his bandanna, "and I determined to aid you with a sortie, which, when judiciously timed, has been the means of raising many a siege; though, had Montcalm rested quietly within his walls, the plains of Abr'am might never have drunk his blood."

"Oh! his decision was soldierly, and according to all the rules of war," exclaimed Manual; "and, had I followed his example, this day might have produced a different tale!"

"Why, who have we here?" cried the colonel in astonishment; "who is it that pretends to criticise battles and sieges, dressed in such a garb?"

" 'Tis a *dux incognitorum*, my worthy host," said Borroughcliffe; "which means, in our English language, a captain of marines in the service of the American Congress."

"What! have you then met the enemy? ay! and, by the fame of the immortal Wolfe, you have captured them!" cried the delighted veteran. "I was pressing on with a part of my garrison to your assistance, for I had seen that you were marching in this direction, and even the report of a few muskets was heard."

"A few!" interrupted the conqueror; "I know not what you call a few, my gallant and ancient friend; you may possibly have shot at each other by the week in the days of Wolfe, and Abercrombie, and Braddock; but I too have seen smart firing, and can hazard an opinion on such matters. There was as pretty a roll made by fire-arms at the battles on the Hudson as ever rattled from a drum; it is all over, and many live to talk of it; but this has been the most desperate affair, for the numbers, I ever was engaged in! I speak always with reference to the numbers. The wood is pretty well sprinkled with dead; and we have contrived to bring off a few of the desperately wounded with us, as you may perceive."

"Bless me!" exclaimed the surprised veteran, "that such an engagement should happen within musket shot of the Abbey, and I know so little of it! My faculties are on the wane, I fear, for the time has been when a single discharge would rouse me from the deepest sleep."

"The bayonet is a silent weapon," returned the composed captain, with a significant wave of his hand; " 'tis the Englishman's pride, and every experienced officer knows that one thrust from it is worth the fire of a whole platoon."

"What! did you come to the charge?" cried the colonel, "by the Lord, Borroughcliffe, my gallant young friend, I would have given twenty tierces of rice, and two able-bodied Negroes, to have seen the fray!"

"It would have been a pleasant spectacle to witness, sans disputation," returned the captain; "but victory is ours without the presence of Achilles, this time. I have them, all that survive the affair; at least, all that have put foot on English soil."

"Ay! and the king's cutter has brought in the schooner!" added Colonel Howard. "Thus perish all rebellion for evermore! Where's Kit! my kinsman, Mr. Christopher Dillon; I would ask him what the laws of the realm next prescribe to loyal subjects. Here will be work for the jurors of Middlesex, Captain Borroughcliffe, if not for a secretary of state's warrant. Where is Kit, my kinsman; the ductile, the sagacious, the loyal Christopher?"

"The cacique '*non est*,' as more than one bailiff has said of sundry clever fellows in our regiment, when there has been a pressing occasion for their appearance," said the soldier; "but the cornet of horse has given me reason to believe that his provincial lordship, who repaired on board the cutter to give intelligence of the position of the enemy, continued there to share the dangers and honors of naval combat."

"Ay, 'tis like him!" cried the colonel, rubbing his hands with glee; " 'tis like him! he has forgotten the law and his peaceful occupations, at the sounds of military preparations, and has carried the head of a statesman into the fight, with the ardor and thoughtlessness of a boy."

"The cacique is a man of discretion," observed the captain, with all his usual dryness of manner, "and will, doubtless, recollect his obligations to posterity and himself, though he be found entangled in the mazes of a combat. But I marvel that he does not return, for some time has now elapsed since the schooner struck her flag, as my own eyes have witnessed."

"You will pardon me, gentlemen," said Griffith, advancing toward them with uncontrollable interest; "but I have unavoidably heard part of your discourse, and cannot think you will find it necessary to withhold the whole truth from a disarmed captive: say you that a schooner has been captured this morning?"

"It is assuredly true," said Borroughcliffe, with a display of nature and delicacy in his manner that did his heart infinite credit; "but I forbore to tell you, because I thought your own misfortunes would be enough for one time. Mr. Griffith, this gentleman is Colonel Howard, to whose hospitality you will be indebted for some favors before we separate."

"Griffith!" echoed the colonel, in quick reply; "Griffith! what a sight for my old eyes to witness!—the child of worthy, gallant, loyal Hugh Griffith a captive, and taken in arms against his prince! Young man, young man, what would thy honest father, what would his bosom friend, my own poor brother, Harry, have said, had it pleased God that they had survived to witness this burning shame and lasting stigma on thy respectable name?"

"Had my father lived, he would now have been upholding the independence of his native land," said the young man, proudly. "I wish to respect even the prejudices of Colonel Howard, and beg he will forbear urging a subject on which I fear we never shall agree."

"Never, while thou art to be found in the ranks of rebellion!" cried the colonel. "Oh! boy, boy! how I could have loved and cherished thee, if the skill and knowledge obtained in the service of thy prince were now devoted to the maintenance of his unalienable rights! I loved thy father, worthy Hugh, even as I loved my own brother Harry."

"And his son should still be dear to you," interrupted Griffith, taking the reluctant hand of the colonel into both his own.

"Ay, Edward, Edward!" continued the softened veteran, "how many of my day-dreams have been destroyed by thy perversity! Nay, I know not that Kit, discreet and loyal as he is, could have found such favor in my eyes as thyself; there is a cast of thy father in that face and smile, Ned, that might have won me to anything short of treason—and then Cicely, provoking, tender, mutinous, kind, affectionate, good Cicely, would have been a link to unite us forever."

The youth cast a hasty glance at the deliberate Borroughcliffe, who, if he had obeyed the impatient expression of his eye, would have followed the party that was slowly bearing the wounded toward the Abbey, before he yielded to his feelings, and answered:

"Nay, sir; let this, then, be the termination of our misunderstanding—your lovely niece shall be that link, and you shall be to me as your friend Hugh would have been had he lived, and to Cecilia twice a parent."

"Boy, boy," said the veteran, averting his face to conceal the workings of his muscles, "you talk idly; my word is now plighted to my kinsman Kit, and thy scheme is impracticable."

"Nothing is impracticable, sir, to youth and enterprise, when aided by age and experience like yours," returned Griffith; "this war must soon terminate."

"This war!" echoed the colonel, shaking loose the grasp which Griffith held on his arm; "ay! what of this war, young man? Is it not an accursed attempt to deny the rights of our gracious sovereign, and to place tyrants, reared in kennels, on the throne of princes! a scheme to elevate the wicked at the expense of the good! a project to aid unrighteous ambition, under the mask of sacred liberty and the popular cry of equality! as if there could be liberty without order! or equality of rights, where the privileges of the sovereign are not as sacred as those of the people!"

"You judge us harshly, Colonel Howard," said Griffith.

"I judge you!" interrupted the old soldier, who by this time thought the youth resembled any one rather than his friend Hugh; "it is not my province to judge you at all; if it were!—but the time will come, the time will come. I am a patient man, and can wait the course of things; yes, yes, age cools the blood, and we learn to suppress the passions and impatience of youth; but if the ministry would issue a commission of justice for the colonies, and put the name of old George Howard in it, I am a dog, if there should be a rebel alive in twelve months!—Sir," turning sternly to Borroughcliffe, "in such a cause, I could prove a Roman, and hang—hang—yes, I do think, sir, I could hang my kinsman, Mr. Christopher Dillon!"

"Spare the cacique such an unnatural elevation before his time," returned the captain, with a grave wave of the hand; "behold," pointing toward the wood, "there is a more befitting subject for the gallows! Mr. Griffith, yonder man calls himself your comrade?"

The eyes of Colonel Howard and Griffith followed the direction of his finger, and the latter instantly recognized the pilot, standing in the skirts of the wood, with his arms folded, apparently surveying the condition of his friends.

"That man," said Griffith, in confusion and hesitating to utter even the equivocal truth that suggested itself, "that man does not belong to our ship's company."

"And yet he has been seen in *your* company," returned the incredulous Borroughcliffe; "he was the spokesman in last night's examination, Colonel Howard, and doubtless commands the rear guard of the rebels."

"You say true," cried the veteran. "Pompey! Cæsar! present! fire!"

The blacks started at the sudden orders of their master, of whom they stood in the deepest awe; and presenting their muskets they averted their faces, and shutting their eyes, obeyed the bloody mandate.

"Charge!" shouted the colonel, flourishing the ancient sword with which he had armed himself, and pressing forward with all the activity that a recent fit of the gout would allow; "charge and exterminate the dogs with the bayonet! push on, Pompey—dress, boys, dress."

"If your friend stand this charge," said Borroughcliffe to Griffith, with unmoved composure, "his nerves are made of iron; such a charge would break the Coldstreams, with Pompey in the ranks!"

"I trust in God," cried Griffith, "he will have forbearance enough to respect the weakness of Colonel Howard!—he presents a pistol!"

"But he will not fire; the Romans deem it prudent to halt; nay, by Heaven, they countermarch to the rear. Hollo! Colonel Howard, my worthy host, fall back on your reinforcements; the wood is full of armed men; they cannot escape us; I only wait for the horse to cut off the retreat."

The veteran, who had advanced within a short distance of the single man who thus deliberately awaited the attack, halted at this summons; and by a glance of his eye, ascertained that he stood alone. Believing the words of Borroughcliffe to be true, he slowly retired, keeping his face manfully toward his enemy, until he gained the support of the captain.

"Recall the troops, Borroughcliffe!" he cried, "and let us charge into the wood; they will fly before his majesty's arms, like guilty scoundrels, as they are. As for the Negroes, I'll teach the black rascals to desert their master at such a moment! They say Fear is pale, but, damme, Borroughcliffe, if I do not believe his skin is black."

"I have seen him of all colors; blue, white, black, and party-colored," said the captain. "I must take the command of matters on myself, however, my excellent host; let us retire into the Abbey, and trust me to cut off the remainder of the rebels."

In this arrangement the colonel reluctantly acquiesced, and the three followed the soldier to the dwelling, at a pace that was adapted to the infirmities of its master. The excitement of the onset, and the current of his ideas, had united, however, to banish every amicable thought from the breast of the colonel, and he entered the Abbey with the resolute determination of seeing justice dealt to Griffith and his companions, even though it should push them to the foot of the gallows.

As the gentlemen disappeared from his view, among the shrubbery of the grounds, the pilot replaced the weapon that was hanging from his hand in his bosom, and, turning with a saddened and thoughtful brow, he slowly re-entered the wood.

21

Casca: *When these prodigies*
Do so conjointly meet, let not men say,
These are their reasons, they are natural.
For I believe they are portentous things
Unto the climate that they point upon.

SHAKESPEARE

THE reader will discover, by referring to the time consumed in the foregoing events, that the Ariel, with her prize, did not anchor in the bay already mentioned, until Griffith and his party had been for several hours in the custody of their enemies. The supposed capture of the rebel schooner was an incident that excited but little interest, and no surprise among the people who were accustomed to consider their seamen as invincible; and Barnstable had not found it a difficult task to practise his deception on the few rustics whom curiosity induced to venture alongside the vessels during the short continuance of daylight. When, however, the fogs of evening began to rise along the narrow basin and the curvatures of its margin were lost in the single outline of its dark and gloomy border, the young seaman thought it time to apply himself in earnest to his duty. The Alacrity, containing all his own crew, together with the Ariel's wounded, was gotten silently under way; and driven easily before the heavy air that swept from the land, she drifted from the harbor, until the open sea lay before her, when her sails were spread, and she continued to make the best of her way in quest of the frigate. Barnstable had watched this movement with breathless anxiety; for, on an eminence that completely commanded the waters to some distance, a small but rude battery had been erected for the purpose of protecting the harbor against the depredations and insults of the smaller vessels of the enemy, and a guard of sufficient force to manage the two heavy guns it contained, was maintained in the work at all times. He was ignorant how far his stratagem had been successful, and it was only when he heard the fluttering of the Alacrity's canvas, as she opened it to the breeze, that he felt he was yet secure.

" 'Twill reach the Englishmen's ears," said the boy Merry, who stood on the forecastle of the schooner, by the side of his commander, listening with breathless interest to the sounds; "they set a sentinel on the point, as the sun went down, and if he is a trifle better than a dead man, or a marine asleep, he will suspect something is wrong."

"Never!" returned Barnstable, with a long breath, that announced all his apprehensions were removed; "he will be more likely to believe it a mermaid fanning herself this cool evening, than to suspect the real fact. What say you, Master Coffin?—will the soldier smell the truth?"

"They're a dumb race," said the cockswain, casting his eyes over his shoulders to ascertain that none of their own marine guard was near him; "now there was our sergeant, who ought to know something, seeing that he has been afloat these four years, maintained, dead in the face and eyes of what every man, who has ever doubled Good Hope, knows to be true, that there was no such vessel to be fallen in with in them seas, as the Flying Dutchman! and then, again, when I told him that he was a 'know-nothing,' and asked him if the Dutchman was a more unlikely thing than that there should be places where the inhabitants split the year into two watches, and had day for six months and night the rest of the time, the greenhorn laughed in my face, and I do believe he would have told me I lied, but for one thing."

"And what might that be?" asked Barnstable, gravely.

"Why, sir," returned Tom, stretching his bony fingers, as he surveyed his broad palm by the little light that remained, "though I am a peaceable man, I can be roused."

"And you have seen the Flying Dutchman?"

"I never doubled the East Cape, though I can find my way through Le Maire in the darkest night that ever fell from the heavens; but I have seen them that have seen her, and spoken her too."

"Well, be it so; you must turn flying Yankee, yourself, to-night, Master Coffin. Man your boat at once, sir, and arm your crew."

The cockswain paused a moment before he proceeded to obey this unexpected order, and, pointing toward the battery, he inquired with infinite phlegm:

"For shore-work, sir? Shall we take the cutlasses and pistols? or shall we want the pikes?"

"There may be soldiers in our way, with their bayonets," said Barnstable, musing; "arms as usual, but throw a few long pikes into the boat; and harkye, Master Coffin, out with your tub and whale-line; for I see you have rigged yourself anew in that way."

The cockswain, who was moving from the forecastle, turned short at this new mandate, and, with an air of remonstrance, ventured to say:

"Trust an old whaler, Captain Barnstable, who has been used to these craft all his life. A whale-boat is made to pull with a tub and line in it, as naturally as a ship is made to sail with ballast, and—"

"Out with it, out with it," interrupted the other, with an impatient gesture, that his cockswain knew signified a positive determination. Heaving a sigh at what he deemed his commander's prejudice, Tom applied himself without further delay to the execution of the orders. Barnstable laid his hand familiarly on the shoulder of the boy, and led him to the stern of his little vessel in profound silence. The canvas hood that covered the entrance to the cabin was thrown partly aside; and, by the light of the lamp that was burning in the small apartment, it was easy to overlook, from the deck, what was passing beneath them. Dillon sat supporting his head with his hands, in a manner that shaded his face, but in an attitude that denoted deep and abstracted musing.

"I would that I could see the face of my prisoner," said Barnstable, in an undertone, that was audible only to his companion. "The eye of a man is a sort of light-house, to tell one how to steer into the haven of his confidence, boy."

"And sometimes a beacon, sir, to warn you there is no safe anchorage near him," returned the ready boy.

"Rogue!" muttered Barnstable, "your cousin Kate spoke there."

"If my cousin Plowden were here, Mr. Barnstable, I know that her opinion of yon gentleman would not be at all more favorable."

"And yet, I have determined to trust him! Listen, boy, and tell me if I am wrong; you have a quick wit, like some others of your family, and may suggest something advantageous." The gratified midshipman swelled with the conscious pleasure of possessing his commander's confidence, and followed to the taffrail, over which Barnstable leaned, while he delivered the remainder of his communication. "I have gathered from the longshoremen who have come on this evening to stare at the vessel which the rebels have been able to build, that a party of seamen and marines have been captured in an old ruin near the Abbey of St. Ruth, this very day."

" 'Tis Mr. Griffith!" exclaimed the boy.

"Ay! the wit of your cousin Katherine was not necessary to discover that. Now I have proposed to this gentleman with the Savannah face, that he should go into the Abbey and negotiate an exchange. I will give him for Griffith, and the crew of the Alacrity for Manual's command and the Tigers."

"The Tigers!" cried the lad, with emotion; "have they got my Tigers, too! would to God that Mr. Griffith had permitted me to land!"

"It was no boy's work they were about, and room was scarcer in their boat than live lumber! But this Mr. Dillon has accepted my proposition, and has pledged himself that Griffith shall return within an hour after he is permitted to enter the Abbey; will he redeem his honor from the pledge?"

"He may," said Merry, musing a moment; "for I believe he thinks the presence of Mr. Griffith under the same roof with Miss Howard a thing to be prevented, if possible; he may be true in this instance, though he has a hollow look."

"He has bad-looking light-houses, I will own," said Barnstable; "and yet he is a gentleman, and promises fair; 'tis unmanly to suspect him in such a matter, and I will have faith! Now listen, sir. The absence of older heads must throw great responsibility on your young shoulders; watch that battery as closely as if you were at the mast-head of your frigate, on the look-out for an enemy; the instant you see lights moving in it, cut, and run into the offing; you will find me somewhere under the cliffs, and you will stand off and on, keeping the Abbey in sight, until you fall in with us."

Merry gave an attentive ear to these and divers other solemn injunctions that he received from his commander, who, having sent the officer next to himself in authority in charge of the prize (the third in command being included in the list of the wounded), was compelled to intrust his beloved schooner to the vigilance of a lad whose years gave no promise of the experience and skill that he actually possessed.

When his admonitory instructions were ended, Barnstable stepped again to the opening in the cabin hood, and, for a single moment before he spoke, once more examined the countenance of his prisoner with a keen eye. Dillon had removed his hands from before his sallow features; and, as if conscious of the scrutiny his looks were to undergo, had concentrated the whole expression of his forbidding aspect in a settled gaze of hopeless submission to his fate. At least, so thought his captor, and the idea touched some of the finer feeling in the bosom of the generous young seaman. Discarding, instantly, every suspicion of his prisoner's honor, as alike unworthy of them both, Barnstable summoned him, in a cheerful voice, to the boat. There was a flashing of the features of Dillon at this call, which gave an indefinable expression to his countenance that again startled the sailor; but it was so very transient, and could so easily be mistaken for a smile of pleasure at his promised liberation, that the doubts it engendered passed away almost as speedily as the equivocal expression itself. Barnstable was in the act of following his companion into the boat, when he felt himself detained by a slight hold of his arm.

"What would you have?" he asked of the midshipman who had given him the signal.

"Do not trust too much to that Dillon, sir," returned the anxious boy in a whisper. "If you had seen his face, as I did, when the binnacle-light fell upon it, as he came up the cabin-ladder, you would put no faith in him."

"I should have seen no beauty," said the generous lieutenant, laughing; "but there is Long Tom, as hard-featured a youth of two score and ten as ever washed in brine, who has a heart as big, ay, bigger, than that of a kraken. A bright watch to you, boy, and remember, a keen eye on the battery." As he was yet speaking, Barnstable crossed the gunwale of his little vessel, and it was not until he was seated by the side of his prisoner that he continued aloud:

"Cast the stops off your sails, Mr. Merry, and see all clear to make a run of everything. Recollect, you are short-handed, sir. God bless ye! and d'ye hear? if there is a man among you who shuts more than one eye at a time, I'll make him, when I get back, open both wider than if Tom Coffin's friend, the Flying Dutchman, was booming down upon him. God bless ye, Merry, my boy; give 'em the square-sail, if this breeze off-shore holds on till morning—shove off."

As Barnstable gave the last order he fell back on his seat, and, drawing back his boat-cloak around him, maintained a profound silence until they had passed the two small headlands that formed the mouth of the harbor. The men pulled, with muffled oars, their long, vigorous strokes, and the boat glided with amazing rapidity past the objects that could be yet indistinctly seen along the dim shore. When, however, they gained the open ocean, and the direction of their little bark changed to one that led them in line with the coast, and within the shadows of the cliffs, the cockswain, deeming that the silence was no longer necessary to their safety, ventured to break it, as follows:

"A square-sail is a good sail to carry on a craft, dead afore it, and in a heavy sea; but if fifty years can teach a man to know the weather, it's my judgment that, should the Ariel break ground after the night turns at eight bells, she'll need her mainsail to hold her up to her course."

The lieutenant started at this sudden interruption, and, casting his cloak from his shoulders, he looked abroad on the waters, as if seeking those portentous omens which disturbed the imagination of his cockswain.

"How, now, Tom," he said, sharply; "have ye turned croaker in your old age? What see you, to cause such an old-woman ditty?"

" 'Tis no song of an old woman," returned the cockswain, with solemn earnestness, "but the warning of an old man; and one who has spent his days where there were no hills to prevent the winds of heaven from blowing on him, unless they were hills of salt water and foam. I judge, sir, there'll be a heavy northeaster setting in upon us afore the morning watch is called."

Barnstable knew the experience of his old messmate too well not to feel uneasiness at such an opinion, delivered in so confident a manner; but after again surveying the horizon, the heavens and the ocean, he said, with a continued severity of manner:

"Your prophecy is idle this time, Master Coffin; everything looks like a dead calm. This swell is what is left from the last blow; the mist overhead is nothing but the nightly fog, and you can see, with your own eyes, that it is driving seaward; even this land breeze is nothing but the air of the ground mixing with that of the ocean; it is heavy with dew and fog, but it's as sluggish as a Dutch galiot."

"Ay, sir, it is damp, and there is little of it," rejoined Tom; "but, as it comes only from the shore, so it never goes far on the water. It is hard to learn the true signs of the weather, Captain Barnstable, and none get to know them well but such as study little else or feel but little else. There is only One who can see the winds of heaven, or who can tell when a hurricane is to begin, or where it will end. Still, a man isn't like a whale or a porpoise, that takes the air in his nostrils, but never knows whether it is a southeaster or a northwester that he feeds upon. Look broad off to leeward, sir; see the streak of clear sky shining under the mists; take an old seafaring man's word for it, Captain Barnstable, that, whenever the light shines out of the heavens in that fashion, 'tis never done for nothing; besides, the sun set in a dark bank of clouds, and the little moon we had was dry and windy."

Barnstable listened attentively, and with increasing concern, for he well knew that his cockswain possessed a quick and almost unerring judgment of the weather, notwithstanding the confused medley of superstitious omens and signs with which it was blended; but, again throwing himself back in his boat, he muttered:

"Then let it blow; Griffith is worth a heavier risk, and, if the battery can't be cheated, it can be carried."

Nothing further passed on the state of the weather. Dillon had not ventured a single remark since he entered the boat, and the cockswain had the discretion to understand that his officer was willing to be left to his own thoughts. For nearly an hour they pursued their way with diligence; the sinewy seamen who wielded the oars, urging their light boat along the edge of the surf with unabated velocity, and apparently with untired exertions. Occasionally Barnstable would cast an inquiring glance at the little inlets that they passed, or would note, with a seaman's eye, the small portions of sandy beach that were scattered here and there along the rocky boundaries of the coast. One, in particular, a deeper inlet than common, where a run of fresh water was heard gurgling as it met the tide, he pointed out to his cockswain, by significant but silent gestures, as a place to be especially noted. Tom, who understood the signal as intended for his own eye alone, made his observations on the spot with equal taciturnity, but with all the minuteness that would distinguish one long accustomed to find his way, whether by land or water, by landmarks and the bearings of different objects. Soon after this silent communication between the lieutenant and his cockswain, the boat was suddenly turned, and was in the act of dashing upon the spit of sand before it, when Barnstable checked the movement by his voice:

"Hold water!" he said; " 'tis the sound of oars!"

The seamen held their boat at rest, while a deep attention was given to the noise that had alarmed the ears of their commander.

"See, sir," said the cockswain, pointing toward the eastern horizon; "it is just rising into the streak of light to seaward of us—now it settles in the trough—ah, here you have it again!"

"By heaven!" cried Barnstable, " 'tis a man-of-war's stroke it pulls; I saw the oar-blades as they fell! and, listen to the sound! neither your fisherman nor your smuggler pulls such a regular oar."

Tom had bowed his head nearly to the water, in the act of listening, and now, raising himself, spoke with confidence:

"That is the Tiger; I know the stroke of her crew as well as I do of my own. Mr. Merry has made them learn the new-fashioned jerk, as they dip their blades, and they feather with such a roll in their rowlocks. I could swear to the stroke."

"Hand me the night-glass," said the commander, impatiently; "I can catch them, as they are lifted into the streak. You are right, by every star in our flag, Tom!—but there is only one man in her stern-sheets. By my good eyes, I be-

lieve it is that accursed pilot, sneaking from the land, and leaving Griffith and Manual to die in English prisons. To the shore with you—beach her at once!"

The order was no sooner given that it was obeyed, and, in less than two minutes, the impatient Barnstable, Dillon and the cockswain, were standing together on the sands.

The impression he had received, that his friends were abandoned to their fate by the pilot, urged the generous young seaman to hasten the departure of the prisoner as he was fearful every moment might interpose some new obstacle to the success of his plans.

"Mr. Dillon," he said, the instant they were landed, "I exact no new promise—your honor is already plighted—"

"If oaths can make it stronger," interrupted Dillon, "I will take them."

"Oaths cannot—the honor of a gentleman is, at all times, enough. I shall send my cockswain with you to the Abbey, and you will either return with him, in person, within two hours, or give Mr. Griffith and Captain Manual to his guidance. Proceed, sir—you are conditionally free; there is an easy opening by which to ascend the cliffs."

Dillon once more thanked his generous captor, and then proceeded to force his way up the rough eminence.

"Follow and obey his instructions," said Barnstable to his cockswain, aloud.

Tom, long accustomed to implicit obedience, handled his harpoon, and was quietly following in the footsteps of his new leader, when he felt the hand of the lieutenant on his shoulder.

"You saw where the brook emptied over the hillock of sand?" said Barnstable, in an undertone.

Tom nodded assent.

"You will find us there riding without the surf; 'twill not do to trust too much to an enemy."

The cockswain made a gesture of great significance with his weapon, that was intended to indicate the danger their prisoner would incur should he prove false; when, applying the wooden end of the harpoon to the rocks, he ascended the ravine at a rate that soon brought him to the side of his companion.

22

Falstaff:

Ay, marry, let me have him to sit under;
He's like to be a cold soldier.

Henry IV

BARNSTABLE lingered on the sands for a few minutes, until the footsteps of Dillon and the cockswain were no longer audible, when he ordered his men to launch their boat once more into the surf. While the seamen pulled leisurely toward the place he had designated as the point where he would await the return of Tom, the lieutenant first began to entertain serious apprehensions concerning the good faith of his prisoner. Now that Dillon was beyond his control, his imagination presented, in very vivid colors, several little circumstances in the other's conduct, which might readily excuse some doubts of his good faith; and, by the time they had reached the place of rendezvous, and had cast a light grapnel into the sea, his fears had rendered him excessively uncomfortable. Leaving the lieutenant to his reflections on this unpleasant subject, we shall follow Dillon and his fearless and unsuspecting companion in their progress toward St. Ruth.

The mists to which Tom had alluded in his discussion with his commander on the state of the weather, appeared to be settling nearer to the earth, and assuming more decidedly the appearance of a fog, hanging above them in sluggish volumes, but little agitated by the air. The consequent obscurity added deeply to the gloom of the night, and it would have been difficult for one less acquainted than Dillon with the surrounding localities, to find the path which led to the dwelling of Colonel Howard. After some little search this desirable object was effected; and the civilian led the way, with rapid strides, toward the Abbey.

"Ay, ay?" said Tom, who followed his steps, and equalled his paces without any apparent effort, "you shore-people have an easy way to find your course and distance when you get into the track. I was once left by the craft I belonged to, in Boston, to find my way to Plymouth, which is a matter of fifteen leagues, or thereaway; and so, finding nothing was bound up the bay, after laying-by for a week, I concluded to haul aboard my land-tacks. I spent the better part of another week in a search for some hooker on board which I might work my passage across the country, for money was as scarce then with old Tom Coffin as it is now, and is likely to be, unless the fisheries get a good luff soon; but it seems that nothing but your horse-flesh, and horned cattle, and jackasses, are privileged to do the pulling and hauling in your shore-hookers; and I was forced to pay a week's wages for a berth, besides keeping a banyan on a mouthful of bread and cheese, from the time we hove-up in Boston till we came to Plymouth town."

"It was certainly an unreasonable exaction on the part of the wagoners, from a man in your situation," said Dillon, in a friendly, soothing tone of voice, that denoted a willingness to pursue the conversation.

"My situation was that of a cabin passenger," returned the cockswain; "for there was but one hand forward, besides the cattle I mentioned—that was he who steered—and an easy berth he had of it; for there his course lay atween walls of stone and fences; and, as for his reckoning, why, they had stuck up bits of stone on an end, with his day's work footed up, ready to his hand, every half league or so. Besides, the landmarks were so plenty, that a man with half an eye might steer her, and no fear of getting to leeward."

"You must have found yourself, as it were, in a new world," observed Dillon.

"Why, to me, it was pretty much the same as if I had been set afloat in a strange country, though I may be said to be a native of those parts, being born on the coast. I had often heard shore-men say that there was as much 'arth as water in the world, which I always set down as a rank lie, for I've sailed with a flowing sheet months an-end without falling in with as much land or rock as would answer a gull to lay its eggs on; but I will own that atween Boston and Plymouth we were out of sight of water for as much as two full watches!"

Dillon pursued this interesting subject with diligence; and by the time they reached the wall, which enclosed the large paddock that surrounded the Abbey, the cockswain was deeply involved in a discussion of the comparative magnitude of the Atlantic Ocean and the Continent of America.

Avoiding the principal entrance of the building, through the great gates which communicated with the court in front, Dillon followed the windings of the wall until it led them to a wicket, which he knew was seldom closed for the night until the hour for general rest had arrived. Their way now lay in the rear of the principal edifice, and soon conducted them to the confused pile which contained the offices. The cockswain followed his companion with a confiding reliance on his knowledge and good faith, that was somewhat increased by the freedom of communication that had been maintained during their walk from the cliffs. He did not perceive anything extraordinary in the other's stopping at the room, which had been provided as a sort of barracks for the soldiers of Captain Borroughcliffe. A conference which took place between Dillon and the sergeant was soon ended, when the former beckoned to the cockswain to follow, and, taking a circuit round the whole of the offices, they entered the Abbey together, by the door through which the ladies had issued, when in quest of the three prisoners, as has been already related. After a turn or two among the narrow passages of that part of the edifice, Tom, whose faith in the facilities of land navigation began to be a little shaken, found himself following the guide through a long dark gallery, that was terminated at the end toward which they were approaching, by a half-open door, that admitted a glimpse into a well-lighted and comfortable apartment. To this door Dillon hastily advanced, and, throwing it open, the cockswain enjoyed a full view of the very scene that we have described, in introducing Colonel Howard to the acquaintance of the reader, and under circumstances of great similitude. The cheerful fire of coal, the strong and glaring lights, the tables of polished mahogany, and the blushing fields, were still the same in appearance, while the only perceptible change was the number of those who partook of the cheer. The master of the mansion, and Borroughcliffe, were seated opposite to each other, employed in discussing the events of the day, and diligently pushing to and fro the glittering vessel that contained a portion of the generous liquor they both loved so well; a task which each moment rendered lighter.

"If Kit would but return," exclaimed the veteran, whose back was to the opening door, "bringing with him his honest brows encircled, as they will be, or ought to be, with laurel, I should be the happiest old fool, Borroughcliffe, in his majesty's realm of Great Britain!"

The captain, who felt the necessity for the unnatural restraint he had imposed on his thirst to be removed by the capture of his enemies, pointed toward the door with one hand, while he grasped the sparkling reservoir of the "south side" with the other, and answered:

"Lo! the cacique himself! his brow inviting the diadem—ha! who have we in his highness's train? By the Lord, Sir Cacique, if you travel with a body-guard of such grenadiers, old Frederick of Prussia himself will have occasion to envy you the corps! a clear six-footer in Nature's stockings! and the arms as unique as the armed!"

The colonel did not, however, attend to half of his companion's exclamations, but, turning, he beheld the individual he had so much desired, and received him with a delight proportioned to the unexpectedness of the pleasure. For several minutes Dillon was compelled to listen to the rapid questions of his venerable relative, to all of which he answered with a prudent reserve, that might, in some measure, have been governed by the presence of the cock-swain. Tom stood with infinite composure, leaning on his harpoon, and surveying, with a countenance where wonder was singularly blended with contempt, the furniture and arrangements of an apartment that was far more splendid than any he had before seen. In the meantime, Borroughcliffe entirely disregarded the private communications that passed between his host and Dillon, which gradually became more deeply interesting, and finally drew them to a distant corner of the apartment; but, taking a most undue advantage of the absence of the gentleman, who had so lately been his boon companion, he swallowed one potation after another, as if a double duty had developed on him in consequence of the desertion of the veteran. Whenever his eye did wander from the ruby tint of his glass, it was to survey with unrepressed admiration the inches of the cockswain, about whose stature and frame there were numberless excellent points to attract the gaze of a recruiting-officer. From this double pleasure, the captain was, however, at last summoned to participate in the councils of his friends.

Dillon was spared the disagreeable duty of repeating the artful tale he had found it necessary to palm on the colonel, by the ardor of the veteran himself, who executed the task in a manner that gave to the treachery of his kinsman every appearance of a justifiable artifice, and of unshaken zeal in the cause of his prince. In substance, Tom was to be detained as a prisoner, and the party of Barnstable were to be entrapped, and, of course, share a similar fate. The sunken eye of Dillon cowered before the steady gaze which Borroughcliffe fastened on him as the latter listened to the plaudits the colonel lavished on his cousin's ingenuity; but the hesitation that lingered in the soldier's manner vanished when he turned to their unsuspecting prisoner, who was continuing his survey of the apartment, while he innocently imagined the consultations he witnessed were merely the proper and preparatory steps to his admission into the presence of Mr. Griffith.

"Drill," said Borroughcliffe, aloud, "advance and receive your orders." The cockswain turned quickly at this sudden mandate, and, for the first time, perceived that he had been followed into the gallery by the orderly and two files of recruits armed. "Take this man to the guard-room and feed him, and see that he dies not of thirst."

There was nothing alarming in this order, and Tom was following the soldiers, in obedience to a gesture from their captain, when their steps were arrested in the gallery by the cry of "Halt!"

"On recollection, Drill," said Borroughcliffe, in a tone from which all dictatorial sounds were banished, "show the gentleman into my own room, and see him properly supplied."

The orderly gave such an intimation of his comprehending the meaning of his officer as the latter was accustomed to receive, when Borroughcliffe returned to his bottle, and the cockswain followed his guide, with the alacrity and good-will that were not a little increased by the repeated mention of the cheer that awaited him.

Luckily for the impatience of Tom, the quarters of the captain were at hand, and the promised entertainment by no means slow in making its appearance. The former was an apartment that opened from a lesser gallery, which communicated with the principal passage already mentioned; and the latter was a bountiful but ungarnished supply of that staple of the British isles called roast beef; of which the kitchen of Colonel Howard was never without a due and loyal provision. The sergeant, who certainly understood one of the signs of his captain to imply an attack on the citadel of the cockswain's brain, mingled, with his own hands, a potation that he styled a rummer of grog, and which he thought would have felled the animal itself that Tom was so diligently masticating, had it been alive and in its vigor. Every calculation that was made on the infirmity of the cockswain's intellect, under the stimulus of Jamaica, was, however, futile. He swallowed glass after glass, with prodigious relish, but at the same time, with immovable steadiness; and the eyes of the sergeant, who felt it incumbent to do honor to his own cheer, were already glistening in his head, when, happily for the credit of his heart, a tap at the door announced the presence of his captain, and relieved him from the impending disgrace of being drunk blind by a recruit.

As Borroughcliffe entered the apartment, he commanded his orderly to retire, adding:

"Mr. Dillon will give you instructions, which you are implicitly to obey."

Drill, who had sense enough remaining to apprehend the displeasure of his officer, should the latter discover his condition, quickened his departure, and the cockswain soon found himself alone with the captain. The vigor of Tom's attacks on the remnant of the sirloin was now much abated, leaving in its stead that placid quiet which is apt to linger about the palate long after the cravings of the appetite have been appeased. He had seated himself on one of the trunks of Borroughcliffe, utterly disdaining the use of a chair; and, with the trencher in his lap, was using his own jack-knife on the dilapidated fragment of the ox, with something of that nicety with which the female ghoul of the Arabian Tales might be supposed to pick her rice with the point of her bodkin. The captain drew a seat nigh the cockswain; and, with a familiarity and kindness infinitely condescending, when the difference in their several conditions is considered, he commenced the following dialogue:

"I hope you have found your entertainment to your liking, Mr. a—a I must own my ignorance of your name."

"Tom," said the cockswain, keeping his eyes roaming over the contents of the trencher; "commonly called Long Tom, by my shipmates."

"You have sailed with discreet men, and able navigators, it will seem, as they understood longitude so well," rejoined the captain; "but you have a patronymic—I would say another name?"

"Coffin," returned the cockswain; "I'm called Tom, when there is any hurry, such as letting go the haul-yards, or a sheet; Long Tom, when they want to get to windward of an old seaman, by fair weather; and Long Tom Coffin when they wish to hail me so that none of my cousins of the same name, about the islands, shall answer; for I believe the best man among them can't measure much over a fathom, taking him from his headworks to his heel."

"You are a most deserving fellow," cried Borroughcliffe, "and it is painful to think to what a fate the treachery of Mr. Dillon has consigned you."

The suspicions of Tom, if he ever had any, were lulled to rest too effectually by the kindness he had received, to be awakened by this equivocal lament; he, therefore, after renewing his intimacy with the rummer, contented himself by saying, with a satisfied simplicity:

"I am consigned to no one, carrying no cargo but this Mr. Dillon, who is to give me Mr. Griffith in exchange, or go back to the Ariel himself, as my prisoner."

"Ah! my good friend, I fear you will find, when the time comes to make this exchange, that he will refuse to do either."

"But I'll be d——d if he don't do one of them! my orders are to see it done, and back he goes; or Mr. Griffith, who is as good a seaman, for his years, as ever trod a deck, slips his cable from this here anchorage."

Borroughcliffe affected to eye his companion with great commiseration; an exhibition of compassion that was, however, completely lost on the cockswain, whose nerves were strung to their happiest tension by his repeated libations, while his wit was, if anything, quickened by the same cause, though his own want of guile rendered him slow to comprehend its existence in others. Perceiving it necessary to speak plainly, the captain renewed the attack in a more direct manner:

"I am sorry to say that you will not be permitted to return to the Ariel; and that your commander, Mr. Barnstable, will be a prisoner within the hour; and, in fact, that your schooner will be taken before the morning breaks."

"Who'll take her?" asked the cockswain, with a grim smile, on whose feelings, however, this combination of threatened calamities was beginning to make some impression.

"You must remember that she lies immediately under the heavy guns of a battery that can sink her in a few minutes; an express has already been sent to acquaint the commander of the work with the Ariel's true character; and, as the wind has already begun to blow from the ocean, her escape is impossible."

The truth, together with its portentous consequences, now began to glare across the faculties of the cockswain. He remembered his own prognostics on the weather, and the helpless situation of the schooner, deprived of more than half her crew, and left to the keeping of a boy, while her commander himself was on the eve of captivity. The trencher fell from his lap to the floor, his head sunk on his knees, his face was concealed between his broad palms, and, in spite of every effort the old seaman could make to conceal his emotion, he fairly groaned aloud.

For a moment the better feelings of Borroughcliffe prevailed; and he paused as he witnessed this exhibition of suffering in one whose head was already sprinkled with the marks of time; but his habits, and the impressions left by many years passed in collecting victims for the wars, soon resumed their ascendancy, and the recruiting officer diligently addressed himself to an improvement of his advantage.

"I pity from my heart the poor lads whom artifice or mistaken notions of duty may have led astray, and who will thus be taken in arms against their sovereign; but, as they are found in the very island of Britain, they must be made examples to deter others. I fear that, unless they can make their peace with government, they will all be condemned to death."

"Let them make their peace with God, then; your government can do but little to clear the log account of a man whose watch is up for this world."

"But, by making their peace with those who have the power, their lives may be spared," said the captain, watching, with keen eyes, the effect his words produced on the cockswain.

"It matters but little, when a man hears the messenger pipe his hammock down for the last time; he keeps his watch in another world, though he goes below in this. But to see the wood and iron, that has been put together after such moulds as the Ariel's, go into strange hands, is a blow that a man may remember long after the purser's books have been squared against his name forever! I would rather that twenty shot should strike my old carcass, than one should hull the schooner that didn't pass out above her water-line."

Borroughcliffe replied, somewhat carelessly: "I may be mistaken, after all, and, instead of putting any of you to death, they may place you all on board the prison-ships, where you may yet have a merry time of it these ten or fifteen years to come."

"How's that, shipmate!" cried the cockswain, with a start; "a prison-ship, d'ye say? you may tell them they can save the expense of one man's rations by hanging him, if they please, and that is old Tom Coffin."

"There is no answering for their caprice; to-day they may order a dozen of you to be shot for rebels; to-morrow they may choose to consider you as prisoners of war, and send you to the hulks for a dozen years."

"Tell them, brother, that I'm a rebel, will ye? and ye'll tell 'em no lie—one that has fou't them since Manly's time, in Boston Bay, to this hour. I hope the boy will blow her up! it would be the death of poor Richard Barnstable to see her in the hands of the English!"

"I know of one way," said Borroughcliffe, affecting to muse, "and but one, that will certainly avert the prison-ship; for, on second thoughts, they will hardly put you to death."

"Name it, friend," cried the cockswain, rising from his seat in evident perturbation, "and if it lies in the power of man, it shall be done."

"Nay," said the captain, dropping his hand familiarly on the shoulder of the other, who listened with the most eager attention, " 'tis easily done, and no dreadful thing in itself; you are used to gunpowder, and know its smell from attar of roses!"

"Ay, ay," cried the impatient old seaman; "I have had it flashing under my nose by the hour; what then?"

"Why, then, what I have to propose will be nothing to a man like you—you found the beef wholesome, and the grog mellow?"

"Ay, ay, all well enough: but what is that to an old sailor?" asked the cockswain, unconsciously grasping the collar of Borroughcliffe's coat in his agitation; "what then?"

The captain manifested no displeasure at this unexpected familiarity, but smiled with suavity as he unmasked the battery, from behind which he had hitherto carried on his attacks.

"Why, then, you have only to serve your king as you have before served the Congress—and let me be the man to show you your colors."

The cockswain stared at the speaker intently, but it was evident he did not clearly comprehend the nature of the proposition, and the captain pursued the subject:

"In plain English, enlist in my company, my fine fellow, and your life and liberty are both safe."

Tom did not laugh aloud, for that was a burst of feeling in which he was seldom known to indulge; but every feature of his weather-beaten visage contracted into an expression of bitter, ironical contempt. Borroughcliffe felt the iron fingers, that still grasped his collar, gradually tightening about his throat, like a vice; and, as the arm slowly contracted, his body was drawn, by a power that it was in vain to resist, close to that of the cockswain, who, when their faces were within a foot of each other, gave vent to his emotions in words:

"A messmate before a shipmate; a shipmate before a stranger; a stranger before a dog—but a dog before a soldier!"

As Tom concluded, his nervous arm was suddenly extended to the utmost, the fingers relinquishing their grasp at the same time; and, when Borroughcliffe recovered his disordered facilities, he found himself in a distant corner of the apartment, prostrate among a confused pile of chairs, tables and wearing apparel. In endeavoring to rise from this humble posture, the hand of the captain fell on the hilt of his sword, which had been included in the confused assemblage of articles produced by his overthrow.

"How now, scoundrel!" he cried, baring the glittering weapon, and springing on his feet; "you must be taught your distance, I perceive."

The cockswain seized the harpoon which leaned against the wall, and dropped its barbed extremity within a foot of the breast of his assailant, with an expression of the eye that denoted the danger of a nearer approach. The captain, however, wanted not for courage, and, stung to the quick by the insult he had received, he made a desperate parry, and attempted to pass within the point of the novel weapon of his adversary. The slight shock was followed by a sweeping whirl of the harpoon, and Borroughcliffe found himself without arms, completely at the mercy of his foe. The bloody intentions of Tom vanished with his success; for laying aside his weapon, he advanced upon his antagonist and seized him with an open palm. One more struggle, in which the captain discovered his incompetency to make any defence against the strength of a man who managed him as if he had been a child, decided the matter. When the captain was passive in the hands of his foe, the cockswain produced sundry pieces of sennet, marline and ratlin-stuff, from his pockets, which appeared to contain as great a variety of small cordage as a boatswain's storeroom, and proceeded to lash the arms of the conquered soldier to the posts of his bed, with a coolness that had not been disturbed since the commencement of hostilities, a silence that seemed inflexible, and a dexterity that none but a seaman could equal. When this part of his plan was executed Tom paused a moment and gazed around him as if in quest of something. The naked sword caught his eye, and, with this weapon in his hand, he deliberately approached his captive, whose alarm prevented his observing that the cockswain had snapped the blade asunder from the handle, and that he had already encircled the latter with marline.

"For God's sake," exclaimed Borroughcliffe, "murder me not in cold blood!"

The silver hilt entered his mouth as the words issued from it, and the captain found, while the line was passed and repassed, in repeated involutions across the back of his neck, that he was in a condition to which he often subjected his own men, when unruly, and which is universally called being "gagged." The cockswain now appeared to think himself entitled to all the privileges of a conqueror; for, taking the light in his hand, he commenced a scrutiny into the nature and quality of the worldly effects that lay at his mercy. Sundry articles, that belonged to the equipments of a soldier, were examined and cast aside with great contempt, and divers garments of plainer exterior were rejected as unsuited to the frame of the victor. He, however, soon encountered two articles of a metal that is universally understood. But uncertainty as to their use appeared greatly to embarrass him. The circular prongs of these curiosities were applied to either hand, to the wrists, and even to the nose, and the little wheels at their opposite extremity were turned and examined with as much curiosity and care as a savage would expend on a watch, until the idea seemed to cross the mind of the honest seaman that they formed part of the useless trappings of a military man, and he cast them aside as utterly worthless. Borroughcliffe, who watched every movement of his conqueror, with a good-humor that would have restored perfect harmony between them, could he but have expressed half what he felt, witnessed the safety of a favorite pair of spurs with much pleasure, though nearly suffocated by the mirth that was unnaturally repressed. At length the cockswain found a pair of handsomely-mounted pistols, a sort of weapon with which he seemed quite familiar. They were loaded, and the knowledge of that fact appeared to remind Tom of the necessity of departing, by bringing to his recollection the danger of his commander and of the Ariel. He thrust the weapons into the canvas belt that encircled his body, and, grasping his harpoon, approached the bed, where Borroughcliffe was seated in duress.

"Harkye, friend," said the cockswain, "may the Lord forgive you, as I do, for wishing to make a soldier of a seafaring man, and one who has followed the waters since he was an hour old, and one who hopes to die off soundings, and to be buried in brine! I wish you no harm, friend; but you'll have to keep a stopper on your conversation till such time as some of your messmates call in this way, which I hope will be as soon after I get an offing as may be."

With these amicable wishes the cockswain departed, leaving Borroughcliffe the light, and the undisturbed possession of his apartment, though not in the most easy or the most enviable situation imaginable. The captain heard the bolt of his lock turn, and the key rattle as the cockswain withdrew it from the door—two precautionary steps, which clearly indicated that the vanquisher deemed it prudent to secure his retreat, by insuring the detention of the vanquished, for at least a time.

23

Whilst Vengeance, in the lurid air,
Lifts her red arm, exposed and bare,
Who, Fear, this ghastly train can see,
And look not madly wild, like thee!

COLLINS

IT is certain that Tom Coffin had devised no settled plan of operations, when he issued from the apartment of Borrough-cliffe, if we except a most resolute determination to make the best of his way to the Ariel, and to share her fate, let it be either to sink or swim. But this was a resolution much easier formed by the honest seaman than executed in his present situation. He would have found it less difficult to extricate a vessel from the dangerous shoals of the "Devil's Grip," than to thread the mazes of the labyrinth of passages, galleries, and apartments, in which he found himself involved. He remembered, as he expressed it to himself, in a low soliloquy, "to have run into a narrow passage from the main channel, but whether he had sheered to the starboard or larboard hand," was a material fact that had entirely escaped his memory. Tom was in that part of the building that Colonel Howard had designated as the "cloisters," and in which, luckily for him, he was but little liable to encounter any foe, the room occupied by Borrough-cliffe being the only one in the entire wing that was not exclusively devoted to the service of the ladies. The circumstance of the soldiers being permitted to invade this sanctuary was owing to the necessity, on the part of Colonel

Howard, of placing either Griffith, Manual, or the recruiting-officer, in the vicinity of his wards, or of subjecting his prisoners to a treatment that the veteran would have thought unworthy of his name and character. This recent change in the quarters of Borroughcliffe operated doubly to the advantage of Tom, by lessening the chance of the speedy release of his uneasy captive, as well as by diminishing his own danger. Of the former circumstance he was, however, not aware; and the consideration of the latter was a sort of reflection to which the cockswain was, in no degree, addicted.

Following, necessarily, the line of the wall, he soon emerged from the dark and narrow passage in which he had first found himself, and entered the principal gallery, that communicated with all the lower apartments of that wing, as well as with the main body of the edifice. An open door, through which a strong light was glaring, at a distant end of this gallery, instantly caught his eye, and the old seaman had not advanced many steps toward it before he discovered that he was approaching the very room which had so much excited his curiosity, and by the identical passage through which he had entered the Abbey. To turn and retrace his steps was the most obvious course for any man to take who felt anxious to escape; but the sounds of high conviviality bursting from the cheerful apartment, among which the cockswain thought he distinguished the name of Griffith, determined Tom to advance and reconnoitre the scene more closely. The reader will anticipate that when he paused in the shadow, the doubting old seaman stood once more near the threshold which he had so lately crossed, when conducted to the room of Borroughcliffe. The seat of that gentleman was now occupied by Dillon, and Colonel Howard had resumed his wonted station at the foot of the table. The noise was chiefly made by the latter, who had been enjoying a more minute relation of the means by which his kinsman had entrapped his unwary enemy.

"A nice *ruse!*" cried the veteran, as Tom assumed his post, in ambush—"a most noble and ingenious *ruse*, and such a one as would have baffled Caesar! He must have been a cunning dog, that Caesar; but I do think, Kit, you would have been too much for him; hang me if I don't think you would have puzzled Wolfe himself, had you held Quebec, instead of Montcalm! Ah, boy! we want you in the colonies, with the ermine over your shoulders; such men as you, cousin Christopher, are sadly, sadly wanted there to defend his majesty's rights."

"Indeed, dear sir, your partiality gives me credit for qualities I do not possess," said Dillon, dropping his eyes, perhaps with a feeling of conscious unworthiness, but with an air of much humility; "the little justifiable artifice—"

"Ay! there lies the beauty of the transaction," interrupted the colonel, shoving the bottle from him, with the free, open air of a man who never harbored disguise; "you told no lie; no mean deception, that any dog, however base and unworthy, might invent; but you practised a neat, a military, a—a—yes, a classical deception, on your enemy; a classical deception, that is the very term for it; such a deception as Pompey, or Mark Antony, or—or—you know those old fellows' names, better than I do, Kit; but name the cleverest fellow that ever lived in Greece, or Rome, and I shall say he is a dunce compared to you. 'Twas a real Spartan trick, both simple and honest."

It was extremely fortunate for Dillon that the animation of his aged kinsman kept his head and body in such constant motion, during this apostrophe, as to intercept the aim that the cockswain was deliberately taking at his head with one of Borroughcliffe's pistols; and perhaps the sense of shame which induced him to sink his face on his hands, was another means of saving his life, by giving the indignant old seaman time for reflection.

"But you have not spoken of the ladies," said Dillon, after a moment's pause; "I should hope they have borne the alarm of the day like kinswomen of the family of Howard."

The colonel glanced his eyes around him, as if to assure himself they were alone, and dropped his voice, as he answered:

"Ah, Kit! they have come to, since this rebel scoundrel, Griffith, has been brought into the Abbey; we were favored with the company of even Miss Howard, in the dining-room, to-day. There was a good deal of 'dear-uncleing,' and 'fears that my life might be exposed by the quarrels and skirmishes of these desperadoes who have landed'; as if an old fellow, who served through the whole war, from '56 to '63, was afraid to let his nose smell gunpowder any more than if it were snuff! But it will be a hard matter to wheedle an old soldier out of his allegiance! This Griffith goes to the Tower, at least, Mr. Dillon."

"It would be advisable to commit his person to the civil authority, without delay."

"To the constable of the Tower, the Earl Cornwallis, a good and loyal nobleman, who is, at this moment, fighting the rebels in my own native province, Christopher," interrupted the colonel; "that will be what I call retributive justice; but," continued the veteran, rising with an air of gentlemanly dignity, "it will not do to permit even the constable of the Tower of London to surpass the master of St. Ruth in hospitality and kindness to his prisoners. I have ordered suitable refreshments to their apartments, and it is incumbent on me to see that my commands have been properly obeyed. Arrangements must also be made for the reception of this Captain Barnstable, who will, doubtless, soon be here."

"Within the hour, at farthest," said Dillon, looking uneasily at his watch.

"We must be stirring, boy," continued the colonel, moving toward the door that led to the apartments of his prisoners; "but there is a courtesy due to the ladies, as well as to those unfortunate violators of the laws—go, Christopher, convey my kindest wishes to Cecilia; she don't deserve them, the obstinate vixen, but then she is my brother Harry's child! and while there, you arch dog, plead your own cause. Mark Antony was a fool to you at a *ruse*, and yet Mark was one of your successful suitors, too; there was that Queen of the Pyramids—"

The door closed on the excited veteran, at these words, and Dillon was left standing by himself, at the side of the table, musing, as if in doubt whether to venture on the step that his kinsman had proposed, or not.

The greater part of the preceding discourse was unintelligible to the cockswain, who had waited its termination with extraordinary patience, in hopes he might obtain some information that he could render of service to the captives. Before he had time to decide on what was now best for him to do, Dillon suddenly determined to venture himself in the cloisters; and, swallowing a couple of glasses of wine in a breath, he passed the hesitating cockswain, who was concealed by the opening door, so closely as to brush his person, and moved down the gallery with those rapid strides which men who act under the impulse of forced resolutions are very apt to assume, as if to conceal their weakness from themselves. Tom hesitated no longer; but aiding the impulse given to the door by Dillon, as he passed, so as to darken the passage, he followed the sounds of the other's footsteps, while he trod, in the manner already described, the stone pavement of the gallery. Dillon paused an instant at the turning that led to the room of Borroughcliffe, but whether irresolute which way to urge his steps, or listening to the incautious and heavy tread of the cockswain, is not known; if the latter, he mistook them for the echoes of his own footsteps, and moved forward again without making any discovery.

The light tap which Dillon gave on the door of the withdrawing-room of the cloisters, was answered by the soft voice of Cecilia Howard herself, who bade the applicant enter. There was a slight confusion evident in the manner of the gentleman as he complied with the bidding, and, in its hesitancy, the door was for an instant neglected.

"I come, Miss Howard," said Dillon, "by the commands of your uncle, and, permit me to add, by my own—"

"May Heaven shield us!" exclaimed Cecilia, clasping her hands in affright, and rising involuntarily from her couch, "are we, too, to be imprisoned and murdered?"

"Surely Miss Howard will not impute to me—" Dillon paused, observing that the wild looks, not only of Cecilia, but of Katherine and Alice Dunscombe, also, were directed at some other object, and, turning, to his manifest terror he beheld the gigantic frame of the cockswain, surmounted by an iron visage fixed in settled hostility, in possession of the only passage from the apartment.

"If there's murder to be done," said Tom, after surveying the astonished group with a stern eye, "it's as likely this here liar will be the one to do it as another; but you have nothing to fear from a man who has followed the seas too long, and has grappled with too many monsters, both flesh and fish, not to know how to treat a helpless woman. None, who know him, will say that Thomas Coffin ever used uncivil language, or unseaman-like conduct, to any of his mother's kind."

"Coffin!" exclaimed Katherine, advancing with a more confident air, from the corner into which terror had driven her with her companions.

"Ay, Coffin," continued the old sailor, his grim features gradually relaxing, as he gazed on her bright looks; " 'tis a solemn word, but it's a word that passes over the shoals, among the islands, and along the cape, oftener than any other. My father was a Coffin and my mother was a Joy; and the two names can count more flukes than all the rest in the island together; though the Worths, and the Garners, and the Swaines, dart better harpoons, and set truer lances, than any men who come from the weather-side of the Atlantic."

Katherine listened to this digression in honor of the whalers of Nantucket, with marked complacency; and, when he concluded, she repeated, slowly:

"Coffin! this, then, is Long Tom?"

"Ay, ay, Long Tom, and no sham in the name, either," returned the cockswain, suffering the stern indignation that had lowered around his hard visage to relax into a low laugh as he gazed on her animated features; "the Lord bless your smiling face and bright black eyes, young madam! you have heard of old Long Tom, then? most likely, 'twas something about the blow he strikes at the fish—ah! I'm old and I'm stiff, now, young madam, but, afore I was nineteen, I stood at the head of the dance, at a ball on the cape, and that with a partner almost as handsome as yourself—ay! and this was after I had three broad flukes logged against my name."

"No," said Katherine, advancing in her eagerness a step or two nigher to the old tar, her cheeks flushing while she spoke, "I have heard of you as an instructor in a seaman's duty, as the faithful cockswain, nay, I may say, as the devoted companion and friend of Mr. Richard Barnstable—but, perhaps, you came now as the bearer of some message or letter from that gentleman."

The sound of his commander's name suddenly revived the recollection of Coffin, and with it all the fierce sternness of his manner returned. Bending his eyes keenly on the cowering form of Dillon, he said in those deep, harsh tones, that seem peculiar to men who have braved the elements, until they appear to have imbibed some of their roughest qualities:

"Liar! how now? What brought old Tom Coffin into these shoals and narrow channels? was it a letter? ha! but by the Lord that maketh the winds to blow, and teacheth the lost mariner how to steer over the wide waters, you shall sleep this night, villain, on the planks of the Ariel; and if it be the will of God that beautiful piece of handicraft is to sink at her mooring, like a worthless hulk, ye shall still sleep in her—ay, and a sleep that shall not end till they call all hands to foot up the day's work of this life, at the close of man's longest voyage."

The extraordinary vehemence, the language, the attitude of the old seaman, commanding in its energy, and the honest indignation that shone in every look of his keen eyes, together with the nature of the address, and its paralyzing effect on Dillon, who quailed before it like the stricken deer, united to keep the female listeners, for many moments, silent through amazement. During this brief period, Tom advanced upon his nerveless victim, and, lashing his arms together behind his back, he fastened him, by a strong cord, to the broad canvas belt that he constantly wore around his own body, leaving to himself, by this arrangement, the free use of his arms and weapons of offence, while he secured his captive.

"Surely," said Cecilia, recovering her recollection the first of the astonished group, "Mr. Barnstable has not commissioned you to offer this violence to my uncle's kinsman, under the roof of Colonel Howard?—Miss Plowden, your friend has strangely forgotten himself in this transaction, if this man acts in obedience to his order!"

"My friend, my cousin Howard," returned Katherine, "would never commission his cockswain, or any one, to do an unworthy deed. Speak, honest sailor; why do you commit this outrage on the worthy Mr. Dillon, Colonel Howard's kinsman, and a cupboard cousin of St. Ruth's Abbey?"

"Nay, Katherine—"

"Nay, Cecilia, be patient, and let the stranger have utterance; he may solve the difficulty altogether."

The cockswain, understanding that an explanation was expected from his lips, addressed himself to the task with an energy suitable both to the subject and to his own feelings. In a very few words, though a little obscured by his peculiar diction, he made his listeners understand the confidence that Barnstable had reposed in Dillon, and the treachery of the latter. They heard him with increased astonishment, and Cecilia hardly allowed him time to conclude, before she exclaimed:

"And did Colonel Howard, could Colonel Howard listen to this treacherous project?"

"Ay, they spliced it together among them," returned Tom; "though one part of this cruise will turn out but badly."

"Even Borroughcliffe, cold and hardened as he appears to be by habit, would spurn at such dishonor," added Miss Howard.

"But, Mr. Barnstable," at length Katherine succeeded in saying, when her feelings permitted her utterance, "said you not, that the soldiers were in quest of him?"

"Ay, ay, young madam," the cockswain replied, smiling with grim ferocity, "they are in chase, but he has shifted his anchorage, and, even if they should find him, his long pikes would make short work of a dozen red-coats. The Lord of tempests and calms have mercy, though, on the schooner! Ah, young madam, she is as lovely to the eyes of an old sea-faring man as any of your kind can be to human nature!"

"But why this delay?—away, then, honest Tom, and reveal the treachery to your commander; you may not yet be too late—why delay a moment?"

"The ship tarries for want of a pilot.—I could carry three fathoms over the shoals of Nantucket the darkest night that ever shut the windows of heaven, but I should be likely to run upon breakers in this navigation. At it was, I was near getting into company that I should have had to fight my way out of."

"If that be all, follow me," cried the ardent Katherine; "I will conduct you to a path that leads to the ocean, without approaching the sentinels."

Until this moment, Dillon had entertained a secret expectation of a rescue, but when he heard this proposal, he felt his blood retreating to his heart from every part of his agitated frame, and his last hope seemed wrested from him. Raising himself from the abject, shrinking attitude, in which both shame and dread had conspired to keep him as though he had been fettered to the spot, he approached Cecilia, and cried, in tones of horror:

"Do not, do not consent, Miss Howard, to abandon me to the fury of this man! Your uncle, your honorable uncle even now applauded and united with me in my enterprise, which is no more than a common artifice in war."

"My uncle would unite, Mr. Dillon, in no project of deliberate treachery like this," said Cecilia coldly.

"He did, I swear by—"

"Liar!" interrupted the deep tones of the cockswain.

Dillon shivered with agony and terror, while the sounds of this appalling voice sunk into his inmost soul; but as the gloom of the night, the secret ravines of the cliffs, and the turbulence of the ocean, flashed across his imagination, he again yielded to a dread of the horrors to which he should be exposed, in encountering them at the mercy of his most powerful enemy, and he continued his solicitations:

"Hear me, once more hear me—Miss Howard, I beseech you, hear me! Am I not of your own blood and country? Will you see me abandoned to the wild, merciless, malignant fury of this man, who will transfix me with that—O God! if you had but seen the sight I beheld in the Alacrity!—hear me, Miss Howard; for the love you bear your Maker, intercede for me! Mr. Griffith shall be released—"

"Liar!" again interrupted the cockswain.

"What promises he?" asked Cecilia, turning her averted face once more at the miserable captive.

"Nothing at all that will be fulfilled," said Katherine. "Follow, honest Tom, and I, at least, will conduct you in good faith."

"Cruel, obdurate Miss Plowden; gentle, kind Miss Alice, you will not refuse to raise your voice in my favor, your heart is not hardened by any imaginary dangers to those you love."

"Nay, address me not," said Alice, bending her meek eyes to the floor; "I trust your life is in no danger; and I pray that He who has the power, will have the mercy, to see you unharmed."

"Away!" said Tom, grasping the collar of the helpless Dillon, and rather carrying than leading him into the gallery; "if a sound, one-quarter as loud as a young porpoise makes when he draws his first breath, comes from you, villain, you shall see the sight of the Alacrity over again. My harpoon keeps its edge well, and the old arm can yet drive it to the seizing."

This menace effectually silenced even the hard, perturbed breathings of the captive, who, with his conductor, followed the light steps of Katherine through some of the secret mazes of the building, until, in a few minutes, they issued through a small door into the open air. Without pausing to deliberate, Miss Plowden led the cockswain through the grounds, to a different wicket from the one by which he had entered the paddock, and pointing to the path, which might be dimly traced along the faded herbage, she bade God bless him, in a voice that discovered her interest in his safety, and vanished from his sight like an aërial being.

Tom needed no incentive to his speed, now that the course lay so plainly before him, but loosening his pistols in his belt, and poising his harpoon, he crossed the fields at a gait that compelled his companion to exert his utmost powers, in the way of walking, to equal. Once or twice Dillon ventured to utter a word or two; but the stern "Silence" from the cockswain warned him to cease, until, perceiving that they were approaching the cliffs, he made a final effort to obtain his liberty, by hurriedly promising a large bribe. The cockswain made no reply, and the captive was secretly hoping that his scheme was producing its wonted effect, when he unexpectedly felt the keen, cold edge of the barbed iron of the harpoon pressing against his breast, through the opening of his ruffles, and even raising the skin.

"Liar!" said Tom; "another word, and I'll drive it through your heart!"

From that moment, Dillon was as silent as the grave. They reached the edge of the cliffs, without encountering the party that had been sent in quest of Barnstable, at a point near where they had landed. The old seaman paused an instant on the verge of the precipice, and cast his experienced eyes along the wide expanse of water that lay before him. The sea was no longer sleeping, but already in heavy motion, and rolling its surly waves against the base of the rocks on which he stood, scattering their white crests high in foam. The cockswain, after bending his looks along the whole line of the eastern horizon, gave utterance to a low and stifled groan; and then, striking the staff of his harpoon violently against the earth, he pursued his way along the very edge of the cliffs, muttering certain dreadful denunciations, which the conscience of his appalled listener did not fail to apply to himself. It appeared to the latter, that his angry and excited leader sought the giddy verge of the precipice with a sort of wanton recklessness, so daring were the steps that he took along its brow, notwithstanding the darkness of the hour, and the violence of the blasts that occasionally rushed upon them, leaving behind a kind of reaction, that more than once brought the life of the manacled captive in imminent jeopardy. But it would seem the wary cockswain had a motive for this apparently inconsiderate desperation. When they had made good quite half the distance between the point where Barnstable had landed and that where he had appointed to meet his cockswain, the sounds of voices were brought indistinctly to their ears, in one of the momentary pauses of the rushing winds, and caused the cockswain to make a dead stand in his progress. He listened intently for a single minute, when his resolution appeared to be taken. He turned to Dillon and spoke; though his voice was suppressed and low, it was deep and resolute:

"One word, and you die; over the cliffs! You must take a seaman's ladder: there is footing on the rocks, and crags for your hands. Over the cliffs, I bid ye, or I'll cast ye into the sea, as I would a dead enemy!"

"Mercy, mercy!" implored Dillon; "I could not do it in the day; by this light I shall surely perish."

"Over with ye!" said Tom, "or—"

Dillon waited for no more, but descended, with trembling steps, the dangerous precipice that lay before him. He was followed by the cockswain, with a haste that unavoidably dislodged his captive from the trembling stand he had taken on the shelf of a rock, who, to his increased horror, found himself dangling in the air, his body impending over the sullen surf, that was tumbling in with violence upon the rocks beneath him. An involuntary shriek burst from Dillon, as he felt his person thrust from the narrow shelf; and his cry sounded amid the tempest like the screeching of the spirit of the storm.

"Another such a call, and I cut your tow-line, villain," exclaimed the determined seaman, "when nothing short of eternity will bring you up!"

The sounds of footsteps and voices were now distinctly audible, and presently a party of armed men appeared on the edges of the rocks directly above them.

"It was a human voice," said one of them, "and like a man in distress."

"It cannot be the men we are sent in search of," returned Sergeant Drill; "for no watchword that I ever heard sounded like that cry."

"They say that such cries are often heard in the storms along the coast," said a voice that was uttered with less of military confidence than the two others; "and they are thought to come from drowned seamen."

A feeble laugh arose among the listeners, and one or two forced jokes were made at the expense of their superstitious comrade; but the scene did not fail to produce its effect on even the most sturdy among the unbelievers in the marvellous; for, after a few more similar remarks, the whole party retired from the cliffs, at a pace that might have been accelerated by the nature of their discourse. The cockswain, who had stood all this time, firm as the rock which supported him, bearing up not only his own weight, but the person of Dillon also, raised his head above the brow of the precipice, as they withdrew, to reconnoitre, and then, drawing up the nearly insensible captive, and placing him in safety on the bank, he followed himself. Not a moment was wasted in unnecessary explanation, but Dillon found himself again urged forward, with the same velocity as before. In a few minutes they gained the desired ravine, down which Tom plunged with a seaman's nerve, dragging his prisoner after him, and directly they stood where the waves rose to their feet, as they flowed far and foaming across the sands. The cockswain stooped so low as to bring the crest of the billows in a line with the horizon, when he discovered the dark boat, playing in the outer edge of the surf.

"What hoa! Ariels there!" shouted Tom, in a voice that the growing tempest carried to the ears of the retreating soldiers, who quickened their footsteps, as they listened to sounds which their fears taught them to believe supernatural.

"Who hails?" cried the well-known voice of Barnstable.

"Once your master, now your servant," answered the cockswain, with a watchword of his own invention.

" 'Tis he," returned the lieutenant; "veer away, boys, veer away. You must wade into the surf."

Tom caught Dillon in his arms, and throwing him like a cork across his shoulder, he dashed into the streak of foam that was bearing the boat on its crest, and before his companion had time for remonstrance or entreaty, he found himself once more by the side of Barnstable.

"Who have we here?" asked the lieutenant; "this is not Griffith!"

"Haul out and weigh your grapnel," said the excited cockswain; "and then, boys, if you love the Ariel, pull while the life and the will is left in you."

Barnstable knew his man, and not another question was asked, until the boat was without breakers, now skimming the rounded summits of the waves, or settling into the hollows of the sea, but always cutting the water asunder, as she urged her course, with amazing velocity, toward the haven where the schooner had been left at anchor. Then, in a few bitter sentences, the cockswain explained to his commander the treachery of Dillon and the danger of the schooner.

"The soldiers are slow at a night-muster," Tom concluded; "and from what I overheard, the express will have to make a crooked course to double the head of the bay, so that, but for this northeaster, we might weather upon them yet; but it's a matter that lies altogether in the will of Providence.—Pull, my hearties, pull—everything depends on your oars tonight."

Barnstable listened in deep silence to this unexpected narration, which sounded in the ears of Dillon like his funeral-knell. At length, the suppressed voice of the lieutenant was heard also, uttering:

"Wretch! if I should cast you into the sea, as food for the fishes, who could blame me? But if my schooner goes to the bottom, she shall prove your coffin!"

24

Had I been any god of power, I would
Have sunk the sea within the earth, ere
It should the good ship so have swallowed.

The Tempest

THE arms of Dillon were released from their confinement by the cockswain, as a measure of humane caution against accidents, when they entered the surf; and the captive now availed himself of the circumstance to bury his features in the folds of his attire, when he brooded over the events of the last few hours with that mixture of malignant passion and pusillanimous dread of the future that formed the chief ingredients in his character. From this state of apparent quietude neither Barnstable nor Tom seemed disposed to rouse him by their remarks, for both were too much engaged with their own gloomy forebodings, to indulge in any unnecessary words. An occasional ejaculation from the former, as if to propitiate the spirit of the storm, as he gazed on the troubled appearance of the elements, or a cheering cry from the latter to animate his crew, alone was heard amid the sullen roaring of the waters, and the mournful whistling of the winds that swept heavily across the broad waste of the German Ocean. There might have been an hour consumed thus, in a vigorous struggle between the seamen and the growing billows, when the boat doubled the northern headland of the desired haven, and shot at once, from its boisterous passage along the margin of the breakers into the placid waters of the sequestered bay. The passing blasts were still heard rushing above the highlands that surrounded, and, in fact, formed the estuary; but the profound stillness of deep night pervaded the secret recesses, along the unruffled surface of its waters. The shadows of the hills seemed to have accumulated, like a mass of gloom, in the centre of the basin, and though every eye involuntarily turned to search, it was in vain that the anxious seamen endeavored to discover their little vessel through its density. While the boat glided into this quiet scene, Barnstable anxiously observed:

"Everything is as still as death."

"God send it is not the stillness of death!" ejaculated the cockswain. "Here, here," he continued speaking in a lower tone as if fearful of being overheard, "here she lies, sir, more to port; look into the streak of clear sky above the marsh, on the starboard hand of the wood, there; that long black line is her main-topmast; I know it by the rake; and there is her night-pennant fluttering above the bright star, ay, ay, sir, there go our own stars aloft yet, dancing among the stars in the heavens! God bless her! God bless her! she rides as easy and as quiet as a gull asleep!"

"I believe all in her sleep too," returned his commander. "Ha! by Heaven, we have arrived in good time; the soldiers are moving."

The quick eye of Barnstable had detected the glimmering of passing lanterns, as they flitted across the embrasures of the battery, and at the next moment the guarded but distinct sounds of an active bustle on the decks of the schooner were plainly audible. The lieutenant was rubbing his hands together with a sort of ecstasy that probably will not be understood by the great majority of our readers, while Long Tom was actually indulging in a paroxysm of his low, spiritless laughter, as these certain intimations of the safety of the Ariel and of the vigilance of her crew were conveyed to their ears; when the whole hull and taper spars of their floating home became unexpectedly visible, and the sky, the placid basin, and the adjacent hills were illuminated by a flash as sudden and as vivid as the keenest lightning. Both Barnstable and his cockswain seemed instinctively to strain their eyes toward the schooner with an effort to surpass human vision; but ere the rolling reverberations of the report of a heavy piece of ordnance from the heights had commenced, the dull whistling rush of the shot swept over their heads like the moaning of a hurricane, and was succeeded by the plash of the waters, which was followed, in a breath, by the rattling of the mass of iron, as it bounded with violent fury from rock to rock, shivering and tearing the fragments that lined the margin of the bay.

"A bad aim with the first gun generally leaves your enemy clean decks," said the cockswain, with his deliberate sort of philosophy; "smoke makes but dim spectacles; besides, the night always grows darkest as you call off the morning watch."

"That boy is a miracle for his years!" rejoined the delighted lieutenant. "See, Tom, the yonker has shifted his berth in the dark, and the Englishmen have fired by the day-range they must have taken, for we left him in a direct line between the battery and yon hammock! What would have become of us if that heavy fellow had plunged upon our decks and gone out below the water-line?"

"We should have sunk into English mud, for eternity, as sure as our metal and kentledge would have taken us down," responded Tom; "such a point-blanker would have torn off a streak of our wales, out-board, and not even left the marines time to say a prayer!—Tend bow there!"

It is not to be supposed that the crew of the whale-boat continued idle during this interchange of opinions between the lieutenant and his cockswain; on the contrary, the sight of their vessel acted on them like a charm, and, believing that all necessity for caution was now over, they had expended their utmost strength in efforts that had already brought them, as the last words of Tom indicated, to the side of the Ariel. Though every nerve of Barnstable was thrilling with the excitement produced by his feelings passing from a state of the most doubtful apprehension to that of a revived and almost confident hope of effecting his escape, he assumed the command of his vessel with all that stern but calm authority that seamen find it most necessary to exert in the moment of extremest danger. Any one of the heavy shot that their enemies continued to hurl from their heights into the darkness of the haven he well knew must prove fatal to them, as it would, unavoidably, pass through the slight fabric of the Ariel, and open a passage to the water that no means he possessed could remedy. His mandates were, therefore, issued with a full perception of the critical nature of the emergency, but with that collectedness of manner, and intonation of voice, that were best adapted to enforce a ready and animated obedience. Under this impulse the crew of the schooner soon got their anchor freed from the bottom, and, seizing their sweeps, they forced her by their united efforts directly in the face of the battery, under that shore whose summit was now crowned with a canopy of smoke, that every discharge of the ordnance tinged with dim colors, like the faintest tints that are reflected from the clouds toward a setting sun. So long as the seamen were enabled to keep their little bark under the cover of the hill, they were, of course, safe; but Barnstable perceived, as they emerged from its shadow, and were drawing nigh the passage which led into the ocean, that the action of his sweeps would no longer avail them against the currents of air they encountered; neither would the darkness conceal their movements from his enemy, who had already employed men on the shore to discern the position of the schooner. Throwing off at once, therefore, all appearance of disguise, he gave forth the word to spread the canvas of his vessel, in his ordinary cheerful manner.

"Let them do their worst now, Merry," he added; "we have brought them to a distance that I think will keep their iron above water, and we have no dodge about us, yonker!"

"It must be keener marksmen than the militia, or volunteers, or fencibles, or whatever they call themselves, behind yon grass-bank, to frighten the saucy Ariel from the wind," returned the reckless boy; "but why have you brought Jonah aboard us again, sir? Look at him by the light of the cabin lamp: he winks at every gun, as if he expected the shot would hull his own ugly yellow physiognomy. And what tidings have we, sir, from Mr. Griffith and the marine?"

"Name him not," said Barnstable, pressing the shoulder on which he lightly leaned with a convulsive grasp that caused the boy to yield with pain—"name him not, Merry; I want my temper and my faculties at this moment undisturbed, and thinking of the wretch unfits me for my duty. But there will come a time!—go forward, sir; we feel the wind, and have a narrow passage to work through."

The boy obeyed a mandate which was given in the usual prompt manner of their profesion, and which, he well understood, was intended to intimate that the distance which years and rank had created between them, but which Barnstable often chose to forget while communing with Merry, was now to be resumed. The sails had been loosened and set; and, as the vessel approached the throat of the passage, the gale, which was blowing with increasing violence, began to make a very sensible impression on the light bark. The cockswain, who, in the absence of most of the inferior officers, had been acting, on the forecastle, the part of one who felt, from his years and experience, that he had some right to advise, if not to command, at such a juncture, now walked to the station which his commander had taken, near the helmsman, as if willing to place himself in the way of being seen.

"Well, Master Coffin," said Barnstable, who well understood the propensity his old shipmate had to commune with him on all important occasions, "what think you of the cruise now? Those gentlemen on the hill make a great noise, but I have lost even the whistling of their shot; one would think they

could see our sails against the broad band of light which is opening to seaward."

"Ay, ay, sir, they see us and mean to hit us too; but we are running across
their fire, and that with a ten-knot breeze; but, when we heave in stays, and
get in a line with their guns, we shall see, and it may be feel, more of their
work than we do now; a thirty-two an't trained as easily as a fowling-piece
or a ducking-gun."

Barnstable was struck with the truth of this observation; but as there existed
an immediate necessity for placing the schooner in the very situation to which
the other alluded, he gave his orders at once, and the vessel came about, and
ran with her head pointing toward the sea, in as short a time as we have taken
to record it.

"There, they have us now, or never," cried the lieutenant, when the evolution was completed. "If we fetch to windward off the northern point, we
shall lay out into the offing, and in ten minutes we might laugh at Queen
Anne's pocket-piece, which, you know, old boy, sent a ball from Dover to
Calais."

"Ay, sir, I've heard of the gun," returned the grave seaman, "and a lively
piece it must have been, if the straits were always of the same width they are
now. But I see that, Captain Barnstable, which is more dangerous than a dozen
of the heaviest cannon that were ever cast can be, at half a league's distance.
The water is bubbling through our lee scuppers already, sir."

"And what of that? haven't I buried her guns often, and yet kept every
spar in her without crack or splinter?"

"Ay, ay, sir, you have done it, and can do it again, where there is sea-room,
which is all that a man wants for comfort in this life. But when we are out of
these chops, we shall be embayed, with a heavy northeaster setting dead into
the bight; it is that which I fear, Captain Barnstable, more than all the powder
and ball in the whole island."

"And yet, Tom, the balls are not to be despised, either; those fellows have
found out their range, and send their iron within hail again; we walk pretty
fast, Mr. Coffin, but a thirty-two can out-travel us, with the best wind that
ever blew."

Tom threw a cursory glance toward the battery, which had renewed its
fire with a spirit that denoted they saw their object, as he answered:

"It is never worth a man's while to strive to dodge a shot; for they are all
commissioned to do their work, the same as a ship is commissioned to cruise
in certain latitudes; but for the winds and the weather, they are given for a
seafaring man to guard against, by making or shortening sail, as the case may

be. Now, the headland to the southward stretches full three leagues to wind-ward and the shoals lie to the north; among which God keep us from ever running this craft again!"

"We will beat her out of the bight, old fellow," cried the lieutenant; "we shall have a leg of three leagues in length to do it in."

"I have known longer legs too short," returned the cockswain, shaking his head; "a tumbling sea, with a lee-tide, on a lee shore, makes a sad lee-way."

The lieutenant was in the act of replying to this saying with a cheerful laugh, when the whistling of a passing shot was instantly succeeded by a crash of splintered wood; and at the next moment the head of the main-mast, after tottering for an instant in the gale, fell toward the deck, bringing with it the main-sail, and the long line of topmast that had been bearing the emblems of America, as the cockswain had expressed it, among the stars of the heavens.

"That was a most unlucky hit!" Barnstable suffered to escape him in the concern of the moment; but, instantly resuming all his collectedness of manner and voice, he gave his orders to clear the wreck and secure the fluttering canvas.

The mournful forebodings of Tom seemed to vanish with the appearance of a necessity for his exertions, and he was foremost among the crew in ex-ecuting the orders of their commander. The loss of all the sail on the main-mast forced the Ariel so much from her course as to render it difficult to weather the point that jutted, under her lee, for some distance into the ocean. This desirable object was, however, effected by the skill of Barnstable, aided by the excellent properties of his vessel; and the schooner, borne down by the power of the gale, from whose fury she had now no protection, passed heavily along the land, heading, as far as possible, from the breakers, while the seamen were engaged in making their preparations to display as much of their main-sail as the stump of the mast would allow them to spread. The firing from the battery ceased as the Ariel rounded the little promontory; but Barnstable, whose gaze was now bent intently on the ocean, soon perceived that, as his cockswain had predicted, he had a much more threatening danger to encounter in the elements. When their damages were repaired, so far as circumstances would permit, the cockswain returned to his wonted station near the lieutenant; and after a momentary pause, during which his eyes roved over the rigging with a seaman's scrutiny, he resumed the discourse.

"It would have been better for us that the best man in the schooner should have been dubbed of a limb by that shot, than that the Ariel should have lost her best leg; a main-sail close-reefed may be prudent canvas as the wind blows, but it holds a poor luff to keep a craft to windward."

"What would you have, Tom Coffin?" retorted his commander. "You see she draws ahead, and off-shore; do you expect a vessel to fly in the very teeth of the gale? or would you have we wear and beach her at once?"

"I would have nothing, nothing, Captain Barnstable," returned the old seaman, sensibly touched at his commander's displeasure; "you are as able as any man that ever trod a plank to work her into an offing; but, sir, when that soldier officer told me of the scheme to sink the Ariel at her anchor, there was such feelings come athwart my philosophy as never crossed it afore. I thought I saw her a wrack, as plainly, ay, as plainly as you may see the stump of that mast; and, I will own it, for it's as natural to love the craft you sail in as it is to love one's self, I will own that my manhood fetched a heavy lee-lurch at the sight."

"Away with ye, ye old sea-croaker! forward with ye, and see that the head-sheets are trimmed flat. But hold! come hither, Tom; if you have sights of wrecks, and sharks, and other beautiful objects, keep them stowed in your own silly brain; don't make a ghost-parlor of my forecastle. The lads begin to look to leeward, now, oftener than I would have them. Go, sirrah, go, and take example from Mr. Merry, who is seated on your namesake there, and is singing as if he were a chorister in his father's church."

"Ah, Captain Barnstable, Mr. Merry is a boy, and knows nothing, so fears nothing. But I shall obey your orders, sir; and if the men fall astarn this gale, it sha'n't be for anything they'll hear from old Tom Coffin."

The cockswain lingered a moment, notwithstanding his promised obedience, and then ventured to request that—

"Captain Barnstable would please call Mr. Merry from the gun; for I know, from having followed the seas my natural life, that singing in a gale is sure to bring the wind down upon a vessel the heavier; for He who rules the tempests is displeased that man's voice shall be heard when he chooses to send His own breath on the water."

Barnstable was at a loss whether to laugh at his cockswain's infirmity, or to yield to the impression which his earnest and solemn manner had a powerful tendency to produce amid such a scene. But, making an effort to shake off the superstitious awe that he felt creeping around his own heart, the lieutenant relieved the mind of the worthy old seaman so far as to call the careless boy from his perch to his own side; where respect for the sacred character of the quarter-deck instantly put an end to the lively air he had been humming. Tom walked slowly forward, apparently much relieved by the reflection that he had effected so important an object.

The Ariel continued to struggle against the winds and ocean for several hours longer before the day broke on the tempestuous scene, and the anxious mariners were enabled to form a more accurate estimate of their real danger. As the violence of the gale increased, the canvas of the schooner had been gradually reduced, until she was unable to show more than was absolutely necessary to prevent her driving helplessly on the land. Barnstable watched the appearance of the weather, as the light slowly opened upon them, with an intense anxiety, which denoted that the presentiments of the cockswain were no longer deemed idle. On looking to windward, he beheld the green masses of water that were rolling in toward the land, with a violence that seemed irresistible, crowned with ridges of foam; and there were moments when the air appeared filled with sparkling gems, as the rays of the rising sun fell upon the spray that was swept from wave to wave. Toward the land the view was still more appalling. The cliffs, but a short half-league under the lee of the schooner, were, at all times, nearly hid from the eye by the pyramids of water, which the furious element, so suddenly restrained in its violence, cast high into the air, as if seeking to overlap the boundaries that Nature had fixed to its dominion. The whole coast, from the distant headland at the south to the well-known shoals that stretched far beyond their course in the opposite direction, displayed a broad belt of foam, into which it would have been certain destruction for the proudest ship that ever swam to enter. Still the Ariel floated on the billows, lightly and in safety, though yielding to the impulses of the waters, and, at times, appearing to be engulfed in the yawning chasms, which, apparently, opened beneath her to receive the little fabric. The low rumor of acknowledged danger had found its way through the schooner, and the seamen, after fastening their hopeless looks on the small spot of canvas that they were still able to show to the tempest, would turn to view the dreary line of coast that seemed to offer so gloomy an alternative. Even Dillon, to whom the report of their danger had found its way, crept from his place of concealment in the cabin, and moved about the decks, unheeded, devouring, with greedy ears, such opinions as fell from the lips of the sullen mariners.

At this moment of appalling apprehension, the cockswain exhibited the calmest resignation. He knew all had been done that lay in the power of man to urge their little vessel from the land, and it was now too evident to his experienced eyes that it had been done in vain; but, considering himself as a sort of fixture in the schooner, he was quite prepared to abide her fate, be it for better or for worse. The settled look of gloom that gathered around the frank brow of Barnstable was in no degree connected with any considerations of himself; but proceeded from that sort of parental responsibility from which the sea-commander is never exempt. The discipline of the crew, however, still continued perfect and unyielding. There had, it is true, been a slight movement made by one or two of the older seamen, which indicated an intention to drown the apprehensions of death in inebriety; but Barnstable had called for his pistols, in a tone that checked the procedure instantly, and, although the fatal weapons were, untouched by him, left to lie exposed on the capstan, where they had been placed by his servant, not another symptom of insubordination appeared among the devoted crew. There was even what, to a landsman, might seem an appalling affectation of attention to the most trifling duties of the vessel; and the men who, it should seem, ought to be devoting the brief moments of their existence to the mighty business of the hour, were constantly called to attend to the most trivial details of their profession. Ropes were coiled, and the slightest damages occasioned by the waves, which, at short intervals, swept across the low decks of the Ariel, were repaired, with the same precision and order as if she yet lay embayed in the haven from which she had just been driven. In this manner the arm of authority was kept extended over the silent crew, not with the vain desire to preserve a lingering though useless exercise of power, but with a view to maintain that unity of action that now could alone afford them even a ray of hope.

"She can make no head against this sea, under that rag of canvas," said Barnstable, gloomily, addressing the cockswain, who, with folded arms, and an air of cool resignation, was balancing his body on the verge of the quarter-deck, while the schooner was plunging madly into waves that nearly buried her in their bosom; "the poor little thing trembles like a frightened child, as she meets the water."

Tom sighed heavily, and shook his head, before he answered:

"If we could have kept the head of the main-mast an hour longer, we might have got an offing, and fetched to windward of the shoals; but as it is, sir, mortal man can't drive a craft to windward—she sets bodily in to land, and will be in the breakers in less than an hour, unless God wills that the wind shall cease to blow."

"We have no hope left us but to anchor; our ground tackle may yet bring her up."

Tom turned to his commander, and replied, solemnly, and with that assurance of manner that long experience only can give a man in moments of great danger:

"If our sheet-cable was bent to our heaviest anchor, this sea would bring it home, though nothing but her launch was riding by it. A northeaster in the German Ocean must and will blow itself out; nor shall we get the crown of

the gale until the sun falls over the land. Then indeed it may lull; for the winds do often seem to reverence the glory of the heavens too much to blow their might in its very face!"

"We must do our duty to ourselves and the country," returned Barnstable. "Go, get the two bowers spliced, and have a kedge bent to a hawser; we'll back our two anchors together, and veer to the better end of two hundred and forty fathoms; it may yet bring her up. See all clear there for anchoring, and cutting away the mast! we'll leave the wind nothing but a naked hull to whistle over."

"Ay, if there was nothing but the wind, we might yet live to see the sun sink behind them hills," said the cockswain; "but what hemp can stand the strain of a craft that is buried, half the time, to her foremast in the water?"

The order was, however, executed by the crew, with a sort of desperate submission to the will of their commander; and, when the preparations were completed, the anchors and kedge were dropped to the bottom, and the instant that the Ariel tended to the wind, the axe was applied to the little that was left of her long, raking masts. The crash of the falling spars, as they came, in succession, across the decks of the vessel, appeared to produce no sensation amid that scene of complicated danger; but the seamen proceeded in silence to their hopeless duty of clearing the wrecks. Every eye followed the floating timbers, as the waves swept them away from the vessel, with a sort of feverish curiosity to witness the effect produced by their collision with those rocks that lay so fearfully near them; but long before the spars entered the wide border of foam, they were hid from view by the furious element in which they floated. It was now felt by the whole crew of the Ariel that their last means of safety had been adopted; and, at each desperate and headlong plunge the vessel took, into the bosom of the seas that rolled upon her forecastle, the anxious seamen thought that they could perceive the yielding of the iron that yet clung to the bottom, or could hear the violent surge of the parting strands of the cable, that still held them to their anchors. While the minds of the sailors were agitated with the faint hopes that had been excited by the movements of their schooner, Dillon had been permitted to wander about the deck unnoticed; his rolling eyes, hard breathing, and clinched hands, excited no observation among the men, whose thoughts were yet dwelling on the means of safety. But now, when with a sort of frenzied desperation he would follow the retiring waters along the decks, and venture his person nigh the group that had collected around and on the gun of the cockswain, glances of fierce or of sullen vengeance were cast at him, that conveyed threats of a nature that he was too much agitated to understand.

"If ye are tired of this world, though your time, like my own, is probably but short in it," said Tom to him, as he passed the cockswain in one of his turns, "you can go forward among the men; but if we have need of the moments to foot up the reck'ning of your doings among men, afore ye're brought to face your Maker, and hear the logbook of Heaven, I would advise you to keep as nigh as possible to Captain Barnstable or myself."

"Will you promise to save me if the vessel is wrecked?" exclaimed Dillon, catching at the first sounds of friendly interest that had reached his ears since he had been recaptured. "Oh! if you will, I can secure your future ease, yes, wealth, for the remainder of your days!"

"Your promises have been too ill kept afore this, for the peace of your soul," returned the cockswain, without bitterness, though sternly; "but it is not in me to strike even a whale that is already spouting blood."

The intercessions of Dillon were interrupted by a dreadful cry, that arose among the men forward, and which sounded with increased horror, amid the roarings of the tempest. The schooner rose on the breast of a wave at the same instant, and, falling off with her broadside to the sea, she drove in toward the cliffs, like a bubble on the rapids of a cataract.

"Our ground-tackle has parted," said Tom, with his resigned patience of manner undisturbed; "she shall die as easy as man can make her!"

While he yet spoke, he seized the tiller, and gave to the vessel such a direction as would be most likely to cause her to strike the rocks with her bows foremost.

There was for one moment an expression of exquisite anguish betrayed in the dark countenance of Barnstable; but at the next it passed away, and he spoke cheerfully to his men:

"Be steady, my lads, be calm: there is yet a hope of life for *you*—our light draught will let us run in close to the cliffs, and it is still falling water—see your boats clear, and be steady."

The crew of the whale-boat, aroused by this speech from a sort of stupor, sprang into their light vessel, which was quickly lowered into the sea, and kept riding on the foam, free from the sides of the schooner, by the powerful exertions of the men. The cry for the cockswain was earnest and repeated, but Tom shook his head, without replying, still grasping the tiller, and keeping his eyes steadily bent on the chaos of waters into which they were driving. The launch, the largest boat of the two, was cut loose from the "gripes," and the bustle and exertions of the moment rendered the crew insensible to the horror of the scene that surrounded them. But the loud, hoarse call of the cockswain, to "look out—secure yourselves!" suspended even their efforts, and at that instant the Ariel settled, on a wave that melted from under her, heavily on the rocks. The shock was so violent as to throw all who disregarded the warning cry from their feet, and the universal quiver that pervaded the vessel was like the last shudder of animated nature. For a time long enough to breathe, the least experienced among the men supposed the danger to be past; but a wave of great height followed the one that had deserted them, and, raising the vessel again, threw her roughly still farther on the bed of rocks, and at the same time its crest broke over her quarter, sweeping the length of her decks with a fury that was almost resistless. The shuddering seamen beheld their loosened boat driven from their grasp, and dashed against the base of the cliffs, where no fragment of her wreck could be traced at the receding of the waters. But the passing billow had thrown the vessel into a position which in some measure, protected her decks from the violence of those that succeeded it.

"Go, my boys, go," said Barnstable, as the moment of dreadful uncertainty passed; "you have still the whale-boat, and she, at least, will take you nigh the shore. Go into her, my boys. God bless you, God bless you all! You have been faithful and honest fellows, and I believe He will not desert you; go, my friends, while there is a lull."

The seamen threw themselves, in a mass, into the light vessel, which nearly sank under the unusual burden; but when they looked around them, Barnstable and Merry, Dillon and the cockswain, were yet to be seen on the decks of the Ariel. The former was pacing, in deep and perhaps bitter melancholy, the wet planks of the schooner, while the boy hung, unheeded, on his arm, uttering disregarded petitions to his commander to desert the wreck. Dillon approached the side where the boat lay, again and again, but the threatening countenances of the seamen as often drove him back in despair. Tom had seated himself on the heel of the bowsprit, where he continued, in an attitude of quiet resignation, returning no other answers to the loud and repeated calls of his shipmates, than by waving his hand toward the shore.

"Now hear me," said the boy, urging his request to tears; "if not for my sake or for your own sake, Mr. Barnstable, or for the hope of God's mercy, go into the boat, for the love of my cousin Katherine."

The young lieutenant paused in his troubled walk, and for a moment he cast a glance of hesitation at the cliffs; but at the next instant his eyes fell on the ruin of his vessel, and he answered:

"Never, boy, never; if my hour has come, I will not shrink from my fate."

"Listen to the men, dear sir; the boat will be swamped, alongside the wreck, and their cry is, that without you they will not let her go."

Barnstable motioned to the boat, to bid the boy enter it, and turned away in silence.

"Well," said Merry, with firmness, "if it be right that a lieutenant shall stay by the wreck, it must also be right for a midshipman!—Shove off; neither Mr. Barnstable nor myself will quit the vessel."

"Boy, your life has been entrusted to my keeping, and at my hands will it be required," said the commander, lifting the struggling youth, and tossing him into the arms of the seamen.—"Away with ye, and God be with you; there is more weight in you now than can go safe to land."

Still the seamen hesitated, for they perceived the cockswain moving, with a steady tread, along the deck, and they hoped he had relented, and would yet persuade the lieutenant to join his crew. But Tom, imitating the example of his commander, seized the latter suddenly in his powerful grasp, and threw him over the bulwarks with an irresistible force. At the same moment he cast the fast of the boat from the pin that held it, and, lifting his broad hands high into the air, his voice was heard in the tempest:

"God's will be done with me!" he cried. "I saw the first timber of the Ariel laid, and shall live just long enough to see it torn out of her bottom; after which I wish to live no longer."

But his shipmates were swept far beyond the sound of his voice before half these words were uttered. All command of the boat was rendered impossible by the numbers it contained, as well as the raging of the surf; and, as it rose on the white crest of a wave, Tom saw his beloved little craft for the last time. It fell into a trough of the sea, and in a few moments more its fragments were ground into splinters on the adjacent rocks. The cockswain still remained where he had cast off the rope, and beheld the numerous heads and arms that appeared rising, at short intervals, on the waves; some making powerful and well-directed efforts to gain the sands, that were becoming visible as the tide fell, and others wildly tossed in the frantic movements of helpless despair. The honest old seaman gave a cry of joy, as he saw Barnstable issue from the surf, bearing the form of Merry in safety to the sands, where one by one several seamen soon appeared also, dripping and exhausted. Many others of the crew were carried, in a similar manner, to places of safety; though, as Tom returned to his seat on the bowsprit, he could not conceal from his reluctant eyes the lifeless forms that were, in other spots, driven against the rocks with a fury that soon left them but few of the outward vestiges of humanity.

Dillon and the cockswain were now the sole occupants of their dreadful station. The former stood in a kind of stupid despair, a witness of the scene we have related; but, as his curdled blood began again to flow more warmly through his heart, he crept close to the side of Tom, with that sort of selfish feeling that makes even hopeless misery more tolerable, when endured in participation with another.

"When the tide falls," he said, in a voice that betrayed the agony of fear, though his words expressed the renewal of hope, "we shall be able to walk to land."

"There was One, and only One, to whose feet the waters were the same as a dry deck," returned the cockswain; "and none but such as have His power will ever be able to walk from these rocks to the sands." The old seaman paused, and turning his eyes, which exhibited a mingled expression of disgust and compassion, on his companion, he added, with reverence: "Had you thought more of Him in fair weather, your case would be less to be pitied in this tempest."

"Do you still think there is much danger?" asked Dillon.

"To them that have reason to fear death. Listen; do you hear that hollow noise beneath ye?"

" 'Tis the wind driving by the vessel!"

" 'Tis the poor thing herself," said the affected cockswain, "giving her last groans. The water is breaking up her decks, and, in a few minutes more, the handsomest model that ever cut a wave will be like the chips that fell from her timbers in framing!"

"Why, then, did you remain here?" cried Dillon, wildly.

"To die in my coffin, if it should be the will of God," returned Tom. "These waves, to me, are what the land is to you; I was born on them, and I have always meant that they should be my grave."

"But I—I," shrieked Dillon, "I am not ready to die!—I cannot die!—I will not die!"

"Poor wretch!" muttered his companion; "you must go, like the rest of us; when the death-watch is called, none can sulk from the muster."

"I can swim," Dillon continued, rushing with frantic eagerness to the side of the wreck. "Is there no billet of wood, no rope, that I can take with me?"

"None; everything has been cut away, or carried off by the sea. If ye are about to strive for your life, take with ye a stout heart and a clean conscience, and trust the rest to God!"

"God!" echoed Dillon, in the madness of his frenzy; "I know no God! there is no God that knows me!"

"Peace!" said the deep tones of the cockswain, in a voice that seemed to speak in the elements; "blasphemer, peace!"

The heavy groaning, produced by the water in the timbers of the Ariel, at that moment added its impulse to the raging feelings of Dillon, and he cast himself headlong into the sea.

The water, thrown by the rolling of the surf on the beach, was necessarily returned to the ocean, in eddies, in different places favorable to such an action of the element. Into the edge of one of these counter-currents, that was produced by the very rocks on which the schooner lay, and which the watermen call the "under-tow," Dillon had, unknowingly, thrown his person; and when the waves had driven him a short distance from the wreck, he was met by a stream that his most desperate efforts could not overcome. He was a light and powerful swimmer, and the struggle was hard and protracted. With the shore immediately before his eyes, and at no great distance, he was led, as by a false phantom, to continue his efforts, although they did not advance him a foot. The old seaman, who at first had watched his motions with careless indifference, understood the danger of his situation at a glance; and, forgetful of his own fate, he shouted aloud, in a voice that was driven over the struggling victim to the ears of his shipmates on the sands:

"Sheer to port, and clear the under-tow! sheer to the southward!"

Dillon heard the sounds, but his faculties were too much obscured by terror to distinguish their object; he, however, blindly yielded to the call, and gradually changed his direction, until his face was once more turned toward the vessel. The current swept him diagonally by the rocks, and he was forced into an eddy, where he had nothing to contend against but the waves, whose violence was much broken by the wreck. In this state, he continued still to struggle, but with a force that was too much weakened to overcome the resistance he met. Tom looked around him for a rope, but all had gone over with the spars, or been swept away by the waves. At this moment of disappointment his eyes met those of the desperate Dillon. Calm, and inured to horrors, as was the veteran seaman, he involuntarily passed his hand before his brow to exclude the look of despair he encountered; and when, a moment afterward, he removed the rigid member, he beheld the sinking form of the victim as it gradually settled in the ocean, still struggling, with regular but impotent strokes of the arms and feet, to gain the wreck, and to preserve an existence that had been so much abused in its hour of allotted probation.

"He will soon know his God, and learn that his God knows him!" murmured the cockswain to himself. As he yet spoke, the wreck of the Ariel yielded to an overwhelming sea, and, after a universal shudder, her timbers and planks gave way, and were swept toward the cliffs, bearing the body of the simple-hearted cockswain among the ruins.

25

Let us think of them that sleep
Full many a fathom deep,
By the wild and stormy steep,
Elsinore!

CAMPBELL

LONG and dreary did the hours appear to Barnstable, before the falling tide had so far receded as to leave the sands entirely exposed to his search for the bodies of his lost shipmates. Several had been rescued from the wild fury of the waves themselves; and one by one, as the melancholy conviction that life had ceased was forced on the survivors, they had been decently interred in graves dug on the very margin of that element on which they had passed their lives. But still the form longest known and most beloved was missing, and the lieutenant paced the broad space that was now left between the foot of the cliffs and the raging ocean, with hurried strides and a feverish eye, watching and following those fragments of the wreck that the sea still continued to cast on the beach. Living and dead, he now found that, of those who had lately been in the Ariel, only two were missing. Of the former he could muster but twelve, besides Merry and himself, and his men had already interred more than half that number of the latter, which, together, embraced all who had trusted their lives to the frail keeping of the whale-boat.

"Tell me not, boy, of the impossibility of his being safe," said Barnstable, in deep agitation, which he in vain struggled to conceal from the anxious youth, who thought it unnecessary to follow the uneasy motions of his commander, as he strode along the sands. "How often have men been found floating on pieces of wreck, days after the loss of their vessel! And you can see, with your own eyes, that the falling water has swept the planks this distance; ay, a good half-league from where she struck. Does the lookout, from the top of the cliffs, make no signal of seeing him yet?"

"None, sir, none; we shall never see him again. The men say that he always thought it sinful to desert a wreck, and that he did not even strike out once for his life, though he has been known to swim an hour, when a whale has stove his boat. God knows, sir," added the boy, hastily dashing a tear from his eye by a stolen movement of his hand, "I loved Tom Coffin better than any foremast man in either vessel. You seldom came aboard the frigate but we had him in the steerage among us reefers, to hear his long yarns and share our cheer. We all loved him, Mr. Barnstable; but love cannot bring the dead to life again."

"I know it, I know it," said Barnstable, with a huskiness in his voice that betrayed the depth of his emotion. "I am not so foolish as to believe in impossibilities; but while there is a hope of his living, I will never abandon poor Tom Coffin to such a dreadful fate. Think, boy, he may at this moment be looking at us, and praying to his Maker that we would turn our eyes upon him; ay, praying to his God, for Tom often prayed, though he did it in his watch, standing, and in silence."

"If he had clung to life so strongly," returned the midshipman, "he would have struggled harder to preserve it."

Barnstable stopped short in his hurried walk, and fastened a look of opening conviction on his companion; but, as he was about to speak in reply, the shouts of the seamen reached his ears, and, turning, they saw the whole party running along the beach, and motioning, with violent gestures, to an intermediate point in the ocean. The lieutenant and Merry hurried back, and, as they approached the men, they distinctly observed a human figure borne along by the waves, at moments seeming to rise above them, and already floating in the last of the breakers. They had hardly ascertained so much when a heavy swell carried the inanimate body far upon the sands, where it was left by the retiring waters.

" 'Tis my cockswain!" cried Barnstable, rushing to the spot. He stopped suddenly, however, as he came within view of the features, and it was some little time before he appeared to have collected his faculties sufficiently to add, in tones of deep horror: "What wretch is this, boy? his form is unmutilated, and yet observe the eyes! they seem as if the sockets would not contain them, and they gaze as wildly as if their owner yet had life—the hands are open and spread, as though they would still buffet the waves!"

"The Jonah, the Jonah!" shouted the seamen, with savage exultation, as they successively approached the corpse; "away with his carrion into the sea again! give him to the sharks! let him tell his lies in the claws of the lobsters!"

Barnstable had turned away from the revolting sight in disgust, but when he discovered these indications of impotent revenge in the remnant of his crew, he said, in that voice which all respected and still obeyed:

"Stand back; back with ye, fellows! Would you disgrace your manhood and seamanship by wreaking your vengeance on him whom God has already in judgment?" A silent but significant gesture toward the earth succeeded his words, and he walked slowly away.

"Bury him in the sands, boys," said Merry, when his commander was at some little distance; "the next tide will unearth him."

The seamen obeyed his orders, while the midshipman rejoined his commander, who continued to pace along the beach, occasionally halting to throw his uneasy glances over the water, and then hurrying onward at a rate that caused his youthful companion to exert his greatest power to maintain the post he had taken at his side. Every effort to discover the lost cockswain was, however, after two hours' more search, abandoned as fruitless; and with reason, for the sea was never known to give up the body of the man who might be emphatically called its own dead.

"There goes the sun, already dropping behind the cliffs," said the lieutenant, throwing himself on a rock; "and the hour will soon arrive to set the dog-watches; but we have nothing left to watch over, boy—the surf and rocks have not even left us a whole plank that we may lay our heads on for the night."

"The men have gathered many articles on yon beach, sir," returned the lad; "they have found arms to defend ourselves with, and food to give us strength to use them."

"And who shall be our enemy?" asked Barnstable, bitterly: "shall we shoulder our dozen pikes, and carry England by boarding?"

"We may not lay the whole island under contribution," continued the boy, anxiously watching the expression of his commander's eyes; "but we may still keep ourselves in work until the cutter returns from the frigate. I hope, sir, you do not think our case so desperate as to intend yielding as prisoners."

"Prisoners!" exclaimed the lieutenant; "no, no, lad, it has not got to that yet! England has been able to wreck my craft, I must concede; but she has, as yet, obtained no other advantage over us. She was a precious model, Merry!

the cleanest run, and the neatest entrance, that art ever united on the stem and stern of the same vessel! Do you remember the time, yonker, when I gave the frigate my topsails, in beating out of the Chesapeake! I could always do it, in smooth water with a whole-sail breeze. But she was a frail thing! a frail thing, boy, and could bear but little."

"A mortar-ketch would have thumped to pieces where she lay," returned the midshipman.

"Ay, it was asking too much of her, to expect she could hold together on a bed of rocks. Merry, I loved her; dearly did I love her; she was my first command, and I knew and loved every timber and bolt in her beautiful frame!"

"I believe it is as natural, sir, for a seaman to love the wood and iron in which he has floated over the depths of the ocean for so many days and nights," rejoined the boy, "as it is for a father to love the members of his own family."

"Quite, quite, ay, more so," said Barnstable, speaking as if he were choked by emotion. Merry felt the heavy grasp of the lieutenant on his slight arm, while his commander continued, in a voice that gradually increased in power, as his feelings predominated. "And yet, boy, a human being cannot love the creature of his own formation as he does the works of God. A man can never regard his ship as he does his shipmates. I sailed with him, boy, when every-thing seemed bright and happy, as at your age; when, as he often expressed it, I knew nothing and feared nothing. I was then a truant from an old father and a kind mother, and he did that for me which no parents could have done in my situation—he was my father and my mother on the deep!—hours, days, even months, has he passed in teaching me the arts of our profession; and now, in my manhood, he has followed me from ship to ship, from sea to sea, and has only quitted me to die, where I should have died—as if he felt the disgrace of abandoning the poor Ariel to her fate, by herself!"

"No, no, no—'twas his superstitious pride!" interrupted Merry; but perceiv-ing that the head of Barnstable had sunk between his hands, as if he would conceal his emotion, the boy added no more; but he sat respectfully watching the display of feeling that his officer in vain endeavored to suppress. Merry felt his own form quiver with sympathy at the shuddering which passed through Barnstable's frame; and the relief experienced by the lieutenant him-self was not greater than that which the midshipman felt, as the latter beheld large tears forcing their way through the other's fingers, and falling on the sands at his feet. They were followed by a violent burst of emotion, such as is seldom exhibited in the meridian of life; but which, when it conquers the nature of one who has buffeted the chances of the world with the loftiness of his sex and character, breaks down every barrier, and seems to sweep before it, like a rushing torrent, all the factitious defences which habit and education have created to protect the pride of manhood. Merry had often beheld the commanding severity of the lieutenant's manner in moments of danger, with deep respect; he had been drawn toward him by kindness and affection, in times of gayety and recklessness; but he now sat for many minutes, profoundly silent, regarding his officer with sensations that were nearly allied to awe. The struggle with himself was long and severe in the bosom of Barnstable; but, at length, the calm of relieved passions succeeded to his emotion. When he arose from the rock, and removed his hands from his features, his eye was hard and proud, his brow slightly contracted, and he spoke in a voice so harsh that it startled his companion:

"Come, sir; why are we here and idle? Are not yon poor fellows looking up to us for advice and orders how to proceed in this exigency? Away, away, Mr. Merry, it is not a time to be drawing figures in the sand with your dirk; the flood-tide will soon be in, and we may be glad to hide our heads in some cavern among these rocks. Let us be stirring, sir, while we have the sun, and muster enough food and arms to keep life in us, and our enemies off us, until we can once more get afloat."

The wondering boy, whose experience had not yet taught him to appreciate the reaction of the passions, started at this unexpected summons to his duty, and followed Barnstable toward the group of distant seamen. The lieutenant, who was instantly conscious how far pride had rendered him unjust, soon moderated his long strides, and continued in milder tones, which were quickly converted into his usual frank communications, though they still remained tinged with a melancholy that time only could entirely remove:

"We have been unlucky, Mr. Merry, but we need not despair—these lads have gotten together abundance of supplies, I see, and, with our arms, we can easily make ourselves masters of some of the enemy's smaller craft, and find our way back to the frigate when this gale has blown itself out. We must keep ourselves close, though, or we shall have the red-coats coming down upon us like so many sharks around a wreck. Ah! God bless her, Merry! there is not such a sight to be seen on the whole beach as two of her planks holding together."

The midshipman, without adverting to this sudden allusion to their vessel, prudently pursued the train of ideas in which his commander had started.

"There is an opening into the country but a short distance south of us, where a brook empties into the sea," he said. "We might find a cover in it, or in the wood above, into which it leads, until we can have a survey of the coast, or can seize some vessel to carry us off."

"There would be a satisfaction in waiting till the morning watch, and then carrying that accursed battery, which took off the better leg of the poor Ariel!" said the lieutenant, "the thing might be done, boy, and we could hold the work, too, until the Alacrity and the frigate drew into land."

"If you prefer storming works to boarding vessels, there is a fortress of stone, Mr. Barnstable, which lies directly on our beam. I could see it through the haze, when I was on the cliffs, stationing the lookout and—"

"And what, boy? speak without a fear: this is a time for free consultation."

"Why, sir, the garrison might not all be hostile—we should liberate Mr. Griffith and the marines; besides—"

"Besides what, sir?"

"I should have an opportunity, perhaps, of seeing my cousin Cecilia, and my cousin Katherine."

The countenance of Barnstable grew animated as he listened, and he answered with something of his usual cheerful manner:

"Ay, that, indeed, would be a work worth carrying! and the rescuing of our shipmates, and the marines, would read like a thing of military discretion—ha! hoy! all the rest would be incidental, yonker; like the capture of the fleet, after you have whipped the convoy."

"I do suppose, sir, that if the Abbey be taken, Colonel Howard will own himself a prisoner of war."

"And Colonel Howard's wards! now there is good sense in this scheme of thine, Master Merry, and I will give it proper reflection. But here are our poor fellows; speak cheeringly to them, sir, that we may hold them in temper for our enterprise."

Barnstable and the midshipman joined their shipwrecked companions, with that air of authority which is seldom wanting between the superior and inferior, in nautical intercourse, but at the same time with a kindness of speech and looks that might have been a little increased by the critical situation. After partaking of the food which had been selected from among the fragments that still lay scattered, for more than a mile, along the beach, the lieutenant directed the seamen to arm themselves with such weapons as offered, and also to make sufficient provision, from the schooner's stores, to last them for four-and-twenty hours longer. These orders were soon executed; and the whole party, led by Barnstable and Merry, proceeded along the foot of the cliffs, in quest of the opening in the rocks through which the little rivulet found a passage to the ocean. The weather contributed, as much as the seclusion of the spot, to prevent any discovery of the small party, which pursued its object with a disregard of caution that might, under other circumstances, have proved fatal to its safety. Barnstable paused in his march when they had all entered the deep ravine, and ascended nearly to the brow of the precipice that formed one of its sides, to take a last and more scrutinizing survey of the sea. His countenance exhibited the abandonment of all hope, as his eyes moved slowly from the northern to the southern boundary of the horizon, and he prepared to pursue his march, by moving, reluctantly, up the stream, when the boy, who still clung to his side, exclaimed joyously:

"Sail ho! It must be the frigate in the offing!"

"A sail!" repeated his commander; "whereaway do you see a sail in this tempest? Can there be another as hardy and unfortunate as ourselves?"

"Look to the starboard hand of the point of rock to windward!" cried the boy; "now you lose it—ah! now the sun falls upon it! 'tis a sail, sir, as sure as canvas can be spread in such a gale!"

"I see what you mean," returned the other, "but it seems a gull, skimming the sea! nay, now it rises, indeed, and shows itself like a bellying topsail. Pass up that glass, lads; here is a fellow in the offing who may prove a friend."

Merry waited the result of the lieutenant's examination with youthful impatience, and did not fail to ask immediately:

"Can you make it out, sir? is it the ship or the cutter?"

"Come, there seemeth yet some hope left for us, boy," returned Barnstable, closing the glass; " 'tis a ship lying-to under her main-topsail. If one might but dare to show himself on these heights, he would raise her hull, and make sure of her character! But I think I know her spars, though even her topsail dips, at times, when there is nothing to be seen but her bare poles; and they shortened by the topgallant masts."

"One would swear," said Merry, laughing, as much through the excitement produced by this intelligence, as at his conceit, "that Captain Munson would never carry wood aloft, when he can't carry canvas. I remember, one night, Mr. Griffith was a little vexed, and said, around the capstan, he believed the next order would be, to rig the bowsprit, and house lower-masts!"

"Ay, ay, Griffith is a lazy dog, and sometimes gets lost in the fogs of his own thoughts," said Barnstable; "and I suppose old Moderate was in a breeze. However, this looks as if he were in earnest; he must have kept the ship away, or she would never have been where she is; I do verily believe the old gentleman remembers that he has a few of his officers and men on this accursed island. This is well, Merry; for, should we take the Abbey, we have a place at hand in which to put our prisoners."

"We must have patience till the morning," added the boy, "for no boat would attempt to land in such a sea."

"No boat could land! The best boat that ever floated, boy, has sunk in these breakers! But the wind lessens, and before morning the sea will fall. Let us on, and find a berth for our poor lads, where they can be made more comfortable."

The two officers now descended from their elevation, and led the way still farther up the deep and narrow dell, until, as the ground rose gradually before them, they found themselves in a dense wood, on a level with the adjacent country.

"Here should be a ruin at hand, if I have a true reckoning, and know my courses and distances," said Barnstable; "I have a chart about me that speaks of such a landmark."

The lieutenant turned away from the laughing expression of the boy's eye, as the latter archly inquired:

"Was it made by one who knows the coast well, sir? or was it done by some school-boy, to learn his maps, as the girls work samplers?"

"Come, yonker, no sampler of your impudence. But look ahead; can you see any habitation that has been deserted?"

"Ay, sir, here is a pile of stones before us, that looks as dirty and ragged as if it was a soldier's barrack; can this be what you seek?"

"Faith, this has been a whole town in its day! we should call it a city in America, and furnish it with a mayor, aldermen, and recorder—you might stow old Faneuil Hall in one of its lockers."

With this sort of careless dialogue, which Barnstable engaged in that his men might discover no alteration in his manner, they approached the mouldering walls that had proved so frail a protection to the party under Griffith.

A short time was passed in examining the premises, when the wearied seamen took possession of one of the dilapidated apartments, and disposed themselves to seek that rest of which they had been deprived by the momentous occurrences of the past night.

Barnstable waited until the loud breathing of the seamen assured him that they slept, when he aroused the drowsy boy, who was fast losing his senses, in the same sort of oblivion, and motioned him to follow. Merry arose, and they stole together from the apartment with guarded steps, and penetrated more deeply into the gloomy recesses of the place.

26

Mercury:
I permit thee to be Sosia again.

DRYDEN

WE must leave the two adventurers winding their way among the broken piles, and venturing boldly between the tottering arches of the ruin, to accompany the reader, at the same hour, within the more comfortable walls of the Abbey; where, it will be remembered, Borroughcliffe was left in a condition of very equivocal ease. As the earth had, however, in the interval, nearly run its daily round, circumstances had intervened to release the soldier from his confinement—and no one, ignorant of the fact, would suppose that the gentleman, who was now seated at the hospitable board of Colonel Howard, directing, with so much discretion, the energies of his masticators to the delicacies of the feast, could read in his careless air and smiling visage, that those foragers of Nature had been so recently condemned, for four long hours, to the mortification of discussing the barren subject of his own sword-hilt. Borroughcliffe, however, maintained not only his usual post, but his well-earned reputation, at the table, with his ordinary coolness of demeanor; though at times there were fleeting smiles that crossed his military aspect, which sufficiently indicated that he considered the matter of his reflection to be of a particularly ludicrous character. In the young man who sat by his side, dressed in the deep-blue jacket of a seaman, with the fine white linen of his collar contrasting strongly with the black silk handkerchief that was tied with studied negligence around his neck, and whose easy air and manner contrasted still more strongly with this attire, the reader will discover Griffith. The captive paid much less devotion to the viands than his neighbor, though he affected more attention to the business of the table than he actually bestowed, with a sort of consciousness that it would relieve the blushing maiden who presided. The laughing eyes of Katherine Plowden were glittering by the side of the mild countenance of Alice Dunscombe, and, at times, were fastened in droll interest on the rigid and upright exterior that Captain Manual maintained, directly opposite to where she was seated. A chair had, also, been placed for Dillon—of course it was vacant.

"And so, Borroughcliffe," cried Colonel Howard, with a freedom of voice, and a vivacity in his air, that announced the increasing harmony of the repast, "the sea-dog left you nothing to chew but the cud of your resentment!"

"That and my sword-hilt," returned the immovable recruiting-officer. "Gentlemen, I know not how your Congress rewards military achievements; but if that worthy fellow were in my company, he should have a halberd within a week—spurs I would not offer him, for he affects to spurn their use."

Griffith smiled, and bowed in silence to the liberal compliment of Borroughcliffe; but Manual took on himself the task of replying:

"Considering the drilling the man has received, the conduct has been well enough, sir; though a well-trained soldier would not only have made prisoners, but he would have secured them."

"I perceive, my good comrade, that your thoughts are running on the exchange," said Borroughcliffe, good-humoredly; "we will fill, sir, and, by permission of the ladies, drink to a speedy restoration of rights to both parties—the *status quo ante bellum!*"

"With all my heart!" cried the colonel; "and Cicely and Miss Katherine will pledge the sentiment in a woman's sip; will ye not, my fair wards?—Mr. Griffith, I honor this proposition of yours, which will not only liberate yourself, but restore to us my kinsman, Mr. Christopher Dillon. Kit had imagined the thing well; ha! Borroughcliffe! 'twas ingeniously contrived, but the fortune of war interposed itself to his success; and yet it is a deep and inexplicable mystery to me, how Kit should have been conveyed from the Abbey with so little noise, and without raising the alarm."

"Christopher is a man who understands the philosophy of silence, as well as that of rhetoric," returned Borroughcliffe, "and must have learned, in his legal studies, that it is sometimes necessary to conduct matters *sub silentio.* You smile at my Latin, Miss Plowden, but really, since I have become an inhabitant of this monkish abode, my little learning is stimulated to unwonted efforts—nay, you are pleased to be yet more merry! I used the language, because silence is a theme in which you ladies take but little pleasure."

Katherine, however, disregarded the slight pique that was apparent in the soldier's manner; but, after following the train of her own thoughts in silent enjoyment for a moment longer, she seemed to yield to their drollery, and laughed until her dark eyes flashed with merriment. Cecilia did not assume the severe gravity with which she sometimes endeavored to repress, what she thought, the unseasonable mirth of her cousin; and the wondering Griffith fancied, as he glanced his eye from one to the other, that he could discern a suppressed smile playing among the composed features of Alice Dunscombe. Katherine, however, soon succeeded in repressing the paroxysm, and, with an air of infinitely comic gravity, she replied to the remark of the soldier:

"I think I have heard of such a process in nautical affairs as towing, but I must appeal to Mr. Griffith for the correctness of the term."

"You could not speak with more accuracy," returned the young sailor, with a look that sent the conscious blood to the temples of the lady, "though you had made marine terms your study."

"The profession requires less thought, perhaps, than you imagine, sir; but is this towing often done, as Captain Borroughcliffe—I beg his pardon—as the monks have it, *sub silentio?*"

"Spare me, fair lady," cried the captain, "and we will establish a compact of mutual grace; you to forgive my learning, and I to suppress my suspicions."

"Suspicions, sir, is a word that a lady must defy."

"And defiance a challenge that a soldier can never receive; so I must submit to talk English, though the fathers of the Church were my companions. I suspect that Miss Plowden has it in her power to explain the manner of Mr. Christopher Dillon's departure."

The lady did not reply, but a second burst of merriment succeeded, of a liveliness and duration quite equal to the former.

"How's this?" exclaimed the colonel; "permit me to say, Miss Plowden, your mirth is very extraordinary! I trust no disrespect has been offered to my kinsman?—Mr. Griffith, our terms are, that the exchange shall only be made on condition that equally good treatment has been extended to the parties!"

"If Mr. Dillon can complain of no greater evil than that of being laughed at by Miss Plowden, sir, he has reason to call himself a happy fellow."

"I know not, sir; God forbid that I should forget what is due to my guests, gentlemen! but ye have entered my dwelling as foes to my prince."

"But not to Colonel Howard, sir."

"I know no difference, Mr. Griffith. King George or Colonel Howard—

Colonel Howard or King George. Our feelings, our fortunes, and our fate, are as one; with the mighty odds that Providence has established between the prince and his people! I wish no other fortune than to share, at a humble distance, the weal or woe of my sovereign!"

"You are not called upon, dear sir, to do either, by the thoughtlessness of us ladies," said Cecilia, rising; "but here comes one who should turn our thoughts to a more important subject—our dress."

Politeness induced Colonel Howard, who both loved and respected his niece, to defer his remarks to another time; and Katherine, springing from her chair with childish eagerness, flew to the side of her cousin, who was directing a servant that had announced the arrival of one of those erratic vendors of small articles, who supply, in remote districts of the country, the places of more regular traders, to show the lad into the dining-parlor. The repast was so far ended as to render this interruption less objectionable; and, as all felt the object of Cecilia to be the restoration of harmony, the boy was ushered into the room without further delay. The contents of his small basket, consisting chiefly of essences, and the small articles of female economy, were playfully displayed on the table by Katherine, who declared herself the patroness of the itinerant youth, and who laughingly appealed to the liberality of the gentlemen in behalf of her *protégé*.

"You perceive, my dear guardian, that the boy must be loyal; for he offers, here, perfume that is patronized by no less than two royal dukes: do suffer me to place a box aside for your special use. You consent; I see it in your eye. And, Captain Borroughcliffe, as you appear to be forgetting the use of your own language, here is even a horn-book for you! How admirably provided he seems to be! You must have had St. Ruth in view, when you laid in your stock, child?"

"Yes, my lady," the boy replied, with a bow that was studiously awkward; "I have often heard of the grand ladies that dwell in the old Abbey, and I have journeyed a few miles beyond my rounds, to gain their custom."

"And surely they cannot disappoint you. Miss Howard, that is a palpable hint to your purse; and I know that not even Miss Alice can escape contribution, in these troublesome times. Come, aid me, child; what have you to recommend, in particular, to the favor of these ladies?"

The lad approached the basket and rummaged its contents, for a moment, with the appearance of deep, mercenary interest; and then, without lifting his hand from the confusion he had caused, he said, while he exhibited something within the basket to the view of his smiling observer:

"This, my lady."

Katherine started, and glanced her eyes, with a piercing look, at the countenance of the boy, and then turned them uneasily from face to face, with conscious timidity. Cecilia had effected her object, and had resumed her seat in silent abstraction; Alice was listening to the remarks of Captain Manual and the host, as they discussed the propriety of certain military usages; Griffith seemed to hold communion with his mistress, by imitating her silence; but Katherine, in her stolen glances, met the keen look of Borroughcliffe, fastened on her face in a manner that did not fail instantly to suspend the scrutiny.

"Come, Cecilia," she cried, after a pause of a moment, "we trespass too long on the patience of the gentlemen; not only to keep possession of our seats, ten minutes after the cloth has been drawn, but even to introduce our essences, and tapes, and needles, among the madeira, and—shall I add, cigars, colonel?"

"Not while we are favored with the company of Miss Plowden, certainly."

"Come, my coz; I perceive the colonel is growing particularly polite, which is a never-failing sign that he tires of our presence."

Cecilia rose, and was leading the way to the door, when Katherine turned to the lad, and added:

"You can follow us to the drawing-room, child, where we can make our purchases, without exposing the mystery of our toilets."

"Miss Plowden has forgotten my horn-book, I believe," said Borroughcliffe, advancing from the standing group who surrounded the table; "possibly I can find some work in the basket of the boy better fitted for the improvement of a grown-up young gentleman than the elementary treatise."

Cecilia, observing him to take his basket from the lad, resumed her seat, and her example was necessarily followed by Katherine, though not without some manifest indications of vexation.

"Come hither, boy, and explain the uses of your wares. This is soap, and this a penknife, I know; but what name do you affix to this?"

"That? that is tape," returned the lad, with an impatience that might very naturally be attributed to the interruption that was thus given to his trade.

"And this?"

"That?" repeated the stripling, pausing with a hesitation between sulkiness and doubt; "that—"

"Come, this is a little ungallant!" cried Katherine; "to keep three ladies dying with impatience to possess themselves of their finery, while you detain the boy, to ask the name of a tambouring-needle!"

"I should apologize for asking question that are so easily answered; but perhaps he will find the next more difficult to solve," returned Borroughcliffe, placing the subject of his inquiries in the palm of his hand, in such a manner as to conceal it from all but the boy and himself. "This has a name, too; what is it?"

"That?—that—is sometimes called—white-line."

"Perhaps you mean a white lie!"

"How, sir!" exclaimed the lad, a little fiercely, "a lie?"

"Only a white one," returned the captain. "What do you call this, Miss Dunscombe?"

"We call it bobbin, sir, generally, in the north," said the placid Alice.

"Ay, bobbin, or white-line; they are the same thing," added the young trader.

"They are? I think, now, for a professional man, you know but little of the terms of your art," observed Borroughcliffe, with an affectation of irony; "I never have seen a youth of your years who knew less. What names, now, would you affix to this—and this, and this?"

While the captain was speaking, he drew from his pocket the several instruments that the cockswain had made use of the preceding night to secure his prisoner.

"That," exclaimed the lad, with the eagerness of one who would vindicate his reputation, "is ratlin-stuff; and this is marline; and that is sennit."

"Enough, enough," said Borroughcliffe; "you have exhibited sufficient knowledge to convince me that you *do* know something of your *trade*, and nothing of these articles. Mr. Griffith, do you claim this boy?"

"I believe I must, sir," said the young sea-officer, who had been intently listening to the examination. "On whatever errand you have now ventured here, Mr. Merry, it is useless to affect further concealment."

"Merry!" exclaimed Cecilia Howard; "is it you, then, my cousin? are you, too, fallen into the power of your enemies! Was it not enough that—"

The young lady recovered her recollection in time to suppress the remainder of the sentence, though the grateful expression of Griffith's eye sufficiently indicated that he had, in his thoughts, filled the sentence with expressions abundantly flattering to his own feelings.

"How's this, again?" cried the colonel; "my two wards embracing and fondling a vagrant, vagabond pedlar, before my eyes! Is this treason, Mr. Griffith, or what means the extraordinary visit of this young gentleman?"

"Is it extraordinary, sir," said Merry himself, losing his assumed awkwardness, in the ease and confidence of one whose faculties had been early exercised, "that a boy, like myself, destitute of mother and sisters, should take a like risk on himself, to visit the only two female relatives he has in the world?"

"Why this disguise, then? surely, young gentleman, it was unnecessary to enter the dwelling of old George Howard on such an errand clandestinely, even though your tender years have been practised on, to lead you astray from your allegiance. Mr. Griffith and Captain Manual must pardon me, if I express sentiments, at my own table, that they may find unpleasant; but this business requires us to be explicit."

"The hospitality of Colonel Howard is unquestionable," returned the boy; "but he has a great reputation for his loyalty to the crown."

"Ay, young gentleman; and, I trust, with some justice."

"Would it, then, be safe to intrust my person in the hands of one who might think it his duty to detain me?"

"This is plausible enough, Captain Borroughcliffe, and I doubt not the boy speaks with candor. I would, now, that my kinsman, Mr. Christopher Dillon, were here, that I might learn if it would be misprision of treason to permit this youth to depart, unmolested, and without exchange?"

"Inquire of the young gentleman, after the cacique," returned the recruiting officer, who, apparently satisfied in producing the exposure of Merry, had resumed his seat at the table; "perhaps he is, in verity, an ambassador, empowered to treat on behalf of his highness."

"How say you?" demanded the colonel; "do you know anything of my kinsman?"

The anxious eyes of the whole party were fastened on the boy for many moments, witnessing the sudden change from careless freedom to deep horror expressed in his countenance. At length he uttered, in an undertone, the secret of Dillon's fate.

"He is dead."

"Dead!" repeated every voice in the room.

"Yes, dead," said the boy, gazing at the pallid faces of those who surrounded him.

A long and fearful silence succeeded the announcement of this intelligence, which was only interrupted by Griffith, who said:

"Explain the manner of his death, sir, and where his body lies."

"His body lies interred in the sands," returned Merry, with a deliberation that proceeded from an opening perception that, if he uttered too much, he might betray the loss of the Ariel, and, consequently, endanger the liberty of Barnstable.

"In the sands?" was echoed from every part of the room.

"Ay, in the sands; but how he died, I cannot explain."

"He has been murdered!" exclaimed Colonel Howard, whose command of utterance was now amply restored to him; "he has been treacherously, and dastardly, and basely murdered!"

"He has *not* been murdered," said the boy, firmly; "nor did he meet his death among those who deserve the name neither of traitors nor of dastards."

"Said you not that he was dead? that my kinsman was buried in the sands of the sea-shore?"

"Both are true, sir—"

"And you refuse to explain how he met his death, and why he has been thus ignominiously interred?"

"He received his interment by my orders, sir; and, if there be ignominy about his grave, his own acts have heaped it on him. As to the manner of his death, I cannot and will not speak."

"Be calm, my cousin," said Cecilia, in an imploring voice; "respect the age of my uncle, and remember his strong attachment to Mr. Dillon."

The veteran had, however, so far mastered his feelings as to continue the dialogue with more recollection.

"Mr. Griffith," he said, "I shall not act hastily—you and your companion will be pleased to retire to your several apartments. I will so far respect the son of my brother Harry's friend as to believe your parole will be sacred. Go, gentlemen; you are unguarded."

The two prisoners bowed low to the ladies and their host, and retired. Griffith, however, lingered a moment on the threshold to say:

"Colonel Howard, I leave the boy to your kindness and consideration. I know you will not forget that his blood mingles with that of one who is most dear to you."

"Enough, enough, sir," said the veteran, waving his hand to him to retire; "and you, ladies; this is not a place for you, either."

"Never will I quit this child," said Katherine, "while such a horrid imputation lies on him. Colonel Howard, act your pleasure on us both, for I suppose you have the power; but his fate shall be my fate."

"There is, I trust, some misconception in this melancholy affair," said Borroughcliffe, advancing into the centre of the agitated group; "and I should hope, by calmness and moderation, all may yet be explained. Young gentleman, you have borne arms, and must know, notwithstanding your youth, what it is to be in the power of your enemies?"

"Never!" returned the proud boy; "I am a captive for the first time."

"I speak, sir, in reference to our power."

"You may order me to a dungeon, or, as I have entered the Abbey in disguise, possibly to a gibbet."

"And is that a fate to be met so calmly by one so young?"

"You dare not do it, Captain Borroughcliffe," cried Katherine, involuntarily throwing an arm around the boy, as if to shield him from harm. "You would blush to think of such a cold-blooded act of vengeance, Colonel Howard."

"If we could examine the young man, where the warmth of feeling, which these ladies exhibit, might not be excited," said the captain, apart to his host, "we should gain important intelligence."

"Miss Howard, and you, Miss Plowden," said the veteran, in a manner that long habit had taught his wards to respect, "your young kinsman is not in the keeping of savages, and you can safely confide him to my custody. I am sorry that we have so long kept Miss Alice standing, but she will find relief on the couches of your drawing-room, Cecilia."

Cecilia and Katherine permitted themselves to be conducted to the door by their polite but determined guardian, where he bowed to their retiring persons with the exceeding courtesy that he never failed to use when in the least excited.

"You appear to know your danger, Mr. Merry," said Borroughcliffe, after the door was closed; "I trust you also know what duty would dictate to one in my situation."

"Do it, sir," returned the boy; "you have a king to render an account to, and I have a country."

"I may have a country also," said Borroughcliffe, with a calmness that was not in the least disturbed by the taunting air with which the youth delivered himself. "It is possible for me, however, to be lenient, even merciful, when the interests of that prince to whom you allude are served—you came not on this enterprise alone, sir?"

"Had I come better attended, Captain Borroughcliffe might have heard these questions instead of putting them."

"I am happy, sir, that your retinue has been so small; and yet, even the rebel schooner called the Ariel might have furnished you with more becoming attendance. I cannot but think that you are not far distant from your friends."

"He is near his enemies, your honor," said Sergeant Drill, who had entered the room unobserved; "for here is a boy who says he has been seized in the old ruin, and robbed of his goods and clothes; and by his description this lad should be the thief."

Borroughcliffe signed to the boy, who stood in the background, to advance; and he was instantly obeyed, with all the eagerness which a sense of injury on the part of the sufferer could excite. The tale of this unexpected intruder was soon told, and was briefly this:

He had been assaulted by a man and a boy (the latter was in presence), while arranging his effects, in the ruin, preparatory to exhibiting them to the ladies of the Abbey, and had been robbed of such part of his attire as the boy had found necessary for his disguise, together with his basket of valuables. He had been put into an apartment of an old tower, by the man, for safe keeping; but as the latter frequently ascended to its turret, to survey the country, he had availed himself of his remissness to escape; and, to conclude, he demanded a restoration of his property and vengeance for his wrongs.

Merry heard his loud and angry details with scornful composure, and, before the offended pedlar was through his narrative, had divested himself of the borrowed garments, which he threw to the other with singular disdain.

"We are beleaguered, mine host! beset! besieged!" cried Borroughcliffe, when the other had ended. "Here is a rare plan to rob us of our laurels! ay, and of our rewards! But, hark ye, Drill! they have old soldiers to deal with, and we shall look into the matter. One would wish to triumph on foot; you understand me? there was no horse in the battle. Go, fellow, I see you grow wiser; take this young gentleman—and remember *he is* a young gentleman— put him in safe keeping; but see him supplied with all he wants."

Borroughcliffe bowed politely to the haughty bend of the body with which Merry, who now began to think himself a martyr to his country, followed the orderly from the room.

"There is metal in the lad!" exclaimed the captain; "and if he live to get a beard, 'twill be a hardy dog who ventures to pluck it. I am glad, mine host, that this 'wandering Jew' has arrived, to save the poor fellow's feelings, for I detest tampering with such a noble spirit. I saw, by his eye, that he had squinted oftener over a gun than through a needle!"

"But they have murdered my kinsman!—the loyal, the learned, the ingenious Mr. Christopher Dillon!"

"If they have done so, they shall be made to answer it," said Borroughcliffe, reseating himself at the table, with a coolness that furnished an ample pledge of the impartiality of his judgment; "but let us learn the facts before we do aught hastily."

Colonel Howard was fain to comply with so reasonable a proposition, and he resumed his chair, while his companion proceeded to institute a close examination of the pedlar-boy.

We shall defer, until the proper time may arrive, recording the result of his inquiries; but shall so far satisfy the curiosity of our readers as to tell them that the captain learned sufficient to convince him a very serious attempt was meditated on the Abbey; and, as he thought, enough, also, to enable him to avert the danger.

27

I have not seen
So likely an ambassador of love.

Merchant of Venice

Cecilia and Katherine separated from Alice Dunscombe in the lower gallery of the cloisters, and the cousins ascended to the apartment which was assigned them as a dressing-room. The intensity of feeling that was gradually accumulating in the breasts of the ladies, as circumstances brought those in whom their deepest interests were centred into situations of extreme delicacy, if not of actual danger, perhaps, in some measure, prevented them from experiencing all that concern which the detection and arrest of Merry might be supposed to excite. The boy, like themselves, was an only child of one of those three sisters who caused the close connection of so many of our characters; and his tender years had led his cousins to regard him with an affection that exceeded the ordinary interest of such an affinity; but they knew that in the hands of Colonel Howard his person was safe, though his liberty might be endangered. When the first emotions, therefore, which were created by his sudden appearance after so long an absence had subsided, their thoughts were rather occupied by the consideration of what consequences, to others, might proceed from his arrest, than by any reflections on the midshipman's actual condition. Secluded from the observations of any strange eyes, the two maidens indulged their feelings, without restraint, according to their several temperaments. Katherine moved to and fro in the apartment with feverish anxiety, while Miss Howard, by concealing her countenance under the ringlets of her luxuriant dark hair, and shading her eyes with a fair hand, seemed to be willing to commune with her thoughts more quietly.

"Barnstable cannot be far distant," said the former, after a few minutes had passed; "for he never would have sent that child on such an errand by himself!"

Cecilia raised her mild, blue eyes to the countenance of her cousin, as she answered:

"All thoughts of an exchange must now be abandoned; and perhaps the persons of the prisoners will be held as pledges, to answer for the life of Dillon."

"Can the wretch be dead? or is it merely a threat, or some device of that urchin? He is a forward child, and would not hesitate to speak and act boldly, on emergency."

"He is dead!" returned Cecilia, veiling her face again in horror; "the eyes of the boy, his whole countenance, confirmed his words! I fear, Katherine, that Mr. Barnstable has suffered his resentment to overcome his discretion, when he learned the treachery of Dillon; surely, surely, though the hard usages of war may justify so dreadful a revenge on an enemy, it was unkind to forget the condition of his own friends!"

"Mr. Barnstable has done neither, Miss Howard," said Katherine, checking her uneasy footsteps, her light form swelling with pride; "Mr. Barnstable is equally incapable of murdering an enemy or of deserting a friend!"

"But retaliation is neither deemed nor called murder by men in arms."

"Think it what you will, call it what you will, Cecilia Howard, I will pledge my life that Richard Barnstable has to answer for the blood of none but the open enemies of his country."

"The miserable man may have fallen a sacrifice to the anger of that seaman who led him hence as a captive!"

"That terrific seaman, Miss Howard, has a heart as tender as your own. He is—"

"Nay, Katherine," interrupted Cecilia, "you chide me unkindly; let us not add to our unavoidable misery by such harsh contention."

"I do not contend with you, Cecilia; I merely defend the absent and the innocent from your unkind suspicions, my cousin."

"Say, rather, your sister," returned Miss Howard, their hands involuntarily closing upon each other, "for we are surely sisters! But let us strive to think of something less horrible. Poor, poor Dillon! now that he has met a fate so terrible, I can even fancy him less artful and more upright than we had thought him! You agree with me, Katherine, I see by your countenance, and we will dwell no longer on the subject. Katherine! my cousin Kate, what see you?"

Miss Plowden, as she relinquished her pressure of the hand of Cecilia, had renewed her walk with a more regulated step; but she was yet making her first turn across the room, when her eyes became keenly set on the opposite window, and her whole frame was held in an attitude of absorbed attention. The rays of the setting sun fell bright upon her dark glances, which seemed fastened on some distant object, and gave an additional glow to the mantling color that was slowly stealing across her cheeks, to her temples. Such a sudden alteration in the manner and appearance of her companion had not failed to catch the attention of Cecilia, who, in consequence, interrupted herself by the agitated question we have related. Katherine slowly beckoned her companion to her side, and, pointing in the direction of the wood that lay in view, she said:

"See yon tower, in the ruin! Do you observe those small spots of pink and yellow that are fluttering above its walls?"

"I do. They are the lingering remnants of the foliage of some tree; but they want the vivid tints which grace the autumn of our own dear America!"

"One is the work of God, and the other has been produced by the art of man. Cecilia, those are no leaves, but they are my own childish signals, and without doubt Barnstable himself is on that ruined tower. Merry cannot, will not, betray him!"

"My life should be a pledge for the honor of our little cousin," said Cecilia. "But you have the telescope of my uncle at hand, ready for such an event! one look through it will ascertain the truth—"

Katherine sprang to the spot where the instrument stood, and with eager hands she prepared it for the necessary observation.

"It is he!" she cried, the instant her eye was put to the glass. "I even see his head above the stones. How unthinking to expose himself so unnecessarily!"

"But what says he, Katherine?" exclaimed Cecilia; "you alone can interpret his meaning."

The little book which contained the explanations of Miss Plowden's signals was now hastily produced, and its leaves rapidly run over in quest of the necessary number.

"'Tis only a question to gain my attention. I must let him know he is observed."

When Katherine, as much to indulge her secret propensities as with any hope of its usefulness, had devised this plan for communicating with Barnstable, she had, luckily, not forgotten to arrange the necessary means to reply to his interrogatories. A very simple arrangement of some of the ornamental cords of the window-curtains enabled her to effect this purpose; and her nimble fingers soon fastened the pieces of silk to the lines, which were now thrown into the air, when these signals in miniature were instantly displayed in the breeze.

"He sees them!" cried Cecilia, "and is preparing to change his flags."

"Keep, then, your eye on him, my cousin, and tell me the colors that he shows, with their order, and I will endeavor to read his meaning."

"He is as expert as yourself! There are two more of them fluttering above the stones again: the upper is white, and the lower black."

"White over black," repeated Katherine, rapidly, to herself, as she turned the leaves of her book.—"'*My messenger: has he been seen?*' To that we must answer the unhappy truth. Here it is—yellow, white, and red—'*He is a prisoner.*' How fortunate that I should have prepared such a question and answer! What says he, Cecilia, to this news?"

"He is busy making his changes, dear. Nay, Katherine, you shake so violently as to move the glass! Now he is done; 'tis yellow over black this time."

"'*Griffith, or who?*' He does not understand us; but I had thought of the poor boy in making out the numbers—ah! here it is; yellow, green, and red—'*My cousin Merry.*' He cannot fail to understand us now."

"He has already taken in his flags. The news seems to alarm him, for he is less expert than before. He shows them now—they are green, red, and yellow."

"The question is '*Am I safe?*' 'Tis that which made him tardy, Miss Howard," continued Katherine. "Barnstable is ever slow to consult his safety. But how shall I answer him? should we mislead him now, how could we ever forgive ourselves?"

"Of Andrew Merry there is no fear," returned Cecilia; "and I think if Captain Borroughcliffe had any intimation of the proximity of his enemies, he would not continue at the table."

"He will stay there while wine will sparkle and man can swallow," said Katherine; "but we know, by sad experience, that he is a soldier on emergency; and yet, I'll trust to his ignorance this time—here, I have an answer: '*You are yet safe, but be wary.*'"

"He reads your meaning with a quick eye, Katherine; and he is ready with his answer, too: he shows green over white this time. Well! do you not hear me? 'tis green over white. Why, you are dumb—what says he, dear?"

Still, Katherine answered not, and her cousin raised her eyes from the glass, and beheld her companion gazing earnestly at the open page, while the glow which excitement had before brought to her cheek was increased to a still deeper bloom.

"I hope your blushes and his signals are not ominous, Kate," added Cecilia; "can green imply his jealousy as white does your purity? what says he, coz?"

"He talks, like yourself, much nonsense," said Katherine, turning to her flags, with a pettish air that was singularly contradicted by her gratified countenance; "but the situation of things requires that I should talk to Barnstable more freely."

"I can retire," said Cecilia, rising from her chair with a grave manner.

"Nay, Cecilia, I do not deserve these looks—'tis you who exhibit levity now! But you can perceive for yourself that evening is closing in, and that some other medium for conversation, besides the eyes, may be adopted.—Here is a signal, which will answer: '*When the Abbey clock strikes nine, come with care to the wicket, which opens at the east side of the paddock, on the road; until then, keep secret.*' I had prepared this very signal in case an interview should be necessary."

"Well, he sees it," returned Cecilia, who had resumed her place by the telescope, "and seems disposed to obey you, for I no longer discern his flags or his person."

Miss Howard now arose from the glass, her observations being ended; but Katherine did not return the instrument to its corner, without fastening one long anxious look through it, on what now appeared to be the deserted tower. The interest and anxiety produced by this short and imperfect communication between Miss Plowden and her lover, did not fail to excite reflections in both the ladies, that furnished materials to hold them in earnest discourse, until the entrance of Alice Dunscombe announced that their presence was expected below. Even the unsuspecting Alice, on entering, observed a change in the countenances and demeanor of the two cousins, which betrayed that their secret conference had not been entirely without contention. The features of Cecilia were disturbed and anxious, and their expression was not unlike melancholy; while the dark flashing eye, flushed temples, and proud, determined step of Katherine exhibited in an equal, if not a greater degree, a very different emotion. As no reference to the subject of their conversation was, however, made by either of the young ladies, after the entrance of Alice, she led the way in silence, to the drawing-room.

The ladies were received by Colonel Howard and Borroughcliffe, with marked attention. In the former there were moments when a deep gloom would, in spite of his very obvious exertions to the contrary, steal over his open, generous countenance; but the recruiting officer maintained an air of immovable coolness and composure. Twenty times did he detect the piercing looks of Katherine fastened on him with an intentness that a less deliberative man might have had the vanity to misinterpret; but even this flattering testimonial of his power to attract failed to disturb his self-possession. It was in vain that Katherine endeavored to read his countenance, where everything was fixed in military rigidity, though his deportment appeared more than usually easy and natural. Tired at length with her fruitless scrutiny, the excited girl turned her gaze upon the clock; to her amazement, she discovered that it was on the stroke of nine, and, disregarding a deprecating glance from her cousin, she arose and quitted the apartment. Borroughcliffe opened the door of her exit, and while the lady civilly bowed her head in acknowledgment of his attention, their eyes once more met; but she glided quickly by him, and found herself alone in the gallery. Katherine hesitated, more than a minute, to proceed, for she thought she had detected in that glance a lurking expression, that manifested conscious security mingled with secret design. It was not her nature, however, to hesitate, when circumstances required that she should be both prompt and alert; and throwing over her slight person a large cloak, that was in readiness for the occasion, she stole warily from the building.

Although Katherine suspected most painfully that Borroughcliffe had received intelligence that might prove dangerous to her lover, she looked around her in vain, on gaining the open air, to discover any alteration in the arrangements for the defence of the Abbey, which might confirm her suspicions, or the knowledge of which might enable her to instruct Barnstable how to avoid the secret danger. Every disposition remained as it had been since the capture of Griffith and his companion. She heard the heavy, quick steps of the sentinel, who was posted beneath their windows, endeavoring to warm himself on his confined post; and, as she paused to listen, she also detected the rattling of arms from the soldier, who, as usual, guarded the approach of that part of the building where his comrades were quartered. The night had set in cloudy and dark, although the gale had greatly subsided toward the close of the day; still the wind swept heavily, and at moments, with a rushing noise, among the irregular walls of the edifice; and it required the utmost nicety of ear to distinguish even these well-known sounds, among such accompaniments. When Katherine, however, was satisfied that her organs had not deceived her, she turned an anxious eye in the direction of what Borroughcliffe called his "barracks."

Everything in that direction appeared so dark and still as to create a sensation of uneasiness by its very quiet. It might be the silence of sleep that now pervaded the ordinarily gay and mirthful apartment; or it might be the stillness of a fearful preparation! There was no time, however, for further hesitation, and Katherine drew her cloak more closely about her form, and proceeded with light and guarded steps to the appointed spot. As she approached the wicket the clock struck the hour, and she again paused while the mournful sounds were borne by her on the wind, as if expecting that each stroke on the bell would prove a signal to unmask some secret design of Borroughcliffe. As the last vibration melted away, she opened the little gate, and issued on the highway. The figure of a man sprang forward from behind an angle of the wall, as she appeared; and, while her heart was still throbbing with the suddenness of the alarm she found herself in the arms of Barnstable. After the first few words of recognition and pleasure which the young sailor uttered, he acquainted his mistress with the loss of his schooner, and the situation of the survivors.

"And now, Katherine," he concluded, "you have come, I trust, never to quit me; or, at most, to return no more to that old Abbey, unless it be to aid in liberating Griffith, and then to join me again forever."

"Why, truly, there is so much to tempt a young woman to renounce her home and friends, in the description you have just given of your condition, that I hardly know how to refuse your request, Barnstable. You are very tolerably provided with a dwelling in the ruin; and I suppose certain predatory schemes are to be adopted to make it habitable! St. Ruth is certainly well supplied with the necessary articles, but whether we should not be shortly removed to the castle at York or the jail at Newcastle is a question that I put to your discretion."

"Why yield your thoughts to such silly subjects, lovely trifler!" said Barnstable, "when the time and the occasion both urge us to be in earnest?"

"It is a woman's province to be thrifty, and to look after the comforts of domestic life," returned his mistress; "and I would discharge my functions with credit. But I feel you are vexed, for, to see your dark countenance is out of the question, on such a night. When do you propose to commence housekeeping, if I should yield to your proposals?"

"I have not concluded relating my plans, and your provoking wit annoys me! The vessel I have taken will unquestionably come into the land, as the gale dies; and I intend making my escape in her, after beating this Englishman, and securing the liberty of Miss Howard and yourself. I could see the frigate in the offing, even before we left the cliffs."

"This certainly sounds better!" rejoined Katherine, in a manner that indi-

cated she was musing on their prospects; "and yet there may exist some difficulties in the way that you little suspect."

"Difficulties there are none—there can be none."

"Speak not irreverently of the mazes of love, Mr. Barnstable. When was it ever known to exist unfettered or unembarrassed? Even I have an explanation to ask of you that I would much rather let alone."

"Of me? Ask what you will, or how you will; I am a careless, unthinking fellow, Miss Plowden; but to you I have little to answer for—unless a foolish sort of adoration be an offence against your merits."

Barnstable felt the little hand that was supported on his arm pressing the limb, as Katherine replied, in a tone so changed from its former forced levity that he started as the first sound reached his ears. "Merry has brought in a horrid report!" she said; "I would I could believe it untrue; but the looks of the boy and the absence of Dillon both confirm it."

"Poor Merry! he, too, has fallen into the trap! but they shall yet find one who is too cunning for them. Is it to the fate of that wretched Dillon that you allude?"

"He *was* a wretch," continued Katherine, in the same voice, "and he deserved much punishment at your hands, Barnstable; but life is the gift of God, and is not to be taken whenever human vengeance would appear to require a victim."

"His life was taken by Him who bestowed it," said the sailor. "Is it Katherine Plowden who would suspect me of the deed of a dastard?"

"I do not suspect you—I did not suspect you," cried Katherine; "I will never suspect any evil of you again. You are not, you cannot be, angry with me, Barnstable? Had you heard the cruel suspicions of my cousin Cecilia, and had your imagination been busy in portraying your wrongs and the temptations to forget mercy, like mine, even while my tongue denied your agency in the suspected deed, you would—you would at least have learned how much easier it is to defend those we love against the open attacks of others than against our own jealous feelings."

"Those words, love and jealousy, will obtain your acquittal," cried Barnstable, in his natural voice; and, after uttering a few more consoling assurances to Katherine, whose excited feelings found vent in tears, he briefly related the manner of Dillon's death.

"I had hoped I stood higher in the estimation of Miss Howard than to be subjected to even her suspicions," he said, when he had ended his explanation. "Griffith has been but a sorry representative of our trade, if he has left such an opinion of its pursuits."

"I do not know that Mr. Griffith would altogether have escaped my conjectures, had he been the disappointed commander, and you the prisoner," returned Katherine; "you know not how much we have both studied the usages of war, and with what dreadful pictures of hostages, retaliations, and military executions, our minds are stored; but a mountain is raised off my spirits, and I could almost say that I am now ready to descend the valley of life in your company."

"It is a discreet determination, my good Katherine, and God bless you for it! The companion may not be so good as you deserve, but you will find him ambitious of your praise. Now let us devise means to effect our object."

"Therein lies another of my difficulties. Griffith, I much fear, will not urge Cecilia to another flight, against her—her—what shall I call it, Barnstable—her caprice, or her judgment? Cecilia will never consent to desert her uncle, and I cannot muster the courage to abandon my poor cousin, in the face of the world, in order to take shelter with even Mr. Richard Barnstable!"

"Speak you from the heart now, Katherine?"

"Very nearly—if not exactly."

"Then have I been cruelly deceived! It is easier to find a path in the trackless ocean, without chart or compass, than to know the windings of a woman's heart!"

"Nay, nay, foolish man; you forget that I am but small, and how very near my head is to my heart; too nigh, I fear, for the discretion of their mistress! But is there no method of forcing Griffith and Cecilia to their own good, without undue violence?"

"It cannot be done; he is my senior in rank, and the instant I release him he will claim the command. A question might be raised, at a leisure moment, on the merits of such a claim—but even my own men are, as you know, nothing but a draft from the frigate, and they would not hesitate to obey the orders of the first-lieutenant, who is not a man to trifle on matters of duty."

" 'Tis vexatious, truly," said Katherine, "that all my well-concerted schemes in behalf of this wayward pair should be frustrated by their own wilful conduct! But, after all, have you justly estimated your strength, Barnstable? Are you certain that you would be successful, and that without hazard, too, if you should make the attempt!"

"Morally, and what is better, physically certain. My men are closely hid, where no one suspects an enemy to lie; they are anxious for the enterprise and the suddenness of the attack will not only make the victory sure, but it will be rendered bloodless. You will aid us in our entrance, Katherine. I shall first secure this recruiting-officer, and his command will then surrender without striking a blow. Perhaps, after all, Griffith will hear reason; if he do not, I will not yield my authority to a released captive without a struggle."

"God send that there shall be no fighting!" murmured his companion, a little appalled at the images his language had raised before her imagination; "and, Barnstable, I enjoin you, most solemnly, by all your affection for me, and by everything you deem most sacred, to protect the person of Colonel Howard at every hazard. There must be no excuse, no pretence, for even an insult to my passionate, good, obstinate, but kind old guardian. I believe I have given him already more trouble than I am entitled to give any one, and Heaven forbid that I should cause him any serious misfortune."

"He shall be safe, and not only he, but all that are with him, as you will perceive, Katherine, when you hear my plan. Three hours shall not pass over my head before you will see me master of that old Abbey. Griffith, ay, Griffith must be content to be my inferior, until we get afloat again."

"Attempt nothing unless you feel certain of being able to maintain your advantage, not only against your enemies, but also against your friends," said the anxious Katherine. "Rely on it, both Cecilia and Griffith are refining so much on their feelings, that neither will be your ally."

"This comes of passing the four best years of his life within walls of brick, poring over Latin grammars and syntaxes, and such other nonsense, when he should have been rolling them away in a good box of live-oak, and studying, at most, how to sum up his day's work, and tell where his ship lies after a blow. Your college learning may answer well enough for a man who has to live by his wits, but it can be of little use to one who is never afraid to read human nature, by looking his fellow-creatures full in the face, and whose hand is as ready as his tongue. I have generally found the eye that was good at Latin was dull at a compass, or in a night squall; and yet, Griff is a seaman, though I have heard him even read the testament in Greek! Thank God, I had the wisdom to run away from school the second day they undertook to teach me a strange tongue, and I believe I am the more honest man, and the better seaman, for my ignorance!"

"There is no telling you what might have been, Barnstable, under other circumstances," retorted his mistress, with a playfulness of manner that she could not always repress, though it was indulged at the expense of him she most loved; "I doubt not but, under proper training, you would have made a reasonably good priest."

"If you talk of priests, Katherine, I shall remind you that we carry one in the ship. But listen to my plan; we may talk further of priestcraft when an opportunity may offer."

Barnstable then proceeded to lay before his mistress a project he had formed for surprising the Abbey that night, which was so feasible that Katherine, notwithstanding her recent suspicions of Borroughcliffe's designs, came gradually to believe it would succeed. The young seaman answered her objections with the readiness of an ardent mind, bent on executing its purposes, and with a fertility of resources that proved he was no contemptible enemy in matter that required spirited action. Of Merry's remaining firm and faithful he had no doubt; and, although he acknowledged the escape of the pedlar-boy, he urged that the lad had seen no other of his party besides himself, whom he mistook for a common marauder.

As the disclosure of these plans was frequently interrupted by little digressions, connected with the peculiar emotions of the lovers, more than an hour flew by before they separated. But Katherine at length reminded him how swiftly the time was passing, and how much remained to be done, when he reluctantly consented to see her once more through the wicket where they parted.

Miss Plowden adopted the same precaution in returning to the house she had used on leaving it; and she was congratulating herself on its success, when her eye caught a glimpse of the figure of a man who was apparently following at some little distance, in her footsteps, and dogging her motions. As the obscure form, however, paused also when she stopped to give it an alarmed though inquiring look, and then slowly retired toward the boundary of the paddock, Katherine, believing it to be Barnstable watching over her safety, entered the Abbey, with every idea of alarm entirely lost in the pleasing reflection of her lover's solicitude.

28

He looks abroad, and soon appears,
O'er Horncliffe Hill, a plump of spears,
Beneath a pennon gay.

Marmion

THE sharp sounds of the supper-bell were ringing along the gallery, as Miss Plowden gained the gloomy passage; and she quickened her steps to join the ladies in order that no further suspicions might be excited by her absence. Alice Dunscombe was already proceeding to the dining-parlor, as Katherine passed through the door of the drawing-room; but Miss Howard had loitered behind, and was met by her cousin alone.

"You have then been so daring as to venture, Katherine!" exclaimed Cecilia.

"I have," returned the other, throwing herself into a chair, to recover her agitation—"I have, Cecilia; and I have met Barnstable, who will soon be in the Abbey, and its master."

The blood which had rushed to the face of Cecilia on first seeing her cousin, now retreated to her heart, leaving every part of her fine countenance of the whiteness of her polished temples, as she said:

"And we are to have a night of blood!"

"We are to have a night of freedom, Miss Howard; freedom to you, and to me; to Andrew Merry, to Griffith, and to his companion!"

"What freedom more than we now enjoy, Katherine, is needed by two young women? Think you I can remain silent, and see my uncle betrayed before my eyes?—his life perhaps endangered!"

"Your own life and person will not be held more sacred, Cecilia Howard, than that of your uncle. If you will condemn Griffith to a prison, and perhaps to a gibbet, betray Barnstable, as you have threatened—an opportunity will not be wanting at the supper-table, whither I shall lead the way, since the mistress of the house appears to forget her duty."

Katherine arose, and with a firm step and proud eye she moved along the gallery to the room where their presence was expected by the rest of the family. Cecilia followed in silence, and the whole party immediately took their several places at the board.

The first few minutes were passed in the usual attentions of the gentlemen to the ladies, and the ordinary civilities of the table; during which Katherine had so far regained the equanimity of her feelings as to commence a watchful scrutiny of the manners and looks of her guardian and Borroughcliffe, in which she determined to persevere until the eventful hour when she was to expect Barnstable would arrive. Colonel Howard had, however, so far got the command of himself as no longer to betray his former abstraction. In its place Katherine fancied, at moments, that she could discover a settled look of conscious security, mingled a little with an expression of severe determination; such as, in her earlier days, she had learned to dread as sure indications of the indignant but upright justice of an honorable mind. Borroughcliffe, on the other hand, was cool, polite, and as attentive to the viands as usual, with the alarming exception of discovering much less devotion to the Pride of the Vineyards than he commonly manifested on such occasions. In this manner the meal passed by and the cloth was removed, though the ladies appeared willing to retain their places longer than was customary. Colonel Howard, filling up the glasses of Alice Dunscombe and himself, passed the bottle to the recruiting officer, and, with a sort of effort that was intended to rouse the dormant cheerfulness of his guests, cried:

"Come, Borroughcliffe, the ruby lips of your neighbors would be still more beautiful were they moistened with this rich cordial, and that, too, accompanied by some loyal sentiment.—Miss Alice is ever ready to express her fealty to her sovereign; in her name I can give the health of his most sacred majesty, with defeat and death to all traitors!"

"If the prayers of an humble subject, and one of a sex that has but little need to mingle in the turmoil of the world, and that has less right to pretend to understand the subtleties of statesmen, can much avail a high and mighty prince like him who sits on the throne, then will he never know temporal evil," returned Alice, meekly; "but I cannot wish death to any one, not even to my enemies, if any I have, and much less to a people who are the children of the same family with myself."

"Children of the same family!" the colonel repeated, slowly, and with a bitterness of manner that did not fail to attract the painful interest of Katherine—"children of the same family! Ay! even as Absalom was the child of David, or as Judas was of the family of the holy apostles! But let it pass unpledged—let it pass. The accursed spirit of rebellion has invaded my dwelling, and I no longer know where to find one of my household that has not been assailed by its malign influence!"

"Assailed I may have been among others," returned Alice; "but not corrupted, if purity, in this instance, consists in loyalty—"

"What sound is that?" interrupted the colonel, with startling suddenness. "Was it not the crash of some violence, Captain Borroughcliffe?"

"It may have been one of my rascals who has met with a downfall in passing from the festive board—where, you know, I regale them to-night, in honor of our success—to his blanket," returned the captain, with admirable indifference; "or it may be the very spirit of whom you have spoken so freely, my host, that has taken umbrage at your remarks, and is passing from the hospitable walls of St. Ruth into the open air, without submitting to the small trouble of ascertaining the position of doors. In the latter case there may be some dozen perches or so of wall to replace in the morning."

The colonel, who had risen, glanced his eyes uneasily from the speaker to the door, and was evidently but little disposed to enter into the pleasantry of his guest.

"There are unusual noises, Captain Borroughcliffe, in the grounds of the Abbey, if not in the building itself," he said, advancing, with a fine military air, from the table to the centre of the room, "and, as master of the mansion, I will inquire who it is that thus unseasonably disturbs these domains. If as friends, they shall have welcome, though their visit be unexpected; and if enemies, they shall also meet with such a reception as will become an old soldier!"

"No, no," cried Cecilia, entirely thrown off her guard by the manner and language of the veteran, and rushing into his arms. "Go not out, my uncle; go not into the terrible fray, my kind, my good uncle! You are old, you have already done more than your duty; why should you be exposed to danger?"

"The girl is mad with terror, Borroughcliffe," cried the colonel, bending his glistening eyes fondly on his niece, "and you will have to furnish my good-for-nothing, gouty old person with a corporal's guard to watch my night-cap, or the silly child will have an uneasy pillow till the sun rises once more. But you do not stir, sir?"

"Why should I?" cried the captain; "Miss Plowden yet deigns to keep me company, and it is not in the nature of one of the —th to desert his bottle and his standard at the same moment. For, to a true soldier, the smiles of a lady are as imposing in the parlor as the presence of his colors in the field."

"I continue undisturbed, Captain Borroughcliffe," said Katherine, "because I have not been an inhabitant for so many months of St. Ruth, and not learned to know the tunes which the wind can play among its chimneys and pointed roofs. The noise which has taken Colonel Howard from his seat, and which has so unnecessarily alarmed my cousin Cecily, is nothing but the Æolian harp of the Abbey sounding a double bass."

The captain fastened on her composed countenance, while she was speaking, a look of open admiration, that brought, though tardily, the color more deeply to her cheeks; and he answered with something extremely equivocal, both in his emphasis and his air:

"I have avowed my allegiance, and I will abide by it. So long as Miss Plowden will deign to bestow her company, so long will she find me among her most faithful and persevering attendants, come who may, or what will."

"You compel me to retire," returned Katherine, rising, "whatever may have been my gracious intentions in the matter; for even female vanity must crimson at an adoration so profound as that which can chain Captain Borroughcliff to a supper-table!—As your alarm has now dissipated, my cousin, will you lead the way? Miss Alice and myself attend you."

"But not into the paddock, surely, Miss Plowden," said the captain; "the door, the key of which you have just turned, communicates with the vestibule. This is the passage to the drawing-room."

The lady faintly laughed, as if in derision of her own forgetfulness, while she bowed her acknowledgment, and moved toward the proper passage. She observed: "The madness of fear has assailed some, I believe, who have been able to affect a better disguise than Miss Howard."

"Is it the fear of present danger, or of that which is in reserve?" asked the captain; "but, as you have stipulated so generously in behalf of my worthy host here, and of one also who shall be nameless, because he has not deserved such a favor at your hands, your safety shall be one of my especial duties in these times of peril."

"There is peril, then!" exclaimed Cecilia; "your looks announce it, Captain Borroughcliffe! The changing countenance of my cousin tells me that my fears are too true!"

The soldier had now risen also, and, casting aside the air of badinage, which he so much delighted in, he came forward into the centre of the apartment, with the manner of one who felt it was time to be serious.

"A soldier is ever in peril when the enemies of his king are at hand, Miss Howard," he answered; "and that such is now the case Miss Plowden can testify, if she will. But you are the allies of both parties—retire, then, to your own apartments, and await the result of the struggle which is at hand."

"You speak of danger and hidden perils," said Alice Dunscombe; "know ye aught that justifies your fears?"

"I know all," Borroughcliffe coolly replied.

"All!" exclaimed Katherine.

"All!" echoed Alice, in tones of horror. "If, then, you know all, you must know his desperate courage and powerful hand, when opposed—yield in quiet, and he will not harm ye. Believe me, believe one who knows his very nature, that no lamb can be more gentle than he would be with unresisting women; nor the lion more fierce with his enemies!"

"As we happen not to be of the feminine gender," returned Borroughcliffe, with an air somewhat splenetic, "we must abide the fury of the king of beasts. His paw is, even now, at the outer door; and, if my orders have been obeyed, his entrance will yet be easier than that of the wolf to the respectable female ancestor of the little Red Riding-hood."

"Stay your hand for one single moment!" said Katherine, breathless, with interest; "you are the master of my secret, Captain Borroughcliffe, and bloodshed may be the consequence. I can yet go forward, and, perhaps, save many inestimable lives. Pledge to me your honor that they who came hither as your enemies, this night, shall depart in peace, and I will pledge to you my life for the safety of the Abbey."

"Oh, hear her, and shed not human blood!" cried Cecilia.

A loud crash interrupted further speech, and the sounds of heavy footsteps were heard in the adjoining room, as if many men were alighting on its floor, in quick succession. Borroughcliffe drew back, with great coolness, to the opposite side of the large apartment, and took a sheathed sword from the table, where it had been placed; at the same moment the door was burst open, and Barnstable entered alone, but heavily armed.

"You are my prisoners, gentlemen," said the sailor, as he advanced; "resistance is useless, and without it you shall receive favor. Ha! Miss Plowden, my advice was that you should not be present at this scene."

"Barnstable, we are betrayed!" cried the agitated Katherine. "But it is not yet too late. Blood has not yet been spilt, and you can retire, without that dreadful alternative, with honor. Go, then, delay not another moment; for should the soldiers of Captain Borroughcliffe come to the rescue of their commander, the Abbey would be a scene of horror!"

"Go you away; go, Katherine," said her lover, with impatience; "this is no place for such as you. But Captain Borroughcliffe, if such be your name, you must perceive that resistance is in vain. I have ten good pikes in this outer room, in twenty better hands, and it will be madness to fight against such odds."

"Show me your strength," said the captain, "that I may take counsel with mine honor."

"Your honor shall be appeased, my brave soldier, for such is your bearing, though your livery is my aversion, and your cause most unholy! Heave ahead, boys! but hold your hands for orders."

The party of fierce-looking sailors whom Barnstable led, on receiving this order, rushed into the room in a medley; but, notwithstanding the surly glances and savage characters of their dress and equipments, they struck no blow, nor committed any act of hostility. The ladies shrank back appalled, as this terrific little band took possession of the hall; and even Borroughcliffe was seen to fall back toward a door, which, in some measure, covered his retreat. The confusion of this sudden movement had not yet subsided, when sounds of strife were heard rapidly approaching from a distant part of the building, and presently one of the numerous doors of the apartment was violently opened, when two of the garrison of the Abbey rushed into the hall, vigorously pressed by twice their number of seamen, seconded by Griffith, Manual, and Merry, who were armed with such weapons of offence as had presented themselves to their hands, at their unexpected liberation. There was a movement on the part of the seamen, who were already in possession of the room, that threatened instant death to the fugitives; but Barnstable beat down their pikes with his sword, and sternly ordered them to fall back. Surprise produced the same pacific result among the combatants; and as the soldiers hastily sought a refuge behind their own officers, and the released captives, with their liberators, joined the body of their friends, the quiet of the hall, which had been so rudely interrupted, was soon restored.

"You see, sir," said Barnstable, after grasping the hands of Griffith and Manual in a warm and cordial pressure, "that all my plans have succeeded. Your sleeping guard are closely watched in their barracks by one party; our officers are released and your sentinels cut off by another; while, with a third, I hold the centre of the Abbey, and am, substantially, in possession of your own person. In consideration, therefore, of what is due to humanity, and to the presence of these ladies, let there be no struggle! I shall impose no difficult terms, nor any long imprisonment."

The recruiting-officer manifested a composure throughout the whole scene that would have excited some uneasiness in his invaders had there been opportunity for minute observation; but his countenance now gradually assumed an appearance of anxiety, and his head was frequently turned, as if listening for further and more important interruptions. He answered, however, to this appeal with his ordinary deliberation:

"You speak of conquests, sir, before they are achieved. My venerable host and myself are not so defenceless as you may choose to imagine." While speaking he threw aside the cloth of a side-table, from beneath which the colonel and himself were instantly armed with a brace of pistols each. "Here are the death-warrants of four of your party, and these brave fellows at my back can account for two more. I believe, my transatlantic warrior, that we are now something in the condition of Cortes and the Mexicans, when the former overran part of your continent—I being Cortes, armed with artificial thunder and lightning, and you the Indians, with nothing but pikes and slings, and such other antediluvian inventions. Shipwrecks and sea-water are fatal dampers of gunpower!"

"That we are unprovided with fire-arms I will not deny," said Barnstable; "but we are men who are used, from infancy, to depend on our good right arms for life and safety, and we know how to use them, though we should even grapple with death! As for the trifles in your hands, gentlemen, you are not to suppose that men who are trained to look in at one end of a thirty-two pounder, loaded with grape, while the match is put to the other, will so much as wink at their report, though you fired them by fifties. What say you, boys, is a pistol a weapon to repel boarders?"

The discordant and disdainful laughs that burst from the restrained seamen were a sufficient pledge of their indifference to so trifling a danger. Boroughcliffe noted their hardened boldness, and taking the supper-bell, which was lying near him, he rang it for a minute, with great violence. The heavy tread of trained footsteps soon followed this extraordinary summons; and presently the several doors of the apartment were opened, and filled with armed soldiers, wearing the livery of the English crown.

"If you hold these smaller weapons in such vast contempt," said the recruiting-officer, when he perceived that his men had possessed themselves of all the avenues, "it is in my power to try the virtue of some more formidable. After this exhibition of strength, gentlemen, I presume you cannot hesitate to submit as prisoners of war."

The seamen had been formed in something like military array by the assiduity of Manual, during the preceding dialogue; and, as the different doors had discovered fresh accessions to the strength of the enemy, the marine industriously offered new fronts, the small party was completely arranged in a hollow square that might have proved formidable in a charge, bristled as it was with the deadly pikes of the Ariel.

"Here has been some mistake," said Griffith, after glancing his eye at the formidable array of the soldiers; "I take precedence of Mr. Barnstable, and I shall propose to you, Captain Borroughcliffe, terms that may remove this scene of strife from the dwelling of Colonel Howard."

"The dwelling of Colonel Howard," cried the veteran, "is the dwelling of his king, or of the meanest servant of the crown! So, Borroughcliffe, spare not the traitors on my behalf; accept no other terms than such unconditional submission as is meet to exact from the rebellious subjects of the anointed of the Lord."

While Griffith spoke, Barnstable folded his arms in affected composure, and glanced his eyes expressively at the shivering Katherine, who, with her companions, still continued agitated spectators of all that passed, chained to the spot by their apprehensions; but to this formidable denunciation of the master of the Abbey he deemed proper to reply:

"Now, by every hope I have of sleeping again on salt water, old gentleman, if it were not for the presence of these three trembling females, I should feel tempted to dispute, at once, the title of his majesty. You may make such a covenant as you will with Mr. Griffith, but, if it contain one syllable about submission to your king, or of any other allegiance than that which I owe to the Continental Congress and the State of Massachusetts, you may as well consider the terms violated at once; for not an article of such an agreement will I consider as binding on me, or on any that shall choose to follow me as leader."

"Here are but two leaders, Mr. Barnstable," interrupted the haughty Griffith; "the one of the enemy, and the other of the arms of America.—Captain Borroughcliffe, to you, as the former, I address myself. The great objects of the contest which now unhappily divides England from her ancient colonies, can be, in no degree, affected by the events of this night; while, on the other hand, by a rigid adherence to military notions, much private evil and deep domestic calamity must follow any struggle in such a place. We have but to speak, sir, and these rude men, who already stand impatiently handling their instruments of death, will aim them at each other's lives; and who can say that he shall be able to stay their hands when and where he will? I know you to be a soldier, and that you are not yet to learn how much easier it is to stimulate to blood than to glut vengeance."

Borroughcliffe, unused to the admission of violent emotions, and secure in the superiority of his own party, both in numbers and equipments, heard him with the coolest composure to the end, and then answered in his customary manner:

"I honor your logic, sir. Your premises are indisputable, and the conclusion, most obvious. Commit, then, these worthy tars to the good keeping of honest Drill, who will see their famished natures revived by divers eatables, and a due proportion of suitable fluids; while we can discuss the manner in which you are to return to the colonies, around a bottle of liquor, which my friend Manual there assures me has come from the sunny side of the island Madeira, to be drunk in a bleak corner of that of Britain. By my palate! but the rascals brighten at the thought. They know by instinct, sir, that a shipwrecked mariner is a fitter companion to a ration of beef and a pot of porter than to such unsightly things as bayonets and boarding-pikes!"

"Trifle not unseasonably!" exclaimed the impatient young sailor. "You have the odds in numbers, but whether it will avail you much in a deadly struggle of hand to hand, is a question you must put to your prudence; we stand not here to ask terms, but to grant them. You must be brief, sir; for the time is wasting while we delay."

"I have offered to you the means of obtaining, in perfection, the enjoyment of the three most ancient of the numerous family of the arts—eating, drinking, and sleeping! What more do you require?"

"That you order these men, who fill the pass to the outer door, to fall back and give us room. I would take, in peace, these armed men from before the eyes of those who are unused to such sights. Before you oppose this demand, think how easily these hardy fellows could make a way for themselves against your divided force."

"Your companion, the experienced Captain Manual, will tell you that such a manœuvre would be very unmilitary with a superior body in your rear!"

"I have not leisure, sir, for this folly," cried the indignant Griffith. "Do you refuse us an unmolested retreat from the Abbey?"

"I do."

Griffith turned, with a look of extreme emotion, to the ladies, and beckoned to them to retire, unable to give utterance to his wishes in words. After a moment of deep silence, however, he once more addressed Borroughcliffe in the tones of conciliation:

"If Manual and myself will return to our prisons, and submit to the will of your government," he said, "can the rest of the party return to the frigate unmolested?"

"They cannot," replied the soldier, who perceiving that the crisis approached, was gradually losing his artificial deportment in the interest of the moment. "You, and all others who willingly invade the peace of these realms, must abide the issue!"

"Then God protect the innocent and defend the right!"

"Amen!"

"Give way, villains!" cried Griffith, facing the party that held the outer door—"give way, or you shall be riddled with our pikes!"

"Show them your muzzles, men!" shouted Borroughcliffe; "but pull no trigger till they advance."

There was an instant of bustle and preparation, in which the rattling of fire-arms blended with the suppressed execrations and threats of the intended combatants; and Cecilia and Katherine had both covered their faces to veil the horrid sight that was momentarily expected, when Alice Dunscombe advanced boldly between the points of the threatening weapons, and spoke in a voice that stayed the hands that were already uplifted:

"Hear me, men! if men ye be, and not demons, thirsting for each other's blood; though ye walk abroad in the semblance of Him who died that ye might be elevated to the rank of angels! Call ye this war? Is this the glory that is made to warm the hearts of even silly and confiding women? Is the peace of families to be destroyed to gratify your wicked lust for conquest; and is life to be taken in vain, in order that ye may boast of the foul deed in your wicked revels? Fall back, then, ye British soldiers! if ye be worthy of that name, and give passage to a woman; and remember that the first shot that is fired will be buried in her bosom!"

The men, thus enjoined, shrank before her commanding mien, and a way was made for her exit through the very door which Griffith had in vain solicited might be cleared for himself and party. But Alice, instead of advancing, appeared to have suddenly lost the use of those faculties which had already affected so much. Her figure seemed rooted to the spot where she had spoken, and her eyes were fixed in a settled gaze, as if dwelling on some horrid object. While she yet stood in this attitude of unconscious helplessness, the doorway became again darkened, and the figure of the pilot was seen on its threshold, clad as usual, in the humble vestments of his profession, but heavily armed with the weapons of naval war. For an instant he stood a silent spectator of the scene; and then advanced calmly, but, with searching eyes, into the centre of the apartment.

29

Don Pedro:

Welcome, signior; you are almost come to
part almost a fray.

Much Ado About Nothing

DOWN with your arms, you Englishmen!"
said the daring intruder; "and you, who fight in the cause of sacred liberty,
stay your hands, that no unnecessary blood may flow! Yield yourself, proud
Briton, to the power of the thirteen republics!"

"Ha!" exclaimed Borroughcliffe, grasping a pistol, with an air of great resolution, "the work thickens—I had not included this man in my estimate of
their numbers. Is he a Samson, that his single arm can change the face of
things so suddenly? Down with your own weapon, you masquerader! or, at
the report of this pistol, your body shall be made a target for twenty bullets!"

"And thirty for a hundred!" returned the pilot. "Without there! Wind
your call, fellow, and bring in our numbers! We will let this confident gentleman feel his weakness."

He had not done speaking, before the shrill whistle of a boatswain rose
gradually on the ears of the listeners, until the sense of hearing became painfully oppressed by the piercing sounds that rang under the arched roof of the
hall, and penetrated even to the most distant recesses of the Abbey. A tre-

mendous rush of men followed, who drove in before them the terrified fragment of Borroughcliffe's command, that had held the vestibule; and the outer
room became filled with a dark mass of human bodies.

"Let them hear ye, lads," cried the leader; "the Abbey is your own!"

The roaring of a tempest was not louder than the shout that burst from his
followers, who continued their cheers, peal on peal, until the very roof of
the edifice appeared to tremble with their vibrations. Numerous dark and
shaggy heads were seen moving around the passage; some cased in the iron-
bound caps of the frigate's boarders, and others glittering with the brazen
ornaments of her marine guard. The sight of the latter did not fail to attract
the eye of Manual, who rushed among the throng, and soon reappeared, followed by a trusty band of his own men, who took possession of the post held
by the soldiers of Borroughcliffe, while the dialogue was continued between
the leaders of the adverse parties.

Thus far Colonel Howard had yielded to his guest, with a deep reverence
for the principles of military subordination, the functions of a commander;
but, now that affairs appeared to change so materially, he took on himself the
right to question these intruders into his dwelling.

"By what authority, sir," the colonel demanded, "is it that you dare thus
to invade the castle of a subject of this realm? Do you come backed by the
commission of the lord-lieutenant of the county, or has your warrant the
signature of his majesty's secretary for the home department?"

"I bear no commission from any quarter," returned the pilot; "I rank only
an humble follower of the friends of America; and, having led these gentlemen into danger, I have thought it my duty to see them extricated. They are
now safe; and the right to command all that hear me rests with Mr. Griffith,
who is commissioned by the Continental Congress for such service."

When he had spoken, he fell back from the position he occupied in the
centre of the room, to one of its sides, where, leaning his body against the
wainscot, he stood a silent observer of what followed.

"It appears, then, that it is to you, degenerate son of a most worthy father,
that I must repeat my demand," continued the veteran. "By what right is my
dwelling thus rudely assailed! and why is my quiet and the peace of those I
protect so daringly violated?"

"I might answer you, Colonel Howard, by saying that it is according to the
laws of arms, or rather in retaliation for the thousand evils that your English
troops have inflicted between Maine and Georgia; but I wish not to increase
the unpleasant character of this scene, and I therefore will tell you that our
advantage shall be used with moderation. The instant that our men can be

collected, and our prisoners properly secured, your dwelling shall be restored to your authority. We are no freebooters, sir; and you will find it so after our departure.—Captain Manual, draw off your guard into the grounds, and make your dispositions for a return-march to our boats.—Let the boarders fall back, there! Out with ye! out with ye—tumble out, you boarders!"

The amicable order of the young lieutenant, which was delivered after the stern, quick fashion of his profession, operated on the cluster of dark figures that were grouped around the door like a charm; and as the men whom Barnstable had led followed their shipmates into the courtyard, the room was now left to such only as might be termed the gentlemen of the invading party, and the family of Colonel Howard.

Barnstable had continued silent since his senior officer had assumed command, listening most attentively to each syllable that fell from either side; but now that so few remained, and the time pressed, he spoke again:

"If we are to take boat so soon, Mr. Griffith, it would be seemly that due preparations should be made to receive the ladies, who are to honor us with their presence; shall I take that duty on myself?"

The abrupt proposal produced a universal surprise in his hearers; though the abashed and conscious expression of Katherine Plowden's features sufficiently indicated that to her, at least, it was not altogether unexpected. The long silence that succeeded the question was interrupted by Colonel Howard.

"Ye are masters, gentlemen; help yourselves to whatever best suits your inclinations. My dwelling, my goods, and my wards are alike at your disposal—or, perhaps, Miss Alice here, good and kind Miss Alice Dunscombe, may suit the taste of some among ye!—Ah! Edward Griffith! Edward Griffith! little did I ever—"

"Breathe not that name in levity again, thou scoffer, or even your years may prove a feeble protection!" said a stern, startling voice from behind. All eyes turned involuntarily at the unexpected sounds, and the muscular form of the pilot was seen resuming its attitude of repose against the wall, though every fibre of his frame was working with suppressed passion.

When the astonished looks of Griffith ceased to dwell on this extraordinary exhibition of interest in his companion, they were turned imploringly toward the fair cousins, who still occupied the distant corner, whither fear had impelled them.

"I have said that we are not midnight marauders, Colonel Howard," he replied; "but if any there be here who will deign to commit themselves to our keeping, I trust it will not be necessary to say, at this hour, what will be their reception."

"We have no time for unnecessary compliments," cried the impatient Barnstable; "here is Merry, who, by years and blood, is a suitable assistant for them, in arranging their little baggage.—What say you, urchin, can you play the lady's-maid on emergency?"

"Ay, sir, and better than I acted the pedlar-boy," cried the gay youngster. "To have my merry cousin Kate and my good cousin Cecily for shipmates, I could play our common grandmother!—Come, coz, let us be moving; you will have to allow a little leeway in time, for my awkwardness."

"Stand back, young man," said Miss Howard, repulsing his familiar attempt to take her arm; and then advancing, with a maidenly dignity, nigher to her guardian, she continued: "I cannot know what stipulations have been agreed to by my cousin Plowden, in the secret treaty she has made this night with Mr. Barnstable: this for myself, Colonel Howard—I would have you credit your brother's child when she says that to her the events of the hour have not been more unexpected than to yourself."

The veteran gazed at her for a moment with an expression of his eye that denoted reviving tenderness; but gloomy doubts appeared to cross his mind again, and he shook his head as he walked proudly away.

"Nay, then," added Cecilia, her head dropping meekly on her bosom, "I may be discredited by my uncle, but I cannot be disgraced without some act of my own."

She slowly raised her mild countenance again, and, bending her eyes on her lover, she continued, while a rich rush of blood passed over her fine features:

"Edward Griffith, I will not, I cannot say how humiliating it is to think that you can for an instant believe I would again forget myself so much as to wish to desert him whom God has given me for a protector for one chosen by my own erring passions. And you, Andrew Merry, learn to respect the child of your mother's sister, if not for her own sake, at least for that of her who watched your cradle!"

"Here appears to be some mistake," said Barnstable, who participated, however, in no trifling degree in the embarrassment of the abashed boy; "but, like all other mistakes on such subjects, it can be explained away, I suppose. Mr. Griffith, it remains for you to speak—damn it, man," he whispered, "you are as dumb as a codfish! I am sure so fine a woman is worth a little fair-weather talk. You are muter than a four-footed beast—even an ass can bray!"

"We will hasten our departure, Mr. Barnstable," said Griffith, sighing heavily, and rousing himself as if from a trance. "These rude sights cannot but appall the ladies. You will please, sir, to direct the order of our march to the shore. Captain Manual has charge of our prisoners, who must all be secured, to answer for an equal number of our own countrymen."

"And our countrywomen!" said Barnstable, "are they to be forgotten, in the selfish recollection of our own security?"

"With them we have no right to interfere, unless at their request."

"By Heaven! Mr. Griffith, this may smack of learning," cried the other, "and it may plead bookish authority as its precedent; but let me tell you, sir, it savors but little of a sailor's love."

"Is it unworthy of a seaman, and a gentleman, to permit the woman he calls his mistress to be so, other than in name?"

"Well, then, Griff, I pity you, from my soul. I would rather have had a sharp struggle for the happiness that I shall now obtain so easily than that you should be thus cruelly disappointed. But you cannot blame me, my friend, that I avail myself of Fortune's favor. Miss Plowden, your fair hand. Colonel Howard, I return you a thousand thanks for the care you have taken, hitherto, of this precious charge; and believe me, sir, that I speak frankly, when I say that, next to myself, I should choose to intrust her with you in preference to any man on earth."

The colonel turned to the speaker, and bowed low, while he answered with grave courtesy:

"Sir, you repay my slight services with too much gratitude. If Miss Katherine Plowden has not become under my guardianship all that her good father, Captain John Plowden, of the Royal Navy, could have wished a daughter of his to be, the fault unquestionably is to be attributed to my inability to instruct, and to no inherent quality in the young lady herself. I will not say, 'Take her, sir,' since you have her in your possession already, and it would be out of my power to alter the arrangement; therefore I can only wish that you may find her as dutiful as a wife, as she has been, hitherto, as a ward and a subject."

Katherine had yielded her hand, passively, to her lover, and suffered him to lead her more into the circle than she had before been; but now she threw off his arm, and shaking aside the dark curls which she had invited to fall in disorder around her brow, she raised her face and looked proudly up, with an eye that sparkled with the spirit of its mistress, and a face that grew pale with emotion at each moment as she proceeded:

"Gentlemen, the one may be as ready to receive as the other is to reject; but has the daughter of John Plowden no voice in this cool disposal of her person? If her guardian tires of her presence, other habitations may be found, without inflicting so severe a penalty on this gentleman as to compel him to provide for her accommodation in a vessel that must be already straitened for room!"

She turned and rejoined her cousin with such an air of maidenly resentment as a young woman would be apt to discover who found herself the subject of matrimonial arrangement, without her own feelings being at all consulted. Barnstable, who knew but little of the windings of the female heart, or how necessary to his mistress, notwithstanding her previous declarations, the countenance of Cecilia was to any decided and open act in his favor, stood in stupid wonder at her declaration. He could not conceive that a woman who had already ventured so much in secret in his behalf, and who had so often avowed her weakness, should shrink to declare it again at such a crisis, though the eyes of the universe were on her! He looked from one of the party to the other, and met in every face an expression of delicate reserve, except in those of the guardian of his mistress, and of Borroughcliffe.

The colonel had given a glance of returning favor at her, whom he now conceived to be his repentant ward, while the countenance of the entrapped captain exhibited a look of droll surprise, blended with the expression of bitter ferocity it had manifested since the discovery of his own mishap.

"Perhaps, sir," said Barnstable, addressing the latter fiercely, "you see something amusing about the person of this lady, to divert you thus unseasonably. We tolerate no such treatment of our women in America!"

"Nor do we quarrel before ours in England," returned the soldier, throwing back the fierce glance of the sailor, with interest; "but I was thinking of the revolutions time can produce; nothing more, I do assure you. It is not half an hour since I thought myself a most happy fellow; secure in my plans for overreaching the scheme you had laid to surprise me; and now I am as miserable a dog as wears a single epaulet, and has no hope of seeing its fellow."

"And in what manner, sir, can this sudden change apply to me?" asked Katherine, with all her spirit.

"Certainly not to your perseverance in the project to assist my enemies, madam," returned the soldier with affected humility; "nor to your zeal for their success, or your consummate coolness at the supper-table! But I find it is time that I should be superannuated—I can no longer serve my king with credit, and should take to serving my God, like all other worn-out men of the world! My hearing is surely defective, or a paddock wall has a most magical effect in determining sounds!"

Katherine waited not to hear the close of this sentence, but walked to a distant part of the room to conceal the burning blushes that covered her countenance. The manner in which the plans of Barnstable had become known to his foe was no longer a mystery. Her conscience also reproached her a little with some unnecessary coquetry, as she remembered that quite one-half of the dialogue between her lover and herself, under the shadow of that very wall to which Borroughcliffe alluded, had been on a subject altogether foreign to contention and tumults. As the feelings of Barnstable were by no means so sensitive as those of his mistress, and his thoughts much occupied with the means of obtaining his object, he did not so readily comprehend the indirect allusion of the soldier, but turned abruptly away to Griffith, and observed with a serious air:

"I feel it my duty, Mr. Griffith, to suggest that we have standing instructions to secure all the enemies of America, wherever they may be found, and to remind you that the States have not hesitated to make prisoners of females in many instances."

"Bravo!" cried Borroughcliffe; "if the ladies will not go as your mistresses, take them as your captives!"

" 'Tis well for you, sir, that you are a captive yourself, or you should be made to answer for this speech," retorted the irritated Barnstable.—"It is a responsible command, Mr. Griffith, and must not be disregarded."

"To your duty, Mr. Barnstable," said Griffith, again arousing from deep abstraction; "you have your orders, sir; let them be executed promptly."

"I have also the orders of our common superior, Captain Munson, Mr. Griffith; and I do assure you, sir, that in making out my instructions for the Ariel—poor thing! there are no two of her timbers hanging together—but my instructions were decided particular on that head."

"And my orders now supersede them."

"But am I justifiable in obeying a verbal order from an inferior, in direct opposition to a written instruction?"

Griffith had hitherto manifested in his deportment nothing more than a cold determination to act, but the blood now flew to every vessel in his cheeks and forehead, and his dark eyes flashed fire, as he cried authoritatively:

"How, sir! do you hesitate to obey?"

"By Heaven, sir, I would dispute the command of the Continental Congress itself, should they bid me so far to forget my duty to—to—"

"Add yourself, sir!—Mr. Barnstable, let this be the last of it. To your duty, sir!"

"My duty calls me here, Mr. Griffith."

"I must act, then, or be bearded by my own officers. Mr. Merry, direct Captain Manual to send in a sergeant and a file of marines."

"Bid him come on, himself!" cried Barnstable, maddened to desperation by his disappointment; " 'tis not his whole corps that can disarm me—let them come on!—Here, there, you Ariels! rally around your captain!"

"The man among them who dares to cross that threshold without my orders, dies!" cried Griffith, menacing with a naked hanger the seamen who had promptly advanced at the call of their old commander. "Yield your sword, Mr. Barnstable, and spare yourself the disgrace of having it forced from you by a common soldier."

"Let me see the dog who dare attempt it!" exclaimed Barnstable, flourishing his weapon in fierce anger. Griffith had extended his own arm in the earnestness of his feelings, and their hangers crossed each other. The clashing of the steel operated on both like the sound of the clarion on a war-horse, and there were sudden and rapid blows, and as rapid parries, exchanged between the flashing weapons.

"Barnstable! Barnstable!" cried Katherine, rushing into his arms, "I will go with you to the ends of the earth!"

Cecilia Howard did not speak; but when Griffith recovered his coolness, he beheld her beautiful form kneeling at his feet, with her pale face bent imploringly on his own disturbed countenance. The cry of Miss Plowden had separated the combatants, before an opportunity for shedding blood had been afforded; but the young men exchanged looks of keen resentment, notwithstanding the interference of their mistresses. At this moment Colonel Howard advanced, and, raising his niece from her humble posture, said:

"This is not a situation for a child of Henry Howard, though she knelt in the presence, and before the throne, of her sovereign. Behold, my dear Cecilia, the natural consequences of this rebellion! It scatters discord in their ranks, and, by its damnable levelling principles, destroys all distinction of rank among themselves; even these rash boys know not where obedience is due!"

"It is due to me," said the pilot, who now stepped forward among the agitated group, "and it is time that I enforce it.—Mr. Griffith, sheathe your sword.—And you, sir, who have defied the authority of your senior officer, and have forgotten the obligation of your oath, submit, and return to your duty."

Griffith started at the sounds of his calm voice, as if with sudden recollection; and then, bowing low, he returned the weapon to its scabbard. But Barnstable still encircled the waist of his mistress with one arm, while with the other he brandished his hanger, and laughed with scorn at this extraordinary assumption of authority.

"And who is this," he cried, "who dare give such an order to me?"

The eyes of the pilot flashed with a terrible fire, while a fierce glow seemed to be creeping over his whole frame, which actually quivered with passion. But, suppressing this exhibition of his feelings, by a sudden and powerful effort, he answered in an emphatic manner:

"One who has a right to order, and who *will* be obeyed!"

The extraordinary manner of the speaker contributed as much as his singular assertion to induce Barnstable, in his surprise, to lower the point of his weapon, with an air that might easily have been mistaken for submission. The pilot fastened his glowing eyes on him, for an instant, and then, turning to the rest of the listeners, he continued, more mildly:

"It is true that we came not here as marauders, and that our wish is to do no unnecessary acts of severity to the aged and the helpless. But this officer of the crown, and this truant American in particular, are fairly our prisoners; as such, they must be conducted on board our ship."

"But the main object of our expedition?" said Griffith.

" 'Tis lost," returned the pilot, hastily—" 'tis sacrificed to more private feelings; 'tis like a hundred others, ended in disappointment, and is forgotten, sir, forever. But the interests of the republics must not be neglected, Mr. Griffith. Though we are not madly to endanger the lives of those gallant fellows, to gain a love-smile from one young beauty, neither are we to forget the advantages they may have obtained for us, in order to procure one of approbation from another. This Colonel Howard will answer well in a bargain with the minions of the crown, and may purchase the freedom of some worthy patriot who is deserving of his liberty. Nay, nay, suppress that haughty look, and turn that proud eye on any, rather than me; he goes to the frigate, sir, and that immediately."

"Then," said Cecilia Howard, timidly approaching the spot where her uncle stood, a disdainful witness of the dissensions among his captors; "then will I go with him! He shall never be a resident among his enemies alone!"

"It would be more ingenuous and more worthy of my brother's daughter," said her uncle, coldly, "if she ascribed her willingness to depart to its proper motive." Disregarding the look of deep distress with which Cecilia received this mortifying rejection of her tender attention, the old man walked toward Borroughcliffe, who was gnawing the hilt of his sword, in very vexation at the downfall of his high-raised hopes, and placing himself by his side, with an air of infinitely dignified submission, he continued: "Act your pleasure on us, gentlemen; you are the conquerors and so we must submit. A brave man knows as well how to yield with decorum as to defend himself stoutly, when he is not surprised, as we have been. But if an opportunity should ever offer!

—Act your pleasures, gentlemen; no two lambs were ever half so meek as Captain Borroughcliffe and myself."

The smile of affected but bitter resignation that the colonel bestowed on his fellow-prisoner was returned by that officer with an attempt at risibility that abundantly betokened the disturbed state of his feelings. The two, however, succeeded in so far maintaining appearances as to contemplate the succeeding movement of the conquerors with a sufficient degree of composure.

The colonel steadily and coldly rejected the advances of his niece, who bowed meekly to his will, and relinquished for the present, the hope of bringing him to a sense of his injustice. She, however, employed herself in earnest to give such directions as were necessary to enforce the resolution she had avowed, and in this unexpected employment she found both a ready and a willing assistant in her cousin. The latter, unknown to Miss Howard, had, in anticipation of some such event as the present, long since made, in secret, all those preparations which might become necessary to a sudden flight from the Abbey. In conjunction with her lover, then, who, perceiving that the plan of the pilot was furthering his own views, deemed it most wise to forget his quarrel with that mysterious individual, she flew to point out the means of securing those articles which were already in preparation. Barnstable and Merry accompanied her light steps among the narrow dark passages of the Abbey with the utmost delight; the former repeatedly apostrophizing her wit and beauty, and, indeed, all of her various merits, and the latter laughing and indulging those buoyant spirits that a boy of his years and reflection might be supposed to feel even in such a scene. It was fortunate for her cousin that Katherine had possessed so much forethought; for the attention of Cecilia Howard was directed much more to the comforts of her uncle than to those which were necessary for herself. Attended by Alice Dunscombe, the young mistress of St. Ruth moved through the solitary apartments of the building, listening to the mild religious consolation of her companion, in silence, at times yielding to those bursts of mortified feeling that she could not repress, or again as calmly giving her orders to her maids as if the intended movement was one of but ordinary interest. All this time the party in the dining-hall remained stationary. The pilot, as if satisfied with what he had already done, sank back to his reclining attitude against the wall, though his eyes keenly watched every movement of the preparations in a manner which denoted that his was the master-spirit that directed the whole. Griffith, had, however, resumed, in appearance, the command, and the busy seamen addressed themselves for orders to him alone. In this manner an hour was consumed, when Cecilia and Katherine appearing in succession attired in a suitable manner for their departure, and the baggage of the whole party having been already intrusted to a petty officer and a party of his men, Griffith gave forth the customary order to put the whole in motion. The shrill, piercing whistle of the boatswain once more rang among the galleries and ceilings of the Abbey, and was followed by the deep hoarse cry of:

"Away, there, you shore-draft! away, there, you boarders! ahead, heave ahead, sea-dogs!"

This extraordinary summons was succeeded by the roll of a drum, and the strains of a fife, from without, when the whole party moved from the building in the order that had been previously prescribed by Captain Manual, who acted as the marshal of the forces on the occasion.

The pilot had conducted his surprise with so much skill and secrecy as to have secured every individual about the Abbey, whether male or female, soldier or civilian; and as it might be dangerous to leave any behind who could convey intelligence into the country, Griffith had ordered that every human being found in the building should be conducted to the cliffs; to be held in durance at least until the departure of the last boat to the cutter, which, he was informed, lay close in to the land, awaiting their re-embarkation. The hurry of the departure had caused many lights to be kindled in the Abbey, and the contrast between the glare within and the gloom without attracted the wandering looks of the captives, as they issued into the paddock. One of those indefinable and unaccountable feelings which so often cross the human mind, induced Cecilia to pause at the great gate of the grounds, and look back at the Abbey, with a presentiment that she was to behold it for the last time. The dark and ragged outline of the edifice was clearly delineated against the northern sky, while the open windows and neglected doors permitted a view of the solitude within. Twenty tapers were shedding their useless light in the empty apartments, as if in mockery of the deserted walls; and Cecilia turned shuddering from the sight, to press nigher to the person of her indignant uncle, with a secret impression that her presence would soon be more necessary than ever to his happiness.

The low hum of voices in front, with the occasional strains of the fife, and the stern mandates of the sea-officers soon recalled her, however, from these visionary thoughts to the surrounding realities, while the whole party pursued their way with diligence to the margin of the ocean.

30

A chieftain to the Highlands bound,
Cries, "Boatman, do not tarry!
And I'll give thee a silver pound
To row us o'er the ferry."

Lord Ullin's Daughter

THE sky had been without a cloud during the day, the gale having been dry and piercing, and thousands of stars were now shining through a chill atmosphere. As the eye, therefore, became accustomed to the change of light, it obtained a more distinct view of surrounding objects. At the head of the line that was stretched along the narrow pathway marched a platoon of the marines, who maintained the regular and steady front of trained warriors. They were followed at some little distance by a large and confused body of seamen, heavily armed, whose disposition to disorder and rude merriment, which became more violent from their treading on solid ground, was with difficulty restrained by the presence and severe rebukes of their own officers. In the centre of this confused mass, the whole of the common prisoners were placed, but were not otherwise attended to by their nautical guard than as they furnished the subjects of fun and numberless quaint jokes. At some distance in their rear marched Colonel Howard and Borroughcliffe, arm-in-arm, both maintaining the most rigid and dignified silence, though under the influence of very bitter feelings. Behind these again, and pressing as nigh as possible to her uncle, was Miss Howard, leaning on the arm of Alice Dunscombe, and surrounded by the female domestics of the establishment of St. Ruth. Katherine Plowden moved lightly, by herself, in the shadow of this group, with elastic steps, but with a maiden coyness that taught her to veil her satisfaction with the semblance of captivity. Barnstable watched her movements with delight, within six feet of her, but submitted to the air of caprice in his mistress, which seemed to require that he should come no nearer. Griffith avoiding the direct line of the party, walked on its skirts in such a situation that his eye could command its whole extent, in order, if necessary, to direct the movements. Another body of the marines marched at the close of the procession, and Manual, in person, brought up the rear. The music had ceased by command, and nothing was now audible but the regular tread of the soldiers, with the sighs of the dying gale, interrupted occasionally by the voice of an officer, or the hum of low dialogue.

"This has been a Scotch prize that we have taken," muttered a surly old seaman; "a ship without head-money or cargo! There was kitchen timber enough in the old jug of a place to have given an outfit in crockery and knee-buckles to every lad in the ship; but no! let a man's mouth water ever so much for food and raiment, damme, if the officers would give him leave to steal even so good a thing as a spare Bible."

"You may say all that, and then make but a short yarn of the truth," returned the messmate who walked by his side; "if there had been such a thing as a ready-made prayer handy, they would have choused a poor fellow out of the use of it. I say, Ben, I'll tell ye what; it's my opinion, that if a chap is to turn soldier and carry a musket, he should have soldier's pay, and leave to plunder a little—not the devil a thing have I laid my hands on to-night, except this firelock and my cutlass—unless you call this bit of a table-cloth something of a windfall."

"Ay! you have fallen in there with a fresh bolt of duck, I see!" said the other, in manifest admiration of the texture of his companion's prize; "why, it would spread as broad a clew as our mizzen-royal, if it was loosened! well, your luck hasn't been every man's luck—for my part, I think this here hat was made for some fellow's great toe; I've rigged it on my head both fore and aft, and athwart ships; but curse the inch can I drive it down. I say, Sam! you'll give us a shirt off that table-cloth?"

"Ay, ay, you can have one corner of it; or, for that matter, ye can take the full half, Nick; but I don't see that we go off to the ship any richer than we landed, unless you may muster she-cattle among your prize-money."

"No richer!" interrupted a waggish young sailor, who had been hitherto a silent listener to the conversation between his older and more calculating shipmates; "I think we are set up for a cruise in them seas where the day-watches last six months; don't you see we have caught a double allowance of midnight?"

While speaking, he laid his hands on the bare and woolly heads of Colonel Howard's two black slaves, who were moving near him, both occupied in mournful forebodings on the results that were to flow from this unexpected loss of their liberty. "Slue your faces this way, gentlemen," he added; "there; don't you think that a sight to put out the binnacle-lamps? there's darkness visible for ye!"

"Let the niggers alone," grumbled one of the more aged speakers; "and what are ye skylarking with the like of them for? the next thing they'll sing out, and then you'll hear one of the officers in your wake. For my part, Nick, I can't see why it is that we keep dodging alongshore here, with less than ten fathoms under us, when, by stretching into the broad Atlantic, we might fall in with a Jamaica-man every day or two, and have sugar-hogsheads and rum-puncheons as plenty aboard us as hard fare is now."

"It is all owing to that pilot," returned the other; "for, d'ye see, if there was no bottom, there would be no pilots. This is a dangerous cruising-ground, where we stretch into five fathoms, and then drop our lead on a sand-pit or a rock! Besides, they make night-work of it too! If we had daylight for fourteen hours instead of seven, a man might trust to feeling his way for the other ten."

"Now, a'n't ye a couple of old horse marines!" again interrupted the young sailor; "don't you see that Congress wants us to cut up Johnny Bull's coasters and that old Blow-hard has found the days too short for his business, and so he has landed a party to get hold of night. Here we have him! and when we get off to the ship, we shall put him under hatches, and then you'll see the face of the sun again!—Come, my lilies! let these two gentlemen look into your cabin-windows—what? you won't! Then I must squeeze your woollen nightcaps for ye!"

The Negroes, who had been submitting to his humors with the abject humility of slavery, now gave certain low intimations that they were suffering pain under the rough manipulations of their tormentor.

"What's that!" cried a stern voice, whose boyish tones seemed to mock the air of authority that was assumed by the speaker—"who's that, I say, raising that cry among ye?"

The wilful young man slowly removed his two hands from the woolly polls of the slaves, but, as he suffered them to fall reluctantly along their sable temples, he gave the ear of one of the blacks a tweak that caused him to give vent to another cry, that was uttered with a much greater confidence of sympathy than before.

"Do ye hear, there!" repeated Merry—"who's skylarking with those Negroes?"

"'Tis no one, sir," the sailor answered with affected gravity; "one of the pale-faces has hit his shin against a cobweb, and it has made his ear ache!"

"Harkye, you Mr. Jack Joker! how come you in the midst of the prisoners? did not I order you to handle your pike, sir, and to keep in the outer line?"

"Ay, ay, sir, you did; and I obeyed orders as long as I could; but these niggers have made the night so dark that I lost my way!"

A low laugh passed through the confused crowd of seamen; and even the midshipman might have been indulging himself in a similar manner at this specimen of quaint humor from the fellow, who was one of those licensed men that are to be found in every ship. At length:

"Well, sir," he said, "you have found out your false reckoning now, so get you back to the place where I bade you stay."

"Ay, ay, sir, I'm going. By all the blunders in the purser's book, Mr. Merry, but that cobweb has made one of these niggers shed tears! Do let me stay to catch a little ink, sir, to write a letter with to my poor old mother; devil the line has she had from me since we sailed from the Chesapeake!"

"If ye don't mind me at once, Mr. Jack Joker, I'll lay my cutlass over your head," returned Merry, his voice now betraying a much greater sympathy in the sufferings of that abject race, who are still in some measure, but who formerly were much more, the butts of the unthinking and licentious among our low countrymen; "then ye can write your letter in red ink if ye will!"

"I wouldn't do it for the world," said Joker, sneaking away toward his proper station; "the old lady wouldn't forget the hand, and swear it was a forgery. I wonder, though, if the breakers on the coast of Guinea be black! as I've heard old seamen say who have cruised in them latitudes."

His idle levity was suddenly interrupted by a voice that spoke above the low hum of the march, with an air of authority, and a severity of tone, that could always quell, by a single word, the most violent ebullition of merriment in the crew.

The low buzzing sounds of "Ay, there goes Mr. Griffith!" and of "Jack has woke up the first lieutenant, he had better now go to sleep himself"; were heard passing among the men. But these suppressed communications soon ceased, and even Jack Joker himself pursued his way with diligence, on the skirts of the party, as mutely as if the power of speech did not belong to his organization.

The reader has too often accompanied us over the ground between the Abbey and the ocean to require any description of the route pursued by the seamen during the preceding characteristic dialogue; and we shall at once pass to the incidents which occurred on the arrival of the party at the cliffs. As the man who had so unexpectedly assumed a momentary authority within St. Ruth had unaccountably disappeared from among them, Griffith continued to exercise the right to command, without referring to any other for consultation. He never addressed himself to Barnstable, and it was apparent that both the haughty young men felt that the tie which had hitherto united them in such close intimacy was, for the present at least, entirely severed. Indeed, Griffith was only restrained by the presence of Cecilia and Katherine from arresting his refractory inferior on the spot; and Barnstable, who felt all the consciousness of error, without its proper humility, with difficulty so far repressed his feelings as to forbear exhibiting in the presence of his mistress such a manifestation of his spirit as his wounded vanity induced him to imagine was necessary to his honor. The two, however, acted in harmony on one subject, though it was without concert or communication. The first object with both the young men was to secure the embarkation of the fair cousins; and Barnstable proceeded instantly to the boats, in order to hasten the preparations that were necessary before they could receive these unexpected captives; the descent of the pilot having been made in such force as to require the use of all the frigate's boats, which were left riding in the outer edge of the surf, awaiting the return of the expedition. A loud call from Barnstable gave notice to the officer in command, and in a few moments the beach was crowded with the busy and active crews of the "cutters," "launches," "barges," "jolly-boats," "pinnaces," or by whatever names the custom of the times attached to the different attendants of vessels-of-war. Had the fears of the ladies themselves been consulted, the frigate's launch would have been selected for their use, on account of its size; but Barnstable, who would have thought such a choice on his part humiliating to his guests, ordered the long low barge of Captain Munson to be drawn upon the sand, it being peculiarly the boat of honor. The hands of fifty men were applied to the task, and it was soon announced to Colonel Howard and his wards that the little vessel was ready for their reception. Manual had halted on the summit of the cliffs with the whole body of the marines, where he was busily employed in posting pickets and sentinels, and giving the necessary instructions to his men to cover the embarkation of the seamen, in a style that he conceived to be altogether military. The mass of the common prisoners, including the inferior domestics of the Abbey, and the men of Borroughcliffe, were also held in the same place, under

a suitable guard; but Colonel Howard and his companion, attended by the
ladies and their own maids, had descended the rugged path to the beach, and
were standing passively on the sands, when the intelligence that the boat
waited for them was announced.

"Where is he?" asked Alice Dunscombe, turning her head, as if anxiously
searching for some other than those around her.

"Where is who?" inquired Barnstable; "we are all here, and the boat waits."

"And will he tear me—even me, from the home of my infancy! the land of
my birth and my affections?"

"I know not of whom you speak, madam, but if it be of Mr. Griffith, he
stands there, just without that cluster of seamen."

Griffith, hearing himself thus named, approached the ladies, and, for the
first time since leaving the Abbey, addressed them: "I hope I am already understood," he said, "and that it is unnecessary for me to say that no female
here is a prisoner; though, should any choose to trust themselves on board our
ship, I pledge to them the honor of an officer, that they shall find themselves
protected and safe."

"Then will I not go," said Alice.

"It is not expected of you," said Cecilia; "you have no ties to bind you to
any here." (The eyes of Alice were still wandering over the listeners.) "Go,
then, Miss Alice, and be the mistress of St. Ruth, until my return; or," she
added, timidly, "until Colonel Howard may declare his pleasure."

"I obey you, dear child, but the agent of Colonel Howard, at B——, will un-
doubtedly be authorized to take charge of his effects."

While no one but his niece alluded to his will, the master of the Abbey had
found, in his resentment, a sufficient apology for his rigid demeanor; but he
was far too well bred to bear, in silence, such a modest appeal to his wishes
from so fair and so loyal a subject as Alice Dunscombe.

"To relieve you, madam, and for no other reason, will I speak on this subject," he said; "otherwise, I should leave the doors and windows of St. Ruth
open as a melancholy monument of rebellion, and seek my future compensation from the crown, when the confiscated estates of the leaders of this accursed innovation on the rights of princes shall come to the hammer. But you,
Miss Alice, are entitled to every consideration that a lady can expect from a
gentleman. Be pleased, therefore, to write to my agent, and request him to seal
up my papers, and transmit them to the office of his majesty's secretary of
state. They breathe no treason, madam, and are entitled to official protection.
The house, and most of the furniture, as you know, are the property of my
landlord, who, in due time, will doubtless take charge of his own interest. I

kiss your hand, Miss Alice, and I hope we shall yet meet at St. James's—depend on it, madam, that the royal Charlotte shall yet honor your merits; I know she cannot but estimate your loyalty."

"Here I was born, in humble obscurity—here I have lived, and here I hope to die in quiet," returned the meek Alice; "if I have known any pleasure, in late years, beyond that which every Christian can find in our daily duties, it has been, my sweet friends, in your accidental society. Such companions, in this remote corner of the kingdom, have been a boon too precious to be enjoyed without alloy, it seems; and I have now to exchange the past pleasure for present pain. Adieu! my young friends; let your trust be in Him to whose eyes both prince and peasant, the European and the American, are alike, and we shall meet again, though it be neither in the island of Britain nor on your own wide continent."

"That," said Colonel Howard, advancing, and taking her hand with kindness, "that is the only disloyal sentiment I have ever heard fall from the lips of Miss Alice Dunscombe! Is it to be supposed that Heaven established orders among men, and that it does not respect the works of its own formation! But adieu; no doubt, if time was allowed us for suitable explanations, we should find but little or no difference of opinion on this subject."

Alice did not appear to consider the matter as worthy of further discussion at such a moment; for she gently returned the colonel's leave-taking, and then gave her undivided attention to her female friends. Cecilia wept bitterly on the shoulder of her respected companion, giving vent to her regret at parting, and her excited feelings, at the same moment; and Katherine pressed to the side of Alice, with the kindliness prompted by her warm but truant heart. Their embraces were given and received in silence, and each of the young ladies moved toward the boat, as she withdrew herself from the arms of Miss Dunscombe. Colonel Howard would not precede his wards, neither would he assist them into the barge. That attention they received from Barnstable, who, after seeing the ladies and their attendants seated, turned to the gentlemen, and observed:

"The boat waits."

"Well, Miss Alice," said Borroughcliffe, in bitter irony, "you are intrusted by our excellent host with a message to his agent; will you do a similar service to me, and write a report to the commander of the district, and just tell him what a dolt—ay, use the plainest terms, and say what an ass one Captain Borroughcliffe has proved himself in this affair? You may throw in, by way of episode, that he has been playing bo-peep with a rebellious young lady from the colonies, and, like a great boy, has had his head broken for his pains.

Come, my worthy host, or rather fellow-prisoner, I follow you, as in duty bound."

"Stay," cried Griffith; "Captain Borroughcliffe does not embark in the boat."

"Ha! sir; am I to be herded with the common men? Forget you that I have the honor to bear the commission of his Britannic Majesty, and that—"

"I forget nothing that a gentleman is bound to remember, Captain Borroughcliffe; among other things, I recollect the liberality of your treatment to myself when a prisoner. The instant the safety of my command will justify such a step, not only you, but your men, shall be set at liberty."

Borroughcliffe started in surprise, but his feelings were too much soured by the destruction of those visions of glory, in which he had been luxuriously indulging for the last day or two, to admit of his answering as became a man. He swallowed his emotions, therefore, by a violent effort, and walked along the beach affecting to whistle a low but lively air.

"Well, then," cried Barnstable, "all our captives are seated. The boat waits only for its officers!"

In his turn, Griffith walked away in haughty silence, as if disdaining to hold communion with his former friend. Barnstable paused a moment, from a deference that long habit had created for his superior officer, and which was not to be shaken off by every burst of angry passion; but, perceiving that the other had no intention to return, he ordered the seamen to raise the boat from the sand, and bear it bodily into the water. The command was instantly obeyed; and, by the time the young lieutenant was in his seat, the barge was floating in the still heavy though no longer dangerous surf, and the crew sprang into their places.

"Bear her off, boys!" he cried; "never mind a wet jacket. I've seen many a worthy fellow tumbling on this beach in a worse time than this. Now you have her head to sea; give way, my souls, give way!"

The seamen rose simultaneously at their oars, and, by a united effort, obtained the command of their boat, which, after making a few sudden ascents, and as many heavy pitches in the breakers, gained the smooth seas of the swelling ocean, and stemmed the waters in a direction for the place where the Alacrity was supposed to be in waiting.

31

His only plot was this—that, much provoked,
He raised his vengeful arm against his
country.

THOMPSON

Aᴸɪᴄᴇ DUNSCOMBE remained on the
sands, watching the dark spot that was soon hid amid the waves in the obscurity of night, and listening, with melancholy interest, to the regulated
sounds of the oars, which were audible long after the boat had been blended
with the gloomy outline of the eastern horizon. When all traces of her departed friends were to be found only in her own recollections, she slowly
turned from the sea, and, hastening to quit the bustling throng that were preparing for the embarkation of the rest of the party, she ascended the path that
conducted her once more to the summit of those cliffs, along which she had so
often roved, gazing at the boundless element that washed their base with
sensations that might have been peculiar to her own situation.

The soldiers of Borroughcliffe, who were stationed at the head of the pass,
respectfully made way; nor did any of the sentinels of Manual heed her retiring figure, until she approached the rear-guard of the marines, who were
commanded by their vigilant captain in person.

"Who goes there?" cried Manual, advancing without the dusky group of
soldiers, as she approached them.

"One who possesses neither the power nor the inclination to do ye harm," answered the solitary female; "'tis Alice Dunscombe, returning, by permission of your leader, to the place of her birth."

"Ay," muttered Manual, "this is one of Griffith's unmilitary exhibitions of his politeness! Does the man think that there was ever a woman who had no tongue! Have you the countersign, madam, that I may know you bear a sufficient warrant to pass?"

"I have no other warrant besides my sex and weakness, unless Mr. Griffith's knowledge that I have left him can be so considered."

"The two former are enough," said a voice, that proceeded from a figure which had hitherto stood unseen, shaded by the trunk of an oak, that spread its wide but naked arms above the spot where the guard was paraded.

"Who have we here?" Manual again cried. "Come in; yield, or you will be fired at."

"What! will the gallant Captain Manual fire on his own rescuer?" said the pilot, with cool disdain, as he advanced from the shadow of the tree. "He had better reserve his bullets for his enemies than waste them on his friends."

"You have done a dangerous deed, sir, in approaching, clandestinely, a guard of marines! I wonder that a man who has already discovered, to-night, that he has some knowledge of tactics, by so ably conducting a surprise, should betray so much ignorance in the forms of approaching a picket!"

"'Tis now of no moment," returned the pilot; "my knowledge and my ignorance are alike immaterial, as the command of the party is surrendered to other and perhaps more proper hands. But I would talk to this lady alone, sir; she is an acquaintance of my youth, and I will see her on her way to the Abbey."

"The step would be unmilitary, Mr. Pilot, and you will excuse me if I do not consent to any of our expedition straggling without the sentries. If you choose to remain here to hold your discourse, I will march the picket out of hearing; though I must acknowledge I see no ground so favorable as this we are on, to keep you within the range of our eyes. You perceive that I have a ravine to retreat into in case of surprise, with this line of wall on my left flank and the trunk of that tree to cover my right. A very pretty stand might be made here, on emergency; for even the oldest troops fight the best when their flanks are properly covered, and a way to make a regular retreat is open in their rear."

"Say no more, sir; I would not break up such a position on any account," returned the pilot; "the lady will consent to retrace her path for a short distance."

Alice followed his steps, in compliance with this request, until he had led her to a place, at some little distance from the marines, where a tree had been prostrated by the late gale. She seated herself quietly on its trunk, and appeared to await with patience his own time for the explanation of his motives in seeking the interview. The pilot paced for several minutes back and forth, in front of the place where she was seated, in profound silence, as if communing with himself; when suddenly throwing off his air of absence, he came to her side and assumed a position similar to the one which she herself had taken.

"The hour is at hand, Alice, when we must part," he at length commenced; "it rests with yourself whether it shall be forever."

"Let it then be forever, John," she returned, with a slight tremor in her voice.

"That word would have been less appalling, had this accidental meeting never occurred. And yet your choice may have been determined by prudence —for what is there in my fate that can tempt a woman to wish that she might share it?"

"If ye mean your lot is that of one who can find but few, or even none, to partake of his joys, or to share in his sorrows—whose life is a continual scene of dangers and calamities, of disappointments and mishaps—then do ye know but little of the heart of woman, if ye doubt of either her ability or her willingness to meet them with the man of her choice."

"Say you thus, Alice? Then have I misunderstood your meaning, or misinterpreted your acts. My lot is not altogether that of a neglected man, unless the favor of princes and the smiles of queens are allowed to go for nothing. My life is, however, one of many and fearful dangers; and yet it is not filled altogether with calamities and mishaps; is it, Alice?" He paused a moment, but in vain, for her answer. "Nay, then, I have been deceived in the estimation that the world has affixed to my combats and enterprises! I am not, Alice, the man I would be, or even the man I had deemed myself."

"You have gained a name, John, among the warriors of the age," she answered, in a subdued voice; "and it is a name that may be said to be written in blood!"

"The blood of my enemies, Alice!"

"The blood of the subjects of your natural prince! The blood of those who breathe the air you first breathed, and who were taught the same holy lessons of instructions that you were first taught, but which, I fear, you have too soon forgotten!"

"The blood of the slaves of despotism!" he sternly interrupted her; "the blood of the enemies of freedom! You have dwelt so long in this dull retirement, and you have cherished so blindly the prejudices of your youth, that the promise of those noble sentiments I once thought I could see budding in Alice Dunscombe, has not been fulfilled."

"I have lived and thought only as a woman, as become my sex and station," Alice meekly replied; "and when it shall be necessary for me to live and think otherwise, I should wish to die."

"Ay, there lie the first seeds of slavery! A dependent woman is sure to make the mother of craven and abject wretches, who dishonor the name of man!"

"I shall never be the mother of children, good or bad," said Alice, with that resignation in her tones that showed she had abandoned the natural hopes of her sex. "Singly and unsupported have I lived; alone and unlamented must I be carried to my grave."

The exquisite pathos of her voice, as she uttered this placid speech, blended as it was with the sweet and calm dignity of virgin pride, touched the heart of her listener, and he continued silent many moments, as if in reverence of her determination. Her sentiments awakened in his own breast those feelings of generosity and disinterestedness, which had nearly been smothered in restless ambition and the pride of success. He resumed the discourse, therefore, more mildly, and with a much greater exhibition of deep feeling, and less of passion, in his manner.

"I know not, Alice, that I ought, situated as I am, and contented, if not happy, as you are, even to attempt to revive in your bosom those sentiments which I was once led to think existed there. It cannot, after all, be a desirable fate to share the lot of a rover like myself; one who may be termed a Quixote in the behalf of liberal principles, and who may be hourly called to seal the truth of those principles with his life."

"There never existed any sentiment, in my breast, in which you are concerned, that does not exist there still, and unchanged," returned Alice, with her single-hearted sincerity.

"Do I hear you aright? or have I misconceived your resolution to abide in England? or have I not rather mistaken your early feelings?"

"You have fallen into no error now nor then. The weakness may still exist, John; but the strength to struggle with it has, by the goodness of God, grown with my years. It is not, however, of myself, but of you, that I would speak. I have lived like one of our simple daisies, which in the budding may have caught your eye; and I shall also wilt like the humble flower, when the winter of my time arrives, without being missed from the fields that have known me for a season. But your fall, John, will be like that of the oak that now supports us, and men shall pronounce on the beauty and grandeur of the noble stem while standing, as well as of its usefulness when felled."

"Let them pronounce as they will!" returned the proud stranger. "The truth must be finally known; and when that hour shall come, they will say, he was a faithful and gallant warrior in his day; and a worthy lesson for all who are born in slavery, but would live in freedom, shall be found in his example."

"Such may be the language of that distant people, whom ye have adopted in the place of those who once formed home and kin to ye," said Alice, glancing her eye timidly at his countenance, as if to discern how far she might venture, without awakening his resentment; "but what will the men of the land of your birth transmit to their children, who will be the children of those that are of your own blood?"

"They will say, Alice, whatever their crooked policy may suggest, or their disappointed vanity can urge. But the picture must be drawn by the friends of the hero, as well as by his enemies! Think you that there are not pens as well as swords in America?"

"I have heard that America called a land, John, where God had lavished His favors with an unsparing hand; where He has bestowed many climes with their several fruits, and where His power is exhibited no less than His mercy. It is said her rivers are without any known end, and that lakes are found in her bosom, which would put our German Ocean to shame! The plains, teeming with verdure, are spread over wide degrees; and yet those sweet valleys, which a single heart can hold, are not wanting. In short, John, I hear it is a broad land, that can furnish food for each passion, and contain objects for every affection."

"Ay, you have found those, Alice, in your solitude, who have been willing to do her justice! It is a country that can form a world of itself; and why should they who inherit it look to other nations for their laws?"

"I pretend not to reason on the right of the children of that soil to do whatever they may deem most meet for their own welfare," returned Alice; "but can men be born in such a land and not know the feelings which bind a human being to the place of his birth?"

"Can you doubt that they should be patriotic?" exclaimed the pilot, in surprise. "Do not their efforts in this sacred cause—their patient sufferings—their long privations—speak loudly in their behalf?"

"And will they, who know so well how to love home, sing the praises of him who has turned his ruthless hand against the land of his fathers?"

"Forever harping on that word home!" said the pilot, who now detected the timid approaches of Alice to her hidden meaning. "Is a man a stick or a stone that he must be cast into the fire, or buried in a wall wherever his fate may have doomed him to appear on the earth? The sound of home is said to feed the vanity of an Englishman, let him go where he will; but it would seem to have a still more powerful charm with English women!"

"It is the dearest of all terms to every woman, John, for it embraces the dearest of all its ties! If your dames of America are ignorant of its charm, all the favors which God has lavished on their land will avail their happiness but little."

"Alice," said the pilot, rising in his agitation, "I see but too well the object of your allusions. But on this subject we can never agree; for not even your powerful influence can draw me from the path of glory in which I am now treading. But our time is growing brief; let us, then, talk of other things. This may be the last time that I shall ever put foot on this island of Britain."

Alice paused to struggle with the feelings excited by this remark, before she pursued the discourse. But, soon shaking off the weakness, she added, with a rigid adherence to that course which she believed to be her duty:

"And now, John, that you have landed, is the breaking up of a peaceful family, and the violence ye have shown toward an aged man, a fit exploit for one whose object is the glory of which ye have spoken?"

"Think you that I have landed, and placed my life in the hands of my enemies, for so unworthy an object! No, Alice; my motive for this undertaking has been disappointed, and therefore will ever remain a secret from the world. But duty to my cause has prompted the step you so unthinkingly condemn. This Colonel Howard has some consideration with those in power, and will answer to exchange for a better man. As for his wards, you forget their home; their magical home is in America; unless, indeed, they find it nearer at hand, under the proud flag of a frigate that is now waiting for them in the offing."

"You talk of a frigate!" said Alice, with sudden interest in the subject; "is she your only means of escaping from your enemies?"

"Alice Dunscombe has taken but little heed of passing events to ask such a question of me!" returned the haughty pilot. "The question would have sounded more discreetly, had it been, 'Is she the only vessel with you that your enemies will have to escape from?'"

"Nay, I cannot measure my language at such a moment!" continued Alice, with a still stronger exhibition of anxiety. "It was my fortune to overhear a part of a plan that was intended to destroy, by sudden means, those vessels of America that were in our seas."

"That might be a plan more suddenly adopted than easily executed, my good Alice. And who were these redoubtable schemers?"

"I know not but my duty to the king should cause me to suppress this information," said Alice, hesitating.

"Well, be it so," returned the pilot, coolly; "it may prove the means of saving the persons of some of the royal officers from death or captivity. I have already said, this may be the last of my visits to this island, and consequently, Alice, the last of our interviews—"

"And yet," said Alice, still pursuing the train of her own thoughts, "there can be but little harm in sparing human blood, and least of all in serving those whom we have long known and regarded!"

"Ah, that is a simple doctrine, and one that is easily maintained," he added, with much apparent indifference; "and yet King George might well spare some of his servants—the list of his abject minions is so long!"

"There was a man named Dillon, who lately dwelt in the Abbey, but who has mysteriously disappeared," continued Alice; "or, rather, who was captured by your companions; know you aught of him, John?"

"I have heard there was a miscreant of that name, but we have never met. Alice, if it please Heaven that this should be the last—"

"He was a captive in the schooner called the Ariel," she added, still unheeding his affected indifference to her communication; "and when permitted to return to St. Ruth, he lost sight of his solemn promise, and of his plighted honor, to wreak his malice. Instead of effecting the exchange that he had conditioned to see made, he plotted treason against his captors. Yes; it was most foul treason! for his treatment was generous and kind, and his liberation certain."

"He was a most unworthy scoundrel! But, Alice—"

"Nay, listen, John," she continued, urged to even a keener interest in his behalf by his apparent inattention; "and yet I should speak tenderly of his failings, for he is already numbered with the dead! One part of his scheme must have been frustrated; for he intended to destroy that schooner which you call the Ariel, and to have taken the person of the young Barnstable."

"In both of which he has failed! The person of Barnstable I have rescued, and the Ariel has been stricken by a hand far mightier than any of this world! —she is wrecked."

"Then is the frigate your only means of escape? Hasten, John, and seem not so proud and heedless; for the hour may come when all your daring will not profit ye against the machinations of secret enemies. This Dillon had also planned that expresses should journey to a seaport at the south, with the intelligence that your vessels were in these seas, in order that ships might be dispatched to intercept your retreat."

The pilot lost his affected indifference as she proceeded, and before she ceased speaking his eye was endeavoring to anticipate her words, by reading her countenance through the dusky medium of the starlight.

"How know you this, Alice?" he asked, quickly—"and what vessel did he name?"

"Chance made me an unseen listener to their plan, and—I know not but I forget my duty to my prince!—but, John, 'tis asking too much of a weak woman to require that she shall see the man whom she once viewed with eyes of favor, sacrificed, when a word of caution, given in season, might enable him to avoid the danger!"

"Once viewed with an eye of favor! Is it then so?" said the pilot, speaking in a vacant manner. "But, Alice, heard ye the force of the ships, or their names? Give me their names, and the first lord of your British admiralty shall not give so true an account of their force as I will furnish from this list of my own."

"Their names were certainly mentioned," said Alice, with tender melancholy; "but the name of one far nearer to me was ringing in my ears, and has driven them from my mind."

"You are the same good Alice I once knew! And my name was mentioned? What said they of the pirate? Had his arm stricken a blow that made them tremble in their Abbey? Did they call him coward, girl?"

"It was mentioned in terms that pained my heart as I listened; for it is ever too easy a task to forget the lapse of years, nor are the feelings of youth to be easily eradicated."

"Ay, there is luxury in knowing that, with all their affected abuse, the slaves dread me in their secret holds!" exclaimed the pilot, pacing in front of his listener with quick steps. "This it is to be marked, among men, above all others, in your calling! I hope yet to see the day when the third George shall start at the sound of that name, even within the walls of his palace."

Alice Dunscombe heard him in deep and mortified silence. It was too evident that a link in the chain of their sympathies was broken, and that the weakness in which she had been unconsciously indulging was met by no correspondent emotion in him. After sinking her head for a moment on her bosom, she arose with a little more than her usual air of meekness, and recalled the pilot to a sense of her presence, by saying, in a yet milder voice:

"I have now communicated all that it can profit you to know, and it is meet that we separate."

"What, thus soon?" he cried, starting and taking her hand. "This is but a short interview, Alice, to precede so long a separation."

"Be it short, or be it long, it must now end," she replied. "Your companions are on the eve of departure, and I trust you would be one of the last who would wish to be deserted. If ye do visit England again, I hope it may be with altered sentiments, so far as regards her interests. I wish ye peace, John, and the blessings of God, as ye may be found to deserve them."

"I ask no further, unless it be the aid of your gentle prayers! But the night is gloomy, and I will see you in safety to the Abbey."

"It is unnecessary," she returned, with womanly reserve. "The innocent can be fearless on occasion, as the most valiant among your warriors. But here is no cause for fear. I shall take a path that will conduct me in a different way from that which is occupied by your soldiers, and where I shall find none but Him who is ever ready to protect the helpless. Once more, John, I bid you adieu." Her voice faltered as she continued: "Ye will share the lot of humanity, and have your hours of care and weakness; at such moments ye can remember those ye leave on this despised island, and perhaps among them ye may think of some whose interest in your welfare has been far removed from selfishness."

"God be with you, Alice!" he said, touched with her emotion, and losing all vain images in more worthy feelings—"but I cannot permit you to go alone."

"Here we part, John," she said, firmly, "and forever! 'Tis for the happiness of both, for I fear we have but little in common." She gently wrested her hand from his grasp, and once more bidding him adieu, in a voice that was nearly inaudible, she turned and slowly disappeared, moving, with lingering steps, in the direction of the Abbey.

The first impulse of the pilot was, certainly, to follow, and insist on seeing her on the way; but the music of the guard on the cliffs at that moment sent forth its martial strains, and the whistle of the boatswain was heard winding its shrill call among the rocks, in those notes that his practised ear understood to be the last signal for embarking.

Obedient to the summons, this singular man, in whose breast the natural feelings, that were now on the eve of a violent eruption, had so long been smothered by the visionary expectation of a wild ambition, and perhaps of fierce resentments, pursued his course, in deep abstraction, towards the boats. He was soon met by the soldiers of Borroughcliffe, deprived of their arms, it is true, but unguarded, and returning peacefully to their quarters. The mind of the pilot, happily for the liberty of these men, was too much absorbed in his peculiar reflections to note this act of Griffith's generosity, nor did he arouse from his musing until his steps were arrested by suddenly encountering a human figure in the pathway. A light tap on his shoulder was the first mark of recognition he received; when Borroughcliffe, who stood before him, said:

"It is evident, sir, from what has passed this evening, that you are not what you seem. You may be rebel admiral or general, for aught that I know, the right to command having been strangely contested among ye this night. But let who will own the chief authority, I take the liberty of whispering in your ear that I have been scurvily treated by you—I repeat, most scurvily treated by you all, generally, and by you in particular."

The pilot started at this strange address, which was uttered with all the bitterness that could be imparted to it by a disappointed man; but he motioned with his hand for the captain to depart, and turned aside to pursue his own way.

"Perhaps I am not properly understood," continued the obstinate soldier. "I say, sir, you have treated me scurvily; and I would not be thought to say this to any gentleman without wishing to give him an opportunity to vent his anger."

The eye of the pilot, as he moved forward, glanced at the pistols which Borroughcliffe held in his hands, the one by the handle and the other by its barrel, and the soldier even fancied that his footsteps were quickened by the sight. After gazing at him until his form was lost in the darkness, the captain muttered to himself:

"He is no more than a common pilot, after all! No true gentleman would have received so palpable a hint with such a start. Ah! here comes the party of my worthy friend whose palate knows a grape of the north side of Madeira from one of the south. The dog has the throat of a gentleman; we will see how he can swallow a delicate allusion to his faults!"

Borroughcliffe stepped aside to allow the marines, who were also in motion for the boats, to pass, and watched with keen looks the person of the commander. Manual, who had been previously apprised of the intention of Griffith to release the prisoners, had halted to see that none but those who had been liberated by authority were marching into the country. This accidental circumstance gave Borroughcliffe an opportunity of meeting the other at some little distance from either of their respective parties.

"I greet you sir," said Borroughcliffe, "with all affection. This has been a pleasant forage for you, Captain Manual."

The marine was far from being disposed to wrangle, but there was that in the voice of the other which caused him to answer:

"It would have been far pleasanter, sir, if I had met an opportunity of returning to Captain Borroughcliffe some of the favors that I have received at his hands."

"Nay, then, dear sir, you weigh my modesty to the earth! Surely you forget the manner in which my hospitality has already been requited—by some two hours' mouthing of my sword-hilt; with a very unceremonious ricochet into a corner; together with a love-tap received over the shoulders of one of my men, by so gentle an instrument as the butt of a musket! Damme, sir, but I think an ungrateful man only a better sort of beast!"

"Had the love-tap been given to the officer instead of the man," returned Manual, with all commendable coolness, "it would have been better justice; and the ramrod might have answered as well as the butt, to floor a gentleman who carried the allowance of four thirsty fiddlers under one man's jacket."

"Now, that is rank ingratitude to your own cordial of the south side, and a most biting insult! I really see but one way of terminating this wordy war, which, if not discreetly ended, may lead us far into the morning."

"Elect your own manner of determining the dispute, sir; I hope, however, it will not be by your innate knowledge of mankind, which has already mistaken a captain of marines in the service of Congress for a runaway lover, bound to some green place or other."

"You might just as well tweak my nose, sir," said Borroughcliffe. "Indeed, I think it would be the milder reproach of the two! will you make your selection of these, sir? they were loaded for a very different sort of service, but I doubt not will answer on occasion."

"I am provided with a pair, that are charged for any service," replied Manual, drawing a pistol from his own belt, and stepping backward a few paces.

"You are destined for America, I know," said Borroughcliffe, who stood his ground with consummate coolness; "but it would be more convenient for me, sir, if you could delay your march for a single moment."

"Fire and defend yourself!" exclaimed Manual, furiously, retracing his steps towards his enemy.

The sounds of two pistols were blended in one report, and the soldiers of Borroughcliffe and the marines all rushed to the place on the sudden alarm. Had the former been provided with arms, it is probable that a bloody fray would have been the consequence of the sight that both parties beheld on arriving at the spot, which they did simultaneously. Manual lay on his back, without any signs of life, and Borroughcliffe had changed his cool, haughty, upright attitude for a recumbent posture, which was somewhat between lying and sitting.

"Is the poor fellow actually expended?" said the Englishman, in something like the tones of regret; "well, he had a soldier's mettle in him, and was nearly as great a fool as myself!"

The marines had, luckily for the soldiers and their captain, by this time discovered the signs of life in their own commander, who had been only slightly stunned by the bullet, which had grazed his crown, and who, being assisted to his feet, stood a minute or two rubbing his head, as if awaking from a dream. As Manual came gradually to his senses, he recollected the business in which he had just been engaged, and, in his turn, inquired after the fate of his antagonist.

"I am here, my worthy *incognito*," cried the other, with the voice of perfect good-nature; "lying in the lap of Mother Earth, and all the better for opening a vein or two in my right leg—though I do think that the same effect might have been produced without treating the bone so roughly!—But I opine that I saw you also reclining on the bosom of our common ancestor."

"I was down for a few minutes, I do believe," returned Manual; "there is the path of a bullet across my scalp."

"Humph! on the head!" said Borroughcliffe, dryly; "the hurt is not likely to be mortal, I see.—Well, I shall offer to raffle with the first poor devil I can find that has but one leg, for who shall have them both; and that will just set up a beggar and a gentleman!—Manual, give me your hand; we have drunk together, and we have fought; surely there is nothing now to prevent our being sworn friends."

"Why," returned Manual, continuing to rub his head, "I can see no irremovable objections—but you will want a surgeon? can I order anything to be done? There go the signals again to embark—march the fellows down at quick time, sergeant; my own man may remain with me, or, I can do altogether without assistance."

"Ah! you are what I call a well-made man, my dear friend!" exclaimed Borroughcliffe; "no weak points about your fortress! such a man is worthy to be at the *head* of a whole corps, instead of a solitary company.—Gently, Drill, gently; handle me as if I were made of potter's clay.—I will not detain you longer, my friend Manual, for I hear signal after signal; they must be in want of some of your astonishing reasoning faculties to set them afloat."

Manual might have been offended at the palpable allusions that his new friend made to the firmness of his occiput, had not his perception of things been a little confused by a humming sound that seemed to abide near the region of thought. As it was, he reciprocated the good wishes of the other, whom he shook most cordially by the hand, and once more renewed his offers of service, after exchanging sundry friendly speeches.

"I thank you quite as much as if I were not at all indebted to you for letting blood, thereby saving me a fit of apoplexy; but Drill has already dispatched a messenger to B—— for a leech, and the lad may bring the whole depot upon you. Adieu, once more, and remember that if you ever visit England again as a friend, you are to let me see you."

"I shall do it without fail; and I shall keep you to your promise if you once more put foot in America."

"Trust me for that; I shall stand in need of your excellent head to guide me safely among those rude foresters. Adieu; cease not to bear me in your thoughts."

"I shall never cease to remember you, my good friend," returned Manual, again scratching the member which was snapping in a manner that caused him to fancy he heard it. Once more these worthies shook each other by the hand, and again they renewed their promises of future intercourse; after which they separated like two reluctant lovers—parting in a manner that would have put to shame the friendship of Orestes and Pylades.

32

Nay, answer me: stand and unfold yourself.

Hamlet

DURING the time occupied by the incidents
that occurred after the pilot had made his descent on the land, the Alacrity,
now under the orders of Mr. Boltrope, the master of the frigate, lay off and
on, in readiness to receive the successful mariners. The direction of the wind
had been gradually changing from the northeast to the south during the close
of the day; and long before the middle watches of the night the wary old seaman, who, it may be remembered, had expressed in the council of war such a
determined reluctance to trust his person within the realm of Britain, ordered
the man who steered the cutter to stand in boldly for the land. Whenever the
lead told them that it was prudent to tack, the course of the vessel was
changed, and in this manner the seaman continued to employ the hours in
patient attendance on the adventurers. The sailing-master, who had spent the
early years of his life as the commander of divers vessels employed in trading,
was apt, like many men of his vocation and origin, to mistake the absence of
refinement for the surest evidence of seamanship, and, consequently, he held
the little courtesies and punctilios of a man-of-war in high disdain. His peculiar duties of superintending the expenditure of the ship's stores in their
several departments, of keeping the frigate's log-book, and of making his daily
examinations into the state of her sails and rigging, brought him so little in
collision with the gay, laughing, reckless young lieutenants, who superin-
tended the ordinary management of the vessel, that he might be said to have
formed a distinct species of the animal, though certainly of the same genus

with his more polished messmates. Whenever circumstances, however, required that he should depart from the dull routine of his duty, he made it a rule, as far as possible, to associate himself with such of the crew as possessed habits and opinions the least at variance with his own.

By a singular fatality the chaplain of the frigate was, as respects associates, in a condition nearly assimilated to that of this veteran tar.

An earnest desire to ameliorate the situation of those who were doomed to meet death on the great deep, had induced an experienced and simple-hearted divine to accept this station, in the fond hope that he might be made the favored instrument of salvation to many, who were then existing in a state of the most abandoned self-forgetfulness. Neither our limits, nor our present object, will permit the relation of the many causes that led, not only to an entire frustration of all his visionary expectations, but to an issue which rendered the struggle of the good divine with himself both arduous and ominous, in order to maintain his own claims to the merited distinctions of his sacred office. The consciousness of his backsliding had so far lessened the earthly if not the spiritual pride of the chaplain, as to induce him to relish the society of the rude master, whose years had brought him, at times, to take certain views of futurity that were singularly affected by the peculiar character of the individual. It might have been that both found themselves out of their places—but it was owing to some such secret sympathy, let its origin be what it would, that the two came to be fond of each other's company. On the night in question, Mr. Boltrope had invited the chaplain to accompany him in the Alacrity; adding, in his broad, rough language, that, as there was to be fighting on shore, "his hand might come in play with some poor fellow or other." This singular invitation had been accepted, as well from a desire to relieve the monotony of a sea-life by any change, as perhaps with a secret yearning in the breast of the troubled divine, to get as nigh to *terra firma* as possible. Accordingly, after the pilot had landed with his boisterous party, the sailing-master and the chaplain, together with a boatswain's mate and some ten or twelve seamen, were left in quiet possession of the cutter. The first few hours of this peaceable intercourse had been spent by the worthy messmates, in the little cabin of the vessel, over a can of grog; the savory relish of which was much increased by a characteristic disquisition on polemical subjects, which our readers have great reason to regret it is not our present humor to record. When, however, the winds invited the near approach to the hostile shores already mentioned, the prudent sailing-master adjourned the discussion to another and more suitable time, removing himself and the can, by the same operation, to the quarter-deck.

"There," cried the honest tar, placing the wooden vessel, with great self-contentment, by his side on the deck, "this is ship's comfort! There is a good deal of what I call a lubber's fuss, parson, kept up on board a ship that shall be nameless, but which bears, about three leagues distant, broad off in the ocean, and which is lying-to under a close-reefed maintopsail, foretopmast-staysail and foresail—I call my hand a true one in mixing a can—take another pull at the halyards!—'twill make your eye twinkle like a light-house, this dark morning! You won't? well, we must give no offence to the Englishman's rum." After a potent draught had succeeded this considerate declaration, he added: "You are a little like our first-lieutenant, parson, who drinks, as I call it, nothing but the elements—which is, water stiffened with air."

"Mr. Griffith may indeed be said to set a wholesome example to the crew," returned the chaplain, perhaps with a slight consciousness that it had not altogether possessed its due weight with himself.

"Wholesome," cried Boltrope; "let me tell you, my worthy leaf-turner, that if you call such a light diet wholesome, you know but little of salt-water and sea-fogs! However, Mr. Griffith is a seaman; and if he gave his mind less to trifles and gimcracks, he would be, by the time he got to about our years, a very rational sort of a companion. But you see, parson, just now, he thinks too much of small follies; such as man-of-war discipline. Now there is rationality in giving a fresh nip to a rope, or in looking well at your mats, or even in crowning a cable; but damme, priest, if I see the use— Luff, luff, you lubber! don't you see, sir, you are steering for Garmany?— If I see the use, as I was saying, of making a rumpus about the time when a man changes his shirt; whether it be this week or next week, or, for that matter, the week after, provided it be bad weather. I sometimes am mawkish about attending muster (and I believe I have as little to fear on the score of behavior as any man), lest it should be found I carried my tobacco in the wrong cheek!"

"I have indeed thought it somewhat troublesome to myself, at times; and it is in a striking degree vexatious to the spirit, especially when the body has been suffering under sea-sickness."

"Why, yes, you were a little apt to bend your duds wrong for the first month, or so," said the master. "I remember you got the marine's scraper on your head, once, in your hurry to bury a dead man! Then you never looked as if you belonged to the ship, so long as those cursed black knee-breeches lasted! For my part, I never saw you come up the quarterdeck ladder, but I expected to see your shins give way across the coaming of the hatch—a man does look like the devil, priest, scudding about a ship's decks in that fashion, under bare poles! But now the tailor has found out the articles aren't seaworthy, and we have got your lower stanchions cased in a pair of purser's slops, I am puzzled often to tell your heels from those of a maintop-man!"

"I have good reason to be thankful for the change," said the humbled priest, "if the resemblance you mentioned existed, while I was clad in the usual garb of one of my calling."

"What signifies a calling?" returned Boltrope, catching his breath after a most persevering draught; "a man's shins are his shins, let his upper works belong to what sarvice they may. I took an early prejudyce to knee-breeches, perhaps from a trick I've always had of figuring the devil as wearing them. You know, parson, we seldom hear much said of a man, without forming some sort of an idea concerning his rigging and fashion-pieces; and so, as I had no particular reason to believe that Satan went naked—Keep full, ye lubber; now you are running into the wind's eye, and be d—d to ye!—But, as I was saying, I always took a conceit that the devil wore knee-breeches and a cocked hat. There's some of our young lieutenants, who come to muster on Sundays in cocked hats, just like soldier-officers; but, d'ye see, I would sooner show my nose under a nightcap than under a scraper!"

"I hear the sound of oars!" exclaimed the chaplain, who, finding this image more distinct than even his own vivid conceptions of the great father of evil, was quite willing to conceal his inferiority by changing the discourse—"is not one of our boats returning?"

"Ay, ay, 'tis likely; if it had been me, I should have been land-sick before this. Wear round, boys, and stand by to heave-to on the other tack."

The cutter, obedient to her helm, fell off before the wind; and, rolling an instant in the trough of the sea, came up again easily to her oblique position, with her head toward the cliffs; and, gradually losing her way, as her sails were brought to counteract each other, finally became stationary. During the performance of this evolution, a boat had hove up out of the gloom, in the direction of the land; and by the time the Alacrity was in a state of rest, it had approached so nigh as to admit of hailing.

"Boat ahoy!" murmured Boltrope, through a trumpet, which, aided by his lungs, produced sounds not unlike the roaring of a bull.

"Ay, ay!" was thrown back from a clear voice, that swept across the water with a fulness that needed no factitious aid to render it audible.

"Ay, there comes one of the lieutenants, with his 'ay, ay,'" said Boltrope. "Pipe the side, there, you boatswain's mate! But here's another fellow more on our quarter! Boat ahoy!"

"Alacrity"—returned another voice in a direction different from the other.

"Alacrity! There goes my commission of captain of this craft in a whiff," returned the sailing-master. "That is as much as to say here comes one who will command when he gets on board. Well, well, it is Mr. Griffith, and I can't say, notwithstanding his love of knee-buckles and small wares, but I'm glad he's out of the hands of the English! Ay! here they all come upon us at once! here is another fellow that pulls like the jolly-boat, coming up on our lee-beam, within hail—let us see if he is asleep. Boat ahoy!"

"Flag," answered a third voice from a small, light rowing boat, which had approached very near the cutter, in a direct line from the cliffs, without being observed.

"Flag!" echoed Boltrope, dropping his trumpet in amazement—"that's a big word to come out of jolly-boats! Jack Manly himself could not have spoken it with a fuller mouth—but I'll know who it is that carries such a weather helm, with a Yankee man-of-war's prize! Boat ahoy! I say."

This last call was uttered in those short, menacing tones that are intended to be understood as intimating that the party hailing is in earnest; and it caused the men who were rowing, and who were now quite close to the cutter, to suspend their strokes simultaneously, as if they dreaded that the cry would be instantly succeeded by some more efficient means of ascertaining their character. The figure that was seated by itself in the stern of the boat started at this second summons, and then, as if with sudden recollection, a quiet voice replied:

"No—no."

" 'No—no,' and 'flag' are very different answers," grumbled Boltrope; "what know-nothing have we here?"

He was yet muttering his dissatisfaction at the ignorance of the individual that was approaching, whoever it might be, when the jolly-boat came slowly to their side, and the pilot stepped from her stern-sheets on the deck of the prize.

"Is it you, Mr. Pilot?" exclaimed the sailing-master, raising a battle-lantern within a foot of the other's face, and looking with a sort of stupid wonder at the proud and angry eye he encountered—"is it you! well, I should have rated you for a man of more experience than to come booming down upon a man-of-war in the dark, with such a big word in your mouth, when every boy in the two vessels knows that we carry no swallow-tailed bunting aboard! Flag! why you might have got a shot, had there been soldiers."

The pilot threw him a still fiercer glance, and, turning away with a look of disgust, he walked along the quarter-deck toward the stern of the vessel, with an air of haughty silence, as if disdaining to answer. Boltrope kept his eyes fastened on him for a moment longer, with some appearance of scorn;

but the arrival of the boat first hailed, which proved to be the barge, immediately drew his attention to other matters. Barnstable had been rowing about in the ocean for a long time, unable to find the cutter; and as he had been compelled to suit his own demeanor to those with whom he was associated, he reached the Alacrity in no very good-humored mood. Colonel Howard and his niece had maintained, during the whole period, the most rigid silence, the former from pride, and the latter touched with her uncle's evident displeasure; and Katherine, though secretly elated with the success of all her projects, was content to emulate their demeanor for a short time in order to save appearances. Barnstable had several times addressed himself to the latter, without receiving any other answer than such as was absolutely necessary to prevent her lover from taking direct offence, at the same time that she intimated by her manner her willingness to remain silent. Accordingly, the lieutenant, after aiding the ladies to enter the cutter, and offering to perform the same service to Colonel Howard, which was coldly declined, turned, with that sort of irritation that is by no means less rare in vessels-of-war than with poor human nature generally, and gave vent to his spleen where he dared.

"How's this, Mr. Boltrope?" he cried; "here are boats coming alongside with ladies in them, and you keep your gaff swayed up till the leach of the sail is stretched like a fiddle-string—settle away your peak-halyards, sir, settle away!"

"Ay, ay, sir," grumbled the master; "settle away that peak there; though the craft wouldn't forge ahead a knot in a month, with all her jibs hauled over." He walked sulkily forward among the men, followed by the meek divine; and added, "I should as soon have expected to see Mr. Barnstable come off with a live ox in his boat as a petticoat! The Lord only knows what the ship is coming to next, parson! what between cocked hats and epaulets, and other knee-buckle matters, she was a sort of no-man's land before; and now, what with the women and their band-boxes, they'll make another Noah's ark of her. I wonder they didn't all come aboard in a coach and six, or a one-horse shay!"

It was a surprising relief to Barnstable to be able to give utterance to his humor, for a few moments, by ordering the men to make sundry alterations in every department of the vessel, in a quick, hurried voice that abundantly denoted, not only the importance of his improvements, but the temper in which they were dictated. In his turn, however, he was soon compelled to give way, by the arrival of Griffith in the heavily-rowing launch of the frigate, which was crowded with a larger body of the seamen who had been employed in the expedition. In this manner, boat after boat speedily arrived, and the whole party were once more happily embarked in safety under their national flag.

The small cabin of the Alacrity was relinquished to Colonel Howard and his wards, with their attendants. The boats were dropped astern, each protected by its own keeper; and Griffith gave forth the mandate to fill the sails and steer broad off into the ocean. For more than an hour the cutter held her course in this direction, gliding gracefully through the glittering waters, rising and settling heavily on the long, smooth billows, as if conscious of the unusual burden that she was doomed to carry; but at the end of that period her head was once more brought near the wind, and she was again held at rest, awaiting the appearance of the dawn, in order to discover the position of the prouder vessel to which she was performing the humble duty of a tender. More than a hundred and fifty living men were crowded within her narrow limits; and her decks presented, in the gloom, as she moved along, the picture of a mass of human heads.

As the freedom of a successful expedition was unavoidably permitted, loud jokes and louder merriment broke on the silent waters from the reckless seamen, while the exhilarating can passed from hand to hand, strange oaths and dreadful denunciations breaking forth at times from some of the excited crew against their enemy. At length the bustle of re-embarking gradually subsided, and many of the crew descended to the hold of the cutter, in quest of room to stretch their limbs, when a clear, manly voice was heard rising above the deep in those strains that a seaman most loves to hear. Air succeeded air, from different voices, until even the spirit of harmony grew dull with fatigue, and verses began to be heard where songs were expected, and fleeting lines succeeded stanzas. The decks were soon covered with prostrate men, seeking their natural rest under the open heavens, and perhaps dreaming, as they yielded heavily to the rolling of the vessel, of scenes of other times in their own hemisphere. The dark glances of Katherine were concealed beneath her falling lids; and even Cecilia, with her head bowed on the shoulder of her cousin, slept sweetly in innocence and peace. Boltrope groped his way into the hold among the seamen, where, kicking one of the most fortunate men from his berth, he established himself in his place with all that cool indifference to the other's comfort that had grown with his experience from the time when he was treated thus cavalierly in his own person to the present moment. In this manner head was dropped after head on the planks, the guns, or on whatever first offered for a pillow, until Griffith and Barnstable, alone, were left pacing the different sides of the quarter-deck in a haughty silence.

Never did a morning watch appear so long to the two young sailors, who were thus deprived, by resentment and pride, of that frank and friendly communion that had for so many years sweetened the tedious hours of their long, and, at times, dreary service. To increase the embarrassment of their situation, Cecilia and Katherine, suffering from the confinement of the small and crowded cabin, sought the purer air of the deck, about the time when the deepest sleep had settled on the senses of the wearied mariners. They stood leaning against the taffrail, discussing with each other in low and broken sentences; but a sort of instinctive knowledge of the embarrassment which existed between their lovers caused a guarded control over every look or gesture which might be construed into an encouragement for one of the young men to advance at the expense of the other. Twenty times, however, did the impatient Barnstable feel tempted to throw off the awkward restraint, and approach his mistress; but in each instance was he checked by the secret consciousness of error, as well as by that habitual respect for superior rank that forms a part of the nature of a sea-officer. On the other hand, Griffith manifested no intention to profit by this silent concession in his favor, but continued to pace the quarter-deck, with strides more hurried than ever; and was seen to throw many an impatient glance toward that quarter of the heavens where the first signs of the lingering day might be expected to appear. At length Katherine, with a ready ingenuity, and perhaps with some secret coquetry, removed the embarrassment, by speaking first, taking care to address the lover of her cousin:

"How long are we condemned to these limited lodgings, Mr. Griffith?" she asked. "Truly, there is a freedom in your nautical customs, which, to say the least, is novel to us females who have been accustomed to the division of space!"

"The instant that there is light to discover the frigate, Miss Plowden," he answered, "you shall be transferred from a vessel of a hundred to one of twelve hundred tons. If your situation there be less comfortable than within the walls of St. Ruth, you will not forget that they who live on the ocean claim it as a merit to despise the luxuries of the land."

"At least, sir," returned Katherine, with a sweet grace, which she well knew how to assume on occasion, "what we shall enjoy will be sweetened by liberty and embellished by a sailor's hospitality.—To me, Cicely, the air of this open sea is as fresh and invigorating as if it were wafted from our own distant America."

"If you have not the arm of a patriot, you at least possess a most loyal imagination, Miss Plowden," said Griffith, laughing. "This soft breeze blows in the direction of the fens of Holland, instead of the broad plains of America.

Thank God, there come the signs of day, at last! Unless the currents have swept the ship far to the north, we shall surely see her with the light."

The cheering intelligence drew the eyes of the fair cousins toward the east, where their delighted looks were soon fastened, while they watched the glories of the sun rising over the water. As the morning had advanced, a deeper gloom was spread across the ocean, and the stars were gleaming in the heavens like balls of twinkling fire. But now a streak of pale light showed itself along the horizon, growing brighter and widening at each moment, until long, fleecy clouds became visible, where nothing had been seen before but the dim base of the arch that overhung the dark waters. This expanding light, which, in appearance, might be compared to a silvery opening in the heavens, was soon tinged with a pale flush, which quickened with sudden transitions into glows yet deeper, until a belt of broad flame bounded the water, diffusing itself more faintly toward the zenith, where it melted into the pearl-colored sky, or played on the fantastic volumes of a few light clouds with inconstant glimmering. While these beautiful transitions were still before the eyes of the youthful admirers of their beauties, a voice was heard above them, crying, as if from the heavens:

"Sail—ho! The frigate lies broad off to seaward, sir!"

"Ay, ay; you have been watching with one eye asleep, fellow," returned Griffith, "or we should have heard you before!—Look a little north of the place where the glare of the sun is coming, Miss Plowden, and you will be able to see our gallant vessel!"

An involuntary cry of pleasure burst from the lips of Katherine, as she followed his directions, and first beheld the frigate through the medium of the fluctuating colors of the morning. The undulating outline of the hazy ocean, which rose and fell heavily against the bright boundary of the heavens, was without any relief to distract the eye as it fed eagerly on the beauties of the solitary ship. She was riding sluggishly on the long seas, with only two of her lower and smaller sails spread, to hold her in command; but her tall masts and heavy yards were painted against the fiery sky in strong lines of deep black, while even the smallest cord in mazes of her rigging might be distinctly traced, stretching from spar to spar, with the beautiful accuracy of a picture. At moments when her huge hull rose on a billow, and was lifted against the background of sky, its shape and dimensions were brought into view, but these transient glimpses were soon lost, as it settled into the trough, leaving the waving spars bowing gracefully toward the waters, as if about to follow the vessel into the bosom of the deep. As a clearer light gradually stole on the senses, the delusion of colors and distance vanished together, and when a flood of day preceded the immediate appearance of the sun, the ship became plainly visible within a mile of the cutter, her black hull checkered with ports, and her high, tapering masts exhibiting their proper proportions and hues.

At the first cry of "A sail!" the crew of the Alacrity had been aroused from their slumbers by the shrill whistle of the boatswain, and long before the admiring looks of the two cousins had ceased to dwell on the fascinating sight of morning chasing night from the hemisphere, the cutter was again in motion to join her consort. It seemed but a moment before their little vessel was in, what the timid females thought, a dangerous proximity to the frigate, under whose lee she slowly passed, in order to admit of the following dialogue between Griffith and his aged commander:

"I rejoice to see you, Mr. Griffith!" cried the captain, who stood in the channel of his ship, waving his hat in the way of cordial greeting. "You are welcome back, Captain Manual—welcome, welcome, all of you, my boys! as welcome as a breeze in the calm latitudes." As his eye, however, passed along the deck of the Alacrity, it encountered the shrinking figures of Cecilia and Katherine; and a dark shade of displeasure crossed his decent features, while he added: "How's this, gentlemen? The frigate of Congress is neither a ball-room, nor a church, that it is to be thronged with women!"

"Ay, ay," muttered Boltrope to his friend, the chaplain, "now the old man has hauled out his mizzen, you'll see him carry a weather helm! He wakes up about as often as the trades shift their points, and that's once in six months. But when there has been a neap-tide in his temper for any time, you're sure to find it followed by a flood with a vengeance. Let us hear what the first-lieutenant can say in favor of his petticoat quality!"

The blushing sky had not exhibited a more fiery glow than gleamed in the fine face of Griffith for a moment; but, struggling with his disgust, he answered with bitter emphasis:

" 'Twas the pleasure of Mr. Gray, sir, to bring off the prisoners."

"Of Mr. Gray!" repeated the captain, instantly losing every trace of displeasure in an air of acquiescence. "Come-to, sir, on the same tack with the ship, and I will hasten to order the accommodation-ladder rigged, to receive our guests!"

Boltrope listened to this sudden alteration in the language of his commander with sufficient wonder; nor was it until he had shaken his head repeatedly, with the manner of one who saw deeper than his neighbors into a mystery, that he found leisure to observe:

"Now, parson, I suppose if you held an almanac in your fist, you'd think you could tell which way we shall have the wind to-morrow! but damme, priest, if better calculators than you haven't failed! Because a lubberly—no, he's a thorough seaman, I'll say that for the fellow!—because a pilot chooses to say, 'Bring me off these here women,' the ship is to be so cluttered with she-cattle, that a man will be obligated to spend half his time in making his manners! Now mind what I tell you, priest, this very frolic will cost Congress the price of a year's wages for an able-bodied seaman in bunting and canvas for screens; besides the wear and tear of running-gear in shortening sail, in order that the women need not be 'stericky in squalls!"

The presence of Mr. Boltrope being required to take charge of the cutter, the divine was denied an opportunity of dissenting from the opinions of his rough companion; for the loveliness of their novel shipmates had not failed to plead loudly in their favor with every man in the cutter whose habits and ideas had not become rigidly set in obstinacy.

By the time the Alacrity was hove-to, with her head toward the frigate, the long line of boats that she had been towing during the latter part of the night, were brought to her side, and filled with men. A wild scene of un-bridled merriment and gayety succeeded, while the seamen were exchanging the confinement of the prize for their accustomed lodgings in the ship, during which the reins of discipline were slightly relaxed. Loud laughter was echoed from boat to boat as they glided by each other; and rude jests, interlarded with quaint humors and strange oaths, were freely bandied from mouth to mouth. The noise, however, soon ceased, and the passage of Colonel Howard and his wards was then effected with less precipitancy and due decorum. Captain Munson, who had been holding a secret dialogue with Griffith and the pilot, received his unexpected guests with plain hospitality, but with an evident desire to be civil. He politely yielded to their service his two con-venient state-rooms, and invited them to partake in common with himself of the comforts of the great cabin.

33

Furious press the hostile squadron,
Furious he repels their rage,
Loss of blood at length enfeebles;
Who can war with thousands wage?

Spanish War Song

WE cannot detain the narrative to detail the scenes which busy wonder, aided by the relation of divers marvellous feats, produced among the curious seamen who remained in the ship, and their more fortunate fellows who had returned in glory from an expedition to the land. For nearly an hour the turbulence of a general movement was heard, issuing from the deep recesses of the frigate, and the boisterous sounds of hoarse merriment were listened to by the officers in indulgent silence; but all these symptoms of unbridled humor ceased by the time the morning repast was ended, when the regular sea-watch was set, and the greater portion of those whose duty did not require their presence on the vessel's deck, availed themselves of the opportunity to repair the loss of sleep sustained in the preceding night. Still no preparations were made to put the ship in motion, though long and earnest consultations, which were supposed to relate to their future destiny, were observed by the younger officers to be held between their captain, the first-lieutenant, and the mysterious pilot. The latter threw many an anxious glance along the eastern horizon, searching it minutely with his glass, and then would turn his impatient looks at the low, dense bank of fog, which, stretching across the ocean like a barrier of cloud, entirely intercepted the view toward the south. To the north and along the land the air was clear, and the sea without a spot of any kind; but in the east a small white sail had been discovered since the opening of day, which was gradually rising above the water, and assuming the appearance of a vessel of some size. Every officer on the quarter-deck in his turn had examined this distant sail, and had ventured an opinion on its destination and character; and even Katherine, who with her cousin was enjoying, in the open air, the novel beauties of the ocean, had been tempted to place her sparkling eye to a glass to gaze at the stranger.

"It is a collier," Griffith said, "who has hauled from the land in the late gale, and who is luffing up to his course again. If the wind holds here in the south, and he does not get into that fog-bank, we can stand off for him and get a supply of fuel before eight bells are struck."

"I think his head is to the northward, and that he is steering off the wind," returned the pilot in a musing manner. "If that Dillon succeeded in getting his express far enough along the coast, the alarm has been spread, and we must be wary. The convoy of the Baltic trade is in the North Sea, and news of our presence could easily have been taken off to it by some of the cutters that line the coast. I could wish to get the ship as far south as the Helder!"

"Then we lose this weather-tide!" exclaimed the impatient Griffith; "surely we have the cutter as a lookout! besides, by beating into the fog, we shall lose the enemy, if enemy it be, and it is thought meet for an American frigate to skulk from her foes!"

The scornful expression that kindled the eye of the pilot, like a gleam of sunshine lighting for an instant some dark dell and laying bare its secrets, was soon lost in the usually quiet look of his glance, though he hesitated like one who was struggling with his passions before he answered:

"If prudence and the service of the State require it, even this proud frigate must retreat and hide from the meanest of her enemies. My advice, Captain Munson, is, that you make sail, and beat the ship to windward, as Mr. Griffith has suggested, and that you order the cutter to precede us, keeping more in with the land."

The aged seaman, who evidently suspended his orders only to receive an intimation of the other's pleasure, immediately commanded his youthful assistant to issue the necessary mandates to put these measures in force. Accordingly, the Alacrity, which vessel had been left under the command of the junior lieutenant of the frigate, was quickly under way; and making short stretches to windward, she soon entered the bank of fog, and was lost to the eye. In the meantime the canvas of the ship was loosened, and spread leisurely, in order not to disturb the portion of the crew who were sleeping; and, following her little consort, she moved heavily through the water, bearing up against the dull breeze.

The quiet of regular duty had succeeded to the bustle of making sail; and, as the rays of the sun fell less obliquely on the distant land, Katherine and Cecilia were amusing Griffith by vain attempts to point out the rounded eminences which they fancied lay in the vicinity of the deserted mansion of St. Ruth. Barnstable, who had resumed his former station in the frigate, as her second-lieutenant, was pacing the opposite side of the quarter-deck, holding under his arm the speaking trumpet, which denoted that he held the temporary control of the motions of the ship, and inwardly cursing the restraint that kept him from the side of his mistress. At this moment of universal quiet, when nothing above low dialogues interrupted the dashing of the waves as they were thrown lazily aside by the bows of the vessel, the report of a light cannon burst out of the barrier of fog, and rolled by them on the breeze, apparently vibrating with the rising and sinking of the waters.

"There goes the cutter!" exclaimed Griffith, the instant the sound was heard.

"Surely," said the captain, "Somers is not so indiscreet as to scale his guns, after the caution he has received!"

"No idle scaling of guns is intended there," said the pilot, straining his eyes to pierce the fog, but soon turning away in disappointment at his inability to succeed—"that gun is shotted, and has been fired in the hurry of a sudden signal!—Can your lookouts see nothing, Mr. Barnstable?"

The lieutenant of the watch hailed the man aloft, and demanded if anything were visible in the direction of the wind, and received for answer, that the fog intercepted the view in that quarter of the heavens, but that the sail in the east was a ship, running large, or before the wind. The pilot shook his head doubtingly at this information, but still he manifested a strong reluctance to relinquish the attempt of getting more to the southward. Again he communed with the commander of the frigate, apart from all other ears; and, while they yet deliberated, a second report was heard, leaving no doubt that the Alacrity was firing signal-guns for their particular attention.

"Perhaps," said Griffith, "he wishes to point out his position, or to ascertain ours, believing that we are lost like himself in the mist."

"We have our compasses!" returned the doubting captain; "Somers has a meaning in what he says!"

"See!" cried Katherine, with girlish delight, "see, my cousin! see, Barnstable! how beautifully that vapor is wreathing itself in clouds above the smoky line of fog! It stetches already into the very heavens like a lofty pyramid!"

Barnstable sprang lightly on a gun, as he repeated her words:

"Pyramids of fog! and wreathing clouds! By Heaven!" he shouted, " 'tis a tall ship! Royal, sky-sails, and studding-sails all abroad! She is within a mile of us, and comes down like a race-horse, with a spanking breeze, dead before it! Now know we why Somers is speaking in the mist!"

"Ay," cried Griffith, "and there goes the Alacrity, just breaking out of the fog, hovering in for the land!"

"There is a mighty hull under all that cloud of canvas, Captain Munson," said the observant but calm pilot. "It is time, gentlemen, to edge away to leeward."

"What, before we know from whom we run?" cried Griffith; "my life on it, there is no single ship King George owns, but would tire of the sport before she played a full game of bowls with—"

The haughty air of the young man was daunted by the severe look he encountered in the eye of the pilot, and he suddenly ceased, though inwardly chafing with impatient pride.

"The same eye that detected the canvas above the fog might have seen the flag of a vice-admiral fluttering still nearer the heavens," returned the collected stranger; "and England, faulty as she may be, is yet too generous to place a flag-officer in time of war in command of a frigate, or a captain in command of a fleet. She knows the value of those who shed their blood in her behalf, and it is thus that she is so well served! Believe me, Captain Munson, there is nothing short of a ship-of-the-line under that symbol of rank and that broad show of canvas!"

"We shall see, sir, we shall see," returned the old officer, whose manner grew decided as the danger appeared to thicken. "Beat to quarters, Mr. Griffith, for we have none but enemies to expect on this coast."

The order was instantly issued, when Griffith remarked, with a more temperate zeal:

"If Mr. Gray be right, we shall have reason to thank God that we are so light of heel!"

The cry of "a strange vessel close aboard the frigate," having already flown down the hatches, the ship was in an uproar at the first tap of the drum. The seamen threw themselves from their hammocks, and, lashing them rapidly into long hard bundles, they rushed to the decks, where they were dexterously stowed in the netting, to aid in the defences of the upper part of the vessel. While this tumultuous scene was exhibiting, Griffith gave a secret order to

Merry, who disappeared, leading his trembling cousins to a place of safety in the inmost depths of the ship.

The guns were cleared of their lumber, and loosened. The bulkheads were knocked down and the cabin relieved of its furniture; and the gun-deck exhibited one unbroken line of formidable cannon, arranged in all the order of a naval battery ready to engage. Arm-chests were thrown open, and the decks strewed with pikes, cutlasses, pistols, and all the various weapons of boarding. In short, the yards were slung and every other arrangement was made with a readiness and dexterity that were actually wonderful, though all was performed amid an appearance of disorder and confusion of the preparations. In a very few minutes everything was completed, and even the voices of the men ceased to be heard answering to their names, as they were mustered at their stations by their respective officers. Gradually the ship became as quiet as the grave; and when Griffith or his commander found it necessary to speak, their voices were calmer and their tones more mild than usual. The course of the vessel was changed to an oblique line from that in which their enemy was approaching though the appearance of flight was to be studiously avoided to the last moment. When nothing further remained to be done, every eye became fixed on the enormous pile of swelling canvas that was rising in cloud over cloud far above the fog, and which was manifestly moving, like driving vapor, swiftly to the north. Presently the dull, smoky boundary of the mist which rested on the water was pushed aside in vast volumes, and the long, taper spars that projected from the bowsprit of the strange ship issued from obscurity, and were quickly followed by the whole of the enormous fabric to which they were merely light appendages. For a moment streaks of reluctant vapor clung to the huge floating pile; but they were soon shaken off by the rapid vessel, and the whole of her black hull became distinct to the eye.

"One, two, three rows of teeth!" said Boltrope, deliberately counting the tiers of guns that bristled along the sides of the enemy; "a three-decker! Jack Manly would show his stern to such a fellow! and even the bloody Scotchman would run!"

"Hard up with your helm, quartermaster!" cried Captain Munson; "there is indeed no time to hesitate, with such an enemy within a quarter of a mile!—turn the hands up, Mr. Griffith, and pack on the ship from her trucks to her lower studding-sail booms. Be stirring! Hard up with your helm! Hard up, and be damned to you!"

The unusual earnestness of their aged commander acted on the startled crew like a voice from the deep, and they waited not for the usual signals of the boatswain and drummer to be given, before they broke away from their

guns, and rushed tumultuously to aid in spreading the desired canvas. There
was one minute of ominous confusion, that to an inexperienced eye would
have foreboded the destruction of all order in the vessel, during which every
hand and each tongue seemed in motion; but it ended in opening the immense
folds of light duck which were displayed along the whole line of the masts,
far beyond the ordinary sails, overshadowing the waters for a great distance,
on either side of the vessel. During the moment of inaction that succeeded this
sudden exertion, the breeze, which had brought up the three-decker, fell
fresher on the sails of the frigate, and she started away from the dangerous
enemy with a very perceptible advantage in point of sailing.

"The fog rises!" cried Griffith; "give us but the wind for an hour, and we
shall run her out of gunshot!"

"These nineties are very fast off the wind," returned the captain in a low
tone, that was intended only for the ears of his first-lieutenant and the pilot;
"and we shall have a struggle for it."

The quick eye of the stranger was glancing over the movements of the
enemy, while he answered:

"He finds we have the heels of him already! he is making ready, and we
shall be fortunate to escape a broadside!—Let her yaw a little, Mr. Griffith;
touch her lightly with the helm; if we are raked, sir, we are lost!"

The captain sprang on the taffrail of his ship with the activity of a young
man, and in an instant he perceived the truth of the other's conjecture.

Both vessels now ran for a few minutes, keenly watching each other's motions like two skilful combatants, the English ship making slight deviations
from the line of her course, and then, as her movements were anticipated by
the other, turning as cautiously in the opposite direction, until a sudden and
wide sweep of her huge bows told the Americans plainly on which tack to expect her. Captain Munson made a silent but impressive gesture with his arms,
as if the crisis were too important for speech, which indicated to the watchful
Griffith the way he wished the frigate steered, to avoid the weight of the impending danger. Both vessels whirled swiftly up to the wind, with their heads
toward the land; and as the huge black side of the three-decker, checkered
with its triple batteries, frowned full upon her foe, it belched forth a flood of
fire and smoke, accompanied by a bellowing roar that shook the surly moanings of the sleeping ocean. The nerves of the bravest man in the frigate contracted their fibres, as the hurricane of iron hurtled by them, and each eye
appeared to gaze in stupid wonder, as if tracing the flight of the swift engines
of destruction. But the voice of Captain Munson was heard in the din, shouting while he waved his hat earnestly in the required direction:

"Meet her! meet her with the helm, boy! meet her, Mr. Griffith, meet her!"

Griffith had so far anticipated this movement, as to have already ordered the head of the frigate to be turned in its former course, when, struck by the unearthly cry of the last tones uttered by his commander, he bent his head, and beheld the venerable seaman driven through the air, his hat still waving, his gray hair floating in the wind, and his eye set in the wild look of death.

"Great God!" exclaimed the young man, rushing to the side of the ship, where he was just in time to see the lifeless body disappear in the waters that were dyed in its blood; "he has been struck by a shot! Lower away the boat, lower away the jolly-boat, the barge, the tiger, the—"

" 'Tis useless," interrupted the calm, deep voice of the pilot; "he has met a warrior's end, and he sleeps in a sailor's grave! The ship is getting before the wind again, and the enemy is keeping his vessel away."

The youthful lieutenant was recalled by these words to his duty, and reluctantly turned his eyes away from the bloody spot on the waters, which the busy frigate had already passed, to resume the command of the vessel with a forced composure.

"He has cut some of our running gear," said the master, whose eye had never ceased to dwell on the spars and rigging of the ship: "and there's a splinter out of the maintopmast that is big enough for a fid! He has let daylight through some of our canvas too; but, taking it by-and-large, the squall has gone over, and little harm done. Didn't I hear something said of Captain Munson getting jammed by a shot?"

"He is killed!" said Griffith, speaking in a voice that was yet husky with horror—"he is dead, sir, and carried overboard; there is more need that we forget not ourselves in this crisis."

"Dead!" said Boltrope, suspending the operation of his active jaws for a moment, in surprise; "and buried in a wet jacket! Well, it is lucky 'tis no worse; for damme if I did not think every stick in the ship would have been cut out of her!"

With this consolatory remark on his lips, the master walked slowly forward, continuing his orders to repair the damages with a singleness of purpose that rendered him, however uncouth as a friend, an invaluable man in his station.

Griffith had not yet brought his mind to the calmness that was so essential to discharge the duties which had thus suddenly and awfully devolved on him, when his elbow was slightly touched by the pilot, who had drawn closer to his side.

"The enemy appears satisfied with the experiment," said the stranger; "and as we work the quicker of the two, he loses too much ground to repeat it, if he be a true seaman."

"And yet, as he finds we leave him so fast," returned Griffith, "he must see that all his hopes rest in cutting us up aloft. I dread that he will come by the wind again, and lay us under his broadside; we should need a quarter of an hour to run without his range, if he were anchored!"

"He plays a sure game—see you not that the vessel we made in the eastern board shows the hull of a frigate? 'Tis past a doubt that they are of one squadron, and that the expresses have sent them in our wake. The English admiral has spread a broad clew, Mr. Griffith; and, as he gathers in his ships, he sees that his game has been successful."

The faculties of Griffith had been too much occupied with the hurry of the chase to look at the ocean; but startled at the information of the pilot, who spoke coolly, though like a man sensible of the existence of approaching danger, he took the glass from the other, and with his own eye examined the different vessels in sight. It is certain that the experienced officer, whose flag was flying above the light sails of the three-decker, saw the critical situation of the chase, and reasoned much in the same manner as the pilot, or the fearful expedient apprehended by Griffith would have been adopted. Prudence, however, dictated that he should prevent his enemy from escaping by pressing so closely on his rear as to render it impossible for the American to haul across his bows and run into the open sea between his own vessel and the nearest frigate of his squadron. The unpractised reader will be able to comprehend the case better by accompanying the understanding eye of Griffith as it glanced from point to point, following the whole horizon. To the west lay the land, along which the Alacrity was urging her way industriously, with the double purpose of keeping her consort abeam, and of avoiding a dangerous proximity to their powerful enemy. To the east, bearing off the starboard bow of the American frigate, was the vessel first seen, and which now began to exhibit the hostile appearance of a ship-of-war, steering in a line converging toward themselves, and rapidly drawing nigher; while far in the northeast was a vessel as yet faintly discerned, whose evolutions could not be mistaken by one who understood the movements of nautical warfare.

"We are hemmed in effectually," said Griffith dropping the glass from his eye; "and I know not but our wisest course would be to haul in to the land, and, cutting everything light adrift, endeavor to cross the broadside of the flagship."

"Provided she left a rag of canvas to do it with!" returned the pilot. "Sir, 'tis an idle hope! She would strip your ship, in ten minutes, to her plank-shears. Had it not been for a lucky wave on which so many of her shot struck and glanced upward, we should have nothing to boast of left from the fire she has already given; we must stand on, and drop the three-decker as far as possible."

"But the frigates?" said Griffith, "what are we to do with the frigates?"

"Fight them!" returned the pilot, in a low, determined voice; "fight them! Young man, I have borne the stars and stripes aloft in greater straits than this, and even with honor! Think not that my fortune will desert me now."

"We shall have an hour of desperate battle!"

"On that we may calculate; but I have lived through whole days of blood-shed! You seem not one to quail at the sight of an enemy."

"Let me proclaim your name to the men!" said Griffith; " 'twill quicken their blood, and at such a moment be a host in itself."

"They want it not," returned the pilot, checking the hasty zeal of the other with his hand. "I would be unnoticed, unless I am known as becomes me. I will share your danger, but would not rob you of a tittle of your glory. Should we come to a grapple," he continued, while a smile of conscious pride gleamed across his face, "I will give forth the word as a war-cry, and, believe me, these English will quail before it!"

Griffith submitted to the stranger's will; and, after they had deliberated fur-ther on the nature of their evolutions, he gave his attention again to the man-agement of the vessel. The first object which met his eye on turning from the pilot was Colonel Howard, pacing the quarter-deck with a determined brow and a haughty mien, as if already in the enjoyment of that triumph which now seemed certain.

"I fear, sir," said the young man, approaching him with respect, "that you will soon find the deck unpleasant and dangerous. Your wards are—"

"Mention not the unworthy term!" interrupted the colonel. "What greater pleasure can there be than to inhale the odor of loyalty that is wafted from yonder floating tower of the king? And danger! you know but little of old George Howard, young man, if you think he would for thousands miss seeing that symbol of rebellion levelled before the flag of his majesty!"

"If that be your wish, Colonel Howard," returned Griffith, biting his lip as he looked around at the wondering seamen who were listeners, "you will wait in vain; but I pledge you my word that, when that time arrives, you shall be advised, and that your own hands shall do the ignoble deed."

"Edward Griffith, why not this moment? This is your moment of probation —submit to the clemency of the crown, and yield your crew to the royal mercy! In such a case I would remember the child of my brother Harry's friend; and, believe me, my name is known to the ministry. And you, misguided and ignorant abettors of rebellion! cast aside your useless weapons, or prepare to meet the vengeance of yonder powerful and victorious servant of your prince."

"Fall back! back with ye, fellows!" cried Griffith, fiercely, to the men who were gathering around the colonel, with looks of sullen vengeance. "If a man of you dare approach him, he shall be cast into the sea!"

The sailors retreated at the order of their commander; but the elated veteran had continued to pace the deck for many minutes before stronger interests diverted the angry glances of the seamen to other objects.

Notwithstanding the ship-of-the-line was slowly sinking beneath the distant waves, and in less than an hour from the time she had fired the broadside no more than one of her three tiers of guns was visible from the deck of the frigate, she yet presented an irresistible obstacle against retreat to the south. On the other hand, the ship first seen drew so nigh as to render the glass no longer necessary in watching her movements. She proved to be a frigate, though one so materially lighter than the American, as to have rendered her conquest easy, had not her two consorts continued to press on for the scene of battle with such rapidity. During the chase the scene had shifted from the point opposite to St. Ruth to the verge of those shoals where our tale commenced. As they approached the latter, the smallest of the English ships drew so nigh as to render the combat unavoidable. Griffith and his crew had not been idle in the intermediate time, but all the usual preparations against the casualties of a sea-fight had been duly made, when the drum once more called the men to their quarters, and the ship was deliberately stripped of her unnecessary sails, like a prize-fighter about to enter the arena, casting aside the encumbrances of dress. At the instant she gave the intimation of her intention to abandon flight, and trust the issue to the combat, the nearest English frigate also took in her light canvas in token of her acceptance of the challenge.

"He is but a little fellow," said Griffith to the pilot, who hovered at his elbow with a sort of fatherly interest in the other's conduct of the battle, "though he carries a stout heart."

"We must crush him at a blow," returned the stranger; "not a shot must be delivered until our yards are locking."

"I see him training his twelves upon us already; we may soon expect his fire."

"After standing the brunt of a ninety-gun ship," observed the collected pilot, "we shall not shrink from the broadside of a two-and-thirty."

"Stand to your guns, men!" cried Griffith, through his trumpet—"not a shot to be fired without the order."

This caution, so necessary to check the ardor of the seamen, was hardly uttered, before their enemy became wrapped in sheets of fire and volumes of smoke, as gun after gun hurled its iron missiles at their vessel in quick succession. Ten minutes might have passed, the two vessels sheering close to each other every foot they advanced, during which time the crew of the American were compelled, by their commander, to suffer the fire of their adversary, without returning a shot. This short period, which seemed an age to the seamen, was distinguished in their vessel by deep silence. Even the wounded and dying, who fell in every part of the ship, stifled their groans, under the influence of the severe discipline, which gave a character to every man and each movement of the vessel; and those officers who were required to speak, were heard only in the lowest tones of resolute preparation. At length the ship slowly entered the skirts of the smoke that enveloped their enemy; and Griffith heard the man who stood at his side whisper the word:

"Now!"

"Let them have it!" cried Griffith, in a voice that was heard in the remotest parts of the ship.

The shout that burst from the seamen appeared to lift the decks of the vessel, and the affrighted frigate trembled like an aspen with the recoil of her own massive artillery, that shot forth a single sheet of flame, the sailors having disregarded, in their impatience, the usual order of firing. The effect of the broadside on the enemy was still more dreadful; for a death-like silence succeeded to the roar of the guns, which was only broken by the shrieks and execrations that burst from her, like the moanings of the damned. During the few moments in which the Americans were again loading their cannon, and the English were recovering from their confusion, the vessel of the former moved slowly past her antagonist, and was already doubling across her bows, when the latter was suddenly, and, considering the inequality of their forces, it may be added desperately, headed into her enemy. The two frigates grappled. The sudden and furious charge made by the Englishman, as he threw his masses of daring seamen along his bowsprit and out of his channels, had nearly taken Griffith by surprise; but Manual, who had delivered his first fire with the broadside, now did good service by ordering his men to beat back the intruders by a steady and continued discharge. Even the wary pilot lost sight of their other foes in the high daring of that moment, and smiles of stern pleasure were exchanged between him and Griffith, as both comprehended at a glance their advantages.

"Lash his bowsprit to our mizzen-mast," shouted the lieutenant, "and we will sweep his decks as he lies!" Twenty men sprang eagerly forward to execute the order, among the foremost of whom were Boltrope and the stranger.

"Ay, now he's our own!" cried the busy master, "and we will take an owner's liberties with him, and break him up—for, by the Eternal—"

"Peace, rude man," said the pilot, in a voice of solemn remonstrance; "at the next instant you may face your God; mock not His awful name!"

The master found time, before he threw himself from the spar on the deck of the frigate again, to cast a look of amazement at his companion, who, with a steady mien, but with an eye that lighted with a warrior's ardor, viewed the battle that raged around him like one who marked its progress to control the result.

The sight of the Englishmen rushing onward with shouts and bitter menaces warmed the blood of Colonel Howard, who pressed to the side of the frigate, and encouraged his friends, by his gestures and voice, to come on.

"Away with ye, old croaker!" cried the master, seizing him by the collar; "away with ye to the hold, or I'll order you fired from a gun!"

"Down with your arms, rebellious dog!" shouted the colonel, carried beyond himself by the ardor of the fray; "down to the dust, and implore the mercy of your injured prince!"

Invigorated by a momentary glow, the veteran grappled with his brawny antagonist; but the issue of the short struggle was yet suspended, when the English, driven back by the fire of the marines, and the menacing front that Griffith with his boarders presented, retreated to the forecastle of their own ship, and attempted to return the deadly blows they were receiving, in their hull, from the cannon that Barnstable directed. A solitary gun was all they could bring to bear on the Americans; but this, loaded with canister, was fired so near as to send its glaring flame into the very faces of their enemies. The struggling colonel, who was already sinking beneath the arm of his foe, felt the rough grasp loosen from his throat at the flash, and the two combatants sunk powerless on their knees facing each other.

"How now, brother?" exclaimed Boltrope, with a smile of grim fierceness; "some of that grist is gone to your mill, ha!"

No answer could, however, be given before the yielding forms of both fell to the deck, where they lay helpless amid the din of the battle and the wild confusion of the eager combatants.

Notwithstanding the furious struggle they witnessed, the elements did not cease their functions; and, urged by the breeze, and lifted irresistibly on a wave, the American ship was forced through the water still farther across the bows of her enemy. The idle fastenings of hemp and iron were snapped asunder like strings of tow, and Griffith saw his own ship borne away from the Englishman at the instant that the bowsprit of the latter was torn from its lashings, and tumbled into the sea, followed by spar after spar, until nothing of all her proud tackling was remaining but the few parted and useless ropes that were left dangling along the stumps of her lower masts. As his own stately vessel moved from the confusion she had caused, and left the dense cloud of smoke in which her helpless antagonist lay, the eye of the young man glanced anxiously toward the horizon, where he now remembered he had more foes to contend against.

"We have shaken off the thirty-two most happily!" he said to the pilot, who followed his motions with singular interest; "but here is another fellow sheering in for us, who shows as many ports as ourselves, and who appears inclined for a closer interview; besides, the hull of the ninety is rising again, and I fear she will be down but too soon!"

"We must keep the use of our braces and sails," returned the pilot, "and on no account close with the other frigate; we must play a double game, sir, and fight this new adversary with our heels as well as with our guns."

" 'Tis time then that we were busy, for he is shortening sail, and, as he nears so fast, we may expect to hear from him every minute; what do you propose, sir?"

"Let him gather in his canvas," returned the pilot; "and when he thinks himself snug, we can throw out a hundred men at once upon our yards, and spread everything alow and aloft; we may draw ahead of him by surprise; if we can once get him in our wake I have no fears of dropping them all."

"A stern chase is a long chase," cried Griffith, "and the thing may do! Clear up the decks here, and carry down the wounded; and as we have our hands full, the poor fellows who have done with us must go overboard at once."

This melancholy duty was instantly attended to, while the young seaman who commanded the frigate returned to his duty with the absorbed air of one who felt its high responsibility. These occupations, however, did not prevent his hearing the sounds of Barnstable's voice calling eagerly to young Merry. Bending his head toward the sound, Griffith beheld his friend, looking anxiously up the main hatch, with a face grimed with smoke, his coat off, and his shirt bespattered with human blood. "Tell me, boy," he said, "is Mr. Griffith untouched? They say that a shot came in upon the quarter-deck that tripped up the heels of half a dozen."

Before even Merry could answer, the eyes of Barnstable, which even while he spoke were scanning the state of the vessel's rigging, encountered the kind looks of Griffith, and from that moment perfect harmony was restored between the friends.

"Ah! you are there, Griff, and with a whole skin, I see," cried Barnstable, smiling with pleasure; "they have passed poor Boltrope down into one of his own store-rooms! If that fellow's bowsprit had held on ten minutes longer, what a mark I should have made on his face and eyes!"

" 'Tis perhaps best as it is," returned Griffith; "but what have you done with those whom we are most bound to protect?"

Barnstable made a significant gesture toward the depths of the vessel as he answered:

"On the cables; safe as wood, iron, and water, can keep them—though Katherine has had her head up three times to—"

A summons from the pilot drew Griffith away, and the young officers were compelled to forget their individual feelings in the pressing duties of their stations.

The ship which the American frigate had now to oppose was a vessel of near her own size and equipage; and, when Griffith looked at her again, he perceived that she had made her preparations to assert her equality in manful fight. Her sails had been gradually reduced to the usual quantity, and, by certain movements on her decks, the lieutenant and his constant attendant, the pilot, well understood that she only wanted to lessen her distance a few hundred yards to begin the action.

"Now spread everything," whispered the stranger.

Griffith applied the trumpet to his mouth and shouted in a voice that was carried even to his enemy: "Let fall—out with your booms—sheet home—hoist away of everything!"

The inspiring cry was answered by a universal bustle; fifty men flew out on the dizzy heights of the different spars, while broad sheets of canvas rose as suddenly along the masts as if some mighty bird were spreading its wings. The Englishman instantly perceived his mistake and he answered the artifice by a roar of artillery. Griffith watched the effect of the broadside with an absorbing interest, as the shot whistled above his head; but when he perceived his masts untouched, and the few unimportant ropes only that were cut, he replied to the uproar with a burst of pleasure. A few men were, however, seen clinging with wild frenzy to the cordage, dropping from rope to rope like wounded birds fluttering through a tree, until they fell heavily into the ocean, the sullen ship sweeping by them in cold indifference. At the next instant the spars and masts of their enemy exhibited a display of men similar to their own, when Griffith again placed the trumpet to his mouth and shouted aloud:

"Give it to them; drive them from their yards, boys; scatter them with your grape—unreeve their rigging!"

The crew of the American wanted but little encouragement to enter on this experiment with hearty good-will, and the close of his cheering words were uttered amid the deafening roar of his own cannon. The pilot had, however, mistaken the skill and readiness of their foe; for, notwithstanding the disadvantageous circumstances under which the Englishman increased his sail, the duty was steadily and dexterously performed.

The two ships were now running rapidly on parallel lines, hurling at each other their instruments of destruction with furious industry, and with severe and certain loss to both, though with no manifest advantage in favor of either. Both Griffith and the pilot witnessed with deep concern this unexpected defeat of their hopes; for they could not conceal from themselves, that each moment lessened their velocity through the water, as the shot of their enemy stripped the canvas from the yards, or dashed aside the lighter spars in their terrible progress.

"We find our equal here!" said Griffith to the stranger. "The ninety is heaving up again like a mountain, and, if we continue to shorten sail at this rate, she will soon be down upon us!"

"You say true, sir," returned the pilot, musing, "the man shows judgment as well as spirit; but—"

He was interrupted by Merry, who rushed from the forward part of the vessel, his whole face betokening the eagerness of his spirit and the importance of his intelligence:

"The breakers!" he cried, when nigh enough to be heard amid the din; "we are running dead on a ripple, and the sea is white not two hundred yards ahead."

The pilot jumped on a gun, and, bending to catch a glimpse through the smoke, he shouted, in those clear, piercing tones that could be heard among the roaring of the cannon—"Port, your helm! we are on the Devil's Grip! pass up the trumpet, sir; port your helm, fellow; give it them, boys—give it to the proud English dogs!" Griffith unhesitating relinquished the symbol of his rank, fastening his own firm look on the calm but quick eye of the pilot, and gathering assurance from the high confidence he read in the countenance of the stranger. The seamen were too busy with their cannon and their rigging to regard their new danger, and the frigate entered one of the dangerous passes of the shoals in the heat of a severely-contested battle. The wondering looks of a few of the older sailors glanced at the sheets of foam that flew by them, in doubt whether the wild gambols of the waves were occasioned by the shot of the enemy, when suddenly the noise of the cannon was succeeded by the sullen wash of the disturbed element, and presently the vessel glided out of her smoky shroud, and was boldly steering in the centre of the narrow passages. For ten breathless minutes longer the pilot continued to hold an uninterrupted sway, during which the vessel ran swiftly by ripples and breakers, by streaks of foam and darker passages of deep water, when he threw down his trumpet, and exclaimed:

"What threatened to our destruction has proved our salvation! Keep yonder hill crowned with wood, one point open from the church-tower at its base, and steer east by north; you will run through these shoals on that course in an hour, and by so doing you will gain five leagues of your enemy, who will have to double their tail."

The moment he stepped from the gun, the pilot lost the air of authority that had so singularly distinguished his animated form, and even the close interest he had manifested in the incidents of the day became lost in the cold, settled reserve he had affected during his intercourse with his present associates. Every officer in the ship, after the breathless suspense of uncertainty had passed, rushed to those places where a view might be taken of their enemies. The ninety was still steering boldly onward, and had already approached the two-and-thirty, which lay a helpless wreck, rolling on the unruly seas that were rudely tossing her on their wanton billows. The frigate last engaged was running along the edge of the ripple, with her torn sails flying loosely in the air, her ragged spars tottering in the breeze, and everything above her hull exhibiting the confusion of a sudden and unlooked-for check to her progress. The exulting taunts and mirthful congratulations of the seamen, as they gazed at the English ships, were, however, soon forgotten in the attention that was required to their own vessel. The drums beat the retreat, the guns were lashed, the wounded again removed, and every individual able to keep the deck was required to lend his assistance in repairing the damages of the frigate and securing her masts.

The promised hour carried the ship safely through all the dangers, which were much lessened by daylight; and, by the time the sun had begun to fall over the land, Griffith, who had not quitted the deck during the day, beheld his vessel once more cleared of the confusion of the chase and battle, and ready to meet another foe. At this period he was summoned to the cabin, at the request of the ship's chaplain. Delivering the charge of the frigate to Barnstable, who had been his active assistant, no less in their subsequent labors than in the combat, he hastily divested himself of the vestiges of the fight, and proceeded to obey the repeated and earnest call.

34

Whither, midst falling dew,
While glow the heavens with the last steps
of day,
Far, through their rosy depths, dost thou
pursue
Thy solitary way?

BRYANT

WHEN the young seaman who now commanded the frigate descended from the quarter-deck in compliance with the oft-repeated summons, he found the vessel restored to the same neatness as if nothing had occurred to disturb its order. The gun-deck has been cleansed of its horrid stains, and the smoke of the fight had long since ascended through the hatches and mingled with the clouds that flitted above the ship. As he walked along the silent batteries, even the urgency of his visit could not prevent him from glancing his eyes toward the splintered sides, those terrible vestiges by which the paths of the shot of their enemy might be traced; and by the time he tapped lightly at the door of the cabin, his quick look had embraced every material injury the vessel had sustained in her principal points of defence. The door was opened by the surgeon of the frigate, who, as he stepped aside to permit Griffith to enter, shook his head with the air of meaning which, in one of his profession, is understood to imply the abandonment of all hopes, and then immediately quitted the apartment, in order to attend to those who might profit by his services.

The reader is not to imagine that Griffith had lost sight of Cecilia and her cousin during the occurrences of that eventful day: on the contrary, his troubled fancy had presented her terror and distress, even in the hottest moments of the fight; and the instant that the crew were called from their guns he had issued an order to replace the bulkheads of the cabin, and to arrange its furniture for their accommodation, though the higher and imperious duties of his station had precluded his attending to their comfort in person. He expected, therefore, to find the order of the rooms restored; but he was by no means prepared to encounter the scene he was now to witness.

Between two of the sullen cannon, which gave such an air of singular wildness to the real comfort of the cabin, was placed a large couch, on which the colonel was lying, evidently near his end. Cecilia was weeping by his side, her dark ringlets falling in unheeded confusion around her pale features, and sweeping in their rich exuberance the deck on which she kneeled. Katherine leaned tenderly over the form of the dying veteran, while her dark, tearful eyes seemed to express self-accusation blended with deep commiseration. A few attendants of both sexes surrounded the solemn scene, all of whom appeared to be under the influence of the hopeless intelligence which the medical officer had but that moment communicated. The servants of the ship had replaced the furniture with a care that mocked the dreadful struggle that so recently disfigured the warlike apartment, and the stout, square frame of Boltrope occupied the opposite settee, his head resting on the lap of the captain's steward, and his hand gently held in the grasp of his friend the chaplain. Griffith had heard of the wound of his master, but his own eyes now conveyed the first intelligence of the situation of Colonel Howard. When the shock of this sudden discovery had a little subsided, the young man approached the couch of the latter, and attempted to express his regret and pity, in a voice that afforded an assurance of his sincerity.

"Say no more, Edward Griffith," interrupted the colonel, waving his hand feebly for silence; "it seemeth to be the will of God that this rebellion should triumph, and it is not for vain man to impeach the acts of Omnipotence. To my erring faculties, it wears an appearance of mystery, but doubtless it is to answer the purpose of His own inscrutable providence. I have sent for you, Edward, on business that I would fain see accomplished before I die, that it may not be said that old George Howard neglected his duty, even in his last moments. You see this weeping child at my side; tell me, young man, do you love the maiden?"

"Am I to be asked such a question?" exclaimed Griffith.

"And will you cherish her—will you supply to her the places of father and mother—will you become the fond guardian of her innocence and weakness?"

Griffith could give no other answer than a fervent pressure of the hand he had clasped.

"I believe you," continued the dying man; "for however he may have forgotten to inculcate his own loyalty, worthy Hugh Griffith could never neglect to make his son a man of honor. I had weak and perhaps evil wishes in behalf of my late unfortunate kinsman, Mr. Christopher Dillon; but they have told me that he was false to his faith. If this be true, I would refuse him the hand of the girl, though he claimed the fealty of the British realms. But he has passed away, and I am about to follow him into a world where we shall find but one Lord to serve; and it may have been better for us both had we more remembered our duty to Him, while serving the princes of the earth. One thing further—know you this officer of your Congress well—this Mr. Barnstable?"

"I have sailed with him for years," returned Griffith, "and can answer for him as myself."

The veteran made an effort to rise, which in part succeeded, and he fastened on the youth a look of keen scrutiny, that gave to his pallid features an expression of solemn meaning, as he continued:

"Speak not now, sir, as the companion of his idle pleasures, and as the unthinking associate commends his fellow, but remember that your opinion is given to a dying man who leans on your judgment for advice. The daughter of John Plowden is a trust not to be neglected, nor will my death prove easy, if a doubt of her being worthily bestowed shall remain."

"He is a gentleman," returned Griffith, "and one whose heart is not less kind than gallant—he loves your ward, and, great as may be her merit, he is deserving of it all. Like myself, he has also loved the land that gave him birth, before the land of his ancestors, but—"

"That is now forgotten," interrupted the colonel; "after what I have this day witnessed, I am forced to believe that it is the pleasure of Heaven that you are to prevail! But, sir, a disobedient inferior will be apt to make an unreasonable commander. The recent contention between you—"

"Remember it not, dear sir," exclaimed Griffith, with generous zeal—" 'twas unkindly provoked, and it is already forgotten and pardoned. He has sustained me nobly throughout the day, and my life on it, that he knows how to treat a woman as a brave man should!"

"Then am I content!" said the veteran, sinking back on the couch; "let him be summoned."

The whispering message which Griffith gave, requesting Mr. Barnstable to enter the cabin, was quickly conveyed, and he had appeared before his friend deemed it discreet to disturb the reflections of the veteran by again addressing him. When the entrance of the young sailor was announced, the colonel again roused himself, and addressed his wondering listener, though in a manner much less confiding and familiar than that which he had adopted toward Griffith.

"The declarations you made last night relevant to my ward, the daughter of the late Captain John Plowden, sir, have left me nothing to learn on the subject of your wishes. Here, then, gentlemen, you both obtain the reward of your attention! Let the reverend divine hear you pronounce the marriage vows, while I have strength to listen, that I may be a witness against ye, in Heaven, should ye forget their tenor!"

"Not now, not now," murmured Cecilia; "oh, ask it not now, my uncle!"

Katherine spoke not; but deeply touched by the tender interest her guardian manifested in her welfare, she bowed her face to her bosom, in subdued feeling, and suffered the tears that had been suffusing her eyes to roll down her cheeks in large drops, till they bathed the deck.

"Yes, now, my love," continued the colonel, "or I fail in my duty. I go shortly to stand face to face with your parents, my children; for the man who, dying, expects not to meet worthy Hugh Griffith and honest Jack Plowden in Heaven, can have no clear view of the rewards that belong to lives of faithful service to the country, or of gallant loyalty to the king! I trust no one can justly say that I ever forgot the delicacy due to your gentle sex; but it is no moment for idle ceremony when time is shortening into minutes, and heavy duties remain to be discharged. I could not die in peace, children, were I to leave you here in the wide ocean, I had almost said in the wide world, without that protection which becomes your tender years and still more tender characters. If it has pleased God to remove your guardian, let his place be supplied by those he wills to succeed him!"

Cecilia no longer hesitated, but she arose slowly from her knees, and offered her hand to Griffith with an air of forced resignation. Katherine submitted to be led by Barnstable to her side; and the chaplain, who had been an affected listener to the dialogue, in obedience to an expressive signal from the eye of Griffith, opened the prayer-book from which he had been gleaning consolation for the dying master, and commenced reading, in trembling tones, the marriage-service. The vows were pronounced by the weeping brides in voices more distinct and audible than if they had been uttered amid the gay crowds that usually throng a bridal; for, though they were the irreclaimable words that bound them forever to the men whose power over their feelings they thus proclaimed to the world, the reserve of maiden diffidence was lost in one engrossing emotion of solemnity, created by the awful presence in which they stood. When the benediction was pronounced, the head of Cecilia dropped on the shoulder of her husband, where she wept violently for a moment, and then, resuming her place at the couch, she once more knelt at the side of her uncle. Katherine received the warm kiss of Barnstable passively, and returned to the spot whence she had been led.

Colonel Howard succeeded in raising his person to witness the ceremony, and had answered to each prayer with a fervent "Amen." He fell back with the last words; and a look of satisfaction shone in his aged and pallid features that declared the interest he had taken in the scene.

"I thank you, my children," he at length uttered, "I thank you; for I know how much you have sacrificed to my wishes.—You will find all my papers relative to the estates of my wards, gentlemen, in the hands of my banker in London; and you will also find there my will, Edward, by which you will learn that Cicely has not come to your arms an unportioned bride. What my wards are in persons and manners your eyes can witness, and I trust the vouchers in London will show that I have not been an unfaithful steward to their pecuniary affairs!"

"Name it not—say no more, or you will break my heart," cried Katherine, sobbing aloud, in the violence of her remorse at having ever pained so true a friend. "Oh! talk of yourself, think of yourself; we are unworthy—at least I am unworthy of another thought!"

The dying man extended a hand to her in kindness, and continued, though his voice grew feebler as he spoke:

"Then to turn to myself—I would wish to lie, like my ancestors, in the bosom of the earth—and in consecrated ground."

"It shall be done," whispered Griffith; "I will see it done myself."

"I thank thee, my son," said the veteran; "for such thou art to me in being the husband of Cicely—you will find, in my will, that I have liberated and provided for all my slaves—except those ungrateful scoundrels who deserted their master—they have seized their own freedom, and they need not be indebted to me for the same. There is, Edward, also an unworthy legacy to the king; his majesty will deign to receive it from an old and faithful servant, and you will not miss the trifling gift." A long pause followed, as if he had been summing up the account of his earthly duties, and found them duly balanced, when he added: "Kiss me, Cicely—and you, Katherine—I find you have the genuine feelings of honest Jack, your father. My eyes grow dim—which is the hand of Griffith? Young gentleman, I have given you all that a fond old man had to bestow—deal tenderly with the precious child—we have not properly understood each other—I had mistaken both you and Mr. Christopher Dillon, I believe; perhaps I may also have mistaken my duty to America—but I was too old to change my politics or my religion—I—I—I loved the king—God bless him—"

His words became fainter and fainter as he proceeded; and the breath deserted his body with his benediction on his livid lips, which the proudest monarch might covet from so honest a man.

The body was instantly borne into a state-room by the attendants; and Griffith and Barnstable supported their brides into the after-cabin, where they left them seated on the sofa that lined the stern of the ship, weeping bitterly, in each other's arms.

No part of the preceding scene had been unobserved by Boltrope, whose small, hard eyes were observed by the young men to twinkle, when they returned into the state apartment; and they approached their wounded comrade to apologize for the seeming neglect that their conduct had displayed.

"I heard you were hurt, Boltrope," said Griffith, taking him kindly by the hand; "but, as I know you are not unused to being marked by shot, I trust we shall soon see you again on deck."

"Ay, ay," returned the master, "you'll want no spyglasses to see the old hulk as you launch it into the sea. I have had shot, as you say, before now to tear my running gear, and even to knock a splinter out of some of my timbers; but this fellow has found his way into my bread-room; and the cruise of life is up!"

"Sure the case is not so bad, honest David," said Barnstable; "you have kept afloat, to my knowledge, with a bigger hole in your skin than this unlucky hit has made!"

"Ay, ay," returned the master, "that was in my upper works, where the doctor could get at it with a plug; but this chap has knocked away the shifting-boards, and I feel as if the whole cargo was broken up. You may say that Tourniquet rates me all the same as a dead man; for, after looking at the shot-hole, he has turned me over to the parson here, like a piece of old junk which is only fit to be worked up into something new. Captain Munson had a lucky time of it! I think you said, Mr. Griffith, that the old gentleman was launched overboard with everything standing, and that Death made but one rap at his door, before he took his leave!"

"His end was indeed sudden!" returned Griffith; "but it is what we seamen must expect."

"And for which there is so much the more occasion to be prepared," the chaplain ventured to add, in a low, humble, and, perhaps, a timid voice.

The sailing-master looked keenly from one to the other as they spoke; and, after a short pause, he continued, with an air of great submission:

" 'Twas his luck; and I suppose it is sinful to begrudge a man his lawful luck. As for being prepared, parson, that is your business, and not mine; therefore, as there is but little time to spare, why, the sooner you set about it the better; and, to save unnecessary trouble, I may as well tell you not to strive to make too much of me; for, I must own it to my shame, I never took learning kindly. If you can fit me for some middling berth in the other world, like the one I hold in this ship, it will suit me as well, and perhaps be easier to all hands of us."

If there was a shade of displeasure blended with the surprise that crossed the features of the divine at this extraordinary limitation of his duties, it entirely disappeared when he considered more closely the perfect expression of simplicity with which the dying master uttered his wishes. After a long and melancholy pause, which neither Griffith nor his friend felt any inclination to interrupt, the chaplain replied:

"It is not the province of man to determine on the decrees of the merciful dispensations of the Deity; and nothing that I can do, Mr. Boltrope, will have any weight in making up the mighty and irrevocable decree. What I said to you last night, in our conversation on this very subject, must still be fresh in your memory, and there is no good reason why I should hold different language to you now."

"I can't say that I logged all that passed," returned the master; "and that which I do recollect fell chiefly from myself, for the plain reason that a man remembers his own better than his neighbor's ideas.—And this puts me in mind, Mr. Griffith, to tell you that one of the forty-two's from the three-decker travelled across the forecastle, and cut the best bower within a fathom of the clinch as handily as an old woman would clip her rotten yarn with a pair of tailor's shears!—If you will be so good as to order one of my mates to shift the cable end-for-end, and make a new bend of it, I'll do as much for you another time."

"Mention it not," said Griffith; "rest assured that everything shall be done for the security of the ship in your department—I will superintend the whole duty in person; and I would have you release your mind from all anxiety on the subject, to attend to your more important interests elsewhere."

"Why," returned Boltrope, with a little show of pertinacity, "I have an opinion that the cleaner a man takes his hands into the other world, of the matters of duty in this, the better he will be fitted to handle anything new. Now, the parson, here, undertook to lay down the doctrine last night that it was no matter how well or how ill a man behaved himself, so that he squared his conscience by the lifts and braces of faith; which I take to be a doctrine that is not to be preached on shipboard; for it would play the devil with the best ship's company that was ever mustered."

"Oh! no—no—dear Mr. Boltrope, you mistook me and my doctrine altogether!" exclaimed the chaplain; "at least you mistook—"

"Perhaps, sir," interrupted Griffith, gently, "our honest friend will not be more fortunate now. Is there nothing earthly that hangs upon your mind, Boltrope; no wish to be remembered to any one, nor any bequest to make of your property?"

"He has a mother, I know," said Barnstable, in a low voice; "he often spoke of her to me in the night-watches; I think she must be still living."

The master, who distinctly heard his young shipmates, continued for more than a minute rolling the tobacco, which he still retained, from one side of his mouth to the other, with an industry that denoted singular agitation for the man; and raising one of his broad hands, with the other he picked the worn skin from fingers which were already losing their brownish-yellow hue in the fading color of death, before he answered:

"Why, yes, the old woman still keeps her grip upon life, which is more than can be said of her son David. The old man was lost the time the Susan and Dorothy was wrecked on the back of Cape Cod; you remember it, Mr. Barnstable? you were then a lad, sailing on whaling-voyages, from the island; well, ever since that gale, I've endeavored to make smooth water for the old woman myself, though she has had but a rough passage of it, at the best; the voyage of life, with her, having been pretty much crossed by rugged weather and short stores."

"And you would have us carry some message to her?" said Griffith, kindly.

"Why, as to messages," continued the master, whose voice was rapidly growing more husky and broken, "there never has been many compliments—passed between us, for the reason—that she is not more used to receive them—than I am to make them. But if any of you will overhaul—the purser's books, and see what there is standing there—to my side of the leaf—and take a little pains to get it to the old woman—you will find her moored in the lee side of a house—ay, here it is, No. 10 Cornhill, Boston. I took care—to get her a good warm berth, seeing that a woman of eighty wants a snug anchorage—at her time of life, if ever."

"I will do it myself, David," cried Barnstable, struggling to conceal his emotion; "I will call on her the instant we let go our anchor in Boston harbor; and, as your credit can't be large, I will divide my own purse with her!"

The sailing-master was powerfully affected by this kind offer; the muscles of his hard, weather-beaten face working convulsively, and it was a moment before he could trust his voice in reply.

"I know you would, Dicky, I know you would," he at length uttered, grasping the hand of Barnstable with a portion of his former strength; "I know you would give the old woman one of your own limbs, if it would do a service—to the mother of a messmate—which it would not—seeing that I am not the son of a—cannibal; but you are out of your father's books, and it's too often shoal water in your pockets to help any one—more especially since you have just been spliced to a pretty young body—that will want all your spare coppers."

"But I am master of my own fortune," said Griffith, "and am rich."

"Ay, ay, I have heard it said you could build a frigate and set her afloat all a-taunt-o without thrusting your hand—into any man's purse—but your own!"

"And I pledge you the honor of a naval officer," continued the young sailor, "that she shall want for nothing; not even the care and tenderness of a dutiful son."

Boltrope appeared to be choking; he made an attempt to raise his exhausted frame on the couch; but fell back exhausted and dying, perhaps a little prematurely, through the powerful and unusual emotions that were struggling for utterance. "God forgive me my misdeeds!" he at length said, "and chiefly for ever speaking a word against your discipline; remember the best bower—and look to the slings of the lower yards—and—and—he'll do it, Dicky, he'll do it, Dicky, he'll do it! I'm casting off—the fasts—of life—and so God bless ye all—and give ye good weather—going large—or on a bowline!"

The tongue of the master failed him, but a look of heartfelt satisfaction gleamed across his rough visage, as its muscles suddenly contracted, when the faded lineaments slowly settled into the appalling stiffness of death.

Griffith directed the body to be removed to the apartment of the master, and proceeded with a heavy heart to the upper deck. The Alacrity had been unnoticed during the arduous chase of the frigate, and, favored by daylight, and her light draught of water, she had easily effected her escape also among the mazes of the shoals. She was called down to her consort by signal, and received the necessary instructions how to steer during the approaching night. The British ships were now only to be faintly discovered, like small white specks on the dark sea; and, as it was known that a broad barrier of shallow water lay between them, the Americans no longer regarded their presence as at all dangerous.

When the necessary order had been given, and the vessels were fully prepared, they were once more brought up to the wind, and their heads pointed
in the direction of the coast of Holland. The wind, which freshened toward
the decline of day, hauled round with the sun; and when that luminary retreated from the eye, so rapid had been the progress of the mariners, it seemed
to sink in the bosom of the ocean, the land having long before settled into its
watery bed. All night the frigate continued to dash through the seas with a
sort of sullen silence, that was soothing to the melancholy of Cecilia and
Katherine, neither of whom closed an eye during that gloomy period. In
addition to the scene they had witnessed, their feelings were harrowed by the
knowledge that, in conformity to the necessary plans of Griffith, and in
compliance with the new duties he had assumed, they were to separate in the
morning for an indefinite period, and possibly for ever.

With the appearance of light, the boatswain sent his rough summons
through the vessel, and the crew were collected in solemn silence in her gangways, to "bury the dead." The bodies of Boltrope, of one or two of her inferior officers, and of several common men who had died of their wounds in
the night, were, with the usual formalities, committed to the deep; when the
yards of the ship were again braced by the wind, and she glided along the
trackless waste, leaving no memorial, in the midst of the ever-rolling waters,
to mark the place of their sepulture.

When the sun had gained the meridian, the vessels were once more hove-to,
and the preparations were made for a final separation. The body of Colonel
Howard was transferred to the Alacrity, whither it was followed by Griffith
and his cheerless bride, while Katherine hung fondly from a window of the
ship, suffering her own scalding tears to mingle with the brine of the ocean.
After everything was arranged, Griffith waved his hand to Barnstable, who
had now succeeded to the command of the frigate, and the yards of the latter
were braced sharp to the wind, when she proceeded to the dangerous experiment of forcing her way to the shores of America, by attempting the pass of
the Straits of Dover, and running the gauntlet through the English ships that
crowded their own channel—an undertaking, however, for which she had
the successful example of the Alliance frigate, which had borne the stars of
America along the same hazardous path but a few months previously.

In the meanwhile the Alacrity, steering more to the west, drew in swiftly
toward the shores of Holland; and, about an hour before the setting of the
sun, had approached so nigh as to be once more hove into the wind, in obedience to the mandate of Griffith. A small, light boat was lowered into the
sea, when the young sailor, and the pilot, who had found his way into the

cutter unheeded, and almost unseen, ascended from the small cabin together. The stranger glanced his eyes along the range of the coast, as if he would ascertain the exact position of the vessel, and then turned them on the sea and the western horizon to scan the weather. Finding nothing in the appearance of the latter to induce him to change his determination, he offered his hand frankly to Griffith, and said:

"Here we part. As our acquaintance has not led to all we wished, let it be your task, sir, to forget we ever met."

Griffith bowed respectfully, but in silence, when the other continued, shaking his hand contemptuously toward the land:

"Had I but a moiety of the navy of that degenerate republic, the proudest among these haughty islanders should tremble in his castle, and be made to feel there is no security against a foe that trusts his own strength and knows the weakness of his enemy! But," he muttered, in a lower and more hurried voice, "this has been like Liverpool, and—Whitehaven—and Edinburgh, and fifty more! it is past, sir; let it be forgotten."

Without heeding the wondering crew, who were collected as curious spectators of his departure, the stranger bowed hastily to Griffith, and, springing into the boat, he spread her light sails with the readiness of one who had nothing to learn even in the smallest matters of his daring profession. Once more, as the boat moved briskly away from the cutter, he waved his hand in adieu; and Griffith fancied, that even through the distance he could trace a smile of bitter resignation lighting his calm features with a momentary gleam. For a long time the young man stood an abstracted gazer at his solitary progress, watching the small boat as it glided toward the open ocean; nor did he remember to order the headsheets of the Alacrity drawn, in order to put the vessel again in motion, until the dark speck was lost in the strong glare that fell obliquely across the water from the setting sun.

Many wild and extraordinary conjectures were uttered among the crew of the cutter, as she slowly drew in toward her friendly haven, on the appearance of the mysterious pilot, during their late hazardous visit to the coast of Britain, and on his still more extraordinary disappearance, as it were, amid the stormy wastes of the North Sea. Griffith himself was not observed to smile, nor to manifest any evidence of his being a listener to their rude discourse, until it was loudly announced that a small boat was pressing for their own harbor across the fore-foot of the cutter, under a single lug-sail. Then indeed, the sudden and cheerful lighting of his troubled eye betrayed the vast relief that was imparted to his feelings by the interesting discovery.

35

Come all you kindred chieftains of the deep,
In mighty phalanx round your brother
bend.
Hush every murmur that invades his sleep—
And guard the laurels that o'ershade your
friend!

Lines on Tripp

HERE, perhaps, it would be wise to suffer the curtain of our imperfect drama to fall before the reader, trusting that the imagination of every individual can readily supply the due proportions of health, wealth, and happiness, that the rigid rules of poetic justice would award to the different characters of the legend. But as we are not disposed to part so coldly from those with whom we have long held amicable intercourse, and as there is no portion of that in reservation which is not quite as true as all that has been already related, we see no unanswerable reason for dismissing the *dramatis personæ* so abruptly. We shall, therefore, proceed to state briefly the outlines of that which befell them in afterlife, regretting, at the same time, that the legitimate limits of a modern tale will not admit of such a dilatation of many a merry or striking scene, as might create the pleasing hope of beholding hereafter some more of our rude sketches quickened into life by the spirited pencil of Dunlap.

Following the course of the frigate, then, toward those shores from which, perhaps, we should never have suffered our truant pen to have wandered, we shall commence the brief task with Barnstable, and his laughing, weeping, gay, but affectionate bride—the black-eyed Katherine. The ship fought her way gallantly, through swarms of the enemy's cruisers, to the port of Boston, where Barnstable was rewarded for his services by promotion, and a more regular authority to command his vessel.

During the remainder of the war, he continued to fill that station with ability and zeal; nor did he return to the dwelling of his fathers, which he soon inherited, by regular descent, until after peace had established not only the independence of his country, but his own reputation as a brave and successful sea-officer. When the Federal Government laid the foundation of its present navy, Captain Barnstable was once more tempted by the offer of a new commission to desert his home; and for many years he was employed among that band of gallant seamen who served their country so faithfully in times of trial and high daring. Happily, however, he was enabled to accomplish a great deal of the more peaceful part of his service, accompanied by Katherine, who, having no children, eagerly profited by his consent to share his privations and hardships on the ocean. In this manner they passed, merrily, and we trust happily, down the vale of life together, Katherine entirely discrediting the ironical prediction of her former guardian, by making, everything considered, a very obedient, and certainly, so far as attachment was concerned, a most devoted wife.

The boy, Merry, who in due time became a man, clung to Barnstable and Katherine, so long as it was necessary to hold him in leading strings; and when he received his regular promotion, his first command was under the shadow of his kinsman's broad pennant. He proved to be in his meridian, what his youth had so strongly indicated, a fearless, active, and reckless sailor; and his years might have extended to this hour, had he not fallen untimely in a duel with a foreign officer.

The first act of Captain Manual, after landing once more on his native soil, was to make interest to be again restored to the line of the army. He encountered but little difficulty in this attempt, and was soon in possession of the complete enjoyment of that which his soul had so long pined after, "a steady drill." He was in time to share in all the splendid successes which terminated the war, and also to participate in his due proportion of the misery of the army. His merits were not forgotten, however, in the reorganization of the forces, and he followed both St. Clair and his more fortunate successor, Wayne, in the Western campaigns. About the close of the century, when the

British made their tardy relinquishment of the line of posts along the frontiers, Captain Manual was ordered to take charge, with his company, of a small stockade on our side of one of those mighty rivers that set bounds to the territories of the republic in the North. The British flag was waving over the ramparts of a more regular fortress, that had been recently built, directly opposite, within the new lines of the Canadas. Manual was not a man to neglect the observances of military etiquette; and, understanding that the neighboring fort was commanded by a field-officer, he did not fail to wait on that gentleman, in proper time, with a view to cultivate the sort of acquaintance, that their mutual situations would render not only agreeable, but highly convenient. The American martinet, in ascertaining the rank of the other, had not deemed it at all necessary to ask his name; but when the red-faced comical-looking officer with one leg, who met him, was introduced as Major Borroughcliffe, he had not the least difficulty in recalling to recollection his quondam acquaintance of St. Ruth. The intercourse between these worthies was renewed with remarkable gusto, and at length arrived to so regular a pass, that a log-cabin was erected on one of the islands in the river, as a sort of neutral territory, where their feastings and revels might be held without any scandal to the discipline of their respective garrisons. Here the qualities of many a saddle of savory venison were discussed, together with those of sundry pleasant fowls, as well as of divers strange beasts, that inhabit those Western wilds, while, at the same time, the secret places of the broad river were vexed, that nothing might be wanting that could contribute to the pleasures of their banquets. A most equitable levy was regularly made on their respective pockets, to sustain the foreign expenses of this amicable warfare; and a suitable division of labor was also imposed on the two commandants, in order to procure such articles of comfort as were only to be obtained from those portions of the globe where the art of man had made a nearer approach to the bounties of Nature than in the vicinity of their fortifications. All liquids in which malt formed an ingredient, as well as the deep-colored wines of Oporto, were suffered to enter the Gulf of St. Lawrence, and were made to find their way, under the superintendence of Borroughcliffe, to their destined goal; but Manual was solely intrusted with the more important duty of providing the generous liquor of Madeira, without any other restriction on his judgment than an occasional injunction from his co-adjutor that it should not fail to be the product of the "south side"!

It was not unusual for the young officers of the two garrisons to allude to the battle in which Major Borroughcliffe had lost his limb—the English ensign invariably whispering to the American, on such occasions, that it occurred during the late contest, in a desperate affair in the northeastern coast of their island, in which the major commanded in behalf of his country, with great credit and signal success, and for which service he obtained his present rank "without purchase"! A sort of national courtesy prevented the two veterans, for by this time both had earned that honorable title, from participating at all in these delicate allusions; though, whenever, by any accident, they occurred near the termination of the revels, Borroughcliffe would so far betray his consciousness of what was passing, as to favor his American friend with a leer of singular significance, which generally produced in the other that sort of dull recollection which all actors and painters endeavor to represent by scratching the head. In this manner year after year rolled by, the most perfect harmony existing between the two posts, notwithstanding the angry passions that disturbed their respective countries, when an end was suddenly put to the intercourse by the unfortunate death of Manual. This rigid observer of discipline never trusted his person on the neutral island without being accompanied by a party of his warriors, who were posted as a regular picket, sustaining a suitable line of sentries; a practice which he also recommended to his friend, as being highly conducive to discipline, as well as a salutary caution against a surprise on the part of either garrison. The major, however, dispensed with the formality in his own behalf, but was sufficiently good-natured to wink at the want of confidence it betrayed in his boon companion. On one unhappy occasion, when the discussions of a new importation had made a heavy inroad on the morning, Manual left the hut to make his way toward his picket, in such a state of utter mental aberration, as to forget the countersign when challenged by a sentinel, when, unhappily, he met his death by a shot from a soldier, whom he drilled to such an exquisite state of insensibility, that the man cared but little whether he killed friend or enemy, so long as he kept within military usage, and the hallowed limits established by the articles of war. He lived long enough, however, to commend the fellow for the deed, and died while delivering a eulogium to Borroughcliffe on the high state of perfection to which he had brought his command!

About a year before this melancholy event, a quarter-cask of wine had been duly ordered from the south side of the island of Madeira, which was, at the death of Manual, toiling its weary way up the rapids of the Mississippi and the Ohio; having been made to enter by the port of New Orleans, with the intention of keeping it as long as possible under a genial sun! The untimely fate of his friend imposed on Borroughcliffe the necessity of attending to this precious relic of their mutual tastes; and he procured a leave of absence from his superior, with the laudable desire to proceed down the streams and superintend its further advance in person. The result of his zeal was a high fever, that set in the day after he reached his treasure; and as the doctor and the major espoused different theories, in treating a disorder so dangerous in that climate—the one advising abstemiousness, and the other administering repeated draughts of the cordial that had drawn him so far from home—the disease was left to act its pleasure. Borroughcliffe died in three days; and was carried back and interred by the side of his friend, in the very hut which had so often resounded with their humors and festivities! We have been thus particular in relating the sequel of the lives of these rival chieftains, because, from their want of connection with any kind heart of the other sex, no widows and orphans were left to lament their several ends; and furthermore, as they were both mortal, and might be expected to die at a suitable period, and yet did not terminate their career until each had attained the mature age of threescore, the reader can find no just grounds of dissatisfaction at being allowed this deep glance into the womb of Fate.

The chaplain abandoned the seas in time to retrieve his character, a circumstance which gave no little satisfaction to Katherine, who occasionally annoyed her worthy husband on the subject of the informality of their marriage.

Griffith and his mourning bride conveyed the body of Colonel Howard in safety to one of the principal towns in Holland, where it was respectfully and sorrowfully interred; after which the young man removed to Paris, with a view of erasing the sad images, which the hurried and melancholy events of the few preceding days had left on the mind of his lovely companion. From this place Cecilia held communion, by letter, with her friend Alice Dunscombe; and such suitable provision was made in the affairs of her late uncle as the times would permit. Afterward, when Griffith obtained the command which had been offered him before sailing on the cruise in the North Sea, they returned together to America. The young man continued a sailor until the close of the war, when he entirely withdrew from the ocean, and devoted the remainder of his life to the conjoint duties of a husband and a good citizen.

As it was easy to reclaim the estates of Colonel Howard, which, in fact, had been abandoned more from pride than necessity, and which had never been confiscated, their joint inheritances made the young couple extremely affluent; and we shall here take occasion to say that Griffith remembered his promise to the dying master, and saw such provision made for the childless mother as her situation and his character required.

It might have been some twelve years after the short cruise, which it has been our task to record in these volumes, that Griffith, who was running his eyes carelessly over a file of newspapers, was observed by his wife to drop the bundle from before his face, and pass his hand slowly across his brow, like a man who had been suddenly struck with renewed impressions of some former event, or who was endeavoring to recall to his mind images that had long since faded.

"See you anything in that paper to disturb you, Griffith?" said the still lovely Cecilia. "I hope that now we have our confederate government, the States will soon recover from their losses—but it is one of those plans to create a new navy that has met your eye! Ah! truant! you sigh to become a wanderer again, and pine after your beloved ocean!"

"I have ceased sighing and pining since you have begun to smile," he returned with a vacant manner, and without removing his hand from his brow.

"Is not the new order of things, then, likely to succeed? Does the Congress enter into contention with the President?"

"The wisdom and name of Washington will smooth the way for the experiment, until time shall mature the system. Cecilia, do you remember the man who accompanied Manual and myself to St. Ruth, the night we became your uncle's prisoners, and who afterward led the party which liberated us, and rescued Barnstable?"

"Surely I do; he was the pilot of your ship, it was then said; and I remember the shrewd soldier we entertained even suspected that he was one greater than he seemed."

"The soldier surmised the truth; but you saw him not on that fearful night when he carried us through the shoals; and you could not witness the calm courage with which he guided the ship into those very channels again, while the confusion of battle was among us!"

"I heard the dreadful din! And I can easily imagine the horrid scene," returned his wife, her recollections chasing the color from her cheeks, even at that distance of time; "but what of him? is his name mentioned in those papers? Ah! they are English prints! you called his name Gray, if I remember!"

"That is the name he bore with us. He was a man who had formed romantic notions of glory, and wished everything concealed in which he acted a part that he thought would not contribute to his renown. It has been, therefore, in compliance with a solemn promise made at the time, that I have ever avoided mentioning his name; he is now dead!"

"Can there have been any connection between him and Alice Dunscombe?" said Cecilia, dropping her work in her lap, in a thoughtful manner. "She met him alone, at her own urgent request, the night Katherine and myself saw you in your confinement, and even then my cousin whispered they were acquainted. The letter I received yesterday from Alice was sealed with black, and I was pained with the melancholy though gentle manner in which she wrote of passing from this world into another!"

Griffith glanced his eye at his wife with a look of sudden intelligence, and then answered, like one who began to see with the advantages of a clearer atmosphere:

"Cecilia, your conjecture is surely true. Fifty things rush to my mind at that one surmise—his acquaintance with that particular spot—his early life—his expedition—his knowledge of the Abbey, all confirm it! He, altogether, was indeed a man of marked character!"

"Why has he not been among us?" asked Cecilia; "he appeared devoted to our cause."

"His devotion to America proceeded from desire of distinction, his ruling passion, and perhaps a little also from resentment of some injustice which he claimed to have suffered from his own countrymen. He was a man, and not therefore without foibles—among which may have been reckoned the estimation of his own acts; but they were most daring, and deserving of praise! neither did he at all merit the obloquy that he received from his enemies. His love of liberty may be more questionable; for if he commenced his deeds in the cause of these free States, they terminated in the service of a despot! He is now dead—but had he lived in times and under circumstances when his consummate knowledge of his profession, his cool, deliberate, and even desperate courage, could have been exercised in a regular and well-supported navy, and had the habits of his youth better qualified him to have borne, meekly, the honors he acquired in his age, he would have left behind him no name in its lists that would have descended to the latest posterity of his adopted countrymen with greater renown!"

"Why, Griffith," exclaimed Cecilia, in a little surprise, "you are zealous in his cause! Who was he?"

"A man who held a promise of secrecy while living, which is not at all released by his death. It is enough to know that he was greatly instrumental in procuring our sudden union, and that our happiness might have been wrecked in the voyage of life had we not met the unknown pilot of the German Ocean."

Perceiving her husband to rise, and carefully collect the papers in a bundle, before he left the room, Cecilia made no further remark at the time, nor was the subject ever revived between them.